TROUBLE

Books by Elle Casey

CONTEMPORARY URBAN FANTASY

War of the Fae (10-book series)
Ten Things You Should Know About Dragons
(short story, The Dragon Chronicles)
My Vampire Summer
Aces High

DYSTOPIAN

Apocalypsis (4-book series)

SCIENCE FICTION

Drifters' Alliance (ongoing series)
Winner Takes All (short story prequel to Drifters' Alliance,
Dark Beyond the Stars Anthology)
The Ivory Tower (short story standalone, Beyond the Stars: A
Planet Too Far Anthology)

ROMANCE

By Degrees
Rebel Wheels (3-book series)
Just One Night (romantic serial)
Just One Week
Love in New York (3-book series)
Shine Not Burn (2-book series)
Bourbon Street Boys (4-book series)
Desperate Measures
Mismatched

ROMANTIC SUSPENSE

*All the Glory: How Jason Bradley Went from
Hero to Zero in Ten Seconds Flat*
Don't Make Me Beautiful
Wrecked (2-book series)

PARANORMAL

Duality (2-book series)
Monkey Business (short story)
Dreampath (short story standalone, The
Telepath Chronicles)
Pocket Full of Sunshine (short story & screenplay)

Rebel Wheels

Book 3

TROUBLE

ELLE CASEY

Elle Casey

PO Box 14367

N Palm Beach, FL 33408

Website: www.ElleCasey.com
Email: info@ellecasey.com

ISBN/EAN-13: 978-1-939455-19-2

SECOND EDITION

DEDICATION

Never gonna give you up
Never gonna let you down
Never gonna run around and desert you
Never gonna make you cry
Never gonna say goodbye
Never gonna tell a lie and hurt you.

Dear Reader,
You have just been rickrolled.

"Never Gonna Give You Up"

Lyrics by Rick Astley

CHAPTER
ONE

EVERY BAD THOUGHT I HAVE about myself is confirmed in my mind when I catch Colin looking at me. The expression on his face is just . . . *ugh*. I don't know whether to call it disdain, disapproval or just plain old nausea. I think I literally make him sick to his stomach. Of course there are those times I can tell he's purposely *not* looking at me, staring off in another direction when anyone else would acknowledge my presence. I mean, I am kind of hard to miss being almost eight months pregnant, but he manages to treat me like I'm invisible.

"How are you feeling today?" Teagan asks me, coming in from the kitchen, interrupting my daydreams of the guy who lives next door but who thankfully isn't here right now.

Teagan and I are temporary roommates. To say I'm living with her and her boyfriend Rebel under duress would be an understatement. I cannot stand being a burden to people and that's definitely what I am to them. They might not say that or admit it when I bring it up, but I know it's true. I have no money for rent, no money for food, no money for anything.

My car's been repoed, and my family has completely shut me out of their lives for being pregnant and unwed. I have no idea what I'm going to do when the baby comes. I try not to think about it too much. I'm finding solace in denial. So far I have refused to visit the welfare office. Using food stamps is something I never dreamed I'd have to do to survive, but every day I get closer to my due date, it looks more inevitable. The thought literally makes me ill.

"I'm fine," I say, lying my eyeballs out. My feet are swollen, my belly feels like there are three babies kick-boxing inside it, and I just noticed a stretch mark on one of my thighs. I guess I should be grateful it's not above my bikini line, but all I can think about is how my youth is now gone and how much the real world sucks. This life is nothing like I had planned for myself.

"Rebel and I are going to sign the lease on the house today. Do you want to come?"

I pretend to be very busy reading so I won't have to look her in the eye. "No, thanks. I'll just hang out here."

Teagan drops down on the couch next to me. "You're going to grow roots out of your ass if you stay on this couch much longer, you know."

I can't keep ignoring her. To do that would be rude, and I can't afford to be rude to the people who are keeping a roof over my head. And besides, Teagan is a nice person. Sure, her language leans way more into the foul range than mine does and she has her awkward moments where she puts her foot in her mouth in very public ways, but that doesn't change the basic facts that she's kind and generous and not one bit stuck-up even though she comes from a lot of money. It says a lot about her character that even after losing her father and all his money in one big event, she still has pretty much the same attitude in life. I wish I could be more like her sometimes.

"I get out," I say. It's another lie. I hate leaving the apartment and having people stare at me. It's just a reminder of how stupid I am and how badly I screwed up my life.

"When?" she challenges. "When do you get out?"

"I got out a couple weeks ago. When I went on that road trip with Quin." There. That'll shut her up. We did her a big favor going on that reconnaissance mission and finding that little bit of information her lawyers are busy tracking down now.

"Okay, fine. But that's one trip outside the apartment in two weeks. It's not healthy to stay all closed up in here like a mole rat."

I put my e-reader down. "I'm not a mole rat. I'm just . . . tired."

"You're tired because you're vegging too much. You need to move those muscles." She nudges my leg.

I shove her hand away. "No, I'm tired because I'm *pregnant*." She's annoying me now. Pushing me. She does that every once in a while. She's not as bad as Quin is, but she's bad enough that I try to keep my nose buried in books so I appear unavailable for conversation.

"No, you're tired because you're a cranky butthead who keeps pretending things aren't going on that are."

I sigh heavily and stare at the ceiling, trying to keep a handle on my emotions and temper. "I don't want to talk about this with you right now." Not now. Not ever. Not with Teagan or anyone else. My business is my business and no one else's. I've never been one for sharing secrets.

"You're going to have to talk about it some day. If not to me, then someone else."

"Whatever," I mumble, picking up my e-reader again. The idea of telling anyone what's going through my mind terrifies me. I'm hoping if I try to ignore it hard enough, eventually it'll fade out to a dull roar.

Teagan gets up and leaves the room, and I have to battle not to let out a huge sigh of relief. I know she means well, but I can't handle the stress of having her in my business and trying to connect with me. She's one semester away from graduating and getting her degree. She has a hot boyfriend who thinks she walks on water, a best friend who would step in front of a bus for her, and a future so bright she has to wear shades. I have nothing and no one. My grand sparkling future that included a college degree, a prestigious, high-paying job, and a sophisticated husband and children with our shared, unspoiled DNA . . . is gone. *Poof.* Just like that, one night combined with one bad decision, and my life did a one-eighty. And now I just have to live with that. Life's a B-word.

My melancholy thoughts are interrupted when the door to the apartment opens up. My heart leaps up into my throat when I realize who it is.

Colin.

He just stands there, staring at me.

"Can I help you?" I say, my disconcerting emotions and elevated heart rate showing themselves in an annoyed tone.

"Is Teagan around?"

"I'm in here!" she says from the kitchen. "Just trying this banana bread recipe I found online."

"Oh boy," he says, too quietly for Teagan to hear. I hate that my heart goes even faster at the idea that his comment might have been meant for me.

"She didn't burn the last one so much," I say, before I can stop myself. My face goes red at the realization that I just tried to engage him in conversation when I know darn well he's not interested.

He glances at the kitchen and then at the door behind him, like he's trapped and looking for exits.

"Come try a piece!" Teagan says. "I'll put some butter on it for ya."

His shoulders sink in defeat as he moves farther into the room.

I go back to staring at my e-reader, but I'm not seeing any words there. My eyes are stuck, focusing on my reflection on the screen. It's like I'm starving for words that only he can deliver and he's just about fresh out of them. It's almost painful how much I want to talk to him, while at the same time how much I don't want to. I really wish I could just be somewhere else entirely so I wouldn't have to battle with myself so much over something so stupid. He's just a guy, and a felon at that. Definitely not my type.

I scoff at my own thoughts. As if I have a type. I'm never going to be with another guy ever again, for as long as I live. The price is just too high. I rub my belly as the baby chooses that moment to flip over.

"I can't stay long," says Colin, watching me rub my stomach. "I have to go to the grocery store."

Teagan comes out with two small plates, putting one in front of me on the coffee table and handing one to Colin. She gestures to the small chair next to me. "Here. Sit. Eat."

She leaves us in the room alone.

I look at the slice of bread with trepidation. I'm over the part of my pregnancy where I have a sensitive stomach, but that doesn't mean Teagan's concoctions haven't challenged me. She has gotten better with her cooking, but better than solid-black burnt still isn't edible as far as I'm concerned. So far, I've been able to hide different bites of food in Rebel's potted plants, the toilet, and other places, rather than eat them. I don't have the heart to tell her that her stuff is soooo bad.

"Do we have to eat it?" Colin whispers.

I try not to smile. "Yes."

"You go first," he says.

"Nice. Make the pregnant girl be the taste-tester."

He screws up his mouth. "Fine. But if I keel over, promise me you'll call nine-one-one."

There's no hope of me not smiling now. I can picture him falling over in his chair as he chokes and turns purple. Death by banana bread.

He lifts the bread to his nose and sniffs it. "Smells like bananas."

"That's a plus," I say, still smiling. He really is too cute, especially at times like this when he doesn't realize he's being watched. I'm just a fat old pregnant girl with no future; there's no need for him to pretend to be the dangerous player around me. It makes me feel special, which is really, really pitiful. My smile fades away at the thought.

His tongue comes out and he licks the edge of the bread.

My heart stops beating for a few seconds at the sight of it. Sweat breaks out over my upper lip. I have to look away so I don't have some sort of apoplectic fit. These pregnancy hormones are seriously messing me up.

"Tastes like bananas," he says, oblivious to my distress. "I don't sense anything burned yet."

I nod, still not looking at him. If I see that tongue again I'm going to have to excuse myself to go to the bathroom so I can splash some cold water on my face.

When I catch movement out of the corner of my eye, I look. He's taking a bite. I'm breathless waiting for the verdict. I have no idea why.

He chews.

He chews some more.

His expression tells me nothing.

"So?" I ask.

He gestures at me with his plate. "Go ahead."

I glance once at the kitchen and then at the slice of inno-cent-looking bread on my plate. "If this is inedible, you're in big trouble."

It's possible that I catch a hint of devilry when I look at him, but the expression is gone so fast I'm not sure if I saw it or not. Just in case, I do the same examination he did.

I smell it. I lick it. Colin looks away at that part. When he's no longer watching me, I grab the bread off the plate and take a bite of it.

Colin swallows his bite with effort. "What do you think?" He's smiling, the butthead.

My face twists up as the sourness overwhelms my tastebuds. "Oh my god," I say in a whisper. "What the fudge?"

Colin is laughing silently now, his shoulders shaking with the effort of remaining quiet.

"Oh my gob. Oh my gob . . ." I'm searching the room, desper-ately seeking a container of some sort to hide my bread in. I might be able to swallow this bite, but not the whole thing. No way.

"Here. Give it to me," Colin says, grabbing my plate. He dash-es over to the bathroom and I hear two plops into water and then a flush. He's back to sitting in the chair, his face a mask of inno-cence when Teagan comes into the room.

"Wow, you guys finished that up fast." She's smiling very big.

I feel incredibly guilty. My attempt to return her smile could probably be mistaken for a reaction to an intestinal cramp.

Then she frowns. "Did you think it was a little sour?"

I'm still trying to finish the bite I put in my mouth, so I just shrug and play stupid.

"Maybe a little," Colin says. "Gave it a little extra kick." He does an air punch for effect.

Teagan nods thoughtfully. "Yeah. I guess. The recipe said to use lemon zest so I just squeezed it right in there. Maybe the lemon was too big."

I cringe with the effort of swallowing the hunk of sour banana bread so I can speak. "Did you say *squeezed*?"

"Yeah. So?"

I try very hard not to smile. "Lemon zest can't be squeezed."

"Sure it can," Teagan says, putting her hands on her hips. "I squeezed the ever-loving shit out of it."

I laugh. It's impossible not to when she has that offended look on her face. When I can breathe properly again, I explain.

"Zest is the yellow part of the rind. The part just on top of the white skin under it, just on the *outside* of the part you squeeze. There's no juice in zest. Like . . . ever."

"Well, why the fuck would anyone want to put lemon peels in a damn banana bread?" she says, sounding like she's ready to fight me.

I give her a hesitant shrug to ease the sting of my words. "Maybe because it gives a lemon flavor without the sourness?"

Colin snorts.

Teagan sighs out loud and long. "Fuck me sideways. I screwed up again, didn't I?" She leans over and grabs the plates out of Colin's hand. "Did you guys really eat it?"

We both nod, first at each other and then at her.

"Well, you're just stupid, then, aren't you? I don't know why I'm using *you* guys as taste-testers when you can't even taste a whole buttload of lemon juice in a slice of banana bread." She leaves the room, and only when she's completely gone do Colin and I collapse in giggles.

When we can finally breathe again, I suddenly realize he's on the couch with me and sitting way closer than normal. I try to act cool about it since he seems unfazed by the whole thing. *Breathe in, breathe out. You can do this, Alissa!*

"Shit, I have to go to the grocery store." He stands up at the front of the couch suddenly, making me think that maybe he wasn't as unfazed as he appeared. Looking down at me he smiles kind of awkwardly. "Do you need anything?"

I shake my head, freaking out about the mere idea of him shopping for me. "No. Thanks."

Teagan comes out. "Oh, I need something."

"More lemons?" he asks.

"No, smart ass, I need tampons. Not the super size ones, either. Regular size, since I have such a small vagina."

Colin chokes on his own spit and his face turns bright red as he battles to breathe.

I have to hide my face behind my e-reader so he doesn't see me smiling. Man, she is so bold and rude, but sometimes I can't help but laugh at the stuff that comes flying out of her mouth. I'm pretty sure she's getting back at Colin for fake-eating her bread.

"No way," he finally says. "No way am I buying tampons at the store, of *any* size."

"I have to clean up this mess before Rebel gets home. If he sees it he'll try to eat some of it and then he'll break up with me for being such a horrible cook."

"If being a good cook were the reason he's with you, he'd've broken up with you a long time ago." Colin runs around the back of the couch when Teagan goes after him.

I tuck my legs up around the sides of my belly like a frog, trying to keep from getting tripped over.

Teagan points at him when he finally stops running; they're on opposite sides of the couch with me in the middle. "When I catch you? You die." She leaves the room, but not after issuing her last order. "Better get me those tampons or you're going to be sorry."

Colin's at the door in a flash, looking toward the kitchen and then at me. He's nervous.

"She'll kill you, you know," I say, smiling over the idea that such a small girl can make such a big scary guy actually worried.

"Or make me eat her next meal, which is the same thing but slower and more painful."

I laugh.

"Come with me," he says.

"What? Me? No way." I put my e-reader up to my face so he won't see it going red.

He strides over and yanks it away from me, backing up before I can swipe it back.

"Hey! That's mine!"

"And you can have it back if you get those damn tampons for me."

"That's blackmail." I'm glaring at him, terrified for some stupid reason about the idea of going to the store with him. I'm pregnant. I'm fat. I'm ugly. And he's so darn beautiful!

"I've done much worse," he says, darkness moving over his face for a moment. "Please?" The shadow disappears with that one word and suddenly he's years younger.

It's the politeness that gets me. There's so little of it left in my world. My parents were always sticklers for it, but here in this apartment, I don't hear much in the way of please and thank you. It's not that I'm a hard-butt about that stuff, but it is possible I'm missing my family and their habits. I hate that this is the case. I want to be as free of them as they are of me.

"Fine," I say, admitting defeat. Teagan was right earlier; I do need to get out of the house. I feel like a vegetable - a big leafy green one with zero personality. And it doesn't matter that I'm fat and ugly. Colin would never be interested in me anyway, and I would never be seriously interested in a guy like him either, so who cares if my hair is a mess and I have a stretch mark on my thigh? "Let me get my purse."

"You don't need your purse, I'll get you whatever you want."

I hate the uncomfortable feeling his statement gives me. "I don't need your charity."

"It's not charity. It's paying you off for tampon shopping. Trust me, it'll be worth every penny."

Giving up on finding my purse, I shake my head at him as we walk out of the apartment and down to the car. "I don't see what the big deal is," I say. "They're just tampons."

"Could we please just stop saying that word?" he says, as he walks ahead of me down the stairs.

"What word? Tampon?"

"Yes."

I'm tempted to do a soliloquy on tampons right then and there, but I resist. It would be too much like flirting. Instead, I follow him silently out to his black car and get in the front seat next to him, folding my hands tightly and placing them in my lap.

Just breathe, Alissa. Just breathe. I stare out the window, refusing to give into the temptation and look sideways at him. *He's just a guy bringing you to the grocery store so you can buy tampons for a friend. It's no big deal.* I keep saying that to myself over and over, but by the time we get there, the silence between us has stretched so far and so wide, it's almost suffocatingly stressful.

CHAPTER
TWO

I HAVEN'T BEEN TO THE grocery store in ages, and never to this particular one. It's kind of dirty or old or something - nothing like the place where my family shops, with its shiny chrome surfaces and gourmet cheeses and meats — but the food looks fine. Not that I can afford to be picky anymore.

My mood picks up in the produce section. As I wander over to a giant bin of apples, enthralled by their color and shape, I feel like Snow White must have when the witch dropped by with her poisoned snack. As Colin fills up a plastic bag with bananas, I stand in front of the big, red juicy fruits with my mouth watering.

Unable to help myself, I reach out and touch one. It's shiny and pink, not totally red, reminding me of my favorite summer lipgloss. I've never seen an apple like this before. I wish I had the money for extras, because if I did, I'd buy six of them. There's only seventeen dollars and eighty-one cents left in my purse, and I didn't even bring my wallet with me.

"Pink Lady," a voice says over my shoulder.

I jump to the side in fright.

Colin.

He's really good at sneaking up behind people, making me wonder if cat-burglaring is in his repertoire. Knowing him, it probably is.

"What?" I ask, trying to get control of my racing pulse while acting like he doesn't send my system into complete overload just by being close.

He reaches around me and grabs one of the apples, tossing it up and catching it right in front of my face. "*This . . .* is a Pink Lady apple, a cross between the Golden Delicious and the Lady Williams." He rips a plastic bag off the roll and starts putting some of the rosy apples inside without saying anything else

I stand there staring at him, not sure if he's totally messing with me or if he really knows what he's talking about. He sounded for a brief moment like a science teacher I once had and liked a lot.

"You're staring at me again," he says. He looks over briefly at me and smiles before going back to his apple-bagging. He totally knows what that smile does to girls.

"I'm not staring," I say, my face flaming up to the point that I'm sure it looks like one of those fruits. "And I haven't *been* staring." I'm totally busted. *How many times has he caught me? God, I'm just like every other girl on the planet. Easy to manipulate with just a look. Ugh.*

"Okay, then, stop making gooey eyes at me." He's smiling but that doesn't make me feel any less stupid.

"You are so full of yourself, you know that? And it's not gooey eyes, it's goo-goo eyes." I snort. "Like I'd have goo-goo eyes over someone like *you.*" I walk away, leaving him to suffer my serious burn. *Chew on that for awhile, Colin, you big dummy. You're not so great.*

I want to feel like the champion of all come-backs and satisfied with having knocked him down a peg or two, but instead I feel completely stupid. I'm a pregnant girl with sausagey ankles, accused of checking out a guy who's so far out of her league and even out of her universe it's not even funny. *Yuck.* And I thought my life couldn't get any worse. Wrong again. I used to be so calm.

So cool. So collected. So *focused*. When did everything get so out of control? Why have I let it go this far?

I stop my inner diatribe when I reach the end of the ladies' products aisle and take a left. Upon reaching the tampon section, I realize I might have a problem. My eyes scan the shelves. Which brand does she want? Did she mention it? I don't recall hearing any of the brand names I see here. What style does she prefer? I'm chewing on my lip as I consider my choices when a voice comes from behind me.

"If you need some of those, I'd say you're in a bit of trouble."

I turn around to face the woman standing there. She's tall and thin, with perfectly straight, shoulder-length blonde hair, expertly highlighted. I'm jealous of the ribbon hair-band she's used to keep her long bangs out of her eyes. I used to look like that — perfectly put together and neat— back before I got pregnant and stopped caring about pretty much anything.

"Oh. I don't need any tampons," I say, my face going red. Then I actually snort at the ridiculousness of it. I quickly start talking again to distract her from my eerily good imitation of a potbelly pig. "They're for my friend. Really, they are." I don't know why I'm suddenly nervous and feel the need to convince her. It's not like I'm in the drug aisle.

"Are you okay?" the woman asks. She reaches out as if to touch my arm.

I move away to avoid her, my back hitting the shelves behind me. "I'm fine. Really, I'm fine." I look to the left and right, searching for an escape route. She's not being mean or even overly weird, but I can't help feeling nervous about random acts of niceness. After having been rejected by my own family, it seems like a mean trick.

She smiles and moves to the side a little, giving me more space. I could run down toward the meat counter area if I really wanted to. She's being completely non-threatening.

"Okay," she says, "it just seems like maybe you're a little . . . stressed." She looks down at my belly. "I hear being pregnant can do that to you."

She looks so sad when she says it, I don't run away like my first instinct tells me to. "Do you have kids?" I realize what a stupid question that is as soon as my brain re-processes what she just said. I wish I could take the words back when I see her expression.

"Unfortunately, no. My husband and I have been trying for years, but it looks like it's just not going to happen for us."

"Oh. That's too bad." I feel awkward and silly, having this conversation with a complete stranger. But to leave her in the dust now would be rude, and as much as I seem to have forgotten my manners with Colin, I can't leave them behind now. Not with this lady. Not in this situation.

"Heartbreaking is more the adjective I'd use, but that's neither here nor there." She visibly perks up. "I hope your pregnancy is going well."

"If you count stretch marks and swollen ankles as going well, then I guess I'm in good shape."

The woman sighs, looking at my belly again. "I envy you those things."

The baby takes that moment to do a complete flip and my stomach warps into a weird oval shape. It's really uncomfortable, so I push my hands on either end of the bulges, trying to massage her into a more round shape. She complies within seconds of feeling my pressure, flipping back in the other direction and settling into a ball-shape again.

"Oh my god," the woman whispers. "I just saw it move, didn't I?" She has tears in her eyes.

I want to cry right along with her. The world is so freaking unfair. Here I am standing here regretting my life while this complete stranger envies it. Where is the justice in that?

"Do you want to feel her?" I ask. I've never done that before, offered up my belly to a complete stranger. No one has felt this baby move but me; but for some reason, this feels like the right thing to do.

The woman looks at me, her eyes all shiny and her face practically glowing. "Really? I'd love to."

I shrug. "Sure. Go ahead." I'm nervous, but I don't back away.

The woman wastes no time. Moving over to stand closer, she puts one hand on the front of me, just above my belly-button, which is sticking out like a gross marble.

"It's better if you use two hands," I say, feeling shy and at the same time wanting to get this over with as soon as possible. Now that her hand is on me, I realize how creepy this is. A grocery store aisle. A stranger. My belly in her hands. *What am I doing? Who am I today?* I've never acted so completely out of character in my life. This is Colin's doing. I'm going to blame this entire episode on his influence.

Her second hand comes up and sits next to the first.

I take her wrists and adjust her hands more to the sides, where I think she'll feel some of the movement. The baby tends to kick on the left and right rather than on my bladder, thank goodness.

The woman jumps with surprise a split second after I feel the baby move.

"I felt it! I felt it!" Tears roll down her cheeks as more kicks and bumps happen under her fingers. She doesn't bother to wipe them away; she's too la-la over feeling the baby gymnastics.

I can't stop staring at her. She's a total mess over something completely silly.

"Oh my god, it's a miracle," she says, her voice all weepy. "The miracle of life is *right here* in your body. You are so lucky. You are *so* blessed." She lets go of my stomach and grabs me by the shoulders, pulling me into a hug that's so enthusiastic, I'm afraid she's going mental on me. But then she lets me go and wipes away her tears with shaking fingers. "I'm so sorry. I don't know what's coming over me right now. I'm never so publicly demonstrative."

"Maybe it's baby fever?" I say, worried she's going to start crying again.

She nods as more tears slip out. "Yes. Baby fever is right." She looks up the aisle toward the front of the store before going back to looking at me. "Thank you for sharing that with me."

I shrug. "No big deal."

She stops crying and stares me dead in the eye, now all of a sudden serious. "Don't ever say that. Cherish what you have. Never *ever* forget to be grateful for that which you've been given."

I open my mouth to respond to her almost-sermon, but nothing will come out. And that's probably okay, since she doesn't stick around to hear what's on my mind anyway.

The woman takes off without another word, abandoning her cart in the middle of the aisle and jogging out the front doors. A couple seconds later, she's getting into a silver mini-van and leaving the parking lot going a lot faster than she probably should. She barely stops before jumping out onto the road and speeding off.

Colin comes up next to me. "Who was that?" he asks, watching her go too.

"Some lady who freaked out after she felt the baby move." I look down into her cart. There's fruit, vegetables, and several jars of baby food in there. *Baby food? What would she need baby food for if she doesn't have any kids?*

Colin's gaze drops to my belly. "She felt *your* baby move?"

I look at him and frown. "Yes, my baby. Who else's baby would I be talking about?"

"You can feel it move?"

"Yes, of course."

"I mean, *another* person can feel it move? Like, a stranger?"

"Yeeeess." I feel like this is a trick question.

He's still staring at my belly. It starts to get awkward.

"Are you trying to make her move?" I ask, amused by the expression on his face.

"Her who?"

"Her the baby."

He looks up quickly at me. "Can I do that?"

I laugh. "Not with your Vulcan mind power, no, but with your hands, probably."

"What?"

"You're seriously confused right now, aren't you?" I ask. This is a revelation to me. For some reason I was thinking a guy who knows about hybrid apple types would also know about the wonders of pregnancy, but apparently his knowledge is reserved for the world of botany.

"No, I'm not confused." He looks at me like I'm the stupid one for a few seconds, but when I glare at him, he caves. "Okay, maybe I am a little."

I sigh, feeling like I'm talking to a fourth grader. "She moves all the time, pretty much. But if she's not moving, I can make her move by giving her a poke."

"A poke? You actually *poke* your baby?"

I slap him lightly on the arm. "Don't say it like that. It's not like I'm torturing her."

He shakes his head slowly. "I don't think you should poke her. That doesn't sound good."

"Would you shut up?" I turn away from him and look at the shelf in front of me. "I'm trying to buy tampons right now."

He looks up at the shelves. "Oh, shit. I'm in the tampon aisle."

I can't help but laugh when I look at him and catch his horrified expression. "Yes, you are. Watch out, they're going to *get* you!" Without thinking, I grab a box off the shelf and throw it at him.

It bounces off his massive chest.

"Cut it out," he says in a low whisper. The box clatters to the floor.

"Uh-oh! Here come some pads!" I say, tossing the next item at him.

The soft, plastic pack hits him in the forehead.

"What are those!" he yells, jumping out of the way as the pads bounce off to his right. He's high-stepping as he moves out of the way like he has big, scary football players coming to tackle his stupid butt.

In my deranged mind, I'm a football coach now and he's on my team. *Time for some calisthenics!* "Move! Move! Move!" I yell, nailing him with box after box of tampons, pads and whatever else I can find nearby and grab from the shelves. I'm possessed. I cannot control myself for some reason and I don't want to. This is like getting high without drugs.

"Jesus Christ, Alissa, you're losing it! Stop! You're making a fucking mess!" He's running, jumping, and in between all his evasive maneuvers, picking up the boxes off the floor and holding them in his arms. It's almost like a contest now to see how many boxes and bags I can get him to pick up and hold at one time. We should be on a game show. We'd totally win.

Colin has about ten boxes stacking up in his arms and his face is bright red. My arm is poised over my shoulder as I'm about to launch a super-sized box of old-school sanitary pads, otherwise known in my house as mouse mattresses, at him. I'm sure this will make all the other boxes fall out of his arms. He's like the duck in the county fair midway game and I'm about to nail him with my fake bullet and knock him over. *KA-BLAM!*

"*What* in the sam hill is going on here?" A mostly bald man with a manager's uniform and name-tag is standing at the end of the aisle, glaring at us and waiting for an answer to his question. There are two really greasy clumps of hair trying to do the job of covering his shiny dome-like bald spot, and I'm suddenly possessed by the need to cut them off. I search the aisle for a pair of scissors as I lower the box of pads down to my waist.

Colin interrupts my search when he points at me with a box of panty-liners. "She's pregnant."

The manager puts his hands on his hips. "I can see that. What it doesn't explain, however, is why suddenly all of these feminine products are on the floor."

I start giggling. It's not pretty when my laughter turns quickly into snorts. The potbelly pig is baaaack.

"What's so funny?" the man asks me, his volume going up.

"You said feminine products." I don't know why, but this is hysterical to me. I hold my stomach, afraid I'm going to pull something or possibly pee my pants.

"See? She's pregnant," Colin says. "Explains everything." He starts shoving boxes anywhere on the shelf he can find an empty space. "I'll just clean this up real quick and then we'll go."

"You're darn right you will." The manager shakes a ballpoint pen at us. "You're lucky I don't call law enforcement."

"Law enforcement." I'm giggling even harder now. This guy is so serious. Quin says I have a stick up my butt, but she needs to meet Mr. I'm-Going-To-Call-Law-Enforcement. He makes me look as laid back as her and Teagan.

"I don't see what's so funny about getting arrested," he continues. He gestures at my belly. "I'm surprised you do, seeing as how you're a mother."

That douses my humor like nothing else could. My smile turns upside down and I'm ready to kick him. "I'm not a mother," I say, deciding a kick isn't quite enough for this butthead. I really want to scratch him right now, but I've bitten off all my fingernails in the last few months, leaving me with just nubs.

"Sure looks to me like you are. And what a fine mother you'll make, too." He sneers. "Maybe by the time your kid is two years old he can be pick-pocketing tourists with you on the street corner."

Colin has to hold me back from nubbing the guy's face off.

"Okay, settle down, wild woman," Colin says, pushing me backward, toward the front of the aisle. He doesn't sound mad or freaked out about being pelted with pads anymore. He actually sounds happy.

"You haven't finished cleaning this up!" the manager says, pointing at the last remaining boxes of pads on the floor.

"Pick it up yourself, comb-over," Colin says over his shoulder.

"Yeah! Pick it up yourself, comb-over!" I yell. My voice echoes all over the store and I totally do not care.

I turn around and walk with Colin, moving as fast as my legs will take me without actually running. It's possible there's serious waddling involved. "You told him," I say under my breath.

"Damn straight we did."

I can't stop grinning. "You're my hero."

He lets out a huff of air. "Trust me. I ain't nobody's hero."

I don't argue, even though I know he's wrong.

We get to the parking lot and into the car. Once the doors are shut, we sit there, the silence folding in around us. I'm starting to feel like we're Bonnie and Clyde. The worst part is, I don't know whether to feel ashamed or proud. I'm so confused right now.

"So," Colin says finally, looking over at me.

"So," I say back, meeting his stare without flinching.

"I guess we still need to go shopping."

"Better not go back to Teagan without tampons," I warn.

He's biting the inside of his cheek, I think to keep from smiling. "Can I trust you to behave yourself in the next store?" he asks.

"Probably not," I say, turning to look out the front window. My chin goes up just the slightest bit. I feel completely reckless and wild, and I love it. For the first time in months, I feel alive.

"Good," he says, starting up the car and reversing out of the space. "Behaving is boring."

CHAPTER
THREE

ALL THE EXCITEMENT GENERATED BY my tampon attack has left me exhausted. By the time we get to the second
grocery store, I'm too tired to even shop. I give Colin the best
description I can of the type of tampons he should get for Teagan
and nap in the car, and surprisingly, he gives me no argument
about having to make the purchase alone. When I wake up, we're
at Rebel Wheels again. My elated mood has completely deflated
into nothing. I'm back to being a gray-girl, living in a numb state.

I climb out of the car with regret in my heart. I really don't
want to go back inside this place. Now that I've had a taste of
the real world again and uprooted myself from the couch, I'm
almost regretting my hibernation plan. Too bad my energy levels are more suited to *that* plan than any other. My feet feel like
lead weights.

Colin drops the plastic bag from the store on the armchair when
we get into the apartment and then wanders into the kitchen. I
hear the refrigerator door opening and the clank of beer bottles.

I'm dismayed to find Quin and Mick there, hanging out in

front of the television. My plan to take a nap and sleep off this lethargy, or at least wile away a few more hours of my boring life in unconscious mode, is now on hold. With all these people in the room where I sleep, it's not going to be possible. I sit in the corner of the couch and grab my e-reader from the coffee table, trying not to let my grouchiness show.

"You're not going to bury your nose in another book, are you?" asks Quin, getting up from the nearby armchair.

"Yes," I say simply. I don't even look up at her.

"What are you reading?" Mick asks.

I shrug. I'm actually not reading anything right now. I've been staring at the same page of this book for days. I just look at the black words swimming around on the screen and let my mind wander into happier times, both past and imagined. It's easier than trying to fall into someone else's life on the pages.

"You're not even reading a book, are you?" Quin asks, falling down into a spot on the couch right next to me. She's too close, but I can't move away since I'm stuck in the corner. I try not to let it irritate me, but it's pretty much impossible.

She leans in closer. "*Pride and Prejudice.* Oh, God, are you reading that voluntarily? I mean, not for an English Lit assignment?"

"Some people do that, you know," I say, flipping my tablet over so she'll quit looking at it.

"You should read the sexy stuff. Erotic romance. The hotsy totsy hoochie cootchie stuff."

I sniff a little. "*Pride and Prejudice* is sexy."

She snorts. "My ass."

"How would you know? You've never read it."

"Like hell, I haven't. That Darcy guy was a total pushover and I have no idea why he was okay with sloppy seconds. He deserved better."

I cannot believe her. "Sloppy seconds? Are you serious?" Quin is so obtuse sometimes.

"Yes. Dead serious. Sloppy seconds all the way."

"There are no sloppy seconds in *Pride and Prejudice.*" Now she's just making me mad.

"What do you call Mr. Wickham? He was her first choice. He got the prime beef. Darcy? Sloppy seconds, like I said."

I put my nose in the air. Quin has no idea what she's talking about. "Wickham was a scoundrel and a cheat and not fit to be her husband."

Quin starts laughing. "You sound like Elizabeth Bennet herself."

I push myself up off the couch with effort, dropping my tablet to the table with a clatter. "Oh, shut up, Quin."

I grab my purse that was hiding behind a plant and storm out of the apartment. It's only after getting out into the hallway that I realize what a bad idea that was. Now I have nowhere to go, and I can't very well walk back into the apartment after that kind of exit; I'll look ten times more foolish than I already do.

I walk to the end of the hallway and take the stairs down into the main garage. I've always just cruised through this space without stopping, but since I've been warned about ten times not to touch anything in Teagan's office, this is the only place left to me unless I want to wander around outside, which I don't. It's way too hot outside for a pregnant person.

I sigh as I wander over to a table covered in tools, putting my purse over my head and across my chest so I can be hands-free. There's a car nearby with its hood open and a rag lying over the radiator part. A piece of the engine is resting on the cloth. The car is painted an ugly orange.

Who'd paint a car orange? Not me. I'd go with white or cream. Something clean-looking and elegant. I sigh as I picture it. I had already picked out the perfect car for myself, freshman year, just like I'd picked out everything else I was eventually going to have in my life once I graduated. I even made a vision board with cutout magazine pictures of the car, the house, the husband, the children, the dog and cat. Everything. I had the perfect plan.

I smile with extreme bitterness as the memories fade. All of those dreams are now gone, like car exhaust in my rearview mirror. I don't even have my beater Toyota anymore. *Ugh.*

I run my fingers over one of the tools. It looks so blunt and masculine. It's cold and hard and . . . *ew,* covered in black grease.

Crud. Now I'm dirty. I try to wipe the goop off my fingers on a blue rag nearby, but there's grease on that too. I'm standing there staring at my black-smeared hand when I hear footsteps behind me.

"You going to work on that water pump for me?"

It's Colin. I brace myself as a shiver runs over my skin.

"I don't think so," I say, embarrassed that he witnessed my big exit. I feel bad now for telling Quin to shut up. She was just being Quin and that normally doesn't bother me so much. Today is a weird day for my hormones, apparently.

"Here, let me help you." Colin pulls a wet wipe out of a box and uses it on my fingers. His strong hands massage the grease right off my skin and leave me breathless as a side-effect.

"I'm sorry about being so . . . stupid," I say, wishing I could take the words back as soon as they leave my mouth. Pregnancy has made me lose brain cells, I'm sure of it. No wonder I can't read *Pride and Prejudice.*

"Who's stupid? You? I don't think so." Colin takes a paper towel and wipes my hand dry.

Without thinking, I lean closer to him just the slightest bit and inhale. I love the way he smells. I don't know if it's laundry soap or cologne that keeps going up my nose, but it's amazing. And it's not too strong either, which would be a problem since pregnancy has given my nose superpowers. I step back a couple inches when I realize I'm about to close my eyes and sigh over it.

Shaking my head to get it back to reality, I try to explain myself. "Quin was just playing around like she always does, and I know she didn't mean anything personal by it. I guess I should feel complimented that she teases me like she teases Teagan."

"It means she likes you," Colin says. His voice holds no judgment and for that I'm grateful. He's being way too nice to me, considering I pelted him with about a hundred of his most feared objects today.

"I guess I could do with some less aggressive friendship at this point in my life," I say.

"Maybe. Maybe not."

I look up at him, even though he's standing really close and it's kind of intimate to be face to face like this. "What's that supposed to mean?"

He shrugs. "Dunno."

I pull my hand out of his grip and move back another step. "Huh-uh. You're not going to say something challenging like that and then just let it go." My left hand rests on the edge of the bench and my fingers curl a little as my stress level rises. The nubs that used to be fingernails drag across the scarred wood surface.

"I wasn't challenging you." He moves away, taking a tool off the table and stepping over to the car, sliding the loose engine part over to the corner so he can reach the spot he's aiming for. His broad back muscles stretch and flex under his tight t-shirt. *Holy mackerelandy.*

"Yes, you were, don't lie."

He pauses as he's in the process of leaning over the engine. Twisting his upper body toward me, he fixes hard eyes on me and says, "I don't lie." Then he goes back to his work and proceeds to use his tool somewhere deep inside the mess of hoses and engine parts I can't see very well.

"Well, what do you call that comment, then?" My breathing rate has increased and I can feel the heat rising in my face.

His voice sounds funny, muffled a little by the hood of the car. "Just an alternate way of looking at the situation."

"How so?" I tap my finger over and over on the bench. The rhythm keeps me from wanting to throw things.

He continues working while he answers. "You said you could do with something different. But maybe you say that because you just want to stay miserable. Maybe Quin and Teagan could help you to feel happy again, but you don't want to let them because you're too focused on punishing yourself."

"What?" My blood is starting to boil. I'm not even sure I've fully processed what he's saying, or that I'm sure about what he means, but I have a feeling I'm not going to like it.

He stands up and faces me. "Nobody in this place understands that mindset more than me, okay? I wrote the fucking book on it. You don't need to hide your shit from me."

I huff out a breath of air, trying to stay civil in the face of his rudeness. "I really wish you'd stop swearing like that."

He shrugs. "Don't cloud the issue."

"Cloud the issue? I'm not clouding the issue." My voice is going up in volume, but I can't seem to stop it. It echoes around the large open space. "Everywhere I go around you people I'm hearing the F-word and the S-word and the C-word and the D-word. Teagan and Quin have a swear word for every letter of the alphabet. Why can't any of you express yourselves without using foul language?"

"Somebody used the C-word around you?" He's smiling. He actually has the nerve to *smile* when I'm upset.

"You're surprised about that?" I throw my hands up and let them fall down to slap my legs. "I don't get you, Colin. You paint like a master, you swear like a trucker, and you smile like an angel. You are a walking, talking, out-loud lie of epic proportions."

He stands there for a few long seconds frowning at me before he responds. "Uhhh . . . I'm not exactly sure . . . did you just compliment me or insult me?"

"Arrrgh!" I scream, storming off. I stride through the office and out the front door of the garage. I cannot stand to be in the same room with that man for another second. I'm liable to nub him to death with my pitiful used-to-be fingernails.

"Where are you going?" Colin's behind me, yelling from the doorway as I trudge across the parking lot.

"None of your beeswax! Leave me alone!" I have no idea where I'm going, but he doesn't need to know that.

I spy some golden arches in the distance and decide this is probably the best place for me to burn off my anger. I can get a free ice water and use their bathroom — double score.

Putting all my anger into my stride, I make it to the fast-food place in under five minutes.

CHAPTER
FOUR

I'M SUCKING DOWN THE LAST bits of an ice water delivered through a fat, plastic, yellow-striped straw when I spy a pregnant girl coming in the door. She looks like she's ready to pop, and the minute I spy her cankles I recognize a kindred spirit. I totally feel her pain.

She looks over at me and smiles shyly.

I smile back because for the first time all day, I feel like I'm looking at someone who can understand what I'm going through. It helps to not feel like the only one in the world suffering like I am. There are now two potbelly pigs in the house. I wonder if she snorts when she laughs too. I never used to do that.

She goes up to the counter and orders. When she gets her tray, she walks over in my direction.

I quickly look down at the table, embarrassed about being caught staring. I know I hate it when people do that to me.

"Hi. Is this seat taken?" she asks, gesturing to the spot across from me.

I look around at all the empty tables around us. We're the only ones in the whole place. Why does she want to sit here?

"No, I guess not." I squirm a little in my seat. I'm not used to strangers approaching me, and now this is twice in one day it's happened. Am I wearing a sign that says, *Make friends with me, I'm lonely*?

"Good. Because I am sick and tired of sitting in the corner alone," she says, smiling again. Her teeth are so white they glow. Her hair is pulled back in a slick pony tail and her skin is flawless, the color of dark mahogany. I can't stop staring at her face.

"What? Do I have something on me? A sesame seed?" She wipes at her cheek.

I shake my head. "No. I was just admiring your complexion. You're one of those pregnant girls who glows." I sigh heavily. "I'm the kind that tarnishes and blotches."

"Oh, flub that. You're gorgeous."

I smile. "Flub that? That's original."

She shrugs as she chews a bite of her Happy Meal hamburger. "You know. Gonna have a baby and all. Gotta start going with the Rated-G stuff."

When I see her eating the little kid meal and her round little face, it strikes me how young she looks. "How far along are you?" I ask. What I really want to know is how old she is, but I don't want to be rude.

"Eight months, three days, and forty some minutes. I am *so* done with the pregnancy, you have no idea."

I rub my belly absently. "Oh, yes I do. Believe me."

She grins. "Oh. I guess you do. That's cool."

I glance at her ring finger. It's empty like mine.

Catching me staring, she holds up her left hand. "Nope, not married, in case you were wondering."

My face flames red. "Sorry."

She waves off my embarrassment. "Don't apologize. I'm an open book. My name is Charity, I'm sixteen, I'm not married and I do not want to be. What's your deal?" She dives into her french fries with gusto, holding up the greasy packet toward me.

I shake my head at her offer, but surprise myself as I answer. "My name is Alissa, I'm twenty-one, I'm definitely not married nor do I want to be." I smile a little, moving past my embarrassment. "And I'm almost eight months pregnant and cannot wait to be *not* pregnant."

"Boy or girl?" she asks.

"Girl."

"I'm having a boy."

My next question flies out of my mouth. "What are you going to do? After he's born, I mean?" I can't believe I've asked such a personal question, but I'm dying to know the answer. Maybe she'll have ideas about what I should do once my baby is born, because so far I've come up with nothing.

"Go back to high school. I'm putting him up for adoption."

My jaw drops open.

She looks at me and stops eating. "What? You against that kind of thing?"

I shake my head briskly. "No, no, of course not. I mean, I don't know if I could do it personally, but I'm definitely not against it. There are tons of people out there looking for babies to adopt and love." The lady from the grocery store comes to mind. I can still see her standing there with tears on her cheeks as her hands rest on my belly. I imagine that I can almost feel the warm spots she left still there, handprints of desperate love.

Charity shrugs. "I'm too young and poor as dirt. I need to finish high school and then go to college before I can do a good job as a mom. I live with my grandpa and we don't have the money to raise a baby right." She sighs as she throws the rest of her fries in the box that her meal came in. "Sucks to learn lessons the hard way."

I nod. *Sucks* doesn't even begin to cover it. I'm jealous that she at least knows what she's going to do.

"Have you picked out a family yet?" I ask.

"Nope. I haven't even started. Isn't that crazy?" She smiles at me, but it's not a very happy expression this time. "I know this is what I want to do, but every time I think about it, I see a report on the news about some couple abusing a kid and I worry that will happen with my baby, you know? I mean, how do you know they're good people? 'Cause you can't take the baby back. Once it's done, it's done."

I shake my head. "I don't know. I guess you get to know them a little first." I watch her bag up her garbage, wanting to help her solve her problem. I can't solve my own but maybe I can do something worthwhile for someone else. "They have agencies and stuff, right? People who want to adopt are checked out and fingerprinted and stuff."

"Yeah, probably. And I see ads online and on billboards and stuff from people who want a baby really bad. I don't know. I feel like . . ." She stops and looks down at the table. She seems embarrassed.

"Like what?" I ask.

"I don't know. It's silly."

"Tell me." I smile to encourage her. I really want to know what she's thinking, which is rare these days. Usually I want people to stop sharing with me and just leave me alone.

"I feel like I'm going to meet the right person and have a feeling, you know? Like God will lead me to her or him and then I'll just know."

"Yeah. I know what you mean." I *used* to know what she means, actually, but I'm not going to burst her bubble and say that out loud. I used to believe in magic and true love and everything working out for people who try hard and trust in the process. Now I know better. But she's young and she seems smart, so maybe things can work out differently for her. Just because my life dreams turned into nightmares, it doesn't mean everyone's have to.

"I met a really nice lady today who wants to adopt," I say, trying to drag my brain out of the unhappy place it's straying into.

"Really? But I thought you said you weren't going to do that?"

"Oh, it wasn't because I was looking for that. I was just at the grocery store."

"They have adoption meetings there?" She folds her straw wrapper into tiny squares as she waits for my explanation.

I laugh. "No, no, nothing like that. I was just in the tampon aisle and she commented how I shouldn't need those in my condition and we started talking. She felt the baby move and nearly had an emotional breakdown."

"Oh, that's rough."

"Yeah. It was really sad. She said that she and her husband have been trying for years to have a baby but it just wasn't going to happen." I shrug as my mind travels down memory lane, seeing her face again and her perfect hairband. I don't know why, but that really spoke to me, the way she wore her hair like mothers did fifty years ago. She was so conservative but so open at the same time. "She really, really wanted to be a mom. And I got the idea that she'd make a good one, you know?"

"Yeah. Sometimes ladies just give off a vibe," Charity says. "Like soccer mom stuff going on with a mini-van and stuff."

I point at her in my excitement. "She totally had a mini-van!"

"Seriously?" Charity laughs with me. "That's funny. You should have gotten her number. I could call her up."

An idea begins to form in my mind. "I didn't get her number or even her name. But I do know where she shops." I shrug again, suddenly shy and feeling silly. "I mean, if you're serious about maybe meeting someone to adopt your baby."

Charity picks up a french fry that fell out of its bag and takes a small bite, slowly chewing on it as she thinks. "Well . . . I am almost ready to pop. I should probably find someone before the baby is born."

"I think that's probably best," I say.

"And I did say to myself that I would trust God to put the right person in my path. And here you are having a hamburger when I'm having a hamburger."

I smile weakly. "Actually I'm just having an ice water, but I'm here, right?"

"Exactly. You didn't even want to eat anything, and yet here you are." She smiles. "I'm kind of excited about this."

"I am too." A spark inside me flames up a little. I feel energized, and for the first time in weeks, I don't want to go take a two-month nap after taking a walk.

"You need to give me your number." She pulls out her cell phone and stops, her thumb poised over the keys.

"I don't have one. I had to give it up when I ran out of money." I want to shrivel up at that admission. I've told everyone else I don't have one because the radiation isn't good for the baby.

"You have a friend with a phone though, right?"

Movement outside the window catches my attention. Colin is walking up the sidewalk, staring at me through the glass.

"Yes. I have a friend with a phone." I pray Colin won't mind being an adoption hotline for a few weeks. "He's right there."

Charity looks to where I'm pointing. Her voice goes all soft. "Well, no wonder you aren't giving your baby up." She looks at me. "Girl, are you brain damaged or something?"

"What?" I have no idea what she's talking about.

"Marry that man. Marry him *today*." She looks back at him. "Mmm-mmm-mmm, I don't even like white guys in general, but he is too fine."

I laugh. "And he's deathly afraid of pregnant girls, so don't look him in the eye when he comes in or he's likely to run the other direction. And he's not the father of my child either, so . . . yeah . . ."

He opens the door and comes right for us.

"Lordy, lordy. You need to put some make-up on or something, catch you a husband." Charity finishes giving me advice just as he walks up.

"You okay?" he asks me, barely sparing a glance for Charity.

"Yes." I act like it's no big deal that he tracked me down to check on me. I'm sure he thinks nothing of it. Who cares that my heart is racing a mile a minute? My heart is stupid and doesn't know any better. "Can I use your phone for a minute?" I hold out my hand.

He pulls it out of his front pocket and hands it to me without a word.

"Here," I say, giving it to Charity. "Call yourself and log in the numbers."

"Yes, ma'am," she says, taking the phone from me and grinning.

"What's up?" Colin asks as Charity does her thing. He's looking at her now, watching as she works with his phone.

"This is Charity. She and I are going to stalk a grocery store together."

Colin stares at me for a long time, but he doesn't say anything. His eyes are dark, so I know he's not happy. He's really, really good-looking when he's cranky. Now that I think about it . . . when is he ugly? That's an easy question to answer: *Never. Never ever.*

Charity gives him his phone back. "There you go. You can find me under Charity." She winks at him.

He gives her a small smile, which he knows very well is designed to melt hearts.

"Damn, boy. You're good." She grins at him and then at me. "Welp, I have to go to class. I'll call you later."

"Class? You're still in school?" I ask. I check my watch; it's after four o'clock.

"Yeah. I have night school. That's where they hide all the pregnant girls." She stands. "You know, because pregnancy is contagious." She says the last word right by Colin's ear as she's leaving the table with her tray of garbage.

He moves to the side a little, almost as if he believes her.

I can't help but laugh.

"What just happened in here?" he asks, looking warily at her back as she waddles off.

I stand up and brush invisible crumbs off my clothes. "I just made a friend and started an adoption agency."

He grabs my arm and pulls me to him. It surprises me so much, I fall sideways. The only thing keeping me from hitting the ground is his solid chest.

"Hey!"

"You're not giving your baby up for adoption!" he says loudly right at my face.

I get back solidly on my feet and jerk my arm from his grasp. "That's none of your business, Colin!"

He glares at me and I glare right back, both of us oblivious to anyone who might be watching.

"I'm not kidding," he says in a much quieter voice.

"Me neither. Now *get* out of my way." I try to push him, but it's about as effective as me trying to move one of the bolted-down tables.

"Did you eat?" he asks.

I'm taken aback by the abrupt change of subject. Anger is replaced by confusion. "What?"

"Did you eat?" His jaw is tense and his eyes full of fire. I'm melting under the heat.

I look down at my empty cup. "Kind of."

He follows my gaze and then his expression softens just the smallest bit. "Ice water doesn't count."

"Fine." I lift my chin. "I didn't eat, then."

"Stay here." He leaves me at the table and walks over to the counter.

I'm tempted to abandon ship and walk back to Rebel Wheels. I'm measuring my odds of escape and success when Colin turns around and talks loudly so I'll hear him across the restaurant.

"Just so you know, Teagan just made cranberry bran muffins."

I sit down, knowing I'm defeated. The only way I'm going to get out of taste-testing one of those monstrosities is to be able to say I'm too full from the lunch Colin bought me.

Colin: 1

Me: 0

CHAPTER FIVE

THE BURGER AND FRIES COLIN delivers to me are surprisingly easy to eat. Normally I'd have to choke down any food from a place like this, but for some reason today my appetite is back. It's been missing for several months.

"I'm going to have to take you here more often," Colin says, taking a sip of his drink as he watches me over the lid.

"Ew, why? This place is horrible." I eat three fries at a time. I can't seem to keep from shoving them into my face. My manners have abandoned me, and I just don't care enough right now to do anything about it.

"Because, it's the only time I've actually seen you eat anything. Maybe you need sodium or something. I know you need some fat." He looks down at my legs under the table.

I pull my feet in closer, sliding them as far under the seat as I can. "You must be joking. My legs are like sausages."

"You're too skinny," he says.

My face heats up and I drop the fry I was about to inhale.

"What's wrong?" he asks, putting his drink down.

"I don't know if you're mocking me or being serious." His comment makes me want to cry. Either option is completely terrible.

"I'm dead serious. You hardly eat. You're supposed to be eating for two or whatever." He picks up one of my fries that fell out of the bag and throws it into his mouth.

"I eat plenty. And if I keep eating too much I'm going to weigh two hundred pounds after the baby's born."

"So? Curves are good."

As a girl who's been battling the booty bulge for most of her life, this does not compute. I roll my eyes. "Please. Spare me." This is crap guys say to girls just to make them feel better about being fat. He's not fooling me one bit.

"I'm serious. No guy wants to be with a stick figure."

"Lie. *All* guys want to be with a stick figure. Just look at the magazines and movies and TV shows." I throw the rest of the burger down onto my tray. Even the simple idea of my big old butt makes me lose my appetite. I stopped looking at it in the mirror months ago, but my memory of it is still very clear.

He shakes his head, like he pities me.

"What?" I say, annoyed.

"You girls . . . so clueless. TV shows and magazines put those chicks on there for *you girls*, not for us guys. Give me a girl with some meat on her bones any day of the week and I'll be a happy camper."

I huff out a breath of annoyance. "Colin, I have news for you. Just because you have that face of yours and all that, it doesn't mean you can just say what you want, when you want, to whomever you want, okay? There's such a thing in the world as manners. You should learn some and use them." I start balling up my garbage, annoyed that he's forced me to lecture him. I don't even know that my lecture made sense. He gets me all messed up in the head when he starts looking at me like that.

"I have manners."

It irks me that he's not at all put off by my admonishments. He really is nervy the way he just sits there and smiles all sexy-time at me. He knows way too much about how to charm women;

it's downright annoying to be manipulated like that. *Women with meat on their bones. As if.*

I can't let it go. "Really? You have manners? Because I haven't seen any." I work to get the bun out of my teeth without anyone noticing. My tongue is doing gymnastics inside my mouth, acting as a sorry excuse for a toothpick.

"I bought you lunch."

"That's not manners. That's pity."

"I open doors for you."

"No, you don't. Not all the time."

"Anytime you don't beat me to the punch."

I have to stop and think about that. *Does he open doors for me?* I can't recall if he does or not. Maybe a couple times he has. I'll have to pay better attention.

I continue my laundry list of his faults. It's making me feel better about chastising him when I might have been just a little wrong. "You swear. A *lot*. And you fight. That's zero manners right there."

He shrugs. "Lots of people swear. They're just words."

"Words designed to incite anger and reactions." I nod in triumph.

"All words are designed to incite something. Emotions are good. Being dead inside isn't."

My nostrils flare as I glare at him. He should be just lying down and letting me win this argument. He knows I'm right. "Cuss words are there to add anger and filth to language. They are the ignoramus's excuse for not being better-read."

He laughs. He actually has the nerve to laugh at me.

"You're insufferable," I say, throwing down my paper napkin and standing.

"Where are you going?" he asks, still smiling his stupid face off.

"I'm leaving, you . . . you . . . *turkey!*"

He's walking behind me. I can hear his footsteps. "You just cussed at me," he says. "That's not very good manners, you know. I have it on good authority. You're inciting anger."

I don't even look back at him. He's too ridiculous. "Turkey is not a cuss word."

"When you use it as a derogatory term it becomes one. I don't particularly like being compared to a flightless bird raised solely for the purpose of making your Thanksgiving table look more festive and delicious."

I will not respond. Mostly because he's too annoying and I don't want to encourage him but also because I feel a little bad that I called him that name. Sure, it's just a bird I eat at Thanksgiving, but I did kind of use it in a bad way. *Grrr*, I hate that he's twisting everything around and making it seem wrong.

"So what's this about adoption?" he asks, pulling even with me as I try to walk down the sidewalk. I hate that my belly is so big my legs won't work right. I feel like a flightless bird waddling down the street the way I lurch from side to side and have to point my toes out. My hips just do not want to function like they used to.

"None of your beeswax." I try to say it without the breathlessness that's arising out of my fast pace and the heat of the day.

"Maybe not, but I'd still like to know."

"Too bad."

He puts his hand on my arm, making me stop. I turn to face him, ready to blast him for manhandling me, but the expression on his face makes it impossible.

Having him stare at me like that is too much. I have to stop it from happening. "What?" I finally say, turning my head to stare out toward the road so I won't have to see him looking at me anymore. He's so darn earnest sometimes, and coming from him, that expression is just too weird.

"Are you really going to put your baby up for adoption?"

I shrug. "What does it matter? It's not yours."

"I know that. I'm pretty sure I'd remember if you and I had sex."

He probably meant it as a joke, but it makes me shiver all the same. Sex. I'm never *ever* doing that again. Not that I even decided to in the first place. *Ugh. Do not go there, Alissa. Focus on something else.*

I look back at him and put my hands on my hips, hating where my head is at right now. Memories. Nightmares. Terrible, terrible things are coming back to me. "Listen, Colin . . . I really appreciate the lunch or dinner or whatever that was, but this doesn't make us friends, okay?"

"I thought we already were friends."

I throw up my arms. "You can't even stand to be in the same room as me or look at me most of the time! How does that equate to friendship?!" I want to tear my hair out over this boy. He makes me lose all my good sense every time he's in the same vicinity as me.

Even though I shouldn't want to be his friend because he's bad news and completely incorrigible, I want to be his friend, and that just ticks me off. Because we both know it just can't happen. We're from different worlds, raised in different worlds, and living in different worlds. I might be in his world right now, but it's only temporary. After this baby is born, I'm gone. I have no idea where I'll go, but it won't be here and it won't be with him.

"That's not true," he says, but not very convincingly. "I don't avoid you."

I start walking again. "See? Even you don't believe yourself."

He jogs to catch up. "Okay, fine. That might have been true for the past few weeks, but it's not true anymore."

"Why? What's the big change for? Is it your birthday? Did you confess your sins at church and now you have to repent?"

"No. None of that. I don't know."

"Lie. I can tell you're lying."

"I don't lie."

I won't even dignify that with a response. Instead, I snort. *Dammit. I'm potbelly pigging again.*

"I might be fibbing, but it's for a good reason. My mom used to say white lies aren't real lies."

"A lie is a lie is a lie," I say. "Liars must *die.*" I'm burning with anger right now. I've known one particular liar in my life who I'd happily throw in front of a train if I had the strength. The thought of it clouds everything else out. All I can see is *him.* His face. His hands. His body. All I can feel is *him.* His weight, pushing down on me. His strong arms wrapped around me. His hands, pressing into my body. *Lying, butthole, jerkface, hurting, sneaking, . . .* I don't say the last word that almost comes to mind. I can't even think it clearly, and I could never say it out loud.

I'm crying now and as close to running as I can get while eight months pregnant. My belly swings uncomfortably from side to side as I huff and puff to breathe.

"Hey, slow down, little penguin! You're going to bust something," Colin says, jogging next to me. He's barely having to move his feet to keep up.

"Shut up! Leave me alone!" I sound pitiful, but I can't help it. He's confirmed my fears about looking like a graceless, flightless bird and it's possible a sun-stroke is in my near future. I just need to get away. Back to the couch. Back to my books. Back to ignoring the rest of the world around me.

"Hey, hey, hey," he says, taking me by the elbow and slowing me down, "why are you crying? Is it because I called you little penguin? I'm sorry. I'll never do it again."

"Just go, Colin, okay? Just go." I yank my arm back and continue walking super fast. I'm almost to the Rebel Wheels parking lot when I realize I'm alone. He finally listened to me and did what I asked.

Perfect. Go. I don't need you as a friend or a lunch date or anything else. Just leave. Me. Be. And stop haunting my daydreams and night dreams too while you're at it.

CHAPTER
SIX

WHEN I GET BACK TO the apartment, I pray for some alone time, but God isn't listening. As usual, he has my requests on mute. Teagan is there with a plate of hot muffins in her hands and Quin is on the couch with headphones on.

I have to choose: either sit next to Quin or camp out in the bathroom. I start at the bathroom but quickly decide that the hard seat is worse than anything Quin could come up with.

I go back out into the main living room, choosing the more comfortable option and hoping Quin will take the hint when I turn on my e-reader and put it in front of me.

I want to let out a string of terrible cuss words when I realize my battery is dead, but of course I don't. My lips are sealed. Maybe nobody will notice my book isn't on the screen. I hold the tablet up in front of me and pretend to read.

"Did you just go jogging?" Teagan asks, kind of laughing. "You're seriously out of breath and your face looks like a tomato. Here, have a muffin." She holds out a softball-sized thing that looks like a completely rotten apple with bits of green things stuck in it. I shudder when I imagine what it must taste like.

"No. Thanks. I took a walk and had lunch at a fast food place up the street. It's hot outside."

Quin leans over and taps my screen. "Seems to be broken." She looks at me with her head twisted and tilted to the side, a crazy grin on her face.

I put the tablet on the coffee table, my ruse obviously not working against Quin's evil powers of observation. "Yes, it's out of juice."

"Were you trying to charge it with your wifi brain-connect?" Quin asks.

I know she knows I was faking on purpose, and right now I hate her for that. She can never just let things go. That's why I'm living here in the first place. And maybe I should be grateful for the roof over my head, but right now I'm just finding it suffocating.

"No," I say, totally annoyed, "if you must know, I was just trying to have a little private moment without having to go sit on the toilet to get it."

Teagan sets the plate of scary-looking muffins on the table and lowers herself into an armchair, staring at me. Quin sits up straight and does the same. Neither of them says anything.

The pressure mounts to the point that I cannot stand it anymore. I have no idea what exactly happens to make me snap, since neither of them is saying anything, but suddenly words are pouring out of my mouth and I can't seem to stop them. There is no filter between my brain and my mouth anymore.

"I can't get a moment to myself in this place! I'm under your radar and your thumbs twenty-four seven! And if I have to eat another one of those things you make, Teagan, that you would *like* to call food but they are definitely *not* edible, I'm sorry, but I'm probably going to go into labor. I *wish* you'd quit trying to make me eat them because they're beyond horrible! They taste *bad*, okay?! And I'm sorry I have to be the one to say it, but if you check the houseplants you'll find large pieces of your food in all of them and I'm not the only one putting them there, either!"

I pause only because I've run out of breath and take in the shocked expression on Teagan's face. Then it hits me what I just said. I slap my hands up to my cheeks, horrified at myself. I want desperately to apologize, but my mouth just keeps opening and shutting like a fish out of water.

"Well, somebody got her Wheaties shit in, that's for sure," says Quin. "Was it Colin? Do you want me to talk to him for you? Straighten him out? He can be a bit much sometimes."

"*Gah!* No! It wasn't Colin! It's *you*, Quin . . . and *you*," I point at Teagan. I stand up all of a sudden. "Oh my god," I say, half whispering. "I don't know what's wrong with me. I think I'm having a breakdown."

Retreat. It's all I can focus on. The looks on their faces . . . stunned. I have to get out of here.

Once more, I run from the apartment.

I run and run and run.

It feels like I'm running a lot, but I guess I'm not. I'm only halfway across the floor of the garage when a slicing pain goes through my side and stops me short.

"Ohhh . . . ahhhh!" I gasp, unable to keep the sounds to myself.

A big bang sounds off to my right and I look up, moaning through the pain, to see Colin coming out from under a car's hood. He's rubbing the top of his head as he takes in what he's seeing. Then his expression goes from confused to starkly fearful. He's back to being scared doo-doo-less of me.

I want to explain, but I can't. The pain. It hurts. I'm dying.

"Ohhhh, shhiiiippp," I moan. I pant a few times to work through the pain. "Shiiipp, ship, ship, ship, ship . . ." *Breathe in. Breathe out. You can do this.* Is the baby coming? Am I going to give birth on the floor of this dirty place? *Please, God, I know you don't want to talk to me right now, but could you please at least not let me have a baby in Rebel Wheels? I don't want that on her birth certificate.*

Colin is suddenly at my side. "What's going on? Is the baby coming?"

"No, stupid." I can barely say the words. I'm huffing and puffing. It feels like someone stuck a knife in my left side.

"How do you know?" His hands are hovering all around my body, but not actually touching me, like he's afraid to get too close.

"I don't," I growl out.

"Come on," he says.

The floor switches places with the ceiling and I yelp in fright. "What are you doing?!"

Suddenly we're flying through the garage, the office, and then out the door. Colin only puts me down on my feet again when we're at the side of his car.

"What are you doing?!" I scream again, battering his chest. I don't know why I'm doing it, but it does help me forget the pain a little, so I keep it up. I even nub him a little for good measure.

"I'm taking you to the hospital, what do you think I'm doing?!" he yells back, ducking a little to avoid me but not really doing anything to stop my abuse. He's not mad at me. The panic in his voice is unmistakable; our tones match perfectly.

"No, you can't do that!" I stop beating on him and grab his arm, squeezing it tightly. "Don't bring me there!"

He takes me by the upper arms and gets two inches from my face. "Then where should I bring you?!" He's still yelling.

I have to close my eyes to protect them from the spittle that's coming out at me in a jet stream along with eighty thousand decibels of freaking-out man-volume.

"To the clinic," I whisper. "Take me to the clinic." The pain is leeching my strength. I just want to lie down and wait for it to be over.

I hear a door open and I'm airborne again. Colin deposits me onto the front seat with surprising gentleness and buckles me in. And then before I know it, he's getting in the other side of the car and starting the engine.

"You know where it is?" I ask.

"Yes."

I don't know how he knows, but I don't really care right now. I just want all of this to go away. I want to be twenty again and getting ready to celebrate my twenty-first birthday. I want to be innocent to the ways of guys and the things they'll do to stupid girls who don't know any better. I want to start my life over.

But something tells me God is not listening to me anymore now than he did back then, on the day my life changed forever.

CHAPTER
SEVEN

THE TRIP TO THE CLINIC is a blur. Good thing I'm buckled in, since Colin drives like it's a life or death situation. Red lights? Optional, apparently. Stop signs? Ha! What stop signs? We arrive in record time, and he picks me up to carry me in, despite my protests that I can manage on my own.

"Thank you for the ride, Colin, but you need to let me go in by myself," I protest as he hauls me up the sidewalk.

"Like hell. I'm not leaving you here by yourself. What kind of asshole do you think I am?"

"Manners!" I screech. Everything is falling apart, and now I have to listen to that language too.

"Sorry. Like heck. What kind of guy do you think I am?"

"The kind who doesn't want people looking at him thinking he's the father of this baby," I say, dropping my hand onto my belly. The pain has lessened, making it easier to speak. I'm sure this explanation will scare him off.

"Who cares what they think? We know the truth."

My face twists up in bitterness as his words sink in. I know he didn't mean it the way it feels, but I can't help feeling angry and sad and powerless, and it's awful. No one knows the truth but me. I'm the only one in the whole wide world who knows. *And I will be keeping that dirty little secret to myself forever and ever, amen.* I stop trying to resist his help. We're almost to the door anyway.

As soon as the nurses at the clinic see him carrying me in, they rush over. "Is she in labor?" the first one asks. "Because if she is, she needs to go to the hospital."

"She said to bring her here," Colin explains, not letting me go.

"Come with me," another nurse says, leading us into an exam room.

I open my mouth to speak, but everyone just talks over us.

"What are her symptoms?" the first nurse asks.

"Pain, I think. In her stomach or the place where the baby is," Colin says, placing me on the exam table on my back.

I struggle to sit up a little. I have a hard time breathing with the baby lying on my diaphragm.

"Contractions?" a nurse asks. "How far apart? Have you been timing them?"

"Hello!" I yell. "I'm right here! How about asking me?!"

Everyone stops moving and talking and stares at me. Colin's hand freezes just as it's about to go to my shoulder.

I brush my stringy hair out of my face and take a breath to collect myself. "It's a sharp pain on my left side that feels like someone is stabbing me. It's better now, but not completely gone." A dull ache remains where before I thought I was being torn apart.

A person I know to be a midwife comes in the room and stops the conversation from going further.

"Sounds like round ligament issues," says one of the nurses, looking at the newcomer.

"It's not a *ligament*," I say, annoyed that she's acting like it's no big deal. "Something is wrong. Ruptured or ripped or something." The pain was too much to be a minor issue, and I can tell by the nurse's tone that she considers this a false alarm. I don't do false alarms.

The midwife comes over and smiles at me. "Just lie back and let's see what we see, okay?"

I suddenly feel a lot less tense. This woman is a master at what she does, I can tell by looking in her eyes.

I nod. "Okay." Lying back, I stare at her, putting all my faith in her diagnosis. She's probably going to say I need surgery. The pain was bad. I have no idea how I'll pay for any kind of treatment, let alone a trip to the operating room.

She presses near the center of my belly with both hands. "How does this feel?"

"Fine." No pain. Maybe I won't be dying today.

"And here?" she asks, going over to my right side.

"Nothing."

She moves over to the left side. "How about . . . here?"

Pain slashes though me like a thousand volts of burning electricity, all focused on my side. I slap her hands away while simultaneously screaming, "Get the fuck off me!"

The midwife slowly draws her hands away and the nurses turn their backs to us.

Colin starts laughing and talking at the same time. "Holy shit . . . that was awesome. Guess you found the spot, doc."

I'm furious at both him and the midwife. "Shut up, Colin!" I want to tear his face off, but he's too far away now and my nubs can't do that much damage anyway. I turn my ire on the midwife. "What did you do that for?! You made me swear!"

She steps back, smiling, unfazed by my tirade. "You have round ligament pain, typical in this stage of pregnancy. We're almost to the end, so you should expect more of it."

"More?" This does not compute. Nobody told me this was going to happen. How is this fair? "Are you kidding me?!" I feel like I'm going to lose my mind. I'm so tired of being pregnant and uncomfortable and now I'm going to be in pain too? I didn't sign up for this. I didn't sign up for *any* of this.

She pats me on the hand before walking out. "Give her the info sheet on it so she can treat at home." As she's walking out the door she says, "Rest. Keep your feet up. Use heat to ease the pain. Let your boyfriend do all the work. Orgasms are great pain relievers, by the way."

I'm left with my mouth hanging open as she shuts the door behind both herself and one of the nurses who follows her out; the stupid wench is still giggling out in the hallway. The other one who stayed in the room is fishing around in a drawer, flipping through papers with her back to me. I can't look at Colin, so I stare at the wall that has a poster of a woman's vagina on it.

My alleged *boyfriend* clears his throat.

"Don't say a word," I growl. I'm biting the inside of my cheeks now, trying to keep from saying anything else. I'm pretty certain I've said enough for one day.

"Who me?" Colin asks. "Oh, believe me. I'm not saying anything. Not one word. I'm afraid."

I look at him. It's impossible not to. He's barely holding in a laugh.

"I don't see what's so funny." I'm trying to hold onto my anger, but his stupid beet-red face is making it very difficult. He's way cuter when he's not trying to be.

Then he starts laughing hysterically, and I change my mind. He's not cute at all.

He has to bend over and hold his stomach, he's so out of control. The nurse hands him the paper she was searching for and leaves the room, but he keeps right on laughing, the paper flapping around as he waves his arm.

"What? *What* is so funny?" I really wish he'd step closer to the table. I seriously want to slap him now. I'm pretty sure he's laughing at me and that just makes me mad all over again.

He finally gets control of himself and then stands up straight. After taking a big breath and letting it out, he stares me right in the face and tells me what got him so worked up.

"Have you ever seen an angry penguin before? Because I have."

He runs out of the room before I can get off the table.

CHAPTER
EIGHT

COLIN BRINGS ME HOME, THE mood in the car significant-ly subdued from what it was on our trip over. My head is spinning with the events of the day. I go for weeks without doing anything, sitting on that couch and trying to forget my life, and then in less then twenty-four hours I have doo hitting the fan, a new friend, and Colin. Colin no longer acting weird around me. Colin being my hero. Colin making me feel like I'm on a roller coaster I can't get off of. Colin calling me an angry penguin. Right now, all I want to do is sleep.

Luckily, Rebel jumps on his butt as soon as we get in. "I need you to get on that GTO."

"I know," Colin says, "I just need to . . ."

"Now." Rebel disappears behind a big old truck that's getting worked on.

The jaw muscle twitches in Colin's cheek, so I know he's mad, but he doesn't argue. "You going to be okay?" he asks me.

"Yes, of course." I start to walk away.

"Here," he says, catching up to me. "Do what this says."

I take the white paper from him — instructions about how to care for round ligament pain. I feel like balling it up and throwing it on the floor, but I don't.

Leaving the guys to their car repairs, I go up the stairs. I want to think of nothing, but my head keeps wanting to twist to the right and look at Colin. Maybe he'll be looking at me too. Or maybe he won't. I don't want to know. Either scenario is bad news. My eyes remain forward and I focus on dealing with my next obstacle: Teagan and Quin. The dynamic duo of pains in my butt.

I open the door and peek inside. No one's in the living room. My heart lightens at the idea of getting to bed early. It's dinner time, but I'm not hungry. Maybe I got lucky and they went out somewhere.

I sneak in quietly, taking a quick potty break before claiming the couch. After putting out my sheet and unfolding my blankets, I settle down on my side, resting my giant baby bump on the cushion. My eyes close in blissful silence. Thank God, I'm finally alone.

A few seconds into my relaxation, I hear a noise. I ignore it, hoping it's just the air conditioner kicking on or something. Then I hear another noise. And then the paper I put on the coffee table rustles.

I'm not going to open my eyes. Someone is here, but maybe they'll leave if they think I'm sleeping.

More noises come. Someone is sitting down in the chair near me. I try to keep my eyes from fluttering under my lids, but it's impossible. If I weren't so darn big, I'd roll over and give them a view of my big butt, but moving is a major operation at this point in my life and there's no way I'd be able to play possum and get away with it.

I breathe slowly and deeply, waiting it out. Maybe this person, whoever it is, will get the hint and go far, far away.

Yeah, right. And maybe pigs will start flying and we'll be able to order bacon take-out.

My eyes open slowly and take in the situation. Quin is on my right. Teagan is on my left. They're both staring at me with straight, serious faces. It's more than unnerving. They're almost never serious like this unless they're in the lawyer's office.

"What?" I say. "Who died?"

"Nobody. Yet," says Quin, staring me down.

I roll my eyes. "I'm so scared."

"You should be," says Teagan. "You've been acting like a serious turd mobile and without us you'd be in a homeless shelter."

I get up slowly, using my left arm to leverage myself into a sitting position. "Well, don't candy-coat it," I say, torn between being angry and ashamed. There's just a little too much honesty going on right now for comfort. I'm afraid I'm about to hear about all the terrible things I've done, being ungrateful at the top of the list.

"What's this all about?" Quin asks, waving the paper around. "Colin says you had to do an emergency run to the clinic? Why didn't you call us?"

I hold my hand out for the paper, which she gives to me. "I just had a pain, okay? It was no big deal."

"That's not the way he explained it over the phone," says Teagan.

"Who cares how he explained it? He's not in charge of me or my health." I know I sound childish, but I can't help it.

"He was nice enough to bring you to the clinic," says Quin. "What would you have done without him?"

I refuse to answer. These two are like my conscience speaking out loud, and it's highly irritating.

"Listen, we don't mean to be riding your ass, but we need to get some things straightened out here. We're about to move into our new place, and I want things to go smoothly and for there to be no misunderstandings about what's what." Teagan is looking at me. I'm supposed to be her roommate there too.

Since I don't really disagree with her, I relax a little. "Fine."

The two girls exchange glances and then Teagan speaks. "Who is the father of your baby?"

I try to school my features to remain bland, but the heat in my cheeks makes it not nearly as effective as I want it to be. "That's none of your business," I say, my voice only wavering a little.

"It kind of is our business," says Quin. "Or at least Teagan's business. And whatever you tell her she's going to tell me, so you might as well say it in front of both of us and save her the trouble of repeating everything you say."

"I don't believe it's either of your business. It's mine and mine alone."

"See?" Quin said, looking over at Teagan. "I told you she hasn't told the father."

I struggle to stand up.

"Where are you going?" Teagan asks.

"Away from you guys."

"You're not going anywhere," says Quin, standing up too.

I'm finally on my feet and fuming. "How dare you!" I have my hands on my hips and I'm practically spitting I'm so angry.

"How dare I what? Speak the truth? Hurts sometimes, but that doesn't change what it is." She smiles at me like a total b-word.

"Get out of my way," I say, pushing past her. I briefly consider leaving the apartment, but it's really hot outside and I'm exhausted. I wouldn't make it a mile. So instead, I go to the bathroom.

"Where are you going?" Teagan asks, following Quin who's following me.

I get inside the bathroom and slam the door shut, locking it before Quin can follow me in.

The door handle jiggles. "Open up," Quin demands.

"Go to H-E-double-hockey-sticks!" I yell, sitting down on the closed toilet.

"She just cussed at me. Did you hear it?" Quin doesn't sound very mad about that fact. In fact, I think I hear her giggling.

"Good for you, Alissa!" Teagan says, definitely happy. "Let it all out! Just say what you're thinking!"

"I'm thinking you two need to get psychological help. Now leave me alone." I sit on the toilet and stare at the wall in front of me. I have to open my legs a little so my belly can hang between them. I am the grossest girl on the entire planet, I'm sure of it.

"Actually, this is perfect," Quin says, her voice coming easily through the thin door. "You go ahead and sit right there and we'll do the talking."

"I'm plugging my ears," I say. "I won't hear a word of it." My fingers begin to rise, but just before they get to the sides of my head, Teagan speaks and I do hear it. My hands freeze in midair.

"Better not. You won't want to miss this. Trust me." Her words give me a chill. She is my landlord in a way, and if I make her angry enough, I don't doubt that she'll show me to the door. She's a nice person, but she's no saint. There's a toughness to her that is undeniable. Maybe that's how she was able to pick herself up and dust herself off after her father died and her stepmother put a knife in her back.

My hands lace themselves over my belly and I lean against the toilet tank while I listen to Teagan speak. Her tone is all very reasonable, even while her words cut me open.

"We guessed that you haven't told the father of your baby that he got you pregnant. And since you're the ultra-responsible type and totally uptight about everything, and your parents are religious wack-a-dongs, we figure you getting pregnant wasn't exactly planned. Beyond that, we were thinking maybe it was more than that. You're too sensitive about it. So some guy did you really wrong. Either you told him and he basically told you to eff off, or you're too scared to tell him for another reason. Either way, you need to come out and face the music. The moving truck will be here in a few days and we need to know if your stuff is going to be on it or if you're on your way out of here."

I tap my finger on the toilet paper roll, slowly, slowly unraveling it. The first square hits the floor and then the second joins it, folding over on top and then flopping in another direction. The pile builds as my mind swirls and my finger keeps tapping, tapping, tapping.

Charlie. Charlie. Charlie. Charlie the golden boy. Charlie, the guy who could do no wrong. My future. My everything.

And now, my nightmare. *Charlie.*

How much have they guessed about him?

"Alissa!" Quin's angry voice comes through the door next. "You'd better not have your stupid fingers in your ears, you pregnant . . ."

"Shhh, don't say it." Teagan is putting on the brakes. That's a new one.

"I was just going to call her a . . ."

"Don't. She's freaking out. Just give her a minute."

I almost want to stay in the bathroom so I can hear Teagan being the voice of reason some more. Being with Rebel has completely changed her as a person. She's so much calmer. Wiser. I guess I can appreciate that. Being with Charlie has changed me. I'm not calmer, but I'm definitely wiser. I'm so wise now I feel like I'm a hundred years old.

Quin ignores Teagan's advice. "She doesn't need another minute. She's had tons of minutes. Hours. Days. Weeks! Listen up, Alissa. You better unlock this door and come out here with your lady-balls on and talk to us. You're acting like a child and you're about to give birth to one. Time to grow up and act like a fucking adult."

I wish the door opened out so I could smack her in the forehead with it. "I *am* an adult, Quin, unlike some people around here who can't speak a single sentence without swearing."

"Oh, for chrissake, would you get off your high horse already? Who gives a fuck about a few cuss words? They don't mean shit. Just get out here and talk. Stop playing the fucking martyr and trying to get everyone to join your stupid pity party. No one's interested anymore."

That last line is what does it. I was strong and angry and full of righteous indignation until she said that. Now all I want to do is find a razor or a bottle of pills. She's right. No one is interested in me or my life or my problems. Why am I even here?

I stand up and take a step over to the mirror. Staring at my reflection, I try to see what anyone else might see. Ratty, thin brown hair that hasn't been properly brushed or styled in weeks, with bangs that hang way too low on my face. Sunken, dark blue eyes with matching smudges underneath. Pale skin. Fat, pale lips that used to be my pride and joy but now look chapped and too big for my face. Arms puffy and blotchy. Chewed off fingernails, no good for fighting anyone off. And a great, big, giant watermelon belly. My eyes scan the shelves, looking for pharmaceuticals.

And then the baby moves. I see it happening in the mirror. My belly bulges out one way and then the next as she rolls around inside me. My hand brushes over the front of me, my fingers bumping over my bellybutton. Something, maybe a hand or a foot, pushes out directly under my palm. I feel like she's talking to me. Telling me that she's there. Giving me a teeny, tiny high-five.

Tears come, first just a trickle and then a waterfall. I see a bottle of pills and swipe it off the shelf, sending it flying across the bathroom and into the shower stall. I cannot believe I almost considered taking them and ending not just my life but hers. What kind of monster am I?

I collapse onto the floor, sobs overtaking me. My life is over, but hers is just beginning. How am I ever going to be able to take care of her . . . to show her right from wrong . . . to teach her to be a confident girl who won't get stuck in situations she can't get herself out of, when I can't even do that for myself?

.

CHAPTER
NINE

I DON'T KNOW HOW LONG it is that I'm in the bathroom losing my mind. Maybe it's ten minutes. Maybe it's two hours. There's no way for me to grasp the time since I have no window, no watch, and no phone. Besides, my brain is elsewhere. All I can do is think about my failures and the doom and gloom that is my future and the future of my baby.

The door opens somehow and pushes against me. There's scrambling sounds and then Teagan's head comes around the corner. "You need to get up so we can open the door all the way without hurting you."

I just push against it weakly, shaking my head. I don't have the strength to do anything else.

Her head disappears and a few seconds later another one comes through the door.

Blond hair.

Green eyes.

Worry.

"Liss . . . you need to move so I can come in."

I panic. "Colin, God, go away!" I wipe my face off, desperately hoping that I don't have goop on my face that he can see.

"Not a chance. Open up or I'm going to have to take the door off the hinges."

Humiliation surges through me. As if I'm not trouble enough for them, now they're threatening to take the place apart. I try to get my legs under me so I can stand. It's terribly awkward with my belly in the way, but with the help of the counter I'm gripping with all my strength and the door on my other side, I make it.

"I'm up." I put my foot in front of the door to keep it from opening up anymore. "But don't come in."

"I need to."

"No. You *need* to go away. I'm coming out. Just give me a minute."

He turns his head and looks at the shower. Then he looks back at me, his earlier expression of concern now replaced by one of anger. "Why are those pills over there? Did you take any?"

"No," I say, relieved to be telling the truth about that. "I didn't. Just go." I push the door a little, not wanting to hurt him but needing to be alone. It's bad enough he's seen this much of me. I need to try and fix myself before I come out there and face the music.

As soon as his head withdraws and the door shuts, I start splashing water on my cheeks. I scrub it off hard with the towel, trying to make the blotches all combine into one big, giant tomato-face. It's better than looking like I have a rash, which is what crying always does to me.

I try to ignore the reflection in the mirror in front of me, but it's impossible. My face is swollen everywhere and my eyes are so red I look like I'm on drugs. Oh, how far I have fallen. I believe this is what they call *rock bottom*. It's very lonely down here. And scary. I'm so, so tired of being alone and afraid.

Taking a deep breath and letting it out, I attempt to push the stress out with the air. It's not working. My heart feels like it's in a knot, a lump of lead in my chest.

I drop the towel onto the counter and put my hand on the doorknob. I hate to think the entire Rebel Wheels family is out there waiting for me, but I suppose it's the least I deserve. Time to face the music. Time to be an adult. Time to be a mother.

CHAPTER
TEN

EVERYONE IS SITTING IN CHAIRS around the living room. The couch has one seat left; I suppose it's for me. I go into the room as slowly as I can, dreading the conversation that's about to take place. My face is burning red with shame. Even Rebel is there, staring at me.

I sit down and keep my eyes glued to the table. Mick is next to me and Quin is on his other side. Rebel and Teagan are across from me. Colin is on my left. No one says anything for a little while.

Teagan finally breaks the silence. "I'd offer you a muffin, but apparently my shit is inedible."

I look up sharply, expecting a fight, but she's smiling.

I bite my bottom lip, trying to keep the tears at bay. She's being way more generous than I deserve.

"Word, sister. You needed to hear that about your concoctions. Nowhere to go but up, now, right?" Quin high-fives Teagan before turning to look at me. "Honesty is a good policy when it comes to roommates and friends. Just, next time, maybe come at it a little more from the side instead of straight on."

I nod, not trusting myself to speak. I'm liable to start bawling at any second.

"We just want to help," says Mick. He turns his upper body to face me more. "You get that, right? This isn't supposed to be an intimidation thing."

I nod. "Yeah," I say, my voice rough. I glance up and look at Rebel's expression. His face is blank. I can't tell if he's angry or disappointed or just completely neutral. It intimidates the crud out of me. Looking at Colin is just not an option right now. I cannot handle him. I don't want to know what he thinks of me. I've had enough pain and regret for one lifetime.

Teagan continues. "We are completely cool with you staying with us. For as long as you need. Get your feet back under you and figure out what you're going to do, whether it's to keep the baby or give it up for adoption."

"She's not giving the baby up for adoption." Colin sounds angry.

"Whatever. It's her choice, not yours." Teagan's voice goes softer. "But whatever you decide to do, you have to let the father know about the baby. That's the only fair thing."

My blood pressure goes up into the roof. I can't help but glare at her. "You have no idea what you're talking about."

"Whoa, ease up there, cowgirl," says Quin. "She's talking about the legal reality. Regardless of how you feel about it, he has a right to know."

I stand, unable to remain seated while listening to their well-intentioned baloney. "Don't talk to me about legal rights." I practically spit the next words out. "Legal rights, my backside." I stop myself before I go into a rant about people who don't deserve to have the privilege of certain rights. My newfound friends are already way too far up into my business as it is. I am not going to share what they would need to know in order to agree with me, but that doesn't mean I'm going to change my mind about it. Charlie deserves nothing from me except maybe a two-by-four slammed up into his junk.

And yes, they are my friends. I'm looking at all their faces staring back at me, even Rebel's, and all I see is concern there. It takes some of the fight out of me.

I swallow what little pride I have left and put everything I have into my apology. If it were just about me, I'd bail. I'd tell them to kiss my grits and disappear into the horizon. But it's not for me. It's for my baby. I have to do the right thing by her, even though it's the hardest thing to do.

I clasp my hands tightly under my belly. "I appreciate what you're trying to do here. All of you. Your support is awesome. And . . . needed. So if it's okay with you, I will go to the new house with you for a little while. I'm going to work on finding something else, but in the meantime, it would be good to have a roof over my head and some food. And I promise I'll pay you back, every single cent. I've been keeping track of everything. As soon as I can get a job, I'll start giving you part of my paycheck. And I'm sorry for being rude before." My face is burning. This is so hard. I just want to run away.

"This isn't about the money," says Teagan, sounding tired.

"For me, it is to some degree," I explain. "I don't like owing people things, and you guys just stepped in and took over my life. I appreciate it and I will pay you back."

"No one's taken over your life," says Quin. Her tone tells me she's disgusted. "You're in charge of your life, even when you're fucking it up. At least have the decency to not give people who are helping you a hard time over it."

I breathe in and out a couple times, trying to calm myself. Reacting to her the way my first instinct wants to would be a mistake. I know she means well, and I have been kind of rude. "You're right. Absolutely. I'm going to work on that." My face burns with unspoken retorts. I just have to suck it up and take the abuse. I need these people and so does my baby. I'm going to do whatever I have to for my child.

For some reason, this thought makes my heart lighter. It makes this whole event just a tiny bit less awful. I'm still trying to figure out why when Quin starts talking again.

"Good. Because seriously, we can be fun if you just let us be a part of your life."

My smile is watery. "I'm sure you can. I'm just . . . too pregnant maybe to appreciate it right now."

"I think you guys need to just stop being so fucking pushy with her," says Colin.

I finally look at him, surprised to see his jaw muscle twitching like mad.

"Ease up, dude. No one's harassing her." Mick sits forward a little in his seat.

"Bullshit." Colin stands and points at Quin. "She's at the top of the list, followed right behind by Teagan." He gestures at her too. "Fuck . . . Liss can't even take a nap without them in her face about it. No wonder she hides out in the bathroom."

My jaw drops open when all the brothers are suddenly standing.

"Easy, brother," says Rebel. "This isn't the time or the place."

Colin turns on him, his voice laced with bitterness. "When is the time, *brother*? When it's all over? When she's run out and disappeared because she's tired of being ridden all the time?" He turns his ire on the rest of the group. "None of you know where she's coming from or what she's dealing with. But I can guarantee you this . . . it's a hell of a lot more than what any of you are dealing with." He gestures at Teagan. "You think your father's company shit is harder than becoming a mother? Being homeless and jobless and penniless while pregnant? I don't think so." He looks at Rebel. "You think being a business owner is harder? Yeah, right." He looks at Mick. "And you've got nothing to worry about. You've got a job, a place, a girl. What do you worry about at night? Whether you're going to get laid or not, probably."

Mick roars and jumps at Colin, knocking me back into the couch in the process. I fall down in a poof of cushions and my round ligament pain flares back to life.

"Aaaaah!" I scream, unable to stop myself as waves of agony take over my every thought.

Colin is flipped over the back of the armchair he was standing in front of and Mick is rolling around on top of him. The chair bangs loudly into the table.

Teagan and Quin start squealing and jump over toward me on the couch.

I curl up into as tight a ball as I can while breathing heavily through the pain. "Ohhhh, God, that hurts." I can barely get the words out. My eyes are shut now as the knife-like pain slashes through my side.

"Cut it out!" Rebel yells.

A few grunts and groans later and some banging sounds, and the noise quiets down. All I hear is heavy panting and my own moans of pain.

"What's wrong with her?" Rebel asks.

"Fuck," says Mick. He sounds nervous.

"Alissa? Alissa, are you okay?" It's Teagan and she's very close to my face.

"It's just round ligament pain," I say without looking at her. "Just give me a minute and it'll go away."

"Nice, Mick. Fucking Grade-A. You just kicked a pregnant girl's ass." Colin is completely unconcerned for his own welfare, apparently.

"I didn't mean to. Shit, I'm sorry, Alissa. I lost my temper."

"Just go to work," Rebel says in his quiet, controlled voice. "I'll deal with this."

"You keep cleaning up his messes and he'll never work this out with Colin," Teagan says.

"What the fuck, Tea?" Quin asks, definitely mad. "Messes? Colin is the one making messes, not Mick."

I glance up to find Teagan shaking her head. "I don't think you know everything that's going on here, Quin. Don't be mad at me for being honest. You're the one who said friends should be honest, right?"

Quin stands in the middle of the living room with her hands on her hips. "What the hell, Mick? What's going on?"

No one answers her. Everyone is just gazing around the circle of faces. No one looks sorry or guilty. I'm too intrigued to pay attention to my own pain now. There are family secrets here and they're much more interesting than my stupid problems.

"Maybe you guys should have a little family therapy session," I say, trying to ease the tension in the room with a joke.

"Great idea," says Quin, plopping down in the spot next to me. "You can be our therapist. Start asking questions." She folds her arms across her chest.

"I have to go to work," Mick says.

"Uh, I don't think so," Quin replies. "Sit."

"I'm not a dog," he says.

"No, but you're my boyfriend and if you want me to move into this place with you, then you have to be willing to work family shit out. Trust me, I just had the scare of a lifetime with almost losing Jersey and my mom . . . you don't want that crap on your conscience. Just work it out."

"Yes, I agree," says Teagan, sitting on the couch too. "I wish I'd had something like this with my dad before it was too late. You guys deserve to be happy and honest with each other. Let's fix this once and for all."

CHAPTER
ELEVEN

TO MY AMAZEMENT, EVERYONE SITS down. Rebel looks at his brothers and they all exchange silent nods. Suddenly, I'm in the awkward position of being a completely unqualified therapist for a very strange family. Who does weird stuff like this? No one in my family, that's for sure. We're all about not talking things through and keeping our thoughts and emotions to ourselves.

"You guys can't be serious . . . I hardly know any of you." My pain is receding quickly, so I put my legs back down.

"That's perfect. Therapists aren't supposed to have any preconceived notions about their patients," Teagan says.

Quin snorts. "I'm pretty sure she has some preconceived notions."

"And I'm not qualified," I add.

"So what? Just ask some questions and get the ball rolling. We can take it from there." Teagan nods at me and then the others. "Right? We just need to talk it out."

Colin shakes his head slowly. "That's a chick thing. That's not how we do it."

"Rebel doesn't even really talk," I say. When Teagan glares at me, I add, "Does he? I mean, I never hear him talk much."

"He talks when it's important," Teagan says. "Just ask a question. It doesn't hurt to try."

"Okaaaaay," I say, warming up to the idea. "Just promise me one thing before I start. No . . . two things."

Everyone waits for my conditions. When I'm sure I have all their attention, I say, "No fighting and no cussing."

Mick rolls his eyes. "Jesus Christ."

I grit my teeth to keep from telling him what I think about that comment.

Colin steps in. "Dude, get a fu . . . godda . . . uh . . . grip. Get a grip. You can hold off on the language for ten minutes."

"Fifty bucks says you swear before I do," Mick says, holding out his hand toward his brother.

Colin gets up enough to grab it and shake it. It looks like they're having a quick arm-wrestling competition. "Deal," he says. "Give it your best shot. I need that fifty bucks for art supplies."

"What about you?" I ask Rebel. "Are you okay with these conditions?"

He shrugs ever so slightly. "I don't swear. I don't fight my brothers."

"Oh." I'm kind of taken aback by that. I guess I just assumed he swore, but it's possible he doesn't. He doesn't talk enough for me to know any different. "Okay then. Ummm . . ." I search their faces, looking for direction.

Quin points at Colin. "Why don't you ask him why he's always picking fights with Mick?"

"Hey, that's not allowed," protests Teagan. "You're not the fuggin' therapist."

I nod, knowing that to ask that question right off the bat would cause a war amongst all of them. I speak quickly before the flames get any higher. "Okay, how about this one . . . Rebel, if there was anything you could change about your brothers, what would it be?"

Rebel's nostrils flare as he stares at me, making me wish I could shrink myself down into the size of an ant and scurry off. I've only asked one question and I've already blown it.

"Excellent. Jump right into the heart of things," says Quin, a huge smile on her face. "I like it." She leans over and pats me on the leg, making me feel just a tiny bit better.

"You have to answer," says Teagan, rubbing Rebel's arm gently. "Come on, you can do it."

"It's not going to change anything," Rebel finally says, barely sparing her a glance.

"So? It's just an exercise," Quin says. "Answer the question."

Rebel looks at Mick and stares at him for a while. Everyone starts to get antsy. I can literally see them squirming in their seats.

"If I could change something about Mick, it would be to have him reach higher. Own up to the mistakes he's made and be a better man about it."

Mick stands up. "What the fuck, man?!"

"Fifty bucks! Pay up, asshole!" Colin's standing now too, a big grin splitting his face.

"Both of you can pay me fifty bucks!" I say, trying to stand but failing. I give up and fall back into the cushions. I sigh loudly. "This won't work if you act like fighting cocks. I mean game hens. Or whatever." My face goes pink; I can feel the heat in my cheeks.

The both look at me.

"What?" Mick asks. He looks at Quin. "Did she just swear? She said cock, right?"

"Just sit down," I say, gesturing toward his seat. "You're giving me a neck ache *and* round ligament pain."

He slowly lowers himself into his chair again. Colin does the same. A slight smile plays on his lips as he looks at me. I try very hard to ignore him.

Quin puts her arm around Mick's shoulders and kisses him on the temple. "Come on, babe. Let's do this thing."

He frowns at her. "We'll see if you're so happy about sharing when it's your turn."

"Hey, I'm an open book. Ask me anything. Let's just talk it out." Quin's eyes are sparkling. I'm pretty sure she thinks she's being given a sneak look into Mick's secret life. I kind of feel like I am too.

"Fine. You want to know how I feel about that?" He looks right at Rebel. "I feel like shit hearing that. I work my ass off for you, covering for all of Colin's shit when he's too busy being in jail to do his work. So what if I blow off a little steam at the club? Who does that hurt?"

"You don't cover my ass at work. I do all my work myself," Colin says.

"Bullshit." Mick glares at him.

"You're at a hundred and fifty bucks, man," Colin says, holding out his hand.

"Shut up." Mick gestures at his brother and looks around the room at all of us. "You see? It's not me. He's always picking fights. This is on him, not me."

"You want to know who it hurts?" Rebel asks. He seems completely unaffected by his brothers' bickering.

"Yeah," Mick says. "Tell me one person."

"Sheila. She was a good girl."

Mick doesn't respond except to twist up his mouth.

"Yeah. Sheila," Colin says. "You screwed up with her, man. From day one."

"That's past history," Mick says. He's practically growling.

"So what's the deal with her?" asks Quin. "What's she got to do with anything? They broke up, right?" She looks first at Rebel and then Colin for an answer.

"I'll tell you what the big deal is," says Colin, sounding only too happy to share. "For a year he messed around on her. Even got her pregnant. You don't do that shit to girls, I don't care who you are or who she is."

"That's not how it happened!" Mick yells, sitting forward in his seat. "And if you were around *ever* and bothered to talk to me *ever*, you'd know that!"

Quin looks stricken. "Mick . . . you never told me . . ."

"No!" Mick turns to face her and grabs her arm. "Do *not* listen to this shit. Give me a second to explain."

"Oh, you have a second, alright. You have a whole minute if that's what it's going to take to keep me from slapping your entire face off." Quin jerks her arms out of his grasp and leans far away from him into the couch.

Mick seems to forget the rest of us are in the room. "Sheila was a nice girl, yes. But not just with me, okay? She had lots of boy-friends when we were together. We had an understanding. There was no exclusiveness between us. None."

Colin lets out some annoyed air, but Mick ignores him and continues with his explanation. "You can ask anyone you want at the club. Ask Olga. Shit, you can see it on the video tapes she has of the entire place. Sheila was always getting with other guys. It was no big deal. And when she got pregnant, it was her choice to get an abortion. She didn't even know who the father was. It could have been at least three different guys. And yes, I was one of them, but I left it up to her what to do. She decided. I just helped her by driving her to her appointment. Does that make me a bad guy? I don't think so."

"That's bullshit," Colin says.

Mick spins around. "What do you know about my life, ass-hole?! You're never around long enough to know anything about anybody here. And have you ever gone over to help Olga out? Hell, no. You help no one but *yourself*. And don't act like you're some kind of prince among men over there, dick. You go through chicks like you do underwear."

"I don't wear underwear."

"Exactly. Use 'em and lose 'em. That's your motto." Mick turns back to Quin. "Babe, trust me. I didn't do anything wrong. I was just . . ."

" . . . Being a guy," she finishes for him. Her expression is guarded.

"Maybe. But not a bad guy. If she had wanted to be solo with me, I would have done that. Or maybe I would have just broken up with her. The relationship worked for a while, just the way it was. I know it's not how you and I are. I wouldn't do that stuff with you, and I wouldn't have done it with her if it wasn't okay with her."

Quin looks over at Colin. "Why are you being so harsh with him about all this?"

Colin shrugs. "He's my brother. I don't like it when he does shit that's bad for him. You want me to just keep my mouth shut and let him ruin his life?"

Mick shakes his head. "I'm not ruining my life."

"You aren't doing your best." The fact that it's Rebel talking now gets everyone listening very closely. "You're capable of so much more. You've got a good girl now. Time to move it to the next level."

"I thought I was," says Mick, looking down at the ground. "Moving in here was part of that."

"Fine," Rebel says, nodding, "but go back to school. Move on. You don't want to work for me the rest of your life."

Mick just drops his head down low.

Seconds tick by. Maybe a whole minute does before Colin clears his throat and starts talking again. "Listen, man . . . I'm sorry about giving you sh . . . crap." He leans forward in his seat, looking directly at Mick. "You're just such a sanctimonious prick sometimes, it's hard for me to just not bust your ass once in a while. I care about you, dude. Brothers for life." He holds out a fist.

Mick reaches over and hits it with his own, but doesn't look at his brother while he does it.

"What about you?" I ask Colin, trying to keep my voice even. "Why do you demand so much of Mick but not of yourself? Don't you think that's hard for your family to deal with?"

Colin's mouth drops open and he stares at me. My heart spasms a little as a wave of guilt comes over me. I feel like I've been a traitor to him for some reason.

"*Boom*, goes the honesty," says Teagan. "Excellent question. Take him down to the mat."

"Ka-chow," Quin says, her voice soft. "Do *not* piss off the pregnant lady, people."

"Answer the question, man," says Mick, bringing up his head and settling back into his seat. "I had to."

A mutinous expression takes over Colin's face. "Fine. Whatever. So I like to fight. Who cares? Ain't nobody's business but my own."

"No fair taking the easy way out," says Quin. "You have to share your feeeeeelings." She's grinning way too hard. She's totally enjoying getting under his skin.

I kind of feel the same way. It's strange but also exhilarating to see such a strong rebellious guy forced to reckon with his emotions, especially when he spends probably eighty percent of his day pretending like he doesn't even have any.

"Nah. That's all I got to say." He leans back, his body language showing a carelessness and complete lack of regard for what we think. Too bad his face keeps twitching and giving him away. This means a lot to him; maybe more than anything else he has going on. *Interesting.*

"You asked me what I would change about my brothers," Rebel says. He looks at Colin. "If I could change one thing about Colin, I would bring him peace. He just needs some peace in his life."

I feel like I can't breathe. I both ache for him and for me. The irrational thought flits across my mind that a pregnant girl or a new baby is the last thing a guy needing peace would want in his life. It's the most ridiculous thing on every level. Why do I keep inserting myself into his world like that? What is wrong with me? Don't I have enough pain in my life as it is?

"Man . . . I have peace." Colin rests his head on the chair back behind him and looks at the ceiling. "I'm all about the zen." His arms rise up slowly and come to prayer position in front of his face.

"*Shhh.* Right," says Mick. "You're all about the fighting and hell raising. You're pure trouble, or have you forgotten?"

Colin doesn't even lift his head to respond to his brother. His arms drop onto the sides of the chair. "Fuck off, Hellion. You're no angel yourself and you know it."

"Insulting each other is not helping here," I say, taking up the mantle of therapist to help ease myself past my own hurt feelings. "Why do you think he doesn't have peace in his life?" I ask Rebel.

Rebel looks at Mick first and they exchange some kind of silent message. Mick nods and then Rebel looks at Colin. When he begins to speak, the entire room goes dead silent. Even the birds outside seem to stop chirping as they listen for the words Rebel shares so sparingly.

"Colin's got a big heart. Too big sometimes. He loved our mom with everything he had. He loved our sister like she was a part of him. She got hurt real bad and he wasn't there. He takes that on himself, even though he shouldn't. When they died, he decided for some reason he had to do penance for the rest of his life over it. I wish that he'd let that go and move on with his life. Stop taking everything on his shoulders and let something else in for a change. Something . . . lighter."

Colin swallows over and over. And then he jerks himself upright and stands. "Man, this is bullshit. Bullshit!" he yells. "I'm outta here. Have fun with your therapy session, assholes." And then he storms out of the room.

No one says anything for a few seconds until Quin breaks the silence.

"Holy furry bat balls, *that* went well." She grins at me. "Good job, Alissa. You're awesome at this, you know? You should change your major to psychology."

CHAPTER
TWELVE

MOVING DAY IS FINALLY HERE. Colin has made himself scarce over the past few days, and he's definitely not talking to me. I thought before that my life was lonely and boring, but now it's even more so. I hadn't realized before how a simple conversation with him would brighten up my day so much. I am such a mess.

I've packed all my things into a single trash bag and it's not even half-full. When I left my parents' house I hadn't taken anything but my makeup and toothbrush. With the few maternity outfits I got at a thrift store, I can't even fill one drawer. I guess that's a good thing since I don't even own a chest of drawers.

The rental place is in a much better part of town than the Rebel Wheels shop. I breathe a sigh of relief as we pull into the driveway. The house is white, has two floors, and a pointed roof; it looks like it belongs in the northeast somewhere, not Los Angeles. I love it immediately. I can picture myself in my own room again, the one right there in the front of the house looking out over the lawn and the street. I'll be able to see people coming way before they get to the door.

"Alissa? Hello, Earth to Alissa." Quin is staring at me through the back window of the car. She's standing out on the driveway. "You gonna help us get this crap unloaded or what?"

"Oh, yeah. Sorry." I struggle to get out of the back seat. Seems like it's always difficult to get up from a seated position or pretty much do anything these days. Everything on my body is swollen, and I break into a sweat just thinking about moving a single muscle. On top of all that, the baby has decided she's going to be a gymnast when she grows up. She's super good at the triple flips. She practices all day long and even during the night too.

"Here, take your bag and this box of dishes and you're done," Quin says, handing me the two items I could easily carry with one arm.

"I have to do more than that." Out of the corner of my eye I see Rebel and Mick carrying in a sofa. Their muscles are bulging and I silently thank Mother Nature for making it hot out today. They're both shirtless against the heat. I might be pregnant, but I'm not ready for the nunnery yet, apparently.

"Nope, this is all you're allowed to do. No one wants amniotic fluid on the new floors. Just go up to your room and decide where you want everything to go."

I snort. "That'll take me all of three seconds. I only have one bag."

"That's what you think," she says, winking at me.

Quin has been way calmer around me since our big therapy session. Everyone has been. I guess it was a good idea that we did it; except for the fact that Colin probably feels more alienated now than he ever did before. I have huge regrets over that. I shouldn't have pushed so hard.

I mount the stairs with heavy feet as I remember his angry words and lonely departure. He didn't deserve to feel that way. He's a good person, and all he's ever done is try to help me. I should have been more loyal to him, maybe.

When I reach the room I know to be mine from the description that Teagan gave me, I push open the door. I'm too stunned by what's inside to move any farther.

The room is painted a pale pink with white crown moulding. There's a double bed, a big dresser, and a tiny white dresser with a matching crib in a small alcove in the corner.

I rest my palm on the door jamb as the bag of my clothes falls out of my hand and hits the floor.

"Like it?" Quin asks, coming up the stairs behind me. She stops near my back. "Pretty sweet, eh?"

"Who . . . ? How . . . ?"

"We all chipped in. I didn't have any dough to contribute so I just painted. I kick ass at staying in the lines, believe it or not."

I shake my head slowly, trying to take it all in. "I don't believe it." It's surreal. Their generosity is making me lose my mind. I've been nothing but annoying to them, and yet all they do is forgive me and then give me more. Who *are* these people?

"No, it's true. I know, I'm not generally a stay-in-the-lines kind of girl, but when it comes to painting, I have a knack for it. That's my OCD rearing its ugly head, I guess." She points under my arm to the dresser. "You could put a diaper-changing pad on that if you want. Or just use the bed. We used the bed for Jersey 'til he took a massive shit in it one day. Holy stinky radioactive green goo alert. After that we got a diaper changing pad. They have plastic covers so they're way easier to clean." She's still chuckling as she moves down the hall.

I finally step into the room, almost thinking the whole decor and furniture thing will fade away into nothingness as my hallucination disintegrates.

But no, it's still there even when I'm all the way inside. I reach out and touch the nearest wall. The pink. The baby furniture. It's all real. My eyes fill with tears.

I wander over and sit down on the edge of the bed, letting the sadness come. It wasn't supposed to be near-strangers being kind to me. It was supposed to be the boy I loved. The boy I trusted. The golden boy who was going to be the center of my universe for the rest of my life.

Teagan finds me in the room a couple minutes later and sits down next to me. "Do you hate pink? I'm not a fan of it either, but we figured with the baby . . ."

I shake my head and wave her concerns away with a few flicks of my hand. "No, no, it's not that. I love pink."

Quin appears in the entrance of the room. "She freakin'?"

"Yeah, but I'm not sure what about."

I shake my head, afraid I won't be able to speak properly. But I have to try because they deserve some sort of explanation. "It's just . . . overwhelming. I thought . . . I thought . . ."

"You thought what? That we'd blow you off?" Teagan supplies.

"No." I shake my head vigorously. "I know you guys wouldn't do that."

"Then what? What's so upsetting that you'd sit in this glorious pink room and cry? Hell, it's like a fairy queen ate too much cotton candy and then vomited all over the place. What could be prettier, I'd like to know." Quin comes in and sits on the other side of me, putting her arm around me.

I can't help it. I rest my head on her shoulder. "I just thought it would be someone else doing it for me, that's all."

"Your boyfriend?" Teagan answers.

I laugh. It's not a pretty sound. Picturing Charlie being kind like this makes me feel like I just swallowed a mason jar of acid. "Yeah, right. God. No. Don't even say that."

Quin pats me on the head awkwardly as my tears drip all over her shirt. "Sounds like a real piece of shit, that guy."

I nod, saying nothing else. It feels good to share a little bit of my secret like this. What's the harm in saying he was a jerk? It's not like they know who it is.

"What's his name?" Teagan asks. "Anyone we know?"

Her words yank me out of my foggy haze. All this pink . . . it made me drop my guard. *What was I thinking?* "No. No one you know." I stand up and smear the tears off my face with the palms of my hands. "Oh, man. I'm a total mess of hormones right now." I plaster a fake grin on my face. "Are there any towels unpacked yet? I need to wash my face."

Quin and Teagan exchange a look. I'm expecting the third degree to start happening but instead Teagan just points. "Bathroom in the middle of the hall has everything you should need."

"Great. Thanks so much." I rush over to kiss them both on the cheek before beating it out of there.

Once inside the bathroom, I lock the door and lean against it. I'm breathing like I just ran a marathon, and I feel like I just escaped something really awful. It makes me wonder when I'll ever feel free again instead of like a prisoner.

I take my time getting cleaned up and coming back out into the main part of the house. I'm relieved to find that everyone is too busy moving furniture to pay me any mind.

About an hour later, after I've had a quick nap and finally put the last piece of my clothing into a drawer, Mick shows up in my doorway holding out his phone. "Call for ya."

I walk over and take it from him gently. "For me?" Just the idea makes me nervous. *Is it Colin?*

"Some girl named Charity, I think? Got my number from Colin."

I'm momentarily stunned. But then my brain kicks in. "Oh! Thanks!" I put the phone to my ear. "Charity? Hi, this is Alissa."

"Hey, girl. You sure are hard to find, you know that? Anyway, I'm on break at school so I only have a minute. I just wanted to see if you're available to meet me for a soda or a water one of these days. I've been thinking a lot about what you said, and I think we could do something about this adoption thing. Together, I mean. Like you just helping me and stuff or whatever."

The idea of being able to help someone like I've been helped fills me with instant happiness. Mick looks at me funny as I respond. "Sure, I'd love to. Maybe I can ride with my friend when she goes into work. That's just up the street from where I met you that one time."

"Excellent. Works for me. And I have my grandpa's car, so if you want, I can come get you. If the whole riding with the friend thing doesn't work out."

"Okay. I should be fine. We can discuss everything over a soda."

"Tomorrow okay for you?"

I shrug. "I think so. If not, I'll call you back. What time?"

"Three. I have about an hour then."

"Great!" I'm probably way too excited about the prospect of an ice water with a friend, but so what. "See you tomorrow."

"You too. And don't forget to keep your feet up. Helps with the puffy ankles."

"Thanks for the reminder. Bye." I press the red button and hand the phone over to Mick. "Thanks."

"Who was that?"

"Just a friend." Someone I can help. Someone who knows what I'm going through. Suddenly, my life doesn't feel quite as desperate.

CHAPTER THIRTEEN

DINNER ENDS UP BEING PIZZA, wings and beer. I stick with pizza and water. My stomach isn't much into hot sauce and I'm pretty sure turning my baby into an alcoholic in the third trimester is not a good idea. We're sitting around the family room eating off paper plates when Colin walks in.

"Where've you been?" Mick asks. "We could have used your help lifting the furniture." His tone is missing the anger it usually has when talking to Colin.

"Working. Finishing up that Nova as requested." His words are for Rebel, but he's staring at the pizza boxes.

"Help yourself," Teagan says, gesturing to the food. "Beer's in the fridge."

"No thanks. I'll just stick with water."

My heart leaps up into my throat and sticks there when he takes his two pieces of pizza and comes over to sit on the arm of my chair. He swipes my bottled water off the table in front of me and helps himself to a huge swig of it. I'm afraid I might faint at his familiarity. It's way to comfortable and warm.

"Ew, cooties," Quin says. She walks into the kitchen and comes back with a fresh bottle of water for me. "Here, sweetie cheeks. You can have your own. Wouldn't want you swapping spit with pure Trouble, now would we?" She smiles, but I swear there's a devil inside there just having a ball over my discomfort. I'm actually kind of sad to have my own water.

"Ha, ha. Very funny," I say, wishing I could come up with something snappier. But I don't want to let her know that she's shot an arrow right into the center of my heart. I totally want to swap spit with Colin. It's no use denying it anymore, but the very least I can do is act cool about it. To be a pitiful pregnant mess hanging onto his very shadow would be the worst kind of nightmare.

"She likes my cooties, don't ya, Liss?" He nudges me in the shoulder with his elbow, acting all casual about it.

I look away. "No thanks."

Mick laughs. "You sticking around for the game?"

"Maybe. Who's playing?"

"Spain and Brazil."

"Yeah. I'll stay." Colin looks over at Rebel.

I pretend that the arrangement of olives on my pizza is very, very critical to its enjoyment while I listen for Colin's next words. He seems . . . nervous or unsure of himself.

"Yo, Rebel. I was thinking . . . are you using the attic?"

Rebel stares at his brother for a few seconds before turning to look at Teagan. He says nothing, but she speaks up.

"It's full of dust and rat turds. Why?"

"I was up there the other day and it actually has some great light coming in from those skylights and the round window under the gable. It would make a great painting studio. If you're not using the space, I'd rent it from you."

"What about your apartment?" Quin asks. "Don't you usually paint there?"

"Yeah, but it's getting too crowded. And covered in paint. Got some on my stereo the other day."

"Doesn't bother me," Rebel says, going back to focusing on his pizza.

"Me neither," says Teagan. "But you'd have to clean it up when we move out. I'm not losing my part of the security deposit because you destroyed the upstairs."

"Not a problem." Colin looks to Rebel. "We cool?"

Rebel nods.

No one seems to realize what a bad idea this is but me. I squirm in my seat, wishing someone would ask me for my opinion. I mean, I know I'm not paying rent, but I live here too.

"What's the matter, Alissa? You have a problem with Colin painting here?" It's Quin again. She's like a darn termite in my brain, eating away at my thoughts and making it impossible for me to just live anonymously in this place.

"Well, you know . . . paint fumes aren't good for babies."

"You won't smell a thing," Colin says. "I'll open a window."

"And attics aren't good for your lungs. You know, with all the dust and rat . . . excrement."

"A little rat shit never hurt anyone," he says.

I can hear the smile in his voice, but I can't look at his face. I focus on the fireplace mantle over his shoulder. "I'm pretty sure it can. It can cause diseases."

"As long as I don't go blind, I guess I'll be fine."

I sigh out in annoyance. He's totally not getting the hint.

"If he hasn't gone blind by now, it ain't never gonna happen," says Mick, snickering.

Colin throws a pepperoni at his brother. "Shut it, shrimp."

"Come on over here and say that to my face, painter pansy."

Colin drops his pizza on my plate and leaps up off the chair. Mick is gone and out the back door before I even have time to blink.

The two of them are wrestling on the back lawn by the time we all reach them. This time, though, they're laughing as they exchange insults.

"Painter pansy? Painter pansy? I'll give you a painter pansy. How 'bout this, grease monkey? You like that?" Colin is shoving Mick's face into the grass.

Mick bucks his brother off his back and dives on him before Colin can roll over. "Grease monkey? How about this? You like that?

Fucking twinkle toes I-need-a-painting-studio freak." He smashes a handful of weeds and dirt into the side of his brother's face.

"Oh . . . my . . . goodness," Teagan says, shaking her head. "Brotherly love. Another reminder about how lucky I am to be an only child."

"Not all brothers are as idiotic as these two," says Quin.

No sooner are the words out of her mouth than I hear, "Mick-eeeyyyy!" being shrieked over my shoulder. I turn around in time to see a small boy with his arm wrapped up in a sling flying through the house toward us.

I step to the side so he can run past me and not plow me over.

"No, Jersey!" Quin yells, grabbing the back of his shirt and halting his entry into the wrestling match.

He falls back with his shirt bunched up around his neck.

"Stop!" she yells. "You're not supposed to wrestle until your arm is better."

I look at him and then around behind me. There's no one else there. "Where'd he come from?" I ask, a little bewildered. This place is suddenly a madhouse with Jersey yelling and struggling against his sister's hold.

"He's probably here with her dad," Teagan says, leaving to go to the front of the house.

I stay and watch the scene unfold. My house was never this noisy or out of control, ever. It's like I've stepped into an alternate reality, and it's not entirely unpleasant. It's just . . . different.

As soon as Mick sees Quin's brother, he stops and gets up. Jersey sees it and strains his arms out toward Mick.

Colin grabs Mick by the ankle and yanks him back down, oblivious to what's going on since he still has grass and dirt in his eyes.

"Quit, man!" Mick yells. "It's Jersey. *Quit!*"

Colin freezes, his hand on his brother's leg. When he sees the newcomer, he sits up and then stands, running his fingers through his hair and brushing the dirt away. There are several streaks of brown soil across his nose and forehead. He looks at me and then at Mick, waiting for him to make the next move.

He's breathing heavily, his chest moving in and out. I can't stop staring. If he takes his shirt off, I will surely faint.

Mick goes over to Jersey and offers up a fist for bumping. "J-man, what's up, my brother?"

"Nothin'. Dad says I get to come visit for thirty minutes, no more, no less." He's grinning from ear to ear. "I wanna go to your house, but Daddy says I gotta come here."

"I'm not at my house, so I'm glad you came here." Mick lays his arm over Jersey's shoulders and turns him toward the house. "Want some pizza?"

"Yeah! Pizzzaaaa!" Jersey takes off, brushing past me like I'm invisible.

This house is too far away for Jersey to sneak over here without getting a ride. As I'm trying to puzzle through how he's actually here alone, I catch the voice of an older man in the house. I assume that's Quin's father.

Now that I kind of know what's going on, I can breathe normally again. For a minute there, I thought we were going to have a major family drama on our hands. It's already bad enough that Quin's brother and mother have been barely out of the hospital and have bad burn scars to deal with. I can only imagine what they'd do if the kid ran away. He seems like a really big handful. It makes motherhood even more frightening than usual.

"What's wrong?" Colin asks.

I realize that we're the only ones still out in the backyard. As I'm contemplating an escape plan, he whips off his t-shirt and uses it to wipe the sweat and dirt off his face. My ideas about leaving fly right out of my head as I gape at his muscles and the giant tattoo that takes up most of his chest. My heart is doing a weird staccato rhythm thing that may be a precursor to an actual cardiac arrest.

"A dragon?" I ask, before I can think to keep my thoughts to myself.

"Yep. Big fantasy fan," he says. He takes a couple steps closer to me. "Are you?"

"Am I what?"

"A fan?" He winks at me and my heart does a double flip. Speaking of fans . . . if I had one of those, I'd be blowing it on my face right now full blast. "A fan of what?" Is he asking me if I'm a fan of him? Should I lie?

"Of dragons. You know. Fantastical creatures." He grins all sexy-like. "What did you think I meant?"

I turn away with plans to head inside and halt the humiliation in progress, but he stops me with a hand around my wrist. I look down at it and then at him. "What?"

"I need your help."

He looks so serious and innocent, I stop trying to get away. "With what?"

"Remember how you did all that financial stuff to help Quin and Teagan?"

"I didn't do very much. Quin did almost everything."

"Yeah, well, that's cool. You're good with numbers and you're organized. I need some help with my painting."

"Uhhh . . . painting is a creative endeavor. I'm not a creative person." I pull my wrist out of his grasp and fold my arms over my chest.

"No, I need a business person, not a painter. I'm the painter, but I'm terrible at the business stuff."

"I don't get it. You want me to work for you?"

"Kind of. Just, you know . . . keep track of the money part and maybe make some phone calls to some galleries. Maybe talk to some buyers who keep calling me."

I shake my head. "No. I can't help you." The idea of being around him that much is just too freaky. I'd surely make a fool of myself. Plus I have the baby coming and zero plans for my life. Although . . . some money would be nice . . .

"Can't or won't?" He's using his shirt to rub his head all over. Maybe it's sweaty. Maybe it's itchy. Why does he keep doing it? Does he know that it makes me crazy to watch his muscles flex all over the place like that? Is he manipulating me on purpose?

"Put your stupid shirt on," I say, annoyed. And then I turn and head back into the house without another word, leaving him out in the yard.

"If I put my shirt on, will you help me?!" he shouts, laughter in his voice.

"No!" My heart-rate is way too elevated as I make my way to the stairs. I go up as fast as I can and shut myself in my bedroom. Once inside, I hesitate with my fingers on the knob, wondering if I should lock the door. If I do, he won't be able to come in behind me.

I leave the door unlocked and lie down on my bed, staring at the ceiling and listening for the sounds of footsteps following me up the stairs. I'm trembling over the idea of Colin coming in after me. Fear and excitement sure do create a heady mix of chemicals.

CHAPTER
FOURTEEN

I'M TEMPTED TO LIE IN my bed and daydream or take a nap for the next several hours, but I'm just not tired enough. And since Colin seems to have abandoned the idea of pursuing me, there's no point in lying down and trying to come up with comebacks and responses meant to sound indignant instead of pitiful. Plus, this room is making me crazy. I don't know why. It's arranged all wrong or something.

I get off the bed and try moving the giant mattress and frame. It's either way too heavy or they've glued the wood legs to the floor, because I can't even get it to budge an inch. I try the chest of drawers too, and all I'm able to do is lean it backward and bang it into the freshly painted wall.

"Darn it," I say, nursing the finger that got squashed in the process.

There's a tapping at the door but no voice.

"What?" I ask, not very politely. My finger is pounding with every heartbeat.

"Can I come in?"

ELLE CASEY

Now my head is pounding too. I turn to face the window with my back to the door. "No, Colin. I'm sleeping. Go away."

The door opens and my breath catches in my throat as I imagine him coming in. *Is he going to touch me? Whisper into my neck? Slide his hands under my arms and onto my breasts?*

He stops behind me. "Did I just hear you moving furniture in here?"

My face flushes over the idea that I'm having sexual fantasies about Colin when his only intention is to be helpful to me. And he's standing just inches away; I imagine I can already feel him touching me. I'm definitely delusional and possibly in need of medication.

"I tried, but I gave up pretty quick." I turn partway around and hold up my finger, trying to make light of my efforts and get those thoughts out of my head. "I'm on the injured list now."

He moves closer and takes my finger, bringing it to his lips and kissing it before I can stop him. "There. Now it's all better."

I pull my hand back and move toward the window. "Thanks." Thanks for sending me into cardiac arrest. Thanks for fueling my pregnancy-hormone-induced fantasies and sending them into overdrive. "You can go now."

"Where do you want the bed?" he asks.

"You don't have to do that," I say. I can't turn around and face him until my cheeks are no longer beet-red.

"I want to. You shouldn't do heavy lifting stuff, you could go into labor. Where do you want it?"

I gesture to the other wall and then have to scoot out of the way as the bed swings around in my direction. My sense of survival takes over, and just like that I forget to be embarrassed around him.

"Dresser?" he asks, resting his hand on the top of it. He's breathing heavy again. I wish he'd take his dirty shirt off and give me a cheap thrill. I giggle at the very idea.

I point to the other wall, not trusting myself to speak at this point.

He ignores my nutty mood swings and picks it up like it's made of cardboard and not solid wood, easily transporting it across the room.

"We gonna leave the crib and small dresser there?" he asks.

I nod. "I think it looks good. What do you think?"

He studies it for a few seconds. "Well, if it were me, I'd just turn the crib around a little. Like this." He walks over and shifts it ninety degrees.

I wouldn't have thought to do it like that but I realize instantly that he's right. "I like it. It's perfect now." Sitting on the edge of the bed, I look around the room and smile. This is my place. My little slice of heaven. A raft of tranquility floating on a sea of madness.

He sits next to me and takes my hand, holding it lightly against his thigh.

I do everything in my power to act like it's nothing. Nothing at all. Just like he's thinking. Two friends, just hanging out, moving furniture. No big deal.

"I really do need your help," he says. He's looking at me.

I sigh but don't return his gaze. I stare at my small hand in his giant, callused one. "Why do I get the impression that you're either asking me to work for you so you can spy on me or so that you can stop feeling sorry for me?"

"Because you're having paranoid delusions brought on by elevated estrogen levels?"

I look at him and frown. "Are you serious?"

"What?" He shrugs. "That stuff happens. It's not your fault, you know. It's just hormones."

I yank my hand away. "I'm not having paranoid delusions about anything. And my hormones are my business, not yours."

"Work with me."

"No."

"Please."

"No."

"Okay, fine." He lets out a long and dramatic sigh. "I guess I'll just have to tell the gallery I can't do that show . . . you know . . . the one I was going to donate the proceeds of for Teagan's legal fees."

I narrow my eyes at him. "What are you talking about? I thought they took her case on contingency."

"Oh, you didn't know? Huh." He walks to the door. "Never mind. I'll see you later."

He's out the door and shutting it behind him before I can get my feet under me. "Colin!" I wiggle off the bed and run to the door, throwing it open. He's already down the stairs.

"Come back!"

"Gotta go! Game's on!"

The volume goes up on the television and some announcer is talking about a goalie.

I'm tempted to follow Colin down and insist he tell me what he was talking about, but I don't. Instead, I slowly close the door and lie down on the bed to stare at the ceiling. I'm exhausted and my legs don't want to move.

Before I realize it, I'm drifting off into a nightmare that has me right in the middle of Charlie's arms, and he's staring at me with soulless black eyes once more. Just as I think I'm about to be swallowed whole by them, Colin is there and he's yanked me back from the abyss. Together we run away fast and far. I don't even know where he's taking me, but I don't care. So long as I can be with him, I feel like I can't lose.

CHAPTER
FIFTEEN

I WAKE UP AT SEVEN in the morning still fully dressed. Rushing around and taking the fastest shower a pregnant person is capable of taking, I'm downstairs and ready for the day when Teagan shows up in the kitchen in her pajamas searching for a cup of coffee.

"Hey," I say brightly, handing her a mug I unpacked out of a box just minutes earlier.

"Hey," she says, scowling and looking at me sideways. "Why are you so chipper? It's too early for that nonsense. Don't make me hurt you." She pours herself a cup of coffee from the pot I just made.

"I fell asleep right after dinner, so I've had about twelve hours' sleep. I think it helped clear my head. This is the most awake I've felt in a long time."

She grunts in response and then stirs in about four teaspoons of sugar and a bunch of milk.

"So . . . I was wondering if you could let me ride into work with you today." I think I'm smiling too hard. I try to tone it down when she scowls at me again.

Teagan sits down at the small table against the wall. "Sure. What are you going to do all day, though? You could do some filing if you want, but there's not enough to keep you busier for longer than an hour max."

"No, I'm not going to work. I'm meeting someone."

Suddenly she seems interested, her eyebrow goes up as her cup lowers to the table. "Oh, yeah?"

Shoot. I shouldn't have told her anything. "It's no big deal. If you can't, I can meet her some other time."

"Her? Her who?" She takes a quick sip of her coffee before continuing. "Or is it a big secret?"

I feel busted and then silly because it's not a big deal. "No, it's not a secret. I met another girl who's pregnant and she's giving her baby up for adoption, so we were going to talk about it."

"What . . . she some kind of recruiter or something?"

"What?" Now I'm lost.

"You know . . . trying to convince you to give yours up too. Adoption recruiter. Are you sure she's really pregnant? Maybe she's just stuffing pillows in some Spanx or something."

"Oh, gosh, no. She's really pregnant. You can't fake water retention in the ankles like that. She's no recruiter, she's a high school student. We were just talking and she was trying to figure out what to do and I offered to help her. I'm not going to do it myself." I fiddle with the coffee pot, trying to get it to be centered exactly over the heating part. The idea of giving my baby up makes me feel desperately sad, but I'm not sure why because having her makes me scared to death. There is no winning for me in this situation.

"Why do you think Colin is so freaked out about you doing that?" Teagan asks. "The adoption thing, I mean?"

I look over at her but then quickly avert my gaze again. She's staring holes in my head with her crazy laser-beam eyes. I try to play off her question like its answer means nothing to me. "I don't know. That's his issue, not mine."

"Yeah, but isn't it *funny*?"

"How so?" I can't help but look at her right now, because it *is* kind of weird how he latched onto that, and I'm glad to know I'm not the only one who's noticed.

"How so?" Teagan says. "Well, starting with the fact that he was allergic to you for about a month and now suddenly he's mister interested-in-your-life. Interesting, right?"

I shrug. "Not really. He just feels sorry for me. He's a good person who worries about other people and their welfare." I go back to fiddling with the coffee pot. When it's perfectly straight, I move on to lining up all the mugs on the shelf, just so.

"I'm not sure too many people see Colin like you do." Teagan snorts into her cup as she takes another sip.

I look over at her tone because she sounds like she's testing me.

I chew on my lip as I consider how to respond. She's waiting me out, staring me down again. I know she's not going to let it just drop.

"Well, those people are wrong. Colin is very sensitive and kind when he wants to be. I think he just needs a little understanding from the people who love him." I feel my shoulders going back and my chin going out, but I can't do anything to stop it. It really irks me that they treat him like a criminal.

"He gets plenty of understanding and free passes from the people who love him, trust me." Teagan stands, and before I can jump to Colin's defense, she continues. "But I agree with you. He needs peace in his life, just like Rebel said. Maybe one of these days he'll meet someone who can help him find that." She looks over her shoulder at me as she leaves the kitchen, then turns to walk backward.

I ignore what sounds like an insinuation and change the subject. "Can I come with you? To work today?"

"Sure." She disappears down the hallway. "I'm leaving in an hour!"

"I'm ready now!" I yell back. "I'll be in the living room reading!" My face warms at the idea of meeting with Charity later today. Now I just have to figure out what I'm going to do for six hours before our appointed time.

CHAPTER
SIXTEEN

THE DAY DRAGS. COLIN IS just on the other side of the office wall, but I refuse to allow myself to go look at him. Not only am I trying to convince myself that I don't care about what he does, I'm also just a little worried that I might drool on myself if I see him bent over an engine with his greasy hands and muscular arms at work. I'm better off just keeping this barrier of concrete between us.

I finish all of Teagan's filing and then get on the extra computer she pulls out of a cabinet for me. "Here, make yourself useful," she says. "I need a spreadsheet for all of the expenses on this project." She hands me a file that's about an inch thick, filled with receipts.

I have the project done in half an hour. I use the next hour to make the most tasteful adoption flier I can come up with using the free software that came with the computer.

"Can I print something here?" I ask.

"Just email me the expense file from your yahoo account or whatever," Teagan says, not looking up from her work.

"Okay. But that's not what I want to print." I log-on to my internet email and send the spreadsheet to Teagan using the address on the business card she handed me earlier.

"What is it you want to print?" she asks, looking up at me.

I turn the computer around so she can see. "Flier."

She squints her eyes and then scoots her chair closer, reading out loud from my screen. "Desperately seeking woman wearing blue headband, driving a mini-van, with grocery cart full of baby food." She looks up at me, frowning. "Are you insane?"

I turn the computer back around and try to ignore my first instinctual reaction, which is the desire to hit her over the head with the laptop. "No, I'm not insane, thank you very much." I gather my unruly hair into a ponytail and smooth the sides down until there are no more staticky fly-aways.

She puts down the pen that she'd been holding and leans back in her chair. "What's going on with this whole flier thing?"

"I told you. Charity, my pregnant friend, wants to give her baby up for adoption."

"What's that got to do with headband lady?"

It galls me that I have to tell her, but I know she'll give me crud and tell Rebel all my business and probably Quin too if I don't satisfy her curiosity. It's like living with my mother all over again, only with frequent cuss words added as extra decoration.

I sigh long and loud so Teagan will know I find her constant interrogations irritating. "If you must know, I met her at the grocery store, and I know she wants to adopt a baby, but I didn't get her number. So I'm just trying to find her again."

"She's a stranger you met in the grocery store? How do you know she's not a wack-a-dong nutball baby killer?"

I feel a little sick over that question. Teagan does have a tiny point. "She didn't strike me as nuts. Her headband was really nice." I realize how lame my own words sound, but only after they've left my mouth.

Teagan crosses her arms over her chest. "I'm about to say something you're not going to like."

"Again?" Gripping the arms of my chair hard enough to make my knuckles go white, I grind my teeth together. I can't say anything else because I'm too mad. She's going to blab about whatever it is that's on her mind and short of running out the door, I'm about to hear it.

"I'm not sure you're the best judge of character right now."

I stand up all of a sudden. "If you're talking about Colin again, you can just *stop*."

The soft tone of her voice takes me by surprise. "I'm not talking about Colin."

I frown at her, my body relaxing just a little. "Oh. Well, who are you talking about, then?"

Her gaze drops to my belly and she says nothing.

It slowly comes together for me, and I instantly feel sick to my stomach. "How *dare* you." I lift a trembling hand and point a finger at her. "You have *no* right." My voice is barely above a whisper. She is so lucky I don't have any fingernails left.

Teagan just keeps on daring, though, because she is a mean, jerk-face, busybody, awful person. "Whoever he is, he must be a serious asshole, for you to feel this way about not telling him he's fathered a child."

I leave the office before I can be arrested for committing murder. My legs move quicker than they have in a long time, fueled by my rage and indignation.

How dare she judge me. How *dare* she express disappointment in me. Like she knows anything about me or my life or Charlie and what he did. *Ugh.* I just need to get away and get some fresh air.

"Alissa! Wait!"

Oh, God! Not now! I pick up the pace.

"Liss! Wait! Hey! I need to ask you a question!"

"Leave me alone, Colin! I need some fresh air!" My breath comes in gasps and my fat legs churn up the miles. Well, the feet anyway. Possibly inches. God, I'm so out of shape.

He's at my side in seconds. "What's up? Did Teagan piss you off?"

"Of course she did. Isn't that was she does best?"

"She is pretty good at it."

I won't smile at him. Who cares if he's charming.

"Where you going?" he asks.

"None of your beeswax. Go back to work before you get fired."

"It's my lunch break. How 'bout I buy you a burger?"

"No. I'm not hungry." I'm halfway to the meeting place with Charity. My stomach has a hole in it and I can feel the shakes coming on. That burger is sounding better and better with every step. I imagine I can smell the grease from here and I want to take a bath in it I'm so hungry.

"Bull puckie. You're eating for two and you haven't even had breakfast."

"Yes, I have."

"What'd you eat?"

I roll my eyes. "Food." I think about it for a second and realize that I didn't eat anything. I was too excited about meeting with Charity to focus on breakfast.

"Liar. Come on. There's a double burger, a fish sandwich, and a chicken wrap with my name on it in there. You can get whatever you want, on me."

"You eat enough for three people," I say, impressed with the fact that he's so perfectly in shape regardless of all those calories going into his system on a regular basis.

"Have to. How do you think I'm able to keep up my fighting weight?"

I don't bother answering. Part of me wants to lecture him and tell him he needs to stop worrying about being good at fighting and start worrying more about being good at painting and relaxing ... finding that peace Rebel talked about ... but I don't do it. I don't like being lectured so I'm sure not going to do it to him. Especially when he's offering to buy me a burger. My stomach growls like an angry hyena.

"Okay, fine," I say. "Buy me a burger. But don't harass me."

"Harass you? When have I ever harassed you?" He's laughing at me.

"Every time you've ever opened your mouth in my vicinity," I say petulantly. I'm not being fair to him, but I can't seem to be a good person right now.

"Yes, ma'am. I promise not to harass you the whole time we are dining together."

"We are not *dining* together," I say as he opens the door to the restaurant for me and I precede him inside. "We're just having a burger."

"Yes, ma'am. Whatever you say."

I finally smile as we walk up to the cash registers. I'm kinda liking the whole *ma'am* thing.

CHAPTER SEVENTEEN

COLIN IS SITTING ACROSS FROM me, inhaling food. He's not picky about what's going in that mouth of his. Bit of burger, hunk of chicken, a pile of french fries, lint from the table; he's like a giant food vacuum. I hang onto my tiny kid burger with a tighter grip, just in case.

"What?" he asks after swallowing a lump of food that would have challenged a Great Dane.

"You eat like you're starving to death."

"I am." He wipes some ketchup off his lips and smiles. "I haven't eaten in three hours."

My heart flips over. He looks like a little boy enjoying his meal. I want to smooth down his unruly hair and kiss him lovingly on the cheek. *Gah,* my mothering instincts have apparently kicked in.

He gestures toward my burger with the next pile of fries that he's squeezed between his thumb and forefinger. "That's not enough food right there. You're starving yourself."

"No, I'm not. For your information, my stomach only has so much room in it when a baby is using it as a pillow."

He winces. "Ouch."

I nod. Finally, I've got some understanding from someone.

"What else is going on in there?" He shoves the fries into his mouth and chews while he waits for my answer.

"What do you mean?"

"I mean, what other things are happening to your body that are different?"

I stare at him for a few seconds, trying to read his expression. I see nothing but curiosity there.

"Hello?" He smiles at me and snaps his fingers in the air between us. "Are you lost?"

I shake my head. "No. Just trying to decide if you're mocking me or setting me up."

He shakes his head and smiles a little. His expression looks kind of sad, in a way. "I'm not doing either of those things. I'm just asking a simple question because I want to know the answer."

I shrug. "Well, if you really want to know, there are *lots* of things going on."

"Like what?"

"Like . . . I have cankles."

"Cankles?"

I hold out my foot a little so he can admire the puffy view. "Yeah. That's where your ankles get so swollen that you can't tell the difference between them and your calves."

He looks under the table. "I can tell a difference."

"Liar. I also have spots on my face."

He frowns as he stares at me. "No, you don't."

"Yes, I do. Look." I point to my cheek and lean closer. "It's called the mask of pregnancy."

"If you say so."

"*And*, I have a dark brown line going right down the middle of my belly, from stem to stern." I nod with satisfaction. That one will get him good.

He puts his chicken wrap down. "Say what?"

"Yep." I'm still nodding. "Big old brown line. It's probably permanent."

"Get outta town." He wipes his hands off on his pants and licks his lips, grabbing the bit of lettuce that was sitting there.

"No, I'm serious."

"I want to see it." He leans over sideways so he can look under the table again.

My hands fly up to rest protectively over my belly. "No. No way!"

"Yes, way. Come on. I don't believe you. You're just trying to get me to feel sorry for you."

I snort. "As if. I don't need you to feel sorry for me."

"Then show me the line. Unless you're just making stuff up because you think I'm stupid enough to believe everything I hear."

"No, I don't think you're stupid. But it's true. I have a line. A *big* line."

"Prove it."

My jaw sticks out. "I don't have to prove anything to you."

"No, you don't, that's true. But if you want me to believe these ridiculous stories you're telling, you're going to have to ante up."

I roll my eyes as I toy with a fry. "You really don't want to see it, trust me."

"No, I really do. Trust *me.*"

I chew on the inside of my cheek as I consider my options. For some ridiculous reason, I want to show him the line. I want to *not* be the only one outside of the clinic who's seen it. Plus, there's some weird voice in my head telling me to get naked with Colin. It's getting louder every day.

"Come on, you know you want to show me," he says in a sexy voice.

I laugh. "You are a serious freak, you know that?" *God, it's like he can read my mind.* My ears are burning.

Up next in his attempt to persuade me is his pitiful baby face. It's quite powerful. "Please? I've never seen a brown line before. Heck, I've never seen a pregnant belly before."

"Seriously?" I'm not sure I believe him. He's been with so many girls . . .

He nods. "Dead serious."

"Fine." I roll my eyes. "If you want to see it so bad, you can see it." I'm really embarrassed, but I turn sideways in my seat and lift up my shirt a little.

"What is that?" he asks, leaning over and touching the top of my pants. I have maternity jeans on and the cotton panel in front is covering my bulging belly.

I slap his hands away. "My pants, dummy. Don't touch."

He laughs once. "Those are some high pants, Melvin."

I pause in my undressing. "Excuse me, but if you're going to mock the belly, you will not be permitted to *see* the belly."

He holds his hands up in surrender. "Not mocking the belly. Could be mocking the pants though."

I look down at them. "They are intensely ugly, I'll admit. But they're way more comfortable than regular jeans that cut me in half. I have to push those down below my belly and they slice right into me."

"Can't have that. So where's this mysterious brown line, eh? All I see is pants everywhere."

I can't look at him. I'm about to expose one of the most private parts of my body and I'm in a fast food restaurant. Thank goodness it's too early for the normal lunch crowd. I reach up under the rest of my shirt and grab the top edge of my pants. "Brace yourself," I say. "It's going to be ugly."

I pull the top of the panel down and expose my belly to the cool air of the restaurant. It makes the hair all over my body stand up with shivers. I'm staring down at the bulging skin of my stomach, noticing the line has gotten even darker than it was before. *Dammit. It's going to be black soon.*

"See? Told you so. Brown line." I look up, expecting him to be nodding in appreciation, but instead I'm staring into the face of a ghost.

His mouth his hanging open and he's staring at my belly.

I yank up my pants and pull my shirt down quickly, my face flaming up red. "Told you it was hideous."

His expression makes him appear as if he's still in shock. His voice is strangely flat. "I want to see it again. I didn't get a good look."

Scowling at him, I turn back to face my food and pick up a fry. My appetite is gone, but I'm going to pretend it isn't. "Shut up." I put what tastes like cardboard into my mouth and chew mechanically.

"No, I'm completely serious. One more look." Now he sounds way too animated.

I can't help but laugh. "That sounds creepy."

"Sorry. But seriously, show me one more time. I promise I won't say a thing."

I shake my head. "Nope. Show's over."

"I didn't see the brown line."

"You are such a liar." My smile is coming back, bit by bit, like it or not.

"No, I'm not. I didn't see anything but white. Lots of white." He's back to grinning.

"Nice." I shake my head. "Mock the fat girl. Good plan." I crumple up my garbage and start to throw it into the bag my burger came in, but Colin stops me with his hand over mine.

"You are not fat. Why do you keep saying that?"

I pull my hand away because the warmth makes me uncomfortable when combined with his sincere expression. "I can't even fit behind the wheel of a car right now."

"But that's because there's a baby in the way, not fat. Why are you so mean to yourself?"

Tears rush to my eyes and I have to act very busy with the remnants of my meal to keep them from being too obvious. "I'm not mean to myself. I'm just being honest."

"That's not how I see it."

"Well, maybe your perspective is off."

"Nope. My perspective is perfect. I'm an artist. You're pregnant, you hardly eat, you're retaining water because you don't get enough exercise *and* because you're pregnant, but none of that makes you fat. You're beautiful. Pregnancy looks good on you."

I nearly choke on that word. *Beautiful.* I have nothing to say in response to his outrageousness. I desperately want this to be the truth, but just the same, I desperately know it's all a lie. What I can't figure out is why he's bothering.

"Show me the belly," he says. "One more time, I promise I won't call you fat."

"You never have," I say, my voice not quite right. He's never said anything unkind to me ever. I realize in this moment that he is the nicest person I have ever met in my whole life. As tough and as mean as he can be to other people, he's never been anything but a prince to me. The apocalypse must be coming. Nothing makes sense in this world as it is right now.

"See? I'm a safe bet. Just a peek. If you don't, I'm going to have to Google it and then things could get ugly."

"Google it? What? Google my belly? I'm not on Google." I frown at him. Now he's just being silly.

"No, I'll Google 'brown line on pregnant belly'. Do you know the weird shit that will come up if I do that? I'll be scarred for life. Not every woman has a gorgeous bump like you do. Just show me."

I'm flattered beyond reason. I can't think straight. He's called me beautiful and gorgeous all in the space of five minutes. I know he's a world-class charmer and a player of the highest degree, but that doesn't stop me from feeling like a complete nincompoop. My head is spinning and my hand is already moving toward the bottom of my shirt.

"Fine. One look. Last time ever."

"Okay," he agrees, nodding. "If you say so."

"I *do* say so."

"Fine. I agree to your terms." He folds his hands and puts them on the table in front of him, right on top of all the wrappers and food he still has remaining.

"You're nuts," I say as I lift up my shirt.

This time I look right at him from the start.

This time he doesn't turn into a ghost.

"Well, would you look at that . . . a brown line. Right down the center of your belly." He reaches out to touch it, but I slap his hand away.

"Don't touch."

"Why? Does it hurt?" His hand is still hovering very close.

"No, of course not."

"I just want to . . . feel . . . it . . ." His hand comes closer, and this time I let it.

His finger touches the line and slowly makes its way down toward my protruding belly button.

My whole body is on fire now. Not just my face, but my chest, my breasts, my arms, my legs and the space between them. Colin has found my hot button apparently.

And then he gets to my belly button and I go instantly cold at the idea of him even seeing it, let alone touching it.

I shove my shirt down and knock his hand away at the same time. "Freak show over," I say, standing up and grabbing my tray. The panel of my pants is gathered at my hips, but I leave it. I just want to escape.

"Hey, I was just getting started," he says, standing up too. He walks with me over to the garbage can, full of good humor. He's not one bit uncomfortable, unlike me. I want to lock myself into a closet and not come out until he's two counties away.

"That's what you think," I say, trying to play off my embarrassment. I cannot believe he almost touched my outie. I try to walk back to the table, but he stops me with a hand on my arm.

"You're beautiful, Alissa. Really beautiful. I wish you'd stop being mean to yourself."

I yank my arm away. "Better get back to work. Don't want you to get fired." He's being too nice. It's making me uncomfortable. Before, when he was ignoring me and treating me like I had a disease, he was much easier to handle. Being all nice and caring makes him very threatening all of a sudden. I imagine I can still feel his fingers on my stomach. It makes my heart cramp up in my chest. It means nothing to him, I know it does, but it feels like everything to me.

"Aren't you coming back too?" He stands next to the table as I carefully lower myself back into my chair.

"No. I'm waiting for someone."

"Who?" His happiness is quickly replaced by suspicion.

"Charity. She and I are going to talk about her adoption."

He glances up and looks out the windows of the restaurant. "Speak of the devil."

I twist around in my seat to see her coming up the sidewalk. "She's early," I say, worried at the expression on her face. I get up to meet her at the door. "Are you okay?" I ask as she walks in.

She grins hugely. "Hey! Miss me?" She grabs me into a hug and our bellies bump together.

I squeak and turn sideways at the same time she does. We both laugh.

"Yes, I did miss you, actually." Our bond reconnects and my day is suddenly way brighter.

"I see you brought tall and not too dark but very handsome with you." She looks over my shoulder at Colin standing behind me.

"He followed me here. Can't get rid of him."

He steps up in time to hear me say that, but he smiles anyway.

"Well, don't get rid of him on my account," Charity says. She puts her hand out. "Nice to see you again."

He shakes her hand and nods once. He's back to being Mr. Cool, Mr. Distant. "I have to get back to work. I'll give you a ride home later?" he says to me.

I shake my head. "Nope. I'm riding with Teagan."

"Suit yourself." He leaves without another word, his face set in stone.

I struggle to keep my happy expression going while my heart collapses painfully inside my ribs.

CHAPTER
EIGHTEEN

Y OU'RE EARLY," I SAY, MOVING past my regrets at how I
left things with Colin ten seconds earlier. I try not to stare at
his form moving quickly down the street.

"Yeah, I had one of my classes cancel, so I skipped that
homework."

"I already ate, but I'll sit with you."

"Grab us a table before we get locked out," she says, pointing
to the crowded doorway.

By the time she comes to take to the seat I saved for her, it's the
only one left in the whole place. While Colin was charming my
pants down and feeling me up, the whole world decided it was
time for lunch.

"I'm starving. Are you starving all the time like I am?" she
asks, unwrapping a sandwich.

"No. I don't have much of an appetite."

"Lucky you. You probably haven't gained anything, have
you?" She takes her first bite of her sandwich and winces.

"I have. My butt was only half this big before."

She smiles. "For serious. My butt . . ." She shakes her head slowly. "It's hopeless. I'm going to invest in a lot of spandex after this baby is born. And I'm going to join the track team."

I smile, not sure what to say to that. I have zero plans for my future, but hers sounds so hopeful.

"I made you a flier, by the way." I pull the paper out of my purse and show it to her, covering up the awkward silence.

She looks it over and nods. "You think this will work? I mean, what if some weirdo calls me?"

I'm suddenly not feeling as confident in my flier as I was two minutes ago. Only two people have seen it, and they both think it's terrible. "Well, we could change it. Or we could try something else."

"We could stalk the grocery store," Charity offers. "You know . . . hang out there a lot. Maybe we'll see her shopping again."

I nod. "Yeah, I guess we could. As long as they don't throw us out it could work."

"We can just sit in the parking lot. Want to go right now? I have my grandpa's car."

I gesture to her food. "You haven't finished."

She stands and starts shoving things into the paper bag her food came in. "I'll eat it there. We can do a stake-out like in the movies."

Her grin is impossible to not respond to in kind. "Okay. Sounds like fun." It's way better than filing stuff at Rebel Wheels, that's for sure.

Ten minutes later we're in the grocery store parking lot with the car pointed toward the front doors. If the lady wanting to adopt goes in or comes out, we'll have a clear view of her.

"Want a fry?" Charity asks. The whole interior of the vehicle smells like greasy food. My stomach turns over uncomfortably.

"No, thanks. I'm stuffed." I rub my tummy and am instantly rewarded with a kick.

"So, that guy . . . Colin. He your boyfriend now?"

I smile kind of sadly. I can't help it. "No, not at all. He's the brother of one of my roommates, so I see him a lot, but we're definitely not together."

"He know that?"

I look over in time to catch her grinning.

"Of course." I really want to know why she said that, but I keep my mouth shut about it. There's no point in letting her lead me down that road.

"Do you have a boyfriend?" I ask, trying to throw her off the scent.

"Nope. I slept with one a couple times and ended up learning that lesson the hard way. For some reason my brain took a vacation when he told me it would feel better without protection."

I shake my head, angry at this stranger I've never met. "Why do guys do that to girls?"

"Because they're selfish, immature, and brainless. He didn't mean to get me pregnant."

I look at her sideways.

"I'm not making excuses for him. But fact is, I should have taken responsibility for my body and I didn't. You can bet your sweet buns I'll be carrying condoms with me wherever I go after this baby is born."

I laugh. "So you can just drop and go wherever you are."

"Wherever and whenever," she agrees, giggling.

My face freezes in place as I see a flash of blue in blonde hair across the parking lot.

"What?" Charity says. "Did I offend you? I'm sorry."

"No." I grab her arm with one hand and point with the other. "I think that's her."

Charity's head whips around to follow the direction I'm pointing in. "The lady with the yellow shirt?"

"Yes." I grab the door handle. "Are we going in?"

Charity looks at me, her expression suddenly unsure. "Should we?"

I relax a little in my seat. "Only if you want to. I don't want to push you into doing something you don't want to do." Lord knows, people have been doing that to me enough lately that I don't want to be guilty of it myself. Besides, this isn't some little thing. This is about giving up a child. A life being handed over to another person. My stomach cramps a little at the thought of it.

"No, I do want to. I'm just nervous." Charity holds out a trembling hand. "See? I'm shaking. Wow. What a dork."

"No, it's not dorky." I hold her hand in mine. "I'm with you. If you want to do this, I'm going too."

"Wingman?"

"Yes. Wingman. Wingwoman. Wingmomma." I smile at the idea of us two penguins waddling into the grocery store, on a mission.

Charity opens her door and takes the keys out of the ignition. "Okay. Let's do this before I chicken out."

I get out too, and together, we walk into the air-conditioned grocery store, scanning the aisles for the lady with the blue headband.

CHAPTER
NINETEEN

WE FIND HER IN THE baby food aisle. She's staring at a line of organic fruit jars.

"Just follow my lead," I whisper in Charity's ear. Walking over to the canned vegetables just a few feet away from the woman, I exclaim, "Oh, look! Peeeaas. I wonder when we need to start feeding the babies peas."

Charity jumps right in. "I'm pretty sure it's not until they're like a year old or something."

I tap my finger on my chin as I carefully consider all the labels. Or pretend to. I'm not actually seeing anything. I keep waiting for the woman to notice us being confused and come to our rescue. "Well, you could be right. I wish I knew. I'm kind of clueless about all this *baby* stuff."

"Excuse me. Can I be of help?"

Bingo! Blue headband, nine o'clock!

"Oh, sure, that would be really nice," I say, turning to face her. I wait for the spark of recognition to appear, and I'm not disappointed when it does about five seconds later.

Her eyebrows come together in confusion. "Didn't I . . .?"

"Feel my baby move just a few days ago? Yes. Hi, again." I hold out my hand.

She points at me. "You were in the tampon aisle last time." She takes my hand absently as she waits for me to respond.

"Good memory." I grin like a fool and pump her hand really good.

A tapping in the middle of my back gets my attention and I drop our handshake. "Oh, by the way, this is my friend Charity." Turning to the side, I give the lady a better view of my friend.

"Hello, Charity. I'm Barbara." She looks down. "Oh. Wow. Looks like you're almost ready to go."

"Yes, ma'am, I am."

Barbara looks pained all of a sudden. "You just called me ma'am. Now I feel old."

"Oh, you're not old," I say, false happiness lighting up my voice like neon bulbs on the Vegas Strip. "Didn't you say you were thinking of having kids? You can't be old for that." I cringe at the words coming out of my mouth, a steady stream of verbal vomit. I'm supposed to be going all stealth with her but it's not working.

Both Charity and Barbara are staring at me like I have a single eyeball in the middle of my forehead.

"So . . . you're shopping for baby food," Charity says, glancing nervously between Barbara and me. "We were just doing the same thing. Small world, huh?"

"Yes." Barbara looks first at the food and then at the front of the store. I get the impression that she's about to leave in a hurry. Maybe she's worried we're going to kidnap her. I would be if it were me.

It's time to kick this into high gear before we lose our chance. I jump right back into the conversation. "Yeah, and you know what? We are so clueless. So, so, so, so, so clueless. And for me it's kind of a big deal, because you know I'm going to keep my baby and stuff. But Charity here is going to give her baby up for adoption, so she's just acting as like a consultant for me."

Silence.

The totally awful, creepy, awkward silence is making my ears ring. I am so not the type for stake-out work.

"Listen . . .," Charity starts and then lets out a big sigh. "Let's just cut out the bahoola and get right to the point."

"Bahoola?" Barbara asks, looking once more at the front of the store.

"You know. The games," Charity explains. "We were totally stalking the store waiting for you to come in."

Barbara looks sharply at her. "Excuse me?"

Charity rolls her eyes. "Yeah, I know. Terrible idea."

"I'm sorry, I'm just not following." Barbara looks at me. "What am I missing?"

I open my mouth to speak, but Charity goes first, cutting me off.

"See, I met Alissa the same day you did but after, and we got to talking about adoption, and I told her that's what I want to do and she told me about you wanting a baby and all. But she didn't know your name or anything, so we just came back here . . . hoping to see you."

"Because . . ." Barbara stops and then just trails off, staring first at Charity and then at me.

It's my turn to talk now and make a complete fool out of myself. "Because you said you wanted a baby really bad, and you seem so nice with that blue headband on and stuff . . ." I look out the front window, desperation in my heart. "And you have that nice minivan and some baby food too . . ."

"I don't . . . I don't know what to say," Barbara whispers.

I try to smile but I'm sure I look more like I have a stomachache, which I do. My guts are cramping terribly.

Charity must notice my discomfort because she jumps in again. "I'm sorry we kind of bum rushed you, but you know, I'm giving birth soon and I haven't done anything I need to for the adoption yet. So I guess you could say we just acted without thinking too hard about it."

Barbara is nodding, her hand fluttering to her chest and then her throat. "I need to go," she says in a choked voice, moving down the aisle so fast she's practically a blur.

Charity and I watch her go in silence. She's out the door and in her car before Charity speaks again.

"Well, *that* went well," Charity says.

I put my arm across her shoulders. "I'm sorry. I shouldn't have done that. This was a terrible idea."

She puts her arm on my waist. "Aw, don't worry about it. Maybe she just doesn't like black babies."

I look at her to see if she's serious. I feel positively sick. "No . . . you don't really . . ."

"Nah. I'm just joking." She grins. "Come on. I'll drive you home. I gotta get to class."

She keeps up the chatter all the way to my place, but I can tell she's hurt. I'm dying inside knowing that I made that hurt happen. I wish I knew what to say to her, but I can't think of the right words that won't make me sound like I feel sorry for her. She's too proud for that nonsense, and I don't want to damage our already delicate relationship. I really like Charity and admire her; I almost wish I could be more like her. She's strong and smart and keeps a sense of humor about her even when the picture goes dark.

"Here you are," she says, pulling up to the curb in front of the house. "Want to go have another lunch sometime?"

I'm so relieved that she still wants to hang out with me, my answer comes out in a big rush of air. "Sure. Anytime you want."

"Okay, good." She puts her hand on my arm as I'm struggling to get out of the car. "Listen, if I go into labor, I'll let you know, okay? It's not long for me now. Maybe you can come visit me in the hospital. Maybe bring me some red licorice or something."

"Aren't you going to call your partner?" I ask, getting to my feet in the street. "I mean, I'll come, but you should call your partner first." I shut the door behind me and look at her through the open window.

"Partner? What partner? My square dancing partner?"

I bend over a little so I can see her better. "No, silly, your birth coach partner."

"What's that?"

I lean in the car window and look at her straight on. I can't tell if she's messing with me or not. "Are you serious?"

"Serious about what?"

Someone comes walking up the sidewalk behind me. I turn around to see who it is, but don't recognize him. He's younger than me for sure and wearing a goofy baseball hat turned sideways, so I don't feel threatened. He distracts me from my concern over Charity's lack of birth assistance. I don't have any myself, but she's much younger than me.

"Oh, hey," he says, cheerfully. "You must be the famous Alissa."

My nostrils flare out and my lips press together as I consider his words. I'm not sure how I feel about being famous, but since he's not laughing as he says it, I decide to give him the benefit of the doubt. "I'm Alissa, yes."

He holds out his hand for me to shake. "My name's Rat. I was just in your place doing some handiwork for Teagan."

I shake his hand and notice it has callouses on it. "You seem a bit young to be a handyman."

He grins, his bright teeth lighting up his mocha-colored face. "Don't let the baby-smooth skin fool ya. I'm all man."

I laugh because I can't help it. He still has acne, so I have to wonder how honest he's being about the man thing, but I'm not going to pop his bubble and tell him that. "Nice to meet you, Rat." I turn and gesture into the car. "This is my friend Charity."

"Oh, hey, Charity." He leans down and waves for a second before looking up at me. "We know each other already."

"Hey, Julio," she says. "Long time no see."

He leans on the window opening, sticking his head just inside the car. "Where you been?"

"You know. Pregnant girl prison. Night school."

"Aw, man. That sucks. Chemistry is completely boring without you in it."

"Promise?"

"Swear."

I smile at their easy banter. I wish I could talk to guys like Charity does.

"Yo, can I get a lift?" he asks. "My ride just dumped me for a better lookin' dude."

"Quin?" I ask. "She does that."

"Yeah. Said she had to go knock some skulls or something. I didn't want to get in the way of that."

"I don't blame you." I'm thoroughly excited about being in the house alone. I'm totally going to take a bath and then walk around in my fuzzy robe without anyone bothering me.

Rat gets into the car with Charity.

"See you soon?" I ask.

She grins, much happier now that Rat is with her. Her face is even a little pink. I'm suddenly very happy that Quin left this man-boy behind.

"All good," she says in a singsong voice. "I'll call you. Stay healthy!" she yells as she pulls away from the curb.

CHAPTER
TWENTY

I'M JUST GETTING OUT OF the bath when I hear a thumping outside. The bathroom window looks out over the front lawn, so I quickly wrap a towel around me, ignoring the fact that my belly doesn't even come close to being covered, and peek out of the blinds.

I see nothing at first, but the sounds of footsteps on the front porch come again. *Why doesn't whoever that is ring the dang doorbell?*

I get my answer or at least a good guess at an answer when I see a darkly-dressed figure come out from under the porch and round the side of the house.

Charlie?

Fear makes my heart feel like it's about to explode. *What does he want? Why is he here? How does he know where I live?* None of the answers to those questions could possibly be good.

I grab my robe off the door hook and throw it on over my back. My towel drops to the floor and I just abandon it there. I have to get back to my room before . . . before . . . I don't even know what. My worst nightmares have him breaking into the house and murdering me while I stand naked in the bathroom. It's a ridiculous and probably crazy day-mare, but knowing this doesn't change the fact that I feel like I'm running for my life as I waddle my penguin butt down the hallway.

Once inside my bedroom, I slam the door shut and lock it. Trembles take over my body as I work quickly to find some clean clothes to put on. I'm not even paying attention to what they are; I just want to cover myself as quickly as possible. If I'm going to die, let it be without my giant belly flopping all over the place.

I almost laugh at the ridiculousness of it. No one's going to kill me. I haven't done anything wrong. Being a stupid, naive girl isn't against the law last time I checked.

This line of thinking doesn't make me feel any better when the sound of a door slamming downstairs comes into my room.

I scan the small space I now feel trapped inside. Should I hide? Get a weapon? All I see are pillows, and there's no way any guy intent on killing me is going to lie down and relax so I can suffocate him to death.

I nearly laugh out loud at myself over my paranoid thoughts. Charlie wouldn't be coming over here to hurt me, right? But why is he coming here at all? This makes no sense. He doesn't even know . . .

Someone is coming up the stairs. My bedroom is the first door he'll reach.

I back up without even realizing it and only stop when my butt bangs into the dresser behind me.

The handle on my door rattles a couple times.

I can hear my heart beating in my eardrums; the sound is coming from inside my head.

A few seconds later, there's a knock.

I hold my breath, waiting for his next move.

"Alissa? You asleep?"

All my pent up anxiety leaves with my breath in one big whoosh out of my lungs. I storm across the room and unlock the door, throwing it open with all the force of my distress.

"Colin?! What are you doing?!"

He leans way back with a frown. "Should I take that as a yes?"

"Arrrgh!" I back up a step so I can slam the door in his face. I get very little satisfaction from the loud bang.

My heart is going a mile a minute. I walk backward to the edge of the bed and then angle myself up onto it. Closing my eyes and wrapping my forearms around my belly, I concentrate on slowing my breathing and controlling my blood pressure. The baby is flipping out, causing me to cramp a little. I think I just shot her up with pure adrenaline.

The door opens very slowly, and the sound makes me open my eyes. A portion of Colin's face appears around the corner. "Is it safe to enter?"

"No. Go away."

He pushes the door the rest of the way in and stands there. "Are you mad at me or something?"

I sigh heavily, now feeling just a tad more relaxed. "No. Yes." I shake my head, trying to clear it. "No."

"Oh." He grins. "That makes things clear, doesn't it?"

"Did you need something?" I ask, trying to change the subject.

"I'm supposed to give you a ride."

"A ride? A ride where? I wasn't aware I had an appointment."

"I guess Teagan just got back from her lawyer's office, and she and Quin are over at Quin's place. They were hoping you could come."

I have to blink a few times and go over what he just said again in my head to make sure I understand. "They want me there?"

"Yeah. They said you're a part of all of it and they want your opinion."

"Oh. Okay. Well . . . I guess I could come." I feel important. Needed. This is way better than thinking Charlie is about to kill me. I look down at myself and realize I did a poor job of dressing myself when I was in that panic. "I just need a second."

"You going to change your clothes?"

"Yes. Why?" I cross my arms at the tone of his voice. I sense a joke coming.

"Because I was just wondering if color blindness is another one of those pregnancy symptoms."

He's out the door before I can nail him with my bed pillow.

CHAPTER
TWENTY-ONE

COLIN AND I ARE ALMOST to Rebel Wheels when he changes the subject from the weather to his business.

"So, did you give any more thought to my offer?"

"What offer?" I'm playing dumb. I know exactly what he's talking about. Now I feel a little guilty that I never asked anyone about Teagan's case after Colin said something about her not being able to pay for it.

"To work for me. Part time."

"Nope. I already told you. I can't."

"Why not?"

"Honestly?" I look at him, his profile making me feel all funny inside.

"Yes."

"I can't be around you like that. I have to just bide my time until the baby comes, have her, and then figure out my game plan. I need to have a permanent job, and I need to get away from here."

He frowns, glancing at me a couple times before looking back out to the road. "You're leaving? Why?"

"Just because." I stare out the windshield, willing him not to ask me for details.

When he doesn't, I get angry at myself for being sad about it. I just can't win with him and it's my fault. When I try to analyze why I keep pushing him away, the only thing I can come up with is that I figure it's better if it's me doing it now than him doing it to me later. No point in getting hooked on something that can never be and that will just end up as painful wreckage.

I'm about to become a mother; I cannot afford to just hand my heart over to someone who will most certainly crush it. Besides . . . the idea of being with a guy again *that way* is terrifying. I'm not sure I could ever do that again.

We pull into Rebel Wheels and I get out, not waiting for Colin to come open my door. I move slower than I want to, because I know when I try to fast-walk, I waddle even worse than normal. I'm half afraid that Colin is going to catch up to me and try to talk to me again, but then as I'm going up the stairs, I see him moving over to his workbench. He isn't even looking at me, and it makes me want to cry.

I'm afraid if I don't have this baby soon and get rid of these pregnancy hormones, I'm going to go insane.

I open the door to Mick and Quin's apartment and find Quin, Teagan, and Rebel in the living room. Teagan's eyes are dark, and Quin is pacing. I don't have to hear a single word to know she's angry.

"Good, you're here," Quin says. She stops pacing, leans over and grabs some papers off the table, and then hands them to me. "What do you think about all this?"

I take the papers from her and look first at Teagan before I start reading. "Is it okay with you?"

She nods.

I read the letter from her attorney and then glance at the papers below. "This looks like a bill," I say.

"Yes, it is a bill. A bit fat one," says Quin. "Can you believe that?"

"I thought they said they would wait to be paid." I look to Teagan for answers.

"I guess there were some conditions to that," she says.

I look back at the paper. "They want twenty thousand dollars? Do you have that much money?"

Teagan shakes her head. "Not even close."

I glance at Rebel before looking back at her. "Can you borrow it from someone?"

She shakes her head again but doesn't say anything.

Quin jumps in to respond. "Rebel isn't the full owner of Rebel Wheels. Olga loaned him some money to start it and she decides where their profits go. Rebel has reinvested all his personal money back into expanding the business, so he doesn't have anything to loan Teagan." She looks over at him. "Sorry for sharing your shit, but she needs to know so we can talk to her about it."

He nods, but says nothing out loud. I cannot read his expression other than to see that he's not happy.

"What do you want me to say?" I ask, looking at all of them in turn. "If I had anything at all, I'd give it to you, but I don't."

"Are you saying that if you could do something to help Teagan, you would?" Quin asks. She folds her arms across her chest.

"Yes, I'm saying that." I raise my chin a little at her challenging tone.

"No matter what?" Quin says.

"Quin . . . don't," Teagan says. Her request lacks the strength I'm used to hearing from her.

"What's going on?" I ask, my suspicion taking over. I'm being tricked into something, but I don't know what it is. I don't have a single dime, so I know they're not asking me for money.

"It's all good news," Quin says, suddenly smiling. "Teagan desperately needs help, and you're the only one in a position to help her."

"I doubt that," I say, almost laughing. "Unless you want me to sell my baby, which I'm not going to do." I narrow my eyes at her. If she asks me to sell my baby, I'm leaving and never coming back.

"You didn't really just say that," says Quin.

I shrug. "I never know with you guys. You're crazy."

Quin gives me an evil smile. "Crazy like a fox." She pauses a few seconds before delivering the news. "We need you to work for Colin so he can loan Teagan some money."

I snort. "Yeah, right." Another hare-brained idea, courtesy of Quin, no doubt.

Quin and Teagan just stare at me.

"What?" I look from one to the other. "Are you serious?"

"Deadly so," says Quin.

"No." I shake my head. "I'm not . . . that makes no sense. *You* go work for him." I put the papers back down on the table and step back on my way to leaving the room.

Quin shrugs. "Would if I could, but I can't."

"Why not?" My voice is going up in volume, but I can't stop it. I'm losing my temper because they're backing me into a corner. I'm stuck and everyone knows it.

"Because, my mom and Jersey need lots of physical therapy. I have to take them everywhere *and* I have to take care of my sisters *and* the house *and* the meals *and* all that other crap. I already have a full time job."

"What about you?" I ask, gesturing to Teagan. "You could just make a few phone calls or whatever he needs."

"He needs more than that, and I have to work for Rebel. He needs me full time."

I'm standing there with my mouth hanging open when Colin walks in.

"What's going on?" he asks.

My mouth snaps shut and I glare at him.

"Did I do something?" He takes a step back as if he's going to reverse himself right out of the apartment.

"Yes, apparently, you *did*."

"What?"

"You are blackmailing me into working for you, and getting your family to guilt me into it!" I throw my arms up and let them come down to hit my thighs. "How rude can you be?"

"What?" He walks fully into the room and stares at everyone. He doesn't look happy.

"Yeah. Nice try, by the way," I say in the most sarcastic tone I can muster. Like he's all innocent. *Please.* "Low blow, even for you, Colin."

He holds up a hand in my direction. "Listen, I don't know what anyone in this room has said to you, but I didn't *ask* them to say anything." He glares at Teagan.

"I didn't say anything!" she yells. "You think I want to push her into helping me? Jesus. If she doesn't want to do it, she doesn't want to do it."

"It's me, Colin, not Teagan. Don't get mad at her." Quin glares at me. "I just thought Alissa would want to help the people who've been helping her, but I guess I was wrong about that. My bad."

My hands fly to my hips. "Now wait a second . . ."

Colin looks right at me. "It's fine. Don't worry about it. I've already told the galleries it's a no-go, and I don't need you to work for me anyway, so just go on about your business." He leaves the apartment without another word and the room goes completely silent.

My face burns with shame. I'm standing here inside a circle of friends who have done nothing but provide for me, and all I'm doing is saying no to everything they ask of me. What kind of person am I turning into? What's happened to me?

Tears rush to my eyes and start to overflow down my cheeks. I look at Teagan. "I'm going to fix this," I say, my voice catching in my throat.

"Don't worry about it," she says. She sounds exhausted. "I'm just going to call it all off."

I grab the papers off the table and hug them to my chest. "No. Don't do that. I'll be right back." I rush out of the room, on a mission. I have to make this right. I have to fix what I broke. I cannot let all these people down. They're the only family I have right now, and they don't even have to be. They've chosen me, so now, I have to choose them.

CHAPTER
TWENTY-TWO

"COLIN . . . WAIT!" I YELL, AS he disappears into the office. I'm at the top of the stairs, gripping the railing with one hand while my other holds Teagan's papers against my chest. "I need to talk to you." Tears blur my vision.

I can't see the stairs very well and miss one with my right foot. The sensation of falling with nowhere to go fills my heart with dread. I scream as I feel myself heading downward.

My right hand shoots out and grabs for something, anything. Papers go flying around my head. I find the railing with my fingers and grip on with everything I have.

My body swings to the left with the momentum of gravity and lack of balance and my belly bangs into the railing hard. My arm is behind me, twisted in a very uncomfortable position, but it's the only thing keeping me from tumbling head over belly to the ground below so I don't want to let go.

I try to keep my grip, but my sweaty palm makes that impossible. My hand slips off the railing and I'm heading down the stairs again. My body rolls sideways and I've got the railing at my back.

I'm just a step away from releasing my other hand as my wrist twists around painfully.

Suddenly, Colin is there. His body is like a wall, stopping me from going any farther. I freeze in place, getting my breath back, looking up at the top of the stairs. Several faces are there, staring down at me with shocked expressions.

"I'm okay!" I say, nearly breathless. "I'm okay." I pull on the railing and stand up straighter as Colin supports me at my back. I can still feel the warmth of his body pressed into my skin. I'm not sure if my inability to breathe is from that or all the unintended exercise I just did.

"Wow. That was a close one." I feel ridiculously lucky right now. Lucky and embarrassed; I'm not sure that I've ever been less graceful in my entire life.

"You sure? You hit yourself pretty hard," Colin says.

I turn around and see his worried face right next to mine. "Yeah. I'm fine. Thanks to you." I wave up at my audience, hoping they'll leave me to my embarrassment. "Nothing to see here. I'm good."

"Horror-movie-worthy scream, though," says Quin, smiling.

Teagan and Rebel disappear into the shadows behind them without saying anything.

I nod and wave at Quin before turning around to face down the stairs again. "I'm going to try this one more time." I hang on tight to the railing as Colin hovers nearby. My legs are shaking and I'm pretty sure I'm about to pee myself. It's some kind of miracle that I haven't already.

"I need to get those papers," I say, trying to distract myself from my problems. I gesture to the lawyer's letter and attached financial data that is now spread out over the floor beneath the metal staircase.

Colin leaves me to gather them up, handing them to me when I reach the safety of the ground floor.

"I was serious. I don't need your help anymore." His voice is gruff. He looks off to his right like he's going to leave me standing there.

I put my hand on his forearm to keep him by me. "I want to apologize."

"For what?" He looks down at the ground.

"For being rude. For turning my back on you guys. I want to help."

He takes a step back, pulling out of my grip. "Why the sudden change of heart?"

I force myself to keep looking at his face instead of at the floor like I'm tempted to. I'm reminded of my earlier scare, when I was freaking out thinking that Charlie was stalking me. It's because of my friends here that I have a safe, anonymous place to live, far removed from my old life. I owe them so much.

I wish I could explain all of that to Colin, but I can't. I do my best to convince him I'm serious, though, because I really want to work for him and help him with his career. He really is so talented. "I just . . . opened my eyes a little, I guess. I want to help."

"You're busy with your own stuff. The baby. Your life is about to really change. You don't need a job right now."

"I know my life is about to change in a major way. And for that to happen in the *best* way, I need to be working. Please let me work for you. No one else is going to hire a pregnant girl. I don't even know why you want to . . . or wanted to, but I shouldn't have said no."

He grits his teeth together and stares off into space. His profile is stunningly handsome, even with the scar I can see in his eyebrow and upwards, stretching from forehead to hairline.

I wait for him to respond. I don't want to push him too hard and have him rebel against me. I can see he's right on the edge of blowing me off and telling me to get lost forever. Just the thought of that makes me feel sick to my stomach.

"Fine." He walks away and leaves me standing there.

"Fine? As in, I'm hired?"

He goes around the side of a car he's working on and disappears.

I wait at the stairs to see what he'll do next. Maybe I misunderstood. Maybe he's never going to speak to me again. Do I have time to make it to the bathroom so I can vomit there instead of on the floor?

When he comes back around with a file folder in his hands, I breathe out a huge sigh of relief. My body tingles with the release of stress.

He stops in front of me and holds it out. "Here. All the info is inside. Do what you want with it."

I frown first at him and then at the folder. The outside of it is covered in greasy fingerprints. I take it from him and attempt a smile. "I don't understand."

He walks away, waving carelessly over his shoulder. "Just do whatever."

I could probably push him into giving me a better answer, but I don't. I've hurt his feelings and now it's time to pay my penance. I can do this. I can make him happy without getting instructions on how to do it. Now I just need to figure out how I'm going to get home.

Like a knight in shining armor, Mick walks through the office and out into the main repair area, jingling his car keys in his hand.

"Mick!" I say brightly.

"Hey . . . Alissa." He looks at me with suspicion, stopping before he gets too close. He looks over at his brother who's ignoring both of us, and then he's back to staring at me with a funny look on his face.

"Can you give me a lift back home by any chance? Or are you too busy right now?"

He shrugs, some of his suspicion sliding away. "Sure. Not a problem."

As we're walking out to the car, he looks over his shoulder at me. "You feeling okay?" he asks.

"Yes, why?" The sun is out and it hits me in the face. I feel like a cat must when it wants to lie out on a porch and sleep in the light. I stop outside the passenger door and shut my eyes for a brief moment, smiling as the warmth seeps into my bones.

"Because. You seem . . . happy."

I think about that statement all the way home and the fact that Mick was obviously shocked by the very idea of it. I can't be mad at him; he has a point. I have been unhappy for way too long. My life is what it is, and only I can change it or at least change how I look at it.

As we drive along, and I try to figure out what's stopping me from actually doing that, I come to the conclusion that there is nothing stopping me. There's only some*one*. And that someone . . . is me.

CHAPTER
TWENTY-THREE

I DON'T KNOW WHY I resisted Colin so hard before finally ca-pitulating and becoming his assistant. This work is easy, easier than anything I've ever done for money before. The summer jobs in my father's office, the part-time employment I had at a frozen yogurt place . . . they don't even compare. I feel like I'm finally a part of the adult business world, arranging shows, calculating commissions, planning out his year. It's not only easy, it's fun. I'm actually using some of my college education, something I wasn't sure I'd be doing much of once I left last semester.

Colin is going to be so excited when he hears about my prog-ress. Okay, maybe not excited, but perhaps he'll smile for a second and not be so distant with me anymore. And soon he'll have the money he's promised to loan to Teagan to help pay for some of her legal expenses.

After only five days, I've arranged for a showing of his latest work at one of the biggest and best galleries in the city and a pri-vate showing for a very important client in another. The gallery owner sponsoring the show three weeks from now told me she already has expressions of interest in three pieces. Colin's been too busy to hear my updates, and I wanted to wait and give him the news once everything was confirmed.

The only thing getting in my way of doing more is not having transportation. Thank goodness there's email. I open up the laptop I'm borrowing from Colin and sign onto my account, just to be sure I haven't missed anything. The lunch break I give myself is short, but I still hate leaving messages unanswered for any length of time, and I've been waiting for confirmation of the show coming up and it's killing me not to see it in my inbox every day.

I clap with excitement when I see that there's a fresh new message from the gallery owner Geraldine with an attachment. I click to open it up and read hungrily.

"Thought you'd like to see the mailing piece I sent out a couple days ago (postcard). I felt this was the best piece after seeing what was in Colin's new studio. We're all set to go. Cheers, Geraldine."

I double click on the attached advertisement piece to open it, a little nervous because it's the first show I'm actually responsible for arranging, but knowing that the postcard is going to be beautiful; after all, she's using one of Colin's paintings as the centerpiece. Now I finally have something solid to report to Colin. I'm going to forward this to him as soon as I verify it's all okay.

The attachment opens, and for a moment, I'm not sure what I'm looking at.

And then I realize . . .

Oh my god . . . he didn't!

"Oh, no," I whisper, as I take it all in. My hands fly up to land on my cheeks. I press them in, making my lips go into a fishy-face.

Seeing the postcard is not like looking in a mirror. Not exactly. I mean, the image has detail to it, and the face is unmistakable. But then again, it's not what I'm used to seeing in the morning when I wake up and in the night before I go to bed as I'm brushing my teeth.

This person staring back at me from Colin's painting is obviously pregnant; even though there is no skin showing, the baby bump is unmistakable. She's *me*, but she's a different me. I feel both flattered and sick at the same time.

My hands shake just a little as I grab the disposable phone Colin bought me and press the button for his saved number. He doesn't answer, so I leave him a message.

"Colin, it's me. Alissa. Um . . . I just got the postcard from Geraldine for the show I set up . . . and it's . . . it's . . . Well, just call me, okay? Call me as soon as you get this message. It's urgent. Well, it's not that urgent. No, it is that urgent. Just call me." *God, I'm such an idiot! Why can't I talk?*

I hang up and stare at the computer some more. Why didn't I know he did this piece? Why didn't he tell me? What else is he doing up in that attic studio of his? And why did I let Geraldine select the picture for the promotional piece without checking it? I should have done it myself, but I was at a doctor's appointment so she went into his studio without me. I seriously want to cuss right now. I grit my teeth together to keep myself from doing just that.

I slam the computer lid shut and leave my room, going right for the stairs that will take me to Colin's inner sanctum. He'd better not have any more paintings of me up there. I'm pretty sure he has to ask for permission before painting me like that. Like that . . . Madonna or whatever she was supposed to be.

I push the feelings of flattery away in favor of my indignant emotions. It just feels too strange to have someone take a piece of me like that and put it in paint on a canvas for people to gawk at. That girl . . . I'm not even sure she *is* me. She looks too sad or scared or lonely. *Do I look like that?* My heart sinks as I examine the probable answer. I feel . . . exposed. Vulnerable. Maybe even a little betrayed because he did it in secret and he's been ignoring me for days.

The door is locked. I stare at the tumbler and wonder if this is one of those that a bobby pin could pick.

CHAPTER
TWENTY-FOUR

M Y PHONE RINGS AND I look down at it, hoping to see Colin's name popping up. But it's not him; it's Charity, which is probably a good thing because the things I want to say to him right now are not fit for human ears.

"Hey, Charity," I say as I descend the steps, making a mental note to find a bobby pin later when I'm done speaking with her.

"Hey, Alissa. Do you have time for a quick soda or something?"

"Sure. But I don't have a car, still."

"No big deal. I'll come get you. Are you home?"

"Yep."

The doorbell rings. "Hold on a minute, Charity, someone's at the door."

"I'll hang up and see you in a second," she says.

I close my phone as I race down two sets of stairs and then peek through the curtains next to the front door. Charity is standing on the porch with a big grin on her face.

I fling open the door and smile. "Wow, that was fast."

"I was really close and thought, what the heck . . . I'll go see if she's home."

I swing the door open wider. "Come in. We can have something to drink in here if you want."

"Great." She comes in and stands in the foyer. She suddenly seems nervous.

"What's wrong?" I put my hand on her elbow. She looks so vulnerable standing there with her big belly protruding out. I swear she's even bigger than she was last week, and before I would have said that wouldn't be possible. I'm not even going to look at her ankles, because if they're anything like mine, it's going to be scary.

She gives me a watery smile. "I have something to show you. I need your advice."

I take her by the hand and lead her into the kitchen. "Sit," I say, pointing to the kitchen dining set. "I'll make you some herbal tea." I put the kettle on and busy myself with getting mugs, milk, and sugar out on the table. I'm purposely stalling a little, mentally preparing myself for a big job. When a pregnant, unwedded teen girl says she needs your advice, to me this means I really need to be ready for just about anything.

When the kettle starts whistling, I grab it and bring it over to the table, filling the teapot with the hot water and adding some tea bags. As I lower myself into my seat, I smile encouragingly at my friend. "Okay, shoot. What's on your mind?"

She pulls a folded up piece of paper from her pocket and puts it on the table. "Look what I found."

I can tell it's been folded and unfolded a bunch of times. It's well-worn on all the corners and the paper has gone soft with handling. It's not big, maybe half a piece of regular paper. Opening it, I find a hand-written note inside, in very careful, pretty script.

"To the girl I met who was here with her friend. I am the lady in the blue headband with the minivan, and I would like to speak with you. Here is my number . . ."

I look up at Charity, confused but hopeful. "Is this what I think it is? Where'd you get it?"

Charity grimaces; I think it was supposed to be a smile. "I went back to that grocery store. I don't know why. I tried to stay away, but I couldn't."

"And?"

"And this was there, on the bulletin board by the front door. I don't even know why I saw it. Maybe because I'm always checking them these days looking for those ads by people searching for babies to adopt."

"She left this for you," I say in a soft voice. "That's her."

"I know." Charity starts to cry. "I think so too. What should I do?"

I reach out and put my hand over hers, patting it a few times gently. "Just take a breath and let's talk about it. You don't need to decide anything right this second. You can decide in five minutes, five hours, five days . . ."

She sniffs loudly and wipes her nose with the tissue I hand her. "I don't have a lot of time left. My doctor says I could go at any day now. My cervix is starting to dilate."

"Oh. My. Well, you still have time, okay? This is a big decision." I pull my hand back so I can pour her some of my brew. "Tea will help calm your nerves. Sugar?"

She nods. "Five please."

I raise an eyebrow at that, but dutifully scoop out five teaspoons of the sweet stuff and dump it into her mug. "Milk?"

"I don't know," she says. "Is it good with milk?"

"That's how the English do it, or so I read." I add a bit to both of our cups. "Let's try it."

We both take a sip and nod at the same time. I smile over my cup. "What is your first instinct?"

"Fear. Just bold fear, that's it." She lets out a deep sigh. "I was going to ask Julio what he thinks, but I'm afraid he's too young to understand."

"Julio?"

"You know . . . the guy that was here at your place the other day. He's a friend of mine." She smiles shyly.

"A friend, huh? That's nice." I'm so happy for her. Not many guys would want to be a friend to a pregnant girl like that. "He must be special."

"He is. He's not like other guys." She laughs. "He actually volunteered to be my birth coach. I told him what you said about that stuff."

I grin along with her. "That is really sweet. What did you tell him?"

"I told him no, that they probably wouldn't even let him in the room with me."

I shrug. "Maybe they would. Might as well ask, if that's what you want to do."

Charity pushes the paper on the table a little, flicking it with her finger. "I can't do anything until I deal with this." She takes a careful sip of her hot tea. "I'm scared to death."

"What are you scared of exactly? Tell me."

"That she'll say she was just kidding. That she'll be a crazy person who wants to hurt my baby. That she's not what she seems to be, I guess. I know . . . I'm being ridiculous."

I shake my head. "I think you're being what anyone would be in your situation. *Cautious.*"

She shrugs, looking sad.

"Are you sure you don't want to keep the baby?" I ask.

"Yes. Positively. I want my baby to have all the opportunities he can. He won't get that from me right now. Maybe someday he can meet me and I'll explain, because I really do think it's for the best."

"I just wanted to be sure so I'm not giving you bad advice."

"Which is?"

"To call her. Just see what she has to say. What can it hurt?"

"Nothing, I guess. But what if she wants to meet?" Charity wiggles in her seat.

"Then you agree to meet. Do it at her house so you can see her place and get to know her as a person a little."

"Like a social worker's home visit?"

"Exactly."

"Will you come with me?"

I answer without a second thought. "Of course. That's what friends are for." Now that I've got this whole be-a-better-friend plan in action, decisions are getting a lot easier to make. Besides, no pregnant girl should be alone when she's making this kind of plan for her life. There's just way too much at stake.

Charity pulls her phone out of her purse.

"You're going to call her now?" I ask, panic hitting me in the chest like a pile of bricks.

"Yes. Is that a bad idea?" Her fingers freeze over the buttons.

"No, no, go ahead." I scoot my chair closer to hers. "I want to hear." I shake my head a little to get the nervous feelings out of my brain. I need to be strong for my friend so she has someone to lean on.

She presses in the buttons and connects the call, leaning toward me so I can put my ear near the speaker.

"Hello, Gentry residence, Barbara speaking."

"Uh . . . uh . . ." Charity yanks the phone away from her head and presses the red disconnect button. She stares at the phone for a couple seconds and then drops it on the table. Her hands are shaking like mad.

I pick up the phone with one hand and take her shoulder with the other. "You okay?" I ask.

"Yeah," she whispers, staring at the table. "Just panicked. I'm sorry." She finally looks up at me, her eyes as big as saucers. "Holy freak-out. Did I just hang up on her?"

I laugh. "Yes. But we can call her back. Do you want me to do it?"

Charity nods. "Would you please? I can't. I just can't. I'm about to bust out with some pre-eclampsia or something."

I arrow down to the last number called and press the green button. Charity does not lean forward to hear the call. Instead, she stares down at her belly as her arms rest on the tabletop.

"Gentry residence, Barbara speaking."

"Hello, Barbara. Are you the Barbara who wears the blue headband when she grocery shops?" I feel like a spy, talking in code. Luckily, Barbara doesn't hang up on me for being a total weirdo.

"Yes." Her voice is very soft. I can barely hear it. "Is this the beautiful girl I met that one day in the baby food aisle?"

"Maaaybe . . ." I don't consider myself beautiful, but Charity certainly is. I don't want there to be any confusion. I'm trying to think of a delicate way to ask which girl she's talking about, but Barbara beats me to the punch.

"I met two girls there. I left a note for the second one. The one interested in . . . adoption."

I grin like crazy. "Yeah, that's my friend. She just tried to call you herself, but she kind of froze up."

"I thought that might be the case." Barbara's voice is back to normal now, although she still sounds a little nervous. "Thank you for calling back."

"I just want to help if I can."

An awkward silence ensues. Charity stares at me, her fear palpable. I reach over and pat her shoulder, trying to ease her mind.

"Would she like to meet?" Barbara asks.

"That's a great idea. At your house," I say.

"Oh . . . are you sure? Wouldn't you rather . . . meet somewhere else?"

I shake my head, doing my best to channel Quin's extraordinary powers of bossiness. "Nope. Your house would be fine." I'm being pushy, but I don't care. Charity's baby is almost at her knees, her belly is hanging so low. She could have this puppy any minute. Time's a-wastin'.

"Oh . . . okay . . . um . . . you could come here, I suppose. When?"

"How about right now?" I'm getting excited. My heart is racing and my mouth is going dry. I feel like I'm challenging her, testing her. I pray silently that she meets the challenge.

"My husband isn't home, but I guess we could meet with him another time." She pauses. "Okay, she could come over now. Or you both could. But . . . I mean . . . maybe we should discuss some . . . things, first."

"Things? Like what things?" She's obviously uncomfortable about something, but I have no idea what it is, other than maybe two strange girls with big giant bellies wanting to come to her house.

"I hate to bring this up, but I just want to be sure that we're all of the same understanding."

"Sure. Go ahead. Say whatever you want."

"Okay. I just wanted to say that I . . . want to *adopt* a baby, not purchase a baby."

"What?" I don't get what she's saying at first, but then it hits me. "Are you talking about . . ."

She jumps to explain. "I don't mean to insult anyone! I just . . . I've read horror stories. My friends are always warning me. I just . . . I've been looking for a long time and I've had some bad things happen. My husband has put his foot down and told me to stop looking. I guess I'm just afraid to hope anymore." She begins to cry softly and it melts my heart on the spot.

"Don't worry. We're not scammers. I can vouch for Charity, and even though you don't know me, I'm still going to say you can trust me. Give me your address and you can find out for yourself."

I hang up the phone a minute later, the address written on the note that Charity took from the grocery store.

"You ready to go do this?" I ask, getting to my feet.

"I guess I better be," she says, breathless but looking hopeful.

"Come on," I say, grabbing my purse off the back of the chair. "Let's go do this before we lose our nerve."

Charity stands and puts her hand on my arm. "No. I'll go. Alone."

"Alone?" I frown at her, confused. "Really?"

"Yes, really."

"You're not going to go, are you?" My shoulders sag. I'm so disappointed, I can't keep it out of my voice. And here I thought I'd done so well. Maybe I shouldn't have pushed so much. *Damn you, Quin! Get out of my brain!*

"No, I am, I promise." She's chipper and her tone makes me believe she's telling me the truth. "I wouldn't do that, just not show up like that for something so important. I just . . . I don't want to go there and overwhelm her. I mean, you and I make quite the intimidating picture, you know? She kind of spooked-out at the grocery store. Maybe she's better just one-on-one."

I nod. "Okay, if that's what you want to do." I put my purse back. "Will you call me when it's over?"

"Of course." She leans in and hugs me. "Thank you so much. You're a true friend."

I pat her back and then pull away. "Just call me if you change your mind or need anything else."

"I will." She squeezes my arm gently and then leaves. I walk behind her and lock the door when she's gone.

Then I remember something really important and throw the door open. "Charity!" I yell.

She turns around as she's walking behind her car. "Yeah?"

"Find out why she's buying baby food when she doesn't have a baby!"

"Uhh . . . okay!"

I wave and then go back into the house, shutting the door and locking it.

Standing in the hallway, I look down the corridor and then at the stairs, mulling over my next move. I can either clean up my mess in the kitchen or take a nap.

Just picturing my bed in my mind, I suddenly realize how exhausted I am, and choose the stairs. I can clean up later. Now I'm just going to celebrate the fact that I have both Colin's and Charity's lives on track, simply by making a few phone calls and listening to my conscience. For the first time in a long time, I feel like things are getting back to they way they should be.

CHAPTER
TWENTY-FIVE

I'M IN A WEIRD, HALF-asleep almost drugged-out state when I hear the doorbell ring again. I crack one eye open and see that the sun is still up, but it's lower in the sky now. I have no idea what time it is, but it must be getting close to dinner. Maybe. I sit up and rub my face a little to wake myself up so I can figure out what's going on.

The doorbell rings again.

Getting out of bed is an effort. I'm dizzy from moving too fast, and I have to hold onto the doorframe for a few seconds before heading down the stairs.

The doorbell rings again.

"I'm coming!" I yell. And then I mutter, "Jeepers, keep your pants on." If it's Teagan or Quin I'm going to give them a piece of my mind. I'm pregnant; I need my sleep.

I get to the door and put my hand on the lock. I start to open it as I lean toward the curtained side window and look out. As soon as I see who it is, my heart stops beating for a second and my hand freezes, halfway to unlocking the door.

I can't believe I almost just let him in. I re-lock the door and let my hand fall away, jerking back away from the window and hiding behind the door. *Oh my god, oh my god, oh my god . . . what's he doing here?!*

"Alissa, I just saw you. Open the door. I want to talk to you for a second."

"Go away, Randy." My voice is too high. He'll know I'm afraid. "I don't know why you're here, but you can just leave." Trying to maintain a steady, normal tone of voice instead of the freaked-out shriek that wants to leave my lungs takes supreme effort. Both of my hands are clenched into fists.

"I just need to talk to you, it's no big deal." His voice goes lower, quieter . . . like it's coming directly from my nightmares. "Open the door."

"No. Leave or I'm calling the police."

"Don't be ridiculous. I'm not doing anything illegal. I just want to talk to you."

I've annoyed him. I don't have to open the door or look past the curtain to know what the expression on his face is. Disdain. Supercilious, privileged, thinking he's better than anyone around him. Randy has a very high opinion of himself, just like his best friend, Charlie. They are two awful peas in an even more awful pod.

"Not interested." I pray he'll take the not-so-subtle hints I'm sending and just leave. Teagan and Rebel will be home soon and I don't want them involved in this, but even more, *I* don't want to be involved in this. I just want him to disappear and never come back.

"I saw that postcard with your picture on it. I called the gallery and got your address."

It takes a couple seconds for his statement and its meaning to sink in. And then a loud ringing starts in my ears. I can hear my own heartbeat, and it's going way too fast. I wonder if it's possible to have a heart attack or a stroke just from hearing bad news. If it is possible, I'm probably going to end up in the hospital tonight. This is too much. Too much.

"I'll bet you didn't know our parents are art collectors, did you? Mine and Charlie's. Probably because Charlie never introduced you to his family, did he?"

These words cut me like a knife, as we both know they are meant to.

"Did you ever stop to ask yourself why that was, Alissa? Did it ever occur to you that you were out of your league when you were with him?"

I have to swallow over and over again to keep the bile down. I'm very close to vomiting on the front hall floor, but I can't leave. I'm afraid if I walk away, he'll break in and come after me. I know what he's capable of, and it's frightening me almost as much as I've ever been scared in my life. Almost.

"Just leave, Randy. It's over between me and him, so you have nothing to worry about. He can go back to screwing your sister just like before." I just said *screwing*, and I don't care. Desperate times mean rules can go out the window. Besides, it's not like Charlie ever made love to a woman before. He only knows how to screw, the bastard. *Oh shit. I just said bastard. And shit!* Everything is falling apart in my brain and around me.

Tipping my head back and closing my eyes, I say a silent prayer at the ceiling. *Dear God . . . I know you've put me in a time-out and you don't have any interest in hearing my prayers right now, but just in case you have an angel who's not too busy up there, could you send him my way? Because I'm afraid I'm about to be hurt right now, and I don't want anything to happen to my baby.*

There's a rumbling outside that manages to make its way into my bones. It sounds like there's an earthquake happening and for a moment it makes me think God has answered my prayers by sending a natural disaster over to swallow up my enemies.

My head snaps forward and I blink my eyes a few times. Throwing the curtains to the side, I can see what's out on my front lawn and realize that it's not a natural disaster that God has sent. Not exactly.

CHAPTER
TWENTY-SIX

HEY, BUDDY. CAN I HELP you with something?" Colin says, coming out of his big black car and walking up the pathway cut through the front lawn that leads to the porch. I can hear his raised voice through the closed and locked door. His swagger is unmistakable. It's like he knows there's a problem that needs to be dealt with, and he's just the man to take care of it.

"Just here to see a friend of mine," Randy says, his menacing tone traded in for something a little more genial. His back is to the front door now, but he's not moving away.

I pull back from the window. My heart is going rapid-fire. I want Colin to run! To drive away! This is going to ruin everything! I'm afraid if I had a gun right now, I'd shoot Randy with it to keep him from opening his stupid, ugly mouth. I peek out of the curtains again.

"Who's your friend?" Colin asks. He comes up the three stairs to the porch and stops. His body language is neutral, but the power there is unmistakable. He's got his regular low-waisted jeans on, a black t-shirt, and his hair is a mess. If I didn't know any better, I'd think he just got off a helmet-less motorcycle ride or maybe just rolled out of bed. He could not possibly be more sexy than he is right now. My knight in shining muscles. I cross my legs so I don't pee myself.

"Alissa," Randy says. "You live here with her?"

"Nope." Colin doesn't move. If anything, his chest bulges out just a fraction more than it already was. I never noticed quite how big his muscles are before this moment. They're hugely huge. I think he's been spending more time at the gym.

"So who are you, then?" Randy asks.

Colin shakes his head slowly, a small, humorless smile playing on his lips. Then he just stares at Randy. "Depends."

Randy scoffs, completely oblivious to the danger he's facing right now. That's one of Randy's best qualities as far as I'm concerned; he's always underestimating people. "Depends on *what*, dude?"

"On who you are and why you're here." Colin's voice is completely casual, but his threat is obviously not. "Because if you're here to bother Alissa, and she doesn't want to be bothered, well . . . you can just call me your worst nightmare." He gestures out casually with both hands before letting them hang at his sides again, his arm and side muscles making it impossible for them to rest against his body without curving out. "But if you're here for another reason, and Alissa's cool with that, well, you can just call me Colin."

"I don't appreciate your threat, *Colin*. What I have to talk to Alissa about is none of your business."

"Maybe not. Maybe it is. Depends on what she says."

Colin is still staring the guy down when he raises his voice and addresses me. "Alissa! This guy friend or foe?"

My mouth drops open as I realize he knows I'm standing right here. There's no way I'm going to be able to explain this away. I grip the curtain in panic.

Friend or foe? Can I call Randy a friend and find a way to make this all go away? My ears burn with shame as I think about that stupid, stupid postcard. Why did that happen to me? What have I done that's so wrong? Why is God punishing me like this?

"I'm her friend, Randy. She was just letting me in."

The idea of him coming into the house spurs me into action. "Foe! He's a foe, *not* a friend!" My voice comes out sounding like I'm a little unbalanced. Or maybe a lot unbalanced. And it's possible I am at this moment. Hopefully, it isn't permanent.

"You heard what she said. Time for you to go. *Randolph.*"

It's clear what Colin thinks of my foe's name.

It's also pretty obvious that Randy doesn't appreciate the mockery. "Fuck you, man. I'm not going anywhere. I need to talk to her about something important, and she can hide from it all she wants, but it's not going to go away until she hears what I have to say."

"Not today, you don't." Colin moves so quick I don't really see it happen until it's over. One second he's there at the stairs, the next he's not and a big bang comes from the door as bodies slam into it.

I jump back, even though I know I'm safe inside.

"Colin!" I scream, rushing to the side window when it connects in my brain that he's pounding Randy's head in. Just before I get there, an elbow comes crashing through the glass.

I scream again and leap out of the way. My feet crunch on broken window pieces and a sharp pain slices up through my foot. "Ack! Gah!" I dance away on one foot, falling into the door. I slide over until I can see out the other side window.

Colin is beating Randy's butt out on the lawn. There's blood all over Colin's arm and Randy's face. It's not until I have to take a break to breathe that I realize I'm squealing like a piglet.

"Colin, stop!" I yell. "Stop!" As much as I appreciate what he's doing to Randy's face right now, I don't want him going to jail for me.

I'm trying to figure out how I can stop the train wreck from getting worse when Randy gets to his feet and starts running. He's tripping and falling across the lawn, but getting up again and again, digging in his pocket for his keys.

Colin doesn't pursue him. He waits on the grass, wiping his forehead with the back of his hand, his shoulders moving up and down to accommodate his heavy breathing.

Randy jumps in his car and takes off before he even gets his door shut. His BMW tires squeal on the street, leaving two black streaks behind on the asphalt.

I lean against the window and catch my breath. I cannot believe I haven't peed or barfed yet. Turning my face sideways, I watch Colin to see what he'll do next. My mind swirls with imaginings of our next conversation. He's going to want an explanation. He might even deserve one. Geez, my foot stings.

Once Randy is gone, Colin turns around and starts making his way back up the front walk. I look around in a panic, pushing away from the window. I want to run, to lock myself in my room and not come out until he's gone.

But instead I wait. He's gotten hurt protecting me, and the very least I can do is tend to his injuries. And while I'm doing that, I'm going to try and figure out a way to tell him who Randy is without actually telling him anything at all.

CHAPTER
TWENTY-SEVEN

I UNLOCK THE FRONT DOOR and swing it open for Colin. He barely looks at me as he walks through and down the hall, headed toward the kitchen. I glance outside before shutting the door and locking it behind him. When I turn around, he's already out of sight.

The chicken in me says I should run upstairs and lock myself in my room and feign sleep. But the girl who was just rescued says it's time to face the music. I limp down the hallway and into the kitchen to find Colin at the sink with a dishtowel, wiping the blood off his elbow.

"Let me help you with that," I say, taking the rag away from him and staring at it with dismay. This one is headed to the trash after we're done for sure.

He lifts his elbow and angles it over the sink.

Something sparkles on his skin. "Oh, no, there's glass in your arm," I say, feeling ten times worse than I already did. I look at his bland expression. "What do you want me to do? Should I take it out?"

"Probably a good idea," he says in an emotionless voice.

I cringe at the idea, but use my fingernail nubs to squeeze out the few small pieces I can see easily. "Put your arm down in the water so we can wash it off better. There might be more." I don't see anything that needs to be stitched, but that could be because I'm a complete boob when it comes to injuries or anything medical. "Maybe you should go to the hospital."

"No, thanks."

I frown, trying to concentrate on getting his arm clean instead of feeling terribly guilty. This is all my fault. And he's being so cold, it's almost physically painful to be in the same room with him. I feel like a stranger to him, a girl he has no interest in being around. We're back to acting like pregnancy is a disease that he doesn't want to catch.

I use the first aid kit Teagan put in the kitchen cabinet to finish up my doctoring of both him and me. As I'm putting the last gauze pad bandage on his arm, the front door opens and Teagan and Quin walk in. My heart sinks down into my toes. In an effort to hide my face and reaction, I focus on cleaning up the mess, crumbling up and tossing out bandage wrappers and the ruined towel.

"Hey, what's going on? Why is the front window broken?" Teagan enters the kitchen and sees Colin's arm. "Oh, man. Did you get in another fight?"

The censure in her voice instantly grates on my nerves. "What's that supposed to mean?" I ask, turning around to face her, my annoyance showing through.

Quin snorts. "Plain English. He fights a lot." She looks at Colin, waiting for his answer.

"He wasn't in a fight," I say, acting like it was all just a big joke. I cringe inwardly as I try to come up with a lie that doesn't seem completely self-serving.

"I tripped coming up the front stairs and put my elbow through the front window," Colin says. "I'll replace it tomorrow. Just give me a few minutes and I'll cover it temporarily."

"Wow, that must have been a hell of a trip," Quin says, an eyebrow raised. "Sorry I missed it."

I turn my back on her and act busy at the sink so that I'm not tempted to respond. It's a horrible feeling to know that now I have Colin lying for me too. For a split second I consider just 'fessing up and telling them everything, but just as quickly I dismiss that thought. No way can I open that can of worms in this house with these people. Talk about a nightmare coming to life.

"I'm going upstairs," Colin says. "Have a good night."

He leaves the three of us in the kitchen and we all stand there looking at each other.

"Well, that was abrupt," says Teagan. "What's his problem?"

"I think we walked in on a lover's quarrel," Quin says, looking at me. "Did you break up with him?"

"We're not even together like that," I say, ignoring the funny feeling that idea gives me. "He's just really busy. He has some shows coming up soon. I'll bet he's getting the work ready right now." It makes me think of the stupid postcard and I realize now's my chance to see what else he has going on up there in his secret cave. "I have to go talk to him about it." I walk quickly out of the kitchen, but not quickly enough.

"What about dinner?" Teagan asks, following me down the hall.

"Do you want me to make it?" I ask as I start up the stairs. I'm tired, but I'll sacrifice sleep to have something edible on the table.

Teagan stays down in the hallway looking up at me. "No, I can do it. Any special requests?"

"Nothing fancy," I say, knowing our chances of having something edible improve as long as Teagan doesn't get it into her head to cook something that takes more than two steps.

"Okay, gotcha. So no beef bourguignon?"

"Please, no," I say, chuckling a little at the top of the first set of stairs.

"Enchiladas?" she says louder.

"Too many steps!" I yell.

"On the stairs or in the recipe?" she shouts.

I don't answer because I'm almost to the attic and I need to get my game face on. Besides, Teagan knows exactly what I mean. Ever since my confession about her terrible cooking, she's doubled her efforts to figure it all out. And so far, the results have been . . . mixed. But I have to give her points for effort.

I reach the old door at the top of the narrow stairs and raise my knuckles to give it a good knock. Breathing in and out slowly helps calm my nerves just a fraction as I try to come up with my opening line.

CHAPTER
TWENTY-EIGHT

"COME IN," COLIN SAYS FROM inside his attic studio. I open the door and stick my head inside. "Do you mind if I come in and talk to you about your shows?"

"Nope." His back is to me and he's messing with some paints on a table. He's wearing jeans that he's designated for painting. They're loose and covered in many colors, but still somehow sexy on him. I love the way they hang from his waist, sometimes exposing the top of his butt curve when his shirt is twisted or off. He wasn't lying when he said he doesn't wear underwear.

I walk inside and shut the door behind me. The smells up here remind me of Colin. He always has just the faintest hint of acrylic paint odor on him. It's comforting in a way. This feels like a safe place to me, a hideout where I could come and pretend the world doesn't exist. Something tells me it's the same for him.

"Thanks," I say, without preamble standing behind him.

"For what?" He swirls a paintbrush around inside a can of water, still not looking at me.

"For coming to my rescue."

He turns partway around and sits on a stool, facing a blank canvas. His face is in profile, calling my attention to his strong chin and straight nose. "Is that what I did? Rescue you?" Picking up a rag, he dries off his brush.

"I guess. I mean . . . yes, you did."

I wait for him to respond, but he doesn't. He's too busy selecting paint from different tubes, squeezing blobs out onto a palette. One of his feet is propped up on a rung of the stool while the other rests on the ground. His thigh muscle flexes under the denim of his pants when he leans forward and then back. He goes back to staring at the canvas once he's done finding the right colors.

"You told Quin and Teagan that you tripped."

He doesn't respond.

"Thanks. For . . . lying." My face burns with shame, and it only gets worse when Colin looks over at me, glares a couple seconds, and then goes back to staring at the canvas.

Tears rush to fill my eyes. I made the man who never lies . . . lie. The image of him in front of pure white goes blurry. I blink rapidly, trying to make the evidence of my sadness disappear. Instead, the tears fall from my eyes and tickle my cheeks on the way down. He'll be branded a liar and it's completely my fault. I'm so selfish.

I turn around and casually wipe my tears away so he won't notice. Wandering over to the closest wall, I reach out for the paintings that are leaning there in groups, tipping them toward me so I can see what they are.

"Did you see the postcard that Geraldine sent out?" I ask.

"Nope."

"She used a painting that looked a lot like me." I keep my back to him, afraid to see his face.

He doesn't answer, so I just keep on talking. "I didn't know you did that one. I was kind of shocked, actually." I look over my shoulder at him. He's running his paintbrush down the center of his canvas. It's filled with black paint, leaving a dark streak behind.

"Are there any other paintings of me I should know about?"

His brush freezes almost at the bottom of the canvas, and he finally looks at me. "Who says it was you?"

I snort. "Please. Anyone can see it's me. Stringy hair? Long bangs? Pregnant? Sad as crud?"

He shakes his head and goes back to his black streak, finishing it off and adding more paint to his brush. He goes back over the line, this time putting more pressure on the brush. It's thicker and bolder. Angrier.

My hands go to my hips. "Are you denying it's me?"

"I'm not saying anything about anything."

I walk closer. "Well, that's rude." My arms cross over my chest as I try to figure out what his problem is. It's like he wants to fight with me. This is more than just a simple lie issue.

He flips his paintbrush around so that he's holding it upright in a fist. His closed hand rests on his leg, and he turns to me. "Rude? What's rude? Not telling you things you think you should know? Keeping secrets? What? Which is it? Tell me."

I bite my lip hard to keep from jumping into a response. He's playing word games with me. I suppose I'm expected to feel bad about not telling him about my entire life now. *As if.*

"Yes," I finally say. I can't *not* answer since he's staring holes into me. "It's rude to paint a very intimate picture of me and sell it to some stranger."

"Who says I'm selling it to anyone?"

"You gave it to Geraldine for the show."

"I gave her all of my stuff. It was your job to filter through everything and hold back things you didn't want her to have. And just because she has it doesn't mean it's for sale."

"I don't have a car, as you know, so it's kind of hard for me to filter through anything when I can't physically *get* to it."

He shrugs off my excuses. "You could've asked me for a ride. You could've borrowed my car."

"You're busy. And it's your car, not mine. I don't feel right driving it around. It's too valuable."

He shakes his head as he flips his paintbrush around. "Whatever."

This is going all wrong. I meant to come up here and just thank him. Instead, I feel like slapping him and yelling in his face.

I take a moment to figure out where things went pear-shaped and realize it was when I looked at him and saw anger there on his face. Or maybe it was disappointment. Either way, it felt like a dagger to the heart. But instead of blaming myself, I blamed him. I'm being unfair again, and here he is, cut up and bruised from protecting me, no questions asked. Could I be more of a jerk? I don't think so.

I take a stool from across the room and bring it over to where Colin is, setting it down right next to him. I sit on it, and for a few minutes I just watch him paint. I'm working on getting up the nerve to say something when Colin speaks first.

"Why are you here?"

A sad smile appears on my face as I consider his question. "I've asked myself the same thing about a hundred times in the last few months."

He grunts but doesn't say anything.

"I used to think I was here to make my parents proud. To go to the right schools, to learn all the right skills, and to create a life for myself that's everything my parents and I dreamed of." I sigh as I realize that picture of my life has faded into a blurry gray image when it used to be electric rainbow-bright. "Then I got pregnant and everything went away. I lost everything." A sad sigh and a cough keep the tears at bay. "I guess I don't know the answer to your question. I don't know why I'm here."

His hand pauses in midair as he turns to me. "I meant here in the attic."

His expression is so serious, it takes me a few seconds to figure out he's messing with me. It's only when he cracks a small smile that I can let my air out and breathe again.

I push him in the shoulder. "Jerk."

He cleans his brush and picks up some red on the bristles. A streak of bold color joins the black.

Colin speaks without looking at me. "Why do you think your life is over just because you got pregnant? Girls get pregnant all the time and continue on with their lives."

The fact that he's not looking at me waiting for an answer makes it easier to talk and say things I normally would be more guarded about. I stare at a blob of paint on the floor and let my mind wander. My mouth opens and words just spill out, but I hardly pay them any attention. I'm living my past like an actor plays a role in a film. I can see myself and the other actors talking to each other, interacting with one another. Like it's not real, but it is.

"I had a very specific path. I spent years on that path. Going to school, studying for hours every day, making all the right friends and wearing the right clothes that said the right things to people. I thought I fell in love with the perfect guy too. And one night the path just . . . disappeared. Or I got thrown off it. Or I jumped off it." I sigh in defeat. "I don't know how I got off the path exactly. I just know I can never get back on it again."

"Bullshit." He's painting bold streaks all over the black now. In certain places the colors blend together into something ugly.

"You don't know anything about me," I say, almost wishing it weren't true.

"Who was that guy? . . . Randy. Why was he here? Is he your boyfriend?"

I clench my teeth together, not wanting to answer.

"I got his plate number," Colin says. "I'm going to have Dickerson look him up, I think. Pay him a visit . . . make sure he understands he's not welcome back here."

My hand flies up before I can think to stop it and grabs Colin's upper arm. "No! Don't." I hastily yank my hand back and fold it up with my other one in my lap, squeezing my fingers together. My palms are sweaty. So are my armpits.

He stops painting and turns partway in his stool to face me. "If you don't want me getting involved, then tell me why I shouldn't."

CHAPTER
TWENTY-NINE

I GLANCE UP AT HIM under my lashes. He's staring at me with his dark unwavering green eyes, and I know I'm being tested. Right now I could tell him to leave me the heck alone and go on with his life without me in it, and he'll probably be mad or hurt enough to do it.

But God help me, I don't want him to move on without me. It's stupid and ridiculous and completely not what I ever thought I'd want for myself, but it's true; I want Colin to be in my life, even if it's just as my self-appointed protector. Colin the felon. Colin the fighter. Colin the one they call Trouble.

"You shouldn't get involved because Randy and his friends are bad people who have a lot of money at their disposal and who aren't afraid to use it to hurt other people that make them unhappy."

"What?" Colin laughs. "Are they mafia?"

"Who, Randy? No. Not mafia." If the mafia hung out at the polo club, maybe. I laugh at the idea. "Just people who think they're better than everyone else, that's all."

"Why's he showing up here acting like a prick? That his baby?" Colin points to my belly with the end of the paintbrush.

I don't know why, but I suddenly feel very vulnerable. Wrapping my arms around my big belly, I lean over just a little, my eyes glued to Colin's. "No. I would never . . . " I can't finish.

"Then why's he here threatening you?"

"He was just here . . ." I give up with trying to find a lie that will fit. "He was here to warn me off or something, I don't know. He's friends with someone I know. Or knew. Or thought I knew. I don't know." I finish with a sigh. I'm so confused. I still don't know how I could have been so wrong about Charlie. I have to be the most naive girl who ever walked on two legs.

Colin reaches over and before I realize what he's going to do, he places a hand on my belly, right where the baby has decided to stretch. There are smears of paint on his fingers, but I don't care.

"I can feel her move," he whispers. "I can see her move, too."

I nod, strong, strange emotions making it impossible for me to speak. His hand is so big and so warm. All I feel are good things coming from that sensation. He may be vicious and tough, but I would never know that from his touch on my body.

"What was he warning you off of?" Colin asks.

I shake my head slowly from side to side, staring at his hand on me.

"Tell me, Alissa. I can help you."

I look up at him, tears making my eyesight blurry again. "I don't want anyone to get involved. You could get hurt."

He gives me a wry smile. "Please. You know I'm not happy unless I'm looking for a little trouble."

I slide my hand over in response to the baby moving and my fingers settle in next to his. His skin is so warm and solid. I'd give just about anything to have those arms of his around me. "You should start avoiding trouble, I think, now that you're a serious artist, painter person."

He shrugs, all nonchalant. "You want me to stop, I'll stop."

I stare up in his eyes, his very serious expression making me question what he means by that statement. "Stop what? Getting into trouble or stop painting?"

"Either. Both. I don't care."

A shy smile takes over my face; I can't help it. He's acting like I matter in his life. "Don't be silly."

He puts his paintbrush in the water can and turns more fully in his seat. Both of his hands are on my belly now and they're moving around just the slightest bit as he gets a feel for my baby underneath. "I'm not being silly. I'm being serious. Tell me what I can do to help you. How can I make you happy?"

My brain has gone all mushy. I'm wallowing in the coziness of having him so near, touching me, wanting me to be happy. He's so big. So strong. And he smells like Colin . . .

Oh, God. What in the heck am I doing?!

Emotions hit me full force. I'm getting way too attached to this man, and it feels like it's unstoppable, like I have no control over my life or my heart anymore. And the last time that happened, everything crashed down around my ears and was demolished forever. The very idea of going through that again sends me into panic mode. I push his hands away.

"Why?" I say, a little too forcefully. "I don't understand . . . why are you asking me this?"

He rolls his eyes to the ceiling and tips his head back for a few seconds. His eyes close and he tilts his head down again. As he shakes his head, he opens his eyes. "Jesus, Alissa, can't a guy just want to help? Do you want me to tell you that I *like* you? Confess my feelings and emotions or something?"

Humiliation makes me scowl and stand up off my stool. *How embarrassing! He thinks I'm some sort of school girl begging for confessions of love!* "Oh, shut up, Colin."

"Don't go," he says, grabbing my arm.

I yank it away. "Stop."

He stands too and takes both my forearms. "Please don't go. I'm sorry, I shouldn't have said that."

I twist sideways to walk away, breaking his hold on me. "Sure you should have. Why lie? Just say what you really think and we'll all be better off, trust me." I walk to the door, anxious to put as much distance between us as I can. I'm going to go run my head under ice-cold water in the bathroom so I can try and forget what just happened.

"I didn't lie. I'm not. I will! Tell the truth, I mean!"

His shout has my hand freezing on the door handle. I don't turn to face him, but I don't leave either.

"Alissa, just . . . listen . . . I do like you, okay? Jesus, I can't believe I'm saying this."

My face burns again, but this time not with humiliation. I can't believe he's saying this either. Out of the corner of my eye, I can see him holding out a hand in my direction.

"Don't go," he begs. "I want to talk to you. It's important."

I turn around and rest my back against the door. My hand stays behind me on the handle of the door. I can make my escape quickly if I need to, and the idea of it acts as security for me. I can listen to what he says without fear.

My chin goes up. "Fine. Talk."

He sits back down on his stool, puts his feet up onto the rungs, and slouches, fiddling with his fingers between his legs. "Things are changing really fast for me."

I nod, pretending like I understand when I don't.

"Just a couple months ago I had everything all figured out."

"I know the feeling," I say with only a slight trace of bitterness.

"I had work, I had a hobby, I had . . . girls." He looks up at me. "Sounds great, right?"

I shrug. I don't think he really wants an answer to that question.

"But I was angry all the time. Anytime someone looked at me sideways, I wanted to punch their teeth into their skull. I hated the entire world. I was drinking all the time, trying to drown all that anger or something, I don't know. But it only made it worse."

My eyes widen at that. I'm not sure that I've ever been that angry.

He shakes his head and looks at the floor again. "I miss my mom. I miss my sister. I miss them every single damn day of the week and the month and the year." His voice has gone rough, and the sorrow in his confession loosens my feet. I walk closer to him, my hand leaving the door and my security at having it there.

He looks up again. "My sister was raped. Did anyone tell you that?"

I shake my head as my heart is gripped by icy terror. It's like the Devil himself is holding onto it, squeezing it until I feel like I can't breathe anymore.

"I was supposed to pick her up after work, and I was late. She took a ride home from someone else and he raped her. He beat her ass and left her for dead."

Colin, the biggest, baddest, toughest guy I've ever met is crying. There are no sobs, just tears. His eyes are glowing green. I don't know what to do.

"It's not your fault," I say, my voice barely cracking a whisper.

"Of course it's my fault," he says angrily. His eyes show me the tortured soul that lives inside him. "If I'd been there when I was supposed to be, she'd still be here!"

"You don't know that." I put my hand out toward him, but he scowls at me, so I let it drop. I feel like I'm standing in front of a very angry tiger who might possibly be in the mood to eat me.

"I know it. Everyone knows it. Leave it at that."

"You have a pretty high opinion of yourself," I say, trying to rile him up and throw him off. He's too stuck on that one track to listen otherwise.

My ploy works. The muscles all over his body are tensing up and flexing.

"What?" he grinds out.

I shrug, keeping up the game, keeping him on edge with words that are meant to seem careless. "You think you have direct control over everyone's destiny? Like you're God or something?"

"No. I never said that."

"Well, you claim that you could have changed the direction of your sister's life, as if you made the conscious decision to take her out of this world."

"It wasn't a conscious decision. It was a choice and the consequence of that choice. That was all on me."

"Maybe it wasn't, though," I say, my voice softening.

"How so?" he asks, clearly not ready to believe anything other than the fact that he is the reason she's no longer on this earth.

"We all make choices, don't we? She made a choice to get into someone else's car that night. You didn't make that choice for her, did you?"

"Basically I did."

"No, *basically* you made a choice for *yourself*. She made a choice for *herself*. Her rapist made his choices that had nothing to do with you. Only *she* is responsible for her own choices, as you are for yours, and it was *her* choice that got her . . . in a car with the wrong person." My voice hitches at the end of my sentence because I have the strangest sensation that I'm talking to myself and not Colin. "Girls do that all the time, Colin. They just get into a car with the wrong person." Images flash through my mind. A car. The wrong person. The wrongest person I've ever met.

"But if I hadn't been late . . ."

I snap back to reality. "Maybe she would have gone with you. Or maybe she would have said, 'No thanks, Colin, but I'm going to ride with him instead.'"

He shakes his head. "She wouldn't have said that." His voice is missing some of its earlier conviction.

"Says you. But you can't possibly know that. No one could. Life rolls out the way it does either by grand design or by fate or by chance, but you only have control over yourself. You cannot take responsibility or credit for someone else's choices. You are *not* God. And even if you were, you wouldn't be able to take credit for anyone's choices anyway because we're supposed to have free will."

He stares at the floor for a long time, his mouth twisted up into a half-scowl, half-smile. After wiping off the tears that have made it to his jawline, he looks up at me again. "How'd you get so smart?"

The icy hand that was gripping my heart loosens just a little. "I guess I just live and learn. Or try to learn, anyway. It's not easy. Some of the lessons are very hard to take."

"Painful," he says, his voice still raspy.

I nod. "Very."

He holds out his hands and tilts his head up to look at me.

I'm drawn to him like a magnet. I don't stop until I'm standing in front of him and we're holding hands. My giant belly rests between us and my baby is flipping all over the place. She's apparently very excited about what's happening.

"Will you please tell me why Randy came here to threaten you?" he asks in a gentle tone.

I swallow three times; once to keep the tears away, once to keep the vomit in my stomach, and once to get up the nerve to finally give a voice to the nightmares that have been haunting me for months.

"Yes. I'll tell you. If you promise not to tell anyone else for as long as you live."

He nods once.

"I need to hear you say it out loud. Promise on your life."

His jaw muscles bounce out a few times as if he's about to resist, but then he speaks. "I promise not to tell anyone what you're about to tell me for as long as I live."

A giant sigh escapes me, like it's been pent up in my lungs for days and days and days. "Okay, then. But first I have to tell you about Charlie . . ."

CHAPTER
THIRTY

I GET BACK UP ON my stool so I can tell my story without suffering from my aching ankles.

"Charlie was my first real boyfriend. We started dating almost two years ago."

"He go to school with you?"

"Yes. We met during rush week our second year. He was . . . I guess you could say . . . hazing some students rushing his fraternity, and I was at one of their parties. I wasn't in a sorority because I was afraid all the activities would interfere with my studies, but occasionally I went to different parties when I could afford a break."

He nods to encourage me.

"I can't believe what a dork I was. I had such a crystal clear vision of how I was getting from Point A to Point B back then."

"Don't be mean to yourself. Just tell me what happened."

I nod. It's too late for regret. It's just going to muddy the story anyway, so I steel myself for the reality that is my life and continue.

"After we met, we started seeing each other around a lot. I got the impression that he was making some of those meetings happen on purpose. I was very flattered." My face turns pink. "He's very good-looking. His family is wealthy. He drives a Porche and owns a boat. He could date anyone, but he was choosing me."

Colin doesn't say anything to that, but it doesn't stop me from feeling ashamed that those things meant so much to me. I never considered myself a gold digger until those words came out of my mouth.

"He went to a fancy prep school before college, so he was a little older. He was on the crew team. He had a lot of friends who had families in Congress and other high places. One of them is a heart surgeon up in San Francisco. Charlie's father and mother are both lawyers. It was all a very big deal for me. My family is very religious and set in their ways. They believe it's important to make the right connections and follow a certain path toward success. They were impressed by Charlie's family and background."

"And that path they wanted you to follow included this Charlie person?"

"Yes, but not just as a means to an end. I mean, not really. I loved him. Or I thought I loved him." I sigh with the memory. "Or maybe I didn't. I don't know. It's hard to remember any good feelings where he's concerned these days."

"How does Randy figure into this?" Colin takes one of my hands and laces his fingers in with mine. I don't fight him, instead enjoying the feeling of closeness it brings.

"Randy is Charlie's best friend. He was always around. Sometimes I thought he was jealous that we were together, and other times I thought he encouraged it. I found out later that Charlie used to date Randy's sister and that their families had vacationed together a lot growing up."

"So Randy was jealous?"

"I don't know. But whatever it was, it made him kind of angry. He was rude sometimes, but usually not when Charlie was around. And he'd say things that could be taken different ways, so I was never sure if he meant them in a nasty way or was just being funny."

"Give me an example."

I shrug, feeling uncomfortable as Randy's words come back to me in bits and pieces. "One time we went to the beach together and I wore my favorite bathing suit. Randy took one look at me and said something like I must not get out much."

"Get out much? What's that supposed to mean?"

I shake my head, trying to rid it of the memories. I can still feel the burning pain of embarrassment. "Oh, I don't know. Maybe that my suit was out of style. It definitely was more conservative than the ones their other friends were wearing. But he laughed it off like he was just commenting on my lack of a tan. It was just . . . uncomfortable."

"I'll bet."

"Charlie started asking to sleep with me - have sex - right from the beginning, but I wasn't going to do that until I was married."

Colin's gaze drops to my belly, and I laugh bitterly.

"Yeah. As you can see, that didn't work out quite as I planned."

"Stop," Colin says, putting his free hand on my cheek, forcing me to look up at him. "Just tell *your* story, not the story you think others are telling about you."

My lips tremble over the loving feeling his statement creates in my heart.

"Okay." I take a deep breath and continue, pulling back a little so his hand falls away from my face. "I always told him *no*, that I wasn't ready. He would press me pretty hard about it sometimes and then he would let off the pressure, like it didn't matter and that he was willing to wait." I can't look at Colin anymore, so my gaze shifts to his canvas. The angry black and red mirror the emotions in my soul.

"It was my twenty-first birthday. He told me he was going to take me to a party and then he had a very special gift for me, something to show his commitment to me. I was so excited." A tear slips past my rapidly blinking eyes and slides down my cheek. "I thought he was going to propose or something or maybe give me a promise ring. We're young for that kind of thing, but he fit so perfectly into my life. He understood my drive to succeed and desire to move up the rungs of society. He encouraged me to be better."

"To be someone different, sounds like," Colin says softly.

I shake my head but then realize he might be right. Charlie was always telling me I could be a better person. Before I saw it as encouragement. Now I can see it as the demoralization that it was.

"Anyway, we went to this frat party and he brought me upstairs to one of the bedrooms. He also brought champagne. I thought we were just going to do a private toast and he was going to give me my present. But Randy was up there too." The memory comes back as clear as day, like I'm standing right there in the room again. I shiver with fear.

"When I saw Randy in the room, I looked at Charlie and said, 'Why is Randy here?' And Charlie just smiled and said, 'He's bringing part of your present.' Randy sneered at me. I remember that very clearly. Then he laughed, shook Charlie's hand, and left. I thought I saw him give something to Charlie in his hand, like a small piece of paper or something, but then when I looked at Charlie's hand again, I saw nothing there."

"Charlie poured me a drink, said a toast to us or something, I can't remember, and I drank the bubbly champagne. It was bitter, I remember that, but Charlie told me I had to drink the whole thing or the toast wouldn't come true. And I remember staring into Charlie's eyes as he told me how much he'd been looking forward to my birthday, how we were going to celebrate it in style."

I stand up, feeling agitated about being too still. I want to run. I haven't thought about this night since it happened. It's like a heavy drape has been pulled across this stage, this scene in my life, so that I won't have to look at it. But now Colin is here and he's told me to push the curtain aside so we can both watch the scene play out. My heart-rate picks up and my blood pressure goes through the attic roof as everything comes into view.

"I remember asking him . . . 'Where's the ring?'" I laugh bitterly at my own naivety. "I actually said that. I'm such an idiot."

Pain slices through my heart. "He laughed at me. He said, 'What ring? You want me to wear a cock ring or something?'"

I look up at Colin. He's furious. I'm afraid I'm going to vomit, my stomach is burning so much right now. I rub my belly to try and calm it down. My voice drops to a whisper because I no longer have the energy to speak like a normal person. "I didn't even know what that was. A cock ring. I had to look it up online later. I don't know why I remember that part of our night so clearly when so much more of it is a blurry mess."

Colin stands up and grabs me into a fierce hug around my shoulders, causing my arms to flop out to the sides. I can feel his muscles trembling around me, but it makes me feel safe because I know he's not afraid.

He's angry. And I'm angry too. For the first time in months, I am angry at Charlie instead of demolished by him.

"I don't remember anything much after that. He pushed me onto the bed. I remember his weight on me and telling him *no*. I think I passed out. I remember voices. Laughing. Sounds that don't make any sense in my head right now."

"Jesus Christ," Colin says over my shoulder. "Jesus Christ, God almighty . . ."

I'm on a roll now. I can't stop. I just want to get the words out of my head, hoping once they're gone that they'll stay gone. "I woke up in someone's house with my pants off. I couldn't find my underwear anywhere. I was sore . . . down there . . . and there was some blood. So I knew I'd had sex, even though I don't remember it at all. Charlie was gone."

Colin pulls away, holding onto my shoulders and squeezing. "Tell me you went to the police."

My eyes go wide and panic takes hold. "Of course I didn't go to the police. Are you kidding me? I wanted the whole thing to just go away." Tears flood my eyes and the terror comes back. "I couldn't face anyone and tell them what happened to me. My whole life . . . everything . . . it was taken from me. My choice was *taken* from me. My plan to be a virgin on my wedding night was *taken* from me. He *stole* my life away. Nothing anyone said or did was going to change that." I'm shaking and a couple of hot tears escape.

Colin shakes me once, not unkindly. "But he's a criminal. He needs to be in jail."

I put my hands on Colin's cheeks and stare into his eyes, trying to calm him and the atmosphere that's gotten very tense. My hands are trembling, but I keep them pressed to his face and force myself to speak in a normal tone of voice. "You promised me that you wouldn't say anything to anyone about this. You *promised*."

His eyes are bright with unshed tears and anger. "You're going to hold me to that?"

"Yes," I say firmly. "I am. Charlie does not know that he got me pregnant, do you understand? He doesn't know and I want it to stay that way." I'm hoping Randy hasn't said anything to him. Maybe it's not realistic, but it's the only thing I have to hang onto right now. I have to count on Randy's possessiveness of Charlie to keep my secret.

"But . . ."

"He's rich, Colin. Wealthy. And his family is powerful. They'll take this baby away from me and I'll never see her again. Do you understand what I'm saying?"

"They can't do that."

"You don't know them. Their son raped me. You can imagine what his parents are like."

Colin is shaking his head. "So what about this Randy person? Why did he come here?"

My hands drop away from Colin's face as I re-join the real world, present day. "I guess he found out." I look over my shoulder at Colin's canvasses that didn't make it to Geraldine's gallery. "Randy's parents got the postcard from the gallery with that painting of me on it. It shows me pregnant."

I hear a long sigh come from Colin and turn around to see his shoulders sagging toward the ground. "Son of a bitch," he says quietly.

"Yeah. Literally."

Colin looks up, his face a mask of sorrow and apologies. "So what can we do to fix this?"

I shake my head. "Nothing. I just have to give birth and get the heck out of here. I have to start over somewhere else. Far from Charlie, far from his family's influence."

"Why not go to the police and have them get involved? They're not going to hand over your baby to a rapist's family."

"There is no evidence of rape!" I say, my frustration coming out with the force of my words. "I never told anyone! You're the only person in the entire world outside of me, Charlie, Randy, and whoever else was there that night who knows that this happened to me!" My voice downshifts into pleading as I share the cold hard facts with Colin. "And Charlie and I were dating for over a year. Who dates that long without having sex in this day and age?"

"Well, there you go," says Colin, sounding happy.

"What?"

"Witnesses. You said you have witnesses. Randy and whoever else was there, right?"

I burst out crying. I can't help it.

"Oh, shit, babe, I'm so sorry." Colin rushes over and gathers me into his arms.

I'm too far gone to speak. I sound deranged as the sobs wrack my body and have me shivering all over. I'm very close to vomiting.

"Take a breath, babe. Take a breath," he says.

I try, but I can only gulp hunks of oxygen before sobbing all over again. I try to explain so he can understand, pausing to retch and to try and catch my breath. "All this . . . all this . . . time I . . . I . . . I pictured myself be . . . be . . . being drugged and raped, I . . . I . . . I . . . still kept it in my head that . . . that . . . we were alooooone! That we were *alone!*" My voice goes up a few notches into a shriek. " . . . That it was an intimate moment! That it was a rape between two people, not several of them!" A cramp seizes my side and causes me to buckle in half.

"Aaaaahh owwwwww!" I scream. The blood leaves my face and I suddenly go clammy all over.

"Are you okay?" Colin says, his own voice sounding a little crazy. "Are you in pain?"

"My side . . . " I whisper. "It's my side again . . . ohhh owwww ooohhhh poooooo that hurts."

"Come on," Colin says, sweeping me up into his arms. "Let's go to bed."

He's pounding down the stairs as Teagan's on her way up.

"What's going on? Who's getting stabbed?" she asks.

"No one," Colin says. "Just more of that ligament pain. I'm putting her to bed."

I'm focusing all my attention on not dying, so I can't say anything to her to make her feel any better about my craziness.

"You need my help?" she asks. "I could massage something if she wants."

"NO!" I yell with more force than I mean to. "No massages." I pant like a dog to breathe past the pain.

"Okee dokee." Teagan stands in my doorway as Colin lays me down gently on my bed. "Just call if you need me. I'm going to go dig some holes in the backyard with Quin."

Colin turns around. "Dig some holes?"

She wiggles her eyebrows. "Yep. Some holes."

She's gone before either of us gets an explanation, but I don't care. Because now I'm lying in my bed and Colin is hovering over me with a strange look in his eyes, and I don't know whether I should be running away and screaming for my life or opening my arms and inviting him to join me.

CHAPTER
THIRTY-ONE

COLIN STANDS AT THE EDGE of the bed staring down at me. "I feel helpless," he says. "What should I do?"

"Just . . . be with me," I say, closing my eyes so I can try to focus on something other than him and my ligaments. *What else is there to think about? What I just confessed? No. Not that. God, not that.*

The bed moves and I open my eyes in time to see Colin lying down next to me. He's being very careful not to jiggle the bed. I close my lids again so he won't see me staring and freaking out.

My pain recedes in the wake of the sensations taking over my body. Colin is lying so close I can feel the heat from his body. I can smell his sweet breath on my face. And then his heavy hand is on my hip and he's talking.

"Thanks for telling me all that. About Charlie. I won't say anything to anyone."

I smile weakly. "Thanks." Relief comes as a balm to my jagged heart.

"But I really wish you'd say something to the police. It's not right."

"I know. But I can't." Surprisingly, the very idea doesn't set me off into a wave of panic. For the first time, I can hear those words and not think my world is about to end.

"Have you thought about . . ."

I open my eyes. By his expression I can tell he's holding back, afraid to offend me.

"I know what you're going to say. You're going to say he'll do it to someone else."

"Yes. That is what I was going to say. He will, you know."

"I don't think so."

"Why don't you think so?"

So much for the panic receding. Now the guilt descends like a heavy cloak over my shoulders. "I've had this conversation with myself in my head a hundred times, okay? He's not like that."

Colin hisses out some air. "I'd say he's exactly like that."

"No, I mean, we were together for a long time. And in all that time, he never did anything bad."

"Other than pressure you and take your free will away eventually."

"He was stressed, and I think I'm partially to blame for . . . what happened." *There.* I said it out loud. The piece of my nightmare that has always been the worst part to bear is now out there in the air between us.

"How do you figure that?" Colin's hand leaves my hip and his fingers move some hair out of my face. The cool air hits my exposed skin and gives me a shiver.

"We kissed and did other things that always got him . . . you know. Turned on. It was like a tease. For months it was like that. Months and months."

"And you're saying because you let him kiss you and touch you, he was somehow entitled to take everything from you? Is that what you're saying?"

"No. Not like that." I'm getting frustrated and sad. I thought I'd gotten rid of all my tears but apparently not. They drip down and land on the pillow next to my face.

"I'm not trying to make you sad or feel bad. I just want you to see . . ." He strokes more of my hair, sending shivers down and up my spine. "You're not guilty of doing anything wrong. You should be able to kiss a guy and touch his body all over and still say no at the end of the night. You don't owe a guy anything, I don't care who he is or what he's done for you."

I laugh, sadness with a touch of bitterness to go with it flavoring my voice. "Yeah, right. Like you'd go for that."

"I would. And I have."

"Colin . . ." I sigh out heavily. "No girl says *no* to you, so how do you know what you'd do in that situation?"

He smiles. "I've gotten a few *no*s in my life. I lived through it."

"I don't believe it." My tears have dried up and a real smile is breaking through.

"So you think I'm pretty good-looking then, is that what you're saying?"

My heart skips a beat as my sadness is replaced by embarrassment. I shove his shoulder gently. "Shut up."

"Yeah, I can see it in your eyes." He leans back a little and stares at me. "You're thinkin' I'm pretty studly."

"Studly? Who says that anymore?" I'm trying to play it off. I'm so embarrassed right now. He's caught me staring. He's caught me being a goober over him. *Me.* The pregnant girl with the cankles. Holy potbelly pig crush.

"I think you're pretty cute too," he says, his voice soft. He reaches up to touch my hair again and my eyes follow the motion. I can't look at him straight on.

"You're nuts," I say.

"Nah. I'm perfectly sane. I'm just hoping one of these days I can convince you to give me a kiss."

My entire body turns to stone. I'm solid. Every muscle is tensed, and I'm afraid to breathe. I think he just said he wants to kiss me. *Me!*

"Stop playing," I finally say, rolling over onto my back and doing a pretty darn fine imitation of a person who could give two poops about what he just said.

Two seconds later I realize what a mistake that is, when I find it hard to breathe due to a baby sleeping on my lungs, and keep going over to my other side, my back to him now. My heart is racing but I'm giving it everything I have to remain calm and collected. I settle into a comfortable spot looking at the wall.

The bed jiggles as his body comes up closer behind me.

Oh my god. Is he going to spoon me?

Just the very slightest touch of his leg reaches mine, but otherwise, there is still space between us when he stops moving.

"Are you tired?" he asks. His breath tickles a bit of my exposed shoulder.

It's when I think about it for a moment that I realize I'm beyond tired; I'm exhausted. "Yes," I say with a big sigh.

"Me too. Let's go to sleep." He keeps his hands to himself and he doesn't move.

After a few seconds I realize that he really means it. He's falling asleep. A very light snore drifts over us. It's like a metronome, hypnotizing me. Our breathing patterns begin to synch up and I feel my eyelids falling lower and lower.

My brain goes hazy with sleep. What's the harm in a short little snooze with Colin lying next to me in the bed? Nothing. We're adults, right? It's not like he'd ever do anything. I can trust him.

Smiling in the dark, I realize how happy that makes me. It's one hundred percent true, too. I would trust Colin with anything. He'd never force me to do something I wasn't ready for.

I'll just take a little nap. I wiggle around, trying to get my belly comfortable as it sinks lower into the mattress. *And later, when I'm alone, I'll dissect every single word he said and figure out where I'm going to go from here.*

CHAPTER
THIRTY-TWO

I BLINK MY EYES A few times as I reorient myself to my current situation. I'm in my room, in my bed. But I'm fully clothed?

The memories come rushing back. *Colin slept with me!* I look over my shoulder, but no one's there. It makes me both relieved and sad. I'm glad not to be sharing my morning breath with him, but sad that he left me.

Just that idea makes me mad at myself. As if Colin would sleep with me and get up with me in the morning. It's not like we're a couple or anything. It's not like he was being anything more than a good guy last night.

I struggle into a sitting position and realize that I need to pee probably worse than I ever have before. I barely make it to the bathroom, and end up staying in there to take a shower. I have no idea what time it is, but the sun is on its way up and I have things to get done today. One of the first things is to contact Geraldine and find out what other little surprises she might have in her gallery that I don't know about.

My lack of planning becomes evident when I get out of the shower and realize I don't have a towel big enough to cover myself in here. My eyes scan the room and come with one wash-cloth and one regular sized bath towel that I used the day before on my face. I know for a fact that this puppy is only good enough for about half my body being covered. *Dang.*

Doing my best with what I have, I open the door and streak out, tiptoeing as fast as I can over to my bedroom. Luckily, no one's in the hallway.

Flinging the door open, I jump inside my room, and then turn around, pressing the door closed behind me. *Phew! Made it.*

"Good morning."

I squeak in fright and spin around, the flap on my towel open-ing up for a moment to reveal my giant belly.

"Colin!" I say, out of breath, scrambling to grab the edges of my towel. My breasts are barely covered but my belly . . . not so much.

"Yeah. Sorry. Didn't mean to scare ya." He's staring at my stomach.

My towel has taken on a life of its own. Every time I try to grab one side, the other slips through my grip. I bend over, hoping to make it easier, but all that does is split the two edges farther apart. When I stand back up and finally have the two of them un-der control, the top starts coming undone, so I give up on hiding my belly in favor of covering my chest. I'd turn around but the very last thing I want to do is give him a view of my bare butt with this ultra short towel. Holy big backyard alert.

"Stupid towel," I grumble. My face is already flaming red and I can feel the blush coming up my neck now too.

"Hungry?" he asks, gesturing to a tray of food on the bed.

I freeze in my efforts to organize myself. "You brought me breakfast?"

He grins. "Yeah. Breakfast in bed. What do you think?"

My eyebrows are pretty much up in my hairline now. "I think . . . that I'm lucky?" And confused. Definitely confused. Why is he being so nice? And so . . . un-Colin-like?

"Good. Come eat it before it gets cold."

I look over at the selection on the tray. There's a bowl, a box, a spoon, and a glass of milk. "Uh . . . it's cereal."

"Yeah." He grins. "I'm just trying to get you back into bed."

I know he's just playing around, but for some reason it makes me mad. Maybe because I have a tender heart that should not be played with. Turning my back on him, I readjust my towel and go to my dresser, digging out clothes to wear.

"Did I say something wrong?"

"No. You're fine. Just eat without me. I need to get dressed."

He jumps out of bed as I start to walk toward the door, blocking my path. "Don't go."

I can't look at him so I settle for staring at his shoulder. "Colin, move. I need to get dressed. I have phone calls to make."

"But you have to eat." He gestures toward the food. "I'm going to leave you in peace so you can relax and eat without worrying about your towel." He leans in before I can guess what he plans to do and kisses me quickly on the cheek. Then he throws open the door and walks out into the hallway. "I'll see you later today."

He's on his way down the stairs before I'm over my shock of being kissed by him and have the presence of mind to respond. "Later today? What for?" Did I forget something? Is there a meeting I arranged and then promptly forgot? My pregnancy brain is in full gear, liable to forget anything; that's why I have a whole purse full of sticky-notes. But I don't recall a sticky note with the word *meeting* on it.

"Lunch! My treat!" he yells from the front door.

I back into my bedroom and shut the door behind me, wondering what exactly is going on between us.

Before I can muddle through all the conversations and analyze his every facial expression, my phone rings. I'm still half naked, but as soon as I see it's Charity, I answer it.

"Alissa!" she shouts.

"Yes," I say, smiling. It's impossible not to with the tone of her voice like that. "It's me. You sound happy."

"I am. I really, really am."

"Is this about the adoption?"

"Yes. And other stuff too. Everything is just going perfectly right now."

I reach over and knock on the top of my dresser. "I just knocked on wood for you. Do me a favor and don't tempt Fate like that."

"Oh, right. Okay. Things are going reasonably well. How's that?"

"I liked the other way better." I wander over to my bed and sit down on it. "Tell me what happened."

"Well, I went over to Barbara's house. It's pretty fancy. Not too much, though, which is nice. She and her husband bought a fixer-upper and remodeled it. The neighborhood is really nice. There were kids playing outside."

"I can picture it. It sounds nice."

She sighs happily. "It was. I mean, I know it's crazy, but I took it as a good sign that there were kids playing. Is that nuts?"

"No, it's a good sign. What else happened?"

"Well, she took me on a tour of the house. She already has a nursery totally set up with a crib and everything. The closet is full of clothes for a boy and a girl. She said she just buys stuff and was hoping someday there would be a baby there to wear it."

"She has a ton of baby food, huh?"

"Oh my god, yes. A pantry full of it. All of it is organic too."

"That's good." I hesitate to say my next thought, but decide to express it anyway. Friends don't let friends just do things like this without exploring every nook and cranny. "Was it a little weird? I mean . . . to see her house all set up for a baby but without a baby there?"

She hesitates before answering. "Well . . . I'd say it was more sad than anything. She told me some stuff . . . but I guess I can tell you since I know you'll keep it to yourself and you would understand. She's had a few miscarriages. One of them was really late in the pregnancy. So she's gotten to the point that she's kind of really sad and really desperate for a baby. She's worried that if she gets too much older that it will be too late."

"She isn't that old."

"She's forty. I told her it wasn't old either, but you know . . . you can't tell that to a woman. I know when I'm forty I probably won't listen to teenagers either."

"I get it. Well, I guess you found the perfect situation. Have you met her husband?"

"That's the only glitch."

My heart sinks. "How so?"

"Well, I haven't met him. But he seems . . . harsh."

"In what way?"

"Well, I guess he told Barbara to stop looking and to stop talking about adoption. He just got tired of it, I guess."

"Oh. That's really sad."

"I know, right? I mean, I know Barbara is crushed over it. But she's telling me that he's going to be fine with this."

"You need to find out for sure before you commit," I say.

"I know. She invited me to dinner tomorrow. Can you come?"

My mouth drops open. "Uh, yeah." I can just picture us, two pregnant girls showing up at this guy's house and him flipping his lid. It flashes in my mind that I should ask Colin to come with us, but just as quickly I dismiss that thought as ridiculous. He'd think I'm nuts just for asking. Just because we had a nice moment or two together, fueled by my confession, doesn't mean we're suddenly together or anything. I ignore the slight pang in my chest that appears over that thought.

"Phew! Good. I was so scared you'd say no. I just don't want to go alone. I'm sure it's safe, but I just need some moral support, and I don't think asking my grandpa to go is the right thing now. Not yet anyway."

"No, it's okay. I'm good with it. What time?"

"Six o'clock."

"Okay. Are you picking me up?"

"Yep! See you around five forty-five."

"Okay. Bye. And congratulations!"

"Save that for after the dinner," she says, just before hanging up.

As I finish dressing and get ready to start my day, I think about Charity and the risk she's taking. She's a brave girl, giving up her baby so he can have a better life than she can provide. A piece of me says I should probably do the same thing, but then I can't imagine living without my child while someone else raises her.

It's true that there are plenty of people in a better position than I am to raise a baby. But that doesn't mean for me that it's the right answer to walk away from her. I just need to figure out how I can support myself and my child and make it work. I owe her that at the very least.

I leave my bedroom with my cell phone in hand, ready to make a few important phone calls and take the steps I need to in order to start making this life better suited to having a baby on board.

CHAPTER
THIRTY-THREE

MY FIRST CALL IS TO the gallery. I make an appointment to go view the pieces that Geraldine intends to show to her clients. Hopefully there won't be any more surprises in there, but I plan to minimize the damage if there is. I'm allowing myself to have this irrational thought that Randy will keep my big secret and all of my troubles are now going to go away since he's been run off by Colin. I know it's not very realistic, but I'm going to keep on believing in my fantasy world until reality shows me it's futile.

I do an hour of research online about art shows before making another phone call. The next appointment I set is with the accounting firm that's working with Teagan's lawyers. Quin said that they'd offered her a job based on the work she did for Teagan's case, so I figure it wouldn't hurt to go in there and give them a copy of my CV. Maybe they have two positions open. Quin and I have the same major and I've got grades as good as hers. I could start working part time after the baby is born and finish school at night or on weekends. Hopefully. Fingers crossed. If I can find someone to watch her while I'm not home, that is. *Ugh.* Another bridge to cross. Another obstacle to surmount. *Stop worrying about it. Just get your work done.*

Digging around in my purse for my sticky notes, I come out with one attached to my hand. I read it out loud into the empty kitchen as I peel it off my skin. "Ultrasound. Wednesday. Ten a.m." My eyeballs bulge out of their sockets. "Ten o'clock?" My phone says it's nine thirty already. "Dang it."

My thumb hovers over the keys of my cell. I don't know who to call. Colin's too busy working and besides . . . he's not my taxi. Same goes for everyone else in my life. I have no idea how the bus system works and no money to pay for a ride in a real taxi. I'd call and cancel the appointment altogether, but this one is important. It's my final ultrasound before the baby's born and it's supposed to make sure everything's okay and ready to go. *What to do, what to do, what to do . . . ?*

My phone rings as I'm staring down at it. I don't recognize the number.

"Hello?"

"Hey. It's me. Colin."

I frown, confused. "Hi. Where are you calling me from?"

"Work."

"Oh. What's up?"

"Just calling to see how you're doing."

My belly goes a little warm. He wants to know how I'm doing. Does that mean something? I think it does. "Oh. Well. I'm fine, I guess."

"You guess? What's wrong? That guy come back?"

"No, no, nothing like that. I just . . . have an appointment at the doctor and I'm kind of stuck here without a ride. I forgot all about it until just now."

"I can come get you."

"No, no, don't worry about it. I'll just reschedule."

"I'll be there in ten minutes."

"No, Colin, don't. Really. I don't want you to get in trouble."

"Don't worry about it. I have to make a run out for parts anyway. Rebel won't care."

"He will. He just won't say anything."

"Well, then, that's his problem, isn't it? See you in ten."

He hangs up before I can complain. I stare at the phone and consider calling him back to tell him I've already cancelled the appointment and to not bother coming by. But I really, really want to go and see the baby one more time before she's here. I'm just weeks away now and I'm worried that something will go wrong at the end. The closer she is to being here, the more real she seems. I know that's crazy, even just thinking it like that, but it is what it is. I think I've spent too long living in the land of denial.

I run upstairs to try and wrangle my hair into a decent pony-tail and put on some make-up. I have to talk myself out of cutting my own bangs. The few times I've given into the temptation it hasn't gone well. By the time Colin shows up I've changed my clothes twice.

"You ready?" he asks, standing in my doorway.

"Yep." I grab my phone off my dresser and move toward the door, expecting him to back away.

He doesn't. He stands there waiting for me to get closer.

"You eat that breakfast I made for you?"

"Made for me? It was cereal, Colin. And yes, I ate it."

"Good." He smiles, moving sideways so I can come out of the room.

I gesture with my finger at the doorway. "Keep going. I can't fit through that tiny space."

He goes out into the hallway and waits for me. I breeze past him and go down the stairs, trying not to get too excited over the fact that he's behind me. This feels like more than just a ride, but I'm sure I'm reading too much into it.

"Where are we going?" he asks, moving around me to get to the front door first. He holds it open as I step through and onto the porch.

"The clinic. Same place you took me to before."

He closes and locks the door and then jogs to the curb so he can open the car door for me.

"Wow, what a gentleman." The silly girl in me pretends this is a date.

"Always," he says, shooting me a charming grin before getting into the driver's seat.

"So what's this appointment for?" he asks as he pulls out onto the street.

I fold my hands nervously over my stomach, trying to act casual about going to a doctor's appointment with Colin. "An ultrasound to see the baby once more before she's born."

"You can see her?"

"Kind of. It's not like a photograph or anything but it's good for seeing basic stuff. Haven't you ever seen one before?"

He glances at me before going back to his driving. "No. I've never been with a pregnant girl before."

With a pregnant girl. He said 'with'. My tender heart wants to read all kinds of things into that statement, but I can't let it. He means *with* as in physically present. Not *with* with.

We ride the rest of the way in silence. I can see him looking over at me occasionally, but I don't comment and don't return the gestures. It's too nerve-wracking.

I'm so confused right now. We slept in the same bed last night. He brought me breakfast. He said he wants to kiss me. *Does he like me?* Is that even possible? The dreamer in me says *yes.* The normal human being in me says *no way.*

I must be some kind of weird challenge to him or something. Maybe the idea of bagging a pregnant girl is some kind of Fear Factor thing for him. Like eating bugs or jumping off a bridge with a bungee cord attached to his butt. My heart sinks at the idea. By the time we arrive at the clinic, I'm thoroughly depressed.

CHAPTER THIRTY-FOUR

I'M LYING ON THE EXAM table with my shirt pulled up to my boobs when the door opens and the ultrasound tech comes in. Right behind her is Colin looking very nervous or angry or something. My mouth drops open in shock.

"Didn't want your boyfriend left out there all by himself!" the tech says. "It's no fun just seeing the prints after. Live action is so much better. Go ahead and take that seat over there," she says to him. "You can roll it over to be next to . . ." She looks at my chart. "Alissa." She winks at me and turns out the lights. Then she's too busy at her machine clicking buttons to pay me any attention . . . me and my heart attack.

Even though it's pretty dark and I'm staring at the ceiling, I can tell when Colin is near by his smell. Paint and engines and cologne. All man. I finally look over at him, the green glow of the machine making his face look almost evil-dangerous. I must be high because he looks even better than normal. It makes me wish my stupid belly wasn't rising up off the exam table like Mount Vesuvius. I could not possibly be less sexy than I am now.

"What are you doing in here?" I mouth the words to him.

"What?" he leans in toward my face and whispers back.

I glare at him, going cross-eyed because he's so near, but I don't bother repeating myself. The tech is coming closer with her bottle of goo and I don't want to cause a fuss by having him kicked out. Besides . . . if I'm being honest with myself, I have to admit there's a tiny piece of me that's happy to not be alone in here like I usually am.

The bottle of gel makes an embarrassing farty sound when it runs out of stuff halfway through being dispensed onto my stomach. The tech tries three more times and it happens every one of them. I thought I could handle Colin being in here with me, but apparently not. I start giggling uncontrollably.

"Somebody's excited about her last ultrasound," says the tech, smiling vaguely.

Colin takes me by the hand and just rests his arm on the side of the table next to me. It quiets me down immediately. He's completely serious and somehow has managed to dominate the room. I feel like I just got served a Valium.

As the ultrasound wand moves through the gel over my belly, a vision of my baby girl comes up on the screen. I'm not sure I've ever been involved in such an intimate moment before. It's not like my previous appointments, where everything was so clinical and cold. With a man in the room, especially a man like Colin, it's completely different.

I tear my eyes away from the screen for just a minute to watch him. His expression is set in stone and his jaw muscle bumps out occasionally. I can just see his face in profile and I'm struck once more by how handsome he is. His thumb moves to stroke the back of my hand and it gives me goosebumps all over.

"Head circumference is gooooood," the tech says, clicking on some buttons. I hear paper printing out near her feet.

"Aaaand there's a hand." She reaches up and points to the screen for our benefit.

"You can see the fingers," Colin says, his voice breaking between a whisper and a soft tone. He sounds like a teenager going through puberty.

"Yep. Five on one hand . . . five on the other. As far as we can tell, anyway." The wand moves to another part of my belly.

The screen turns into a mushy image and then another view comes up. The tech points once again. "Abdomen. Heart. See it beating there?"

She turns a knob on her machine and the sound fills the room, the whoosh, whoosh, whoosh telling us that my baby girl is alive and kicking in there. And then she does actually kick and her little body moves around on the screen and on the table.

I start to cry. I've never done that before in here. Usually during these things I find myself feeling detached and absent, but today I'm fully here. I'm deeply grateful for it, that I could participate in the process before she arrives. I'm not sure if it's the fact that I'm so close to being finished that's causing this emotion to take me over or the fact that I'm sharing it with someone special, but whatever it is . . . *Thank you, God.*

I look over at Colin. He appears mesmerized by what's on the screen. "Is that her face?" he asks. "Oh my . . . Jesus, that's her face."

"Language, Colin," I say, a smile taking the sting out of my words.

"I was praying, leave me alone," he says, not even looking at me. "Look, there's her nose." He looks at me, grinning. "She has your nose. All pointy and stuff."

"Colin!" I should be annoyed but I'm secretly thrilled that he's even bothered to look at my face that close.

The tech laughs. "He means perky, I'm pretty sure."

"Yeah, perky. That's what I meant." Colin pats me on the shoulder, back to staring at the screen. "I wonder if she's a wad-dler too."

I shove his shoulder. "Alright, that's it. You're kicked out." And I've been trying so hard *not* to look like a penguin. *Fail.*

The tech puts her wand away and moves the screen back out of sight. "We're all done here. Looks like you're good to go. I'll send my report to the doctor and someone will call you if there are any questions." She pulls some glossy black and white papers from her printer and hands them to me.

Colin stands. "I'll meet you outside." He leans down and kisses me on the forehead before disappearing from the room. It's like he's in a hurry and can't get out of there fast enough. And he kissed me!

I shake my head at his roller coaster reactions. First he's serious, then amazed, then pulling my chain, and back to being all freaked out again. He's worse than me, I think. And he kissed me too. I can't stop smiling.

"Lucky girl," the tech says as she moves to turn on the lights.

I don't argue or try to explain. Because even though he's not my boyfriend, he is my friend and that does make me lucky. "Yeah."

I'm in the car with him, folding up my ultrasound papers when he finally finds it in himself to start talking again. "That was cool."

"Yeah, it was." I'm smiling, staring at the picture of her in profile. "Do you really think she has a pointy nose?"

He reaches over and pats my leg. "Yeah."

"Co-*lin*!" I can't believe the nerve of him. He was supposed to say, *Of course not*. "You're a butthead."

He grins at me for a second and then goes back to looking out the window.

"You're pure trouble, you know that?"

"Hell yeah, I know it." His expression goes cold. Like a light switch - *off*.

"I was just kidding," I say, feeling bad that I ruined the fun we were having. It's not fair that he can call me a pointy-nosed penguin and I can't call him trouble. Talk about double-standards.

A few minutes later he starts talking again, and right out of the blue he floors me. His tone is casual, but his words are anything but. "You should give me one of those pictures you got."

I forget to be annoyed at his sensitivity to name-calling.

"What pictures? These pictures?" I look down at the ultrasound printouts.

"Yeah, those pictures. What other pictures would I be talking about?"

Dread creeps into my chest. I don't know why, but suddenly I feel very worried and scared and . . . sad. "Why?"

He shrugs, still very nonchalant. "I don't know. Because I asked for one."

My ears are burning. I don't know what to think or what to say, so of course I say the stupid thing, because that's what I do best. "Why did you ask for one, though?"

He shakes his head, his bottom jaw off kilter. "Jesus, never mind. If you don't want me to have one just say so."

"It's not . . ." I give up on trying to fix things. I'm sure I'll just muck it up anyway. I don't know why he wants a picture of my baby, and I don't know why I hesitate to give him one. Maybe because it feels like a really big deal. Like a really, *really* big deal.

I'm not sure if he understands how much it means, and that's important. We can't be thinking two different things about sharing baby pictures. People give baby pictures to husbands and fathers and grandparents and lovers. Colin is . . . Colin is . . .. none of those things. He's my employer. He's my friend. He has an art studio above my bedroom. He's . . . never going to fall for a girl like me. *So why on earth would he want a picture of my baby?*

We pull up to the house and I sigh, feeling very alone, even though I'm just two feet away from Colin. I unbuckle my seatbelt and look over at him. "Thanks for the ride."

He doesn't say anything. He just stares out the front window, tapping his thumb on the steering wheel.

I take my purse and my pictures and leave the car, slowly walking up the front yard to the porch. He peels out and is gone before I even reach the door. Tears make my vision too blurry to find the lock with my key.

Rejection. God, why does it have to be so darn painful.

CHAPTER
THIRTY-FIVE

AFTER A NAP, ANOTHER SHOWER, a re-scheduling of my gallery appointment, and some Internet surfing, I'm ready for the dinner with Charity and her prospective baby-parents. I'm nervous, so I can only imagine what shape she's in. When she pulls up to the front of the house and I get in the car, I get the impression she's as bad or worse off than I am.

"Hi," she says, sounding breathless. "Are you ready? Are you sure you want to go? I'm not sure if *I* want to go, so I wondered if you were sure if you wanted to go. You can say no if you want. Or say yes. Or we could reschedule." She grins and then frowns and then tries to smile again.

"Hi, Charity." I settle into my seat and bring the safety belt up and around my belly to connect it. "Yes, I'm sure I want to go." I click the belt in place and put my hand on her arm. "Do me a favor and take a breath so you don't explode your guts all over me."

A big huff of air whooshes out of her lungs. "Yeah. Okay. Breathe." She nods a bunch of times, reminding me of a bobble head.

I jiggle her a little before dropping my hand to the seat. "You already met Barbara. Why are you so nervous?"

Charity shifts the car into drive and pulls away from the curb as she shakes her head. "I have no idea. Maybe because her husband could pull the plug on the whole thing. And the more I thought about it, the more I liked the idea of her being the mom. She's really nice and very organized. She even has matching pillows on the couch."

I stare out the front window, wondering if her attachment to Barbara this quick is a good idea.

"What?" she asks, her tone worried. "I can tell you want to say something."

"No, I was just thinking . . ." I shake my head and stare out the window. I do not want to be the voice of reason right now. I want Charity to be happy and excited.

"About . . .?"

What would a good friend do? Lie? Just let a girl go into an important relationship like this without doing the bare minimum? No. Probably not. "Well, maybe before you commit to anything, you should get a background check on both of them." I look over to see her reaction.

She blinks a few times. "Oh. I guess I never thought about that. I mean . . . their house is nice." She grimaces and glances over at me. "That's probably not a good measuring stick, is it?"

"Well, it's important, sure. But you know, just to be positive, maybe we could have the police look to see if they have records."

"Will it cost money? Because I don't have any. I can barely pay for gas."

I shrug. "Probably will, but they should pay for it, not you."

Charity nods. "I knew there was a reason you and I met." She looks over for a moment and smiles big. "First you find parents for my baby and then you make sure they're good ones."

My heart squeezes in my chest. "Don't give me any credit for anything. If things don't go well, I don't want to be blamed."

"Well, that wasn't very positive," Charity says, going from happy to sad in an instant.

"I'm sorry. I take it back. I'm being a jerk right now."

Charity waves her hand in the air, as if to brush away the bad vibes that are floating between us. "No, Alissa, I'm sorry. I've been going on and on about myself and have completely ignored your life. What's going on? Are you okay?"

I sigh heavily. "Yeah, I'm fine."

"Is that the truuuuth?"

I chew my lip, wondering if I should say anything. I should probably just let her live in her cloud without messing it all up with my negativity. "Yes."

"Liar!" She slaps my leg gently. "Tell me the truth."

My smile refuses to stay away. "Truth is, life is very complicated right now. Too complicated."

"I hear ya. What's so complicated about *your* life, though? I want to know. I really do."

A sigh precedes my confession. "Well, I'm just weeks away from giving birth and I don't have any idea what I'm going to do after. I suppose I can get food stamps so she won't starve, but I need to find a job."

"Didn't you mention having a job already?"

"Yes, but it's working for Colin."

"Oooo, Colin. Lucky girl. Aaaand *why* exactly is that a problem?"

"Don't laugh."

"I'm not." She giggles. "Just tell me."

"You know what the problem is! He's too cute!" I can't look at her.

She laughs more. "Damn straight he's cute. He's actually full outta cute and into hot if you ask me. You should go for that shi . . . stuff."

I snort. "Yeah, right. I'm an elephant with cankles and completely limp hair. A penguin with an actual beak. I couldn't possibly be less attractive than I am right now."

"Oh, you'd be surprised," she says, her tone hinting at more.

"About what?"

"About how sexy some guys think pregnant girls are."

"Not Colin."

"Why do you say that?"

"Well, first of all, he only dates models. And second, he says I walk like a penguin."

"He *said* that?"

"Yes. Twice."

"Okay, that's not good. But that don't mean he isn't likin' the curves. That's all I'm saying." She lowers her voice. "And I heard that orgasms while you're pregnant are better than regular ones."

I laugh, but don't respond. Instead, I think about her curves comment for a few minutes. Houses whiz by my window as I consider whether he might be asking for a kiss because he does like curves. Does that make him a prince among men or a pervert?

"What?" she asks. "What are you thinking over there?"

"Nothing. Just . . . nothing."

"Are you sure there's nothing else bothering you?" she asks, slowing down in front of a nice, two-storey house.

"Yep." I put on a cheery smile so we can focus on her life instead of mine. "That's it. And I'll figure it out, don't worry." I unbuckle my seatbelt. "Come on. Let's go meet the parents."

"Ha, ha. Meet the parents. Good one." Charity tries to laugh but it comes out sounding a little like a hyena. "Oh, boy. That's not good," she whispers.

I laugh. "Don't worry about it. They're not going to stop wanting your baby because you laugh like a . . . silly person."

She frowns at me good naturedly. "Silly person? You were going to say something else, like monkey or something."

"Who me? No way." I'm still grinning when the door opens and a teary-eyed Barbara is standing in the entrance.

CHAPTER
THIRTY-SIX

W HAT'S WRONG?" CHARITY ASKS QUIETLY.
"Nothing, sweetie. Come in, come in." She holds her hand out toward the foyer and we both step inside. "You brought your friend. Alissa, right?"

"Yes. Is that a problem? I can leave." I point to the car that's disappearing from view as Barbara shuts the door.

"No, no, don't be silly. Come in." She wipes at her eyes with a tissue.

Charity puts her hand on Barbara's arm. "Tell me what's going on. I don't want to be blindsided."

Barbara stops and faces us. "My husband is just concerned about . . . the whole process."

"That's understandable." I'm afraid there's more to her statement than she's letting on, and I just pray it has nothing to do with the color of Charity's skin. Because people who have issues like that don't deserve to have her baby in my opinion.

Charity takes my hand and I squeeze her fingers a couple times. "Come on," I say. "Let's go have dinner." I smile as brightly as I know how and lead the way into the living room.

There's a man standing next to the fireplace. I don't know what I expected, but this isn't it. He's huge. He's the size of two men. And his skin is about two shades darker than Charity's.

All the breath whooshes out of me in one big gust. *That's one worry out of the way, at least.*

I can feel Charity relaxing through her hand just before it slides out of mine.

"Charity," Barbara gestures toward my friend, "I'd like you to meet my husband, Michael. Michael, this is Charity, the young lady I told you about."

He walks over and shakes her hand. His fingers could probably go around it twice they're so long. "Nice to meet you."

"You too," Charity says. She has to tilt her head up to meet his eyes.

"And this is . . .?" he asks, turning toward me.

"I'm Alissa. Hi." I hold out my hand and give him the firmest handshake I can, considering it's like holding a baseball glove and not a person's actual hand. "I'm Charity's friend. Just here for moral support." I try to smile past my awkwardness.

"That's a good friend," he says, his low voice a rumble in the room.

"Would you like to have a seat?" Barbara asks, pointing to a small couch.

Charity and I sit down next to each other as Barbara takes an armchair across from us. Michael stands at the fireplace again, a small tumbler of an amber liquid in his hand. Ice tinkles gently inside as his hand moves.

A clock ticks loudly somewhere. Charity and I both jump when a loud cuckoo bird starts squawking.

"Holy . . . moley," she half-whispers.

I don't say out loud what I'm thinking, that the dang thing almost made me pee.

"So, you are *interested* . . . in putting your *child* . . . up for *adoption*," Michael says. He reminds me of an actor making a very important speech in a movie.

"Yes, sir, I am." Charity bobble-head nods for a full fifteen seconds. I know why she's doing it, too. I can't help but nod right along with her. Michael is like Darth Vader or something. I swear he's reading our minds right now. No wonder Barbara was crying. I'd probably cry every day if I lived in this house.

"And can you tell me *why* you've made this very important decision? What has motivated you to choose *this* option and not the others?"

"Others?" Charity squeaks. She recovers before he has time to answer. "Um . . . yes, I can tell you." She sits up straighter. "But before I do, let's get one thing straight, okay?"

He lifts an eyebrow in response.

"I'm not here to be judged by you, okay? I'm the one doing the judging. I'm not going to give my baby up to just anyone. So if you don't want to be a father, you can just save us all the trouble right now and say so and I'll be on my way. With my friend." Charity reaches out blindly, and I take her hand, holding it tight against my leg.

I am so proud of her I could do a cheer. Instead, I just stare at the emotions moving across Michael's face. I see surprise, resistance, and then a cool grace. *Man, he's good.*

He nods and closes his eyes for a split second before going back to staring. "Fair enough. Although I think it would be unrealistic to assume we are not also making assessments of our own. Adopting a child is a very important decision. Raising a child even more so. It requires careful consideration by all parties concerned."

"Agreed," Charity says. "I totally think we're on the same page there."

"Good." He steps around the chair next to Barbara and sits down. "Charity, tell us your story."

Charity sits up straighter and lifts her chin. "Well, I'm sixteen, a junior in high school. I skipped kindergarten, so I'm ahead a year. I take all honors courses and I have a three point five GPA. I think my DNA is pretty good. I don't drink, I don't smoke, and I definitely don't do drugs. I did one time have unprotected sex, though, and believe me, I've learned that lesson."

A ghost of a smile appears on his face and then disappears just as quickly. "Do you have family?"

"I live with my grandpa. Both of my parents were in the military and lost their lives in the Middle East."

My mouth drops open and I gasp a little. I had no idea, and it's clear neither did Barbara. I choke on a bit of drool that gets sucked into my windpipe.

Charity pats me on the back as she continues. "I don't tell a lot of people my business, so if you could keep that to yourselves, that would be great."

"Everything we discuss will be kept in confidence," says Michael. "Our condolences to you and your grandfather."

"Yes," agrees Barbara. "Our sympathies. My goodness. Did this happen a long time ago?"

"A few years ago, yeah. But I'm okay. Thanks."

"And the father of *your* child . . ." Michael asks, " . . . is he in the picture?"

Charity snorts. "No. He knows about the baby but he's not interested in raising it."

"So you've discussed adoption with him?" Michael asks.

"Actually, I tried to discuss it with him but he won't talk to me. He wants to pretend I don't exist and that *this* never happened." She points to her belly.

Michael looks over at Barbara. She looks down into her lap for a moment and then looks up. "Obviously there are some details we need to verify before we can be absolutely assured that it will be legally valid."

"That's normal, right?" I ask. "There's always a mother and father and both have to give up the baby, so no big deal. Just get him to sign a paper."

Michael puts his drink down on the table in front of him and stays there with his arms resting on his thighs. "Charity, this is the stumbling block that I see in this process. You want to give your baby to a loving family for adoption. Barbara and I have been searching for a child for going on five years now. In fact, I gave up about six months ago, but Barbara kept pressing forward." He reaches out to her and she takes his hand. He turns back to us. "We have had our hopes up and then dashed too many times to count. We've had money stolen from us. We've had people try to blackmail us and bribe us and . . . well, I don't want to dwell on the unfortunate things we've dealt with. You get the idea."

"That sounds terrible," Charity says.

"Who would do that with a baby involved?" I ask, horrified at the very idea.

"You have no idea," Michael says, sitting back again and letting his wife's hand go. "As you can imagine, we . . . or I . . . have gotten to the point that I just don't think it can happen. That God has determined for whatever reason that we are just not meant to be parents."

"I don't believe that," says Barbara.

"Neither do I," says Charity. "I don't know you that well, but my gut tells me that you're good people and that you'd make great parents for my baby."

Michael puts his elbows on the chair arms and steeples his fingers together. "So what are your terms? What are you looking for in this arrangement?"

"Do you have to sound so cold, honey?" Barbara asks. She looks embarrassed.

He glances at her and drops his hands. "Forgive me, but we can't just dance around the details. It's better to know up front if we can do what you want us to do."

"That makes sense," I say, trying to smooth over the awkward moment.

Charity shrugs. "I just want my baby to be happy and healthy. So that means . . . I want to know you aren't criminals and you don't hurt kids or other people." She grimaces and her shoulders go up around her ears as she sinks down into her seat. "Like with a police background check?"

"Done." Michael nods. "What else?"

Charity sits up straighter. "Well, I don't need to be involved if you don't want me to be, but maybe if you could agree to tell him when he's eighteen, if he wants to know, who I am? That might be nice."

Barbara sits forward. "We've talked about this a lot. And actually . . ." She looks to her husband who nods her on. " . . . We'd like you to visit when you want. I mean, not every day probably, but maybe we can get together once a month or something kind of regular. You can be like . . . an aunt or a godmother or something. And when the baby is older and can understand, we'll tell him. We'll tell him the truth. All of it."

I swallow the lump in my throat. These people are really nice. It's almost too good to be true. Words come flying out of my mouth before I can stop them. "What's the catch?"

Everyone looks at me. Charity seems surprised. Michael, angry. Barbara, confused.

"Sorry, that came out wrong. I'm just wondering . . . it's not usually this easy." I look at the wall behind Michael, unable to face their judgment.

"You aren't wrong to say that, don't feel bad," Michael says, not sounding angry like I expected him to. "There will be legal fees, which we will pay. Court fees as well. The background check is a good idea. That, again, will be our expense. After we have the baby in our custody and he's legally ours, we will pay for his medical costs and so on. But all of this hinges on the baby's father. If he won't surrender his rights without requiring payment, it cannot go forward. We want a child more than anything in the world, but we will not pay for one. That's illegal and we don't believe it's the right way to start a life together."

We all look to Charity.

"I guess I have my work cut out for me." She looks down at her phone. "I'm going to call him right now." She gets up and walks out of the room before we can stop her. I can hear her in the foyer talking in a low voice just a few seconds later.

"So, how did you and Charity become friends?" Michael asks.

I give up on trying to listen in on her conversation and answer his question. "We met at a fast food place."

"Do you work there?"

"No. I was drinking a glass of water and she was having lunch. I guess we bonded over swollen ankles."

Michael smiles for the first time and it makes me feel a little faint. He's really handsome when he's happy. He reminds me of . . .

I point at him. "Did you ever play sports . . . somewhere?"

"UCLA. Running back. It's been a while." He smiles again. So does Barbara.

"That's where we met," she says. "I was a statistician for the team."

My mouth drops open. "I *knew* it! I've seen pictures of you on campus!"

"Those days are far behind me. I'm in real estate now."

I look around the room. "This place is nice."

"Thank you. But Barbara deserves all the credit. She has an eye for details."

She looks over at him and smiles. "This place has good bones. You can do anything when you have the right foundation."

Charity comes back into the room. "Well, I told him what I want to do. He said he doesn't care and he'll sign whatever we want."

Barbara's hand goes up to her mouth and her eyes fill up with tears. She looks back and forth between her husband and Charity. Suddenly I feel like I'm intruding on a moment I shouldn't be a part of.

Michael stands. "Well, we still have a long way to go, but I think we've done all we can for tonight. Who's in the mood for some chicken Cordon Bleu?"

I raise my hand and my belly grumbles.

Charity helps me to my feet. "I am," she says. "I'm starving."

The four of us move into the dining room for one of the most delicious meals I've ever eaten. Apparently, along with being a math whiz and an interior designer, Barbara is also a gourmet cook. And all that baby food she was buying . . . well, that was for taste tests, so she could learn how to make her own gourmet baby food here at home. She has big plans for mommyhood, and I couldn't be happier for her and my friend Charity. Michael warmed up after the appetizers and gave us the rundown on how he was going to teach his son how to throw a football as soon as he's able to hold one. Charity could not stop bragging about her baby's new parents, all the way back to my place.

No one's home, so I go up to my room and get into my pjs. As I lie in bed thinking about our evening, I can't help but be a tiny bit jealous. Of everyone. Teagan, Quin, Charity . . . I wish I had people standing around me telling me how much they love having me in their lives. But I can hardly blame anyone but myself that this isn't happening to me. I haven't offered anything to anyone. I've been focusing on myself and my situation instead of asking others what I can do for them. Colin's been nice, but I'm pretty sure he just feels sorry for me. He's trying to make me feel better. I think he has a protective heart. Maybe I'm taking the spot left empty by his sister or his mother in a way. Even that makes me sad, to think that I'm just a substitute for someone better, someone more wanted. Charlie used to want me. I swear, he used to love me. I could feel it when he told me.

I'm seized by a sudden bout of madness. I've been avoiding the subject of Charlie not only out loud but in my own head. I haven't seen him in months. And just like we talked about tonight with Barbara and Michael, he has rights. I don't want him to have them, and I'm worried to death about what he might do with them, but it doesn't change anything.

Words spoken by Teagan and Quin come back to haunt me. *He has a right to know.* I'm sick over it. Just plain sick. But there's something inside me that says I need a clean slate. I need to start from zero and work my way up from there, with no skeletons shaking their bones in a closet, threatening to come out and haunt me.

I should call him.

I grab my phone from the bedside table and sit up, staring at the glowing keys. My pulse-rate is twice its normal speed and I'm sweating. I know his number by heart. I could just dial it and say hi. I could test the waters and see what he says. Maybe we could meet for coffee and I could tell him about the baby in a rational, calm way and he might say that he sees the error of his ways and wants to be a good person and do the right thing by us.

The idea makes my throat burn with pre-vomit. He raped me. He forced me into this. He's a monster! He doesn't deserve anything from me!

But still . . . he deserves to know. I shouldn't be alone during this time in my life. What if he realizes he made a mistake? What if he's sorry? I mean, he knows I'm pregnant now. Randy came over here. Maybe he sent Randy to see how I was doing. Maybe Randy had a message for me. He sounded angry, but Randy never liked me. He was always jealous of Charlie and me. I shouldn't let Randy stop me from doing what's right.

I'm not in a good place; I know that. I should put my phone right back down on the table and go to sleep. That would be the smart thing to do. But I'm lonely and stupid and confused about my life, so I don't do the smart thing. I press the buttons and put the phone to my ear.

CHAPTER
THIRTY-SEVEN

I'M GETTING READY TO LEAVE a voicemail message after the fourth ring of the phone when it gets picked up. I panic when I realize it's not Charlie.

"Hi. Charlie's phone." The girl answering giggles.

My mouth opens but nothing comes out. The heat rises up into my face. My ears are burning.

"Hello? Is anyone there?" Her giggling has stopped.

I can hear Charlie in the background. "Who is it? Give me that."

There's some rustling around and then Charlie's voice slams into my ear. "Hello, this is Charlie. Who's this?"

"Uhhh . . . ummm . . ." It's the best I can do. No actual words will form and pass my lips.

"Who is this? Is this a prank? Randy, if this is you . . ."

"It's not Randy," the girl says in the background. "Look at the number."

A pause and then Charlie is back on the phone. "Whoever you are, go to hell." And then he hangs up.

ELLE CASEY

I'm not conscious of taking the phone away from my ear or turning it off, but I look down sometime later and it's there in my lap. And it's buzzing. Someone's calling me.

I pick it up and see Charlie's number there, glowing out from the dark covers around my legs.

My heart seizes up. What? He hasn't destroyed me enough? He wants to do some more damage? I press the green button and answer anyway. Maybe I deserve this.

"Hello?" I hate that my voice wavers and my hand shakes.

"Is this . . . Alissa?" He's almost whispering.

"Yes. It's me." I'm sick. Literally sick to my stomach. I pray I can get to the toilet in time if this goes too far.

"What are you doing?"

I frown over that question. "What am I doing? I don't understand the question."

"Why are you calling me?"

"Because . . . Randy . . ."

"What about Randy?"

"He was here. He told me . . . he said . . ."

"Here? Here where? What are you talking about? Are you on drugs or something?"

I'm suddenly deliriously happy. He didn't send Randy to threaten me! "Sorry. I'm at my house. And Randy came by here so I thought you sent him."

"Who me? Nah. He's a dick."

I can't believe he's saying that about his best friend. Maybe there's hope for Charlie. "Yes, he is . . . a very unpleasant person. I'm happy to hear you realize that."

"So what's up with the call?" he asks.

I can't believe he's being so casual. Like nothing ever happened between us. Like he doesn't know I'm pregnant . . .

That's when it hits me. *Maybe he doesn't know!* My mind is swarming with ideas. I could just hang up now and end this. Stay in hiding. Have my baby anonymously and put no father's name on the birth certificate.

My body sinks down into itself and the baby kicks me hard in the ribs. I can just imagine what Teagan and Quin would say about that. Charlie needs to know. He deserves to know everything.

"I was just thinking maybe you and I could meet for coffee."

"Hold on a second." Charlie's voice comes through the phone muffled as he covers it and talks to someone else. I hear running steps and a slamming door before he talks again. He's slightly breathless.

His voice is different. Changed. No longer breezy, light and open. "Seriously, Alissa, why the fuck are you calling me?"

"What?" My heart sinks. This is the Charlie I had expected to find.

"Thinking you might try to get some money out of me or something?"

"*What?*"

"Yeah, well, if you think you are, think again. I don't owe you shit."

"Excuse me, Charlie, but that's not why I called. As far as I'm concerned you can just stay away from me. You *and* your friends."

"Oh, really? Then why are you calling? You must want something."

I cannot believe how much of a jerk he is. I must have been seriously deluded to ever think he was a nice person. "I'm calling because . . . " I don't have an answer. Why am I calling? Because I'm desperately lonely and wanted to hear the voice of a person who I knew at some point loved me? I seriously need to get my brain examined.

"Actually, Charlie, I don't know why I called. Maybe to say that you raped me and I got pregnant. And I'm having the baby soon and thought you should know. But never mind. I know there's no point in trying to have a civilized conversation with a *rapist*."

His voice is low. Menacing. It sends a chill through my entire body. "What did you just call me?"

I steel myself against the fear. I will not let him do it to me all over again. "I called you what you are. A rapist." I almost choke on that last word. My body is going hot and cold in waves, over and over. I'm sweating. My stomach is churning. I can picture him smiling and handing me champagne. "You did that to me. You raped me." I wish my voice were stronger but it's not. It's weak and pitiful.

He laughs. "You wish. You're a fucking whore and you got what you wanted. Now you have regrets, but that's your problem. Don't try to put your shit on me. My family has lawyers and we're not afraid to use them. You can't prove anything because nothing happened. You hear me? *Nothing happened. You're* nothing."

I want to say something. The perfect come-back is somewhere in my brain. But my brain isn't functioning right now. I just sit there, swallowing over and over, trying not to vomit. *I'm nothing. He's right. I'm really nothing.*

The door to my room opens without any warning. "Alissa, you in here . . .?" Teagan is standing in the entrance, staring at me. "Holy shitcakes, what's wrong?"

"Don't call me anymore," I say quickly into the phone before hanging up. It flips out of my hands and lands in my lap. Scrambling around to get it back under control, I look up at Teagan, trying to put some semblance of coolness into my features while I'm dying inside.

"Who was that?" she asks, taking another step closer.

"No one. Sales call. Tele-marketer," I say, my throat a raw mess. I swallow two more times, trying to keep the bile down. It's not working.

"Alissa, there's no way that was a telemarketer unless it was someone selling dildoes or something, because you're about as white as a sheet right now."

I struggle to get off the bed, rolling off the edge to get to my feet. I have about five seconds before I'm going to blow.

"Where are you going?" Teagan asks, moving sideways so I can get past.

I give up on graceful walking and run to the bathroom, getting there just in time to vomit into the toilet.

Teagan follows me in and turns on the water at the sink.

"Go away," I moan, my face resting on my forearm that's draped across the seat.

"Like hell I'm going away," she says. And then she presses a cool washcloth onto the back of my neck. "What the hell is going on? Who was that on the phone?"

"I don't want to talk about it."

"Tough titties because I do, and this time I'm not letting you blow me off over it."

Ignoring her is my only escape. After flushing the toilet, I get to my feet and use the washcloth she gave me to wipe the cold sweat off my face. Eating half a tube of toothpaste only partially gets the sour taste out of my mouth.

"Come on," Teagan says, standing in the hallway.

"I'm going to bed," I say, not meeting her eyes.

"No, you're not. Not unless you want me sleeping with you, you're not."

I finally look at her. "Teagan, I'm tired. I'm exhausted. I don't feel well, as you can see. I just want to be left alone."

She reaches out and puts her hand on my arm. "I think we've left you alone for way too long as it is. Game over. Time to face the music."

"Says who?"

"Says me. The girl paying your bills. Come downstairs with me and let's chat."

Her bossiness rubs me the wrong way. I grit my teeth and prepare to dig my heels in.

"I'm not kidding, Alissa," she says in an angry voice. "Stop fucking around and feeling sorry for yourself."

Something flicks on in me and takes over. I become a screaming maniac. "I am *not* feeling sorry for myself!" Spittle flies out of my mouth. "This is *not* a pity party! This is my *life*, okay?! This is my *life*! It's not *yours*! It's not *Colin's*! It's not . . . anyone *else's*! Okay?!"

Teagan smiles, completely unfazed by my outburst. "There's the spirit." She waves her hand in front of her face. "Maybe more toothpaste wouldn't be a bad idea, though."

"What?!" I'm ready to punch something. Hard.

She's still smiling. "I was wondering when you were going to wake up in there. Come on. Let's go have some cookies."

I shake my head at her, all the steam leaving in the face of confusion. She makes zero sense. "You are insane."

"In a good way, right?" She winks. "Come on. They're not home made. I bought them at the store."

"So they won't kill me, is that what you're saying?"

"Brat. Good one, though. Come on, pregnant girl. Come downstairs and keep me company. The guys are working late and I'm bored." She walks ahead of me and starts down the stairs.

I could follow her or go to my room and lock the door. My gaze flicks from my room to Teagan's disappearing back. Do I want to be alone so I can wallow in my misery or do I want some cookies with a side of interrogation? Both sound pretty awful.

Echoes of Charlie's voice bounce around in my head and make the decision for me. *You are nothing.*

Maybe eating a cookie and listening to Teagan come up with creative swear words will keep that monster at bay for a little while longer.

I follow her down the stairs and into the kitchen.

CHAPTER
THIRTY-EIGHT

TEAGAN PUTS A MUG OF tea and a plate with two cookies down in front of me.

"Thank you," I say, sniffing the tea.

"It's chamomile. Perfectly safe for you and the bambino." She sits across from me. She's already bitten into a cookie and has crumbs on her face. I stare as they fall away and land on the table.

"So, who were you talking to on the phone that had you throwing up? Must be a real dickcheese."

I nod, pretending to be too busy with my cookie to answer.

"Family?"

I shake my head, *no.*

"Hmmm. Not family. Ex boyfriend, maybe?"

I keep chewing.

"That's what I thought. That was my first guess, but I wanted to ease into it." She gives me her evil genius grin. At least, I think that's what that look is on her face.

"So, what's his story? He know about your . . . situation?" She wiggles her eyebrows up and down. For some reason it makes her questioning seem not nearly as invasive.

"His story . . . is that he's a jerk. That's his story." I push a few cookie crumbs around on the table between us, arranging them into patterns.

"I have a little confession to make," Teagan says.

My eyes go up in time to catch her sheepish look. "A confession? For me to hear?"

"Yes."

This is way better than being questioned. I nod to encourage her. "Okay. Tell me. What did you do?"

"Forgive me father, for I have sinned," she says, grinning. "But I'm not feeling all that bad about it, to be honest."

"I'm not sure about the technicalities of going to confession, but I'm pretty sure you have to feel sorry for what you did." I roll my eyes. *Typical Teagan.*

"You see that vent over there?" She points to a metal grate in the ceiling behind us that I'm pretty sure is for the air-conditioning.

"Yeeees." I cannot imagine why she feels like a discussion of air vents is appropriate right now. I suppose I should be thankful that she's completely changing the subject. Maybe she has ADD.

"Well, you know, all the vents have ductwork connecting them to the a/c unit."

"Okaaaay." I shrug. *And I care about that because . . . ?*

"And I guess when the system was being put together, some of those ducts kind of were connected *together*."

I wait for the big reveal. She seems to be getting worked up about something, the way she's staring at me, but I have no idea what it is.

"And so it turns out that when a person is having a conversation in the *attic*, a person sitting down *here* in the *kitchen* can hear it." Her eyebrows are wiggling again.

It takes a few seconds for her words to process.

The attic.

The kitchen.

They're connected.

"They're *connected*?" I ask, fear taking my heart. "The attic and the kitchen are connected by the ducts?"

She nods. "Yeah. Connected. Like a giant belly button cord is between them. Or a telephone line."

"So what does that mean?" I ask, already knowing the answer.

She taps the edge of her tea mug. "It means that nothing you say up there is private if there are people here in the kitchen."

"You heard me," I whisper. "When I was talking to Colin. You heard me." I get halfway up out of my seat.

"No! Sit!" Teagan says, jumping up and pushing down on my shoulder. "No freaking out allowed."

I let her push me back down, but I'm not happy about staying. "I can't believe you eavesdropped on me. That's so rude!"

"I didn't!" She sits back down. "You were talking and we heard some of it. Not all of it. And it's only eavesdropping if a person does it on purpose."

"We? Who's *we*?"

She cringes. "Pretty much all of us."

My head drops down to rest on the back of my arm that's propped up on the table. "God, why do you keep torturing me like this?"

"Are you calling me God now? Because it's flattering, but I'm not sure I'm ready for the responsibility."

"Shut up, Teagan."

"I have a surprise for you," she says, sounding mischievous again.

"I don't want it. I don't want to see it, I don't want to taste it, I don't want to even know what it is. I'm too young to die."

"I think you might change your miiiind." She's almost singing.

I lift my head just enough to see her face. "You sound way too happy. It makes me very nervous."

She stands. "Come on. I want to show you something." She leaves the kitchen and goes to the back door.

Deciding she can't do too much harm in the backyard, I follow her out. She's standing on the edge of the deck, pointing out into the darkness.

"What am I looking at?" I ask.

"See that hole?"

I squint to try and focus past the light thrown from the back door. There's a rectangular dark space over in the corner, near the fence line. "Is that a hole? It's hard to see it from here."

"It's not just a hole," she says in a loud whisper. "It's a *grave*."

My head whips sideways to look at her. "A grave? For what?"

"Not for what," she says. "For *who*."

"For *whom*," I correct.

"For who, for whom. Who cares about prepositions? I'm talking about a graaave."

"It's not a preposition, you dope, it's a relative pronoun."

"Whatever! The point is . . . it's a grave." She's wiggling her eyebrows again. I can catch the movement just barely in the dim glow of the porch light.

"Why on earth is there a grave in our backyard?"

She shrugs as she looks out into the darkness. "Oh, I don't know. Just in case there are any rapists out there in the world who need to be gotten rid of."

I nearly choke. "Teagan!"

"What?" She's the picture of innocence. "Doesn't hurt to be prepared, does it?"

"I swear to God . . . you're completely and totally nuts." I look from her face to the grave and back again. This can't be real. It's probably just a flowerbed or something.

"Not nuts. Angry." She turns to look at me. "I heard what you said, Alissa. That guy deserves to be in that grave, face down, dirt up his asscrack, and his dick in a separate county."

My emotions are all over the place. Hurt. Angry. Frustrated. Sad. And loved. I feel loved. There's no denying it. Without thinking too hard about it, I grab Teagan into a hug, doing the best I can with this giant belly between us.

She pats me on the back. "See? That's what I'm talking about. Some enthusiasm over vengeful thoughts. *Finally*. That shit is healthy, I don't care what anyone says. I felt tons better after three hours of digging. I call it shovel therapy."

I pull back, smiling. "You don't care who says what?"

Teagan sighs. "Quin. She's a big time downer when it comes to the grave. She's anti-grave. Anti shovel-therapy, too. I had to do it all by myself."

"Really? That's surprising." I can picture both of them with a shovel in their hands. I'm almost able to see myself with one, too.

"She watches too many Bones episodes." Teagan sighs while staring out at her creation. "Apparently, there's no way I can use that grave and get away with it. Too much forensic evidence working against me." She shakes her head slowly. "Fucking science. Always was my downfall." She puts her arm around my shoulders and leads me back to the kitchen. "Come on. Those cookies are calling to me and my ass isn't quite big enough yet."

We're back in the kitchen with our cold tea and cookies, but my heart is about a pound lighter than it was before I left. "I can't believe you dug a grave." I shake my head at the craziness. I seriously love her right now.

"Okay, so I really wasn't going to kill your boyfriend and bury him, but it was a symbolic thing. I was angry and I had to do something constructive with all that energy. Rebel says I need to channel my shit."

"Rebel's probably right, but . . . a grave?" I giggle a little. The demon in me can see Charlie's face staring up at me from inside and I don't hate the vision.

"I heard what you said, okay? A grave seemed the most appropriate reaction at the time."

I try to keep smiling, but I can't hold it.

"Don't get all watery on me," Teagan says. "Let's just talk about where we go from here."

"There's no *we*. It's just me."

"Oh, bull testicles. Stop with the Oh-Poor-Me program, will ya? It's old. It's out of style. It's used up. We're all in this with you, okay? We all heard the story. We can't un-hear it. So let *us* channel our collective energy into some serious action." She reaches out and holds my wrist. "I'm not playing, okay? Let's be adults about this. Let's do the right thing by you and your baby. What's her name, by the way? Is it Teagan? Quin and I have a bet going."

I laugh. "You're too much."

"It better not be Quin. I'm serious. I probably won't get over that, like ever. I'm a seriously jealous person when it comes to baby names."

"Since when?"

"Since right this second. I just pictured your baby and you calling her Quin and I barfed a little in my mouth."

"No, you didn't." I'm still laughing. She's so ridiculous.

"Was that him on the phone?"

My laughs completely dry up and disappear. I take a long drink of my tea.

"You were talking to him when I walked into your room, weren't you?"

I sigh heavily and roll my eyes. "Can we not talk about this right now?"

"EEErrrrp! Wrong answer." She takes my remaining cookie. "Stop stalling and start talking, sister. I had a nap today. I can go all night. I will wear you down to a speck of a person. All the forensic teams will find is a hair follicle."

"Ew. Okay, fine. Yes. It was him."

"Did he call you or you call him?"

"I called him."

"Why?"

I throw up my hands and lean back in my chair. "I don't know! Moment of weakness! I wasn't miserable enough!"

"Was it because of Colin?"

I frown. "What? No. It has nothing to do with Colin."

"Be honest."

"I am being honest." Now I'm annoyed. "Colin has been nothing but sweet and kind and understanding about everything."

"And he fought Randy off, don't forget that part. By the way, is that Randy Buttermaker?"

"Butterman, not Buttermaker."

"Stupid name either way. Was that him?"

"Yes. Charlie's best friend." My voice is dripping with sarcasm. "They should marry each other."

Teagan snorts. "Randy wants to, I'm sure."

"What do you mean?" I lean forward, intrigued.

"What do you mean, what do I mean? He's as gay as the day is long. He wants Charlie's dick so bad it's embarrassing to watch. He totally stares at his crotch, like, all the time."

I put my tea mug down carefully. "You're joking, right?"

"Hell no, I'm not joking." She leans in closer. "Don't tell me you didn't ever see that?"

"Actually, I didn't." I grimace. Now that Teagan mentions it, it's not really out of the realm of possibility in my mind. "He was really jealous of me. Or always seemed mad at me."

"There you go."

"But . . . Charlie dated his sister."

"Randy was probably jealous of her too. But he for sure preferred having Charlie over at their place instead of yours. At least there he stood a chance at seeing Charlie's dick."

"That's just . . . strange. I mean, I never thought of it like that. Charlie's straight, though."

"Doesn't mean Randy wouldn't jump at the chance of giving him a BJ. Probably thinks he can convert him over to his team with one good suck-a-roo."

"Ew, Teagan. Ew. Please don't go there."

"Anyway, the question is, what happened during the phone call? Your face looked like a horror show, so I have to assume it wasn't good."

"It wasn't." It feels good to say it to someone other than myself. "It was a big mistake. I shouldn't have called him."

"Why do you say that?"

"Because. If he didn't know I was pregnant before, he does now."

"Good. He needed to know."

"No, not good! Before, I could do things my way and not worry about lawyers and him and his family and . . . all that."

"Bullshit, Alissa. You did have to worry about that. You can't hide that shit from them. But you can prepare yourself and do the right thing and have everything turn out okay. I promise."

"You're living in a fantasy world."

"Nope. I'm living in the real world. We need to get you a lawyer."

"Yeah, right. I can't afford a lawyer. You know that."

She sighs. "I probably shouldn't be telling you this, but what the hell. We have a legal fund set up for you already."

"What? Who does?"

"We do. The family. The Rebel Wheels family."

"None of you have the extra money for this."

"Well, apparently we do, since we're all set to pay your retainer. You just have to decide which lawyer you want."

"What? What? I don't . . . ? That . . ." I can do nothing but sputter.

She pats my hand and stands up. "I think I've done enough for one day." She takes our mugs and plates to the sink. "Why don't you go to sleep and we'll figure the rest of this out tomorrow."

I just sit there staring at her. I don't know what to say. Like I'll be able to sleep after all this. Graves . . . Randy . . . legal funds . . .

When she's done loading the dishes into the dishwasher, she turns to face me. "Everything is going to work out okay. Just leave it to us."

"I'm pretty sure that statement is going to go down in history as famous last words."

"Nah," she says, folding up a kitchen towel and pressing it into the counter. "I believe in the system. It's going to get my father's company back where it belongs and it's going to get your life back where *it* belongs."

"Yeah, right. That system you trust already let you down."

"How so?" she asks.

"Those lawyers, charging you all that money. They said they'd pay for it and wait to have you pay them back."

She grins. "You're right. They did." She walks past me and pats me on the shoulder. "G'night, pregnant lady! See you in the morning."

She's halfway up the stairs before I'm on my feet. "Wait! What?"

The only response I get is the sound of the bathroom door shutting.

I walk up to my room and go inside, slowly closing the door behind me. Staring at the rumpled sheets, I remember how I felt the last time I was in here, less than an hour before. As I climb into bed, I fantasize about getting a full night's sleep without any nightmares torturing my overworked and exhausted brain. As my eyes drift shut, I consider the idea of trying some of that shovel-therapy. Seems like it could have some benefits.

CHAPTER
THIRTY-NINE

THE DAY DAWNS BRIGHT AND sunny. "Just another day in paradise," I mutter, getting out of bed and gathering my things for the shower. I'm shocked when my phone says it's eleven already. *Wow. Were there drugs in those cookies?*

Colin greets me outside the door, dressed in his painting clothes, his hair all over the place. "Morning."

"Morning," I say, trying to keep my horrible breath to myself.

"Got time for lunch with the boss today?"

Butterflies start doing their thing in my stomach. "My boss? Would that be you?"

"Last time I checked," he says, smiling. "Unless you found another job already."

His comment reminds me of the appointment I have at the accounting firm next week. "No, not yet."

"Good." He looks at his phone. "Half hour?"

I nod.

"Okay. My car's out front."

"We're going somewhere?"

"Yep. Thought we'd stop off at the gallery and check on things."

"Okay, good." That scratches one task off my list. "I'll be ready."

Leaving him out in the hallway, I busy myself with getting presentable. A half hour later, I'm out the front door and walking to his car. He's got it in park, but the engine is rumbling.

"You're good," he says through the open window. "I don't know any other chick on the planet who can get ready as fast as you." He moves some papers off the passenger seat so I can sit down.

"I'm low maintenance, what can I say." I click my seatbelt into place and try to smile casually at him. It's hard because all I can do is think how gorgeous he looks. And how he wants a picture of my baby. *Sigh.*

"Good. I like low maintenance." He shifts the car into drive and we leave the neighborhood.

He stops not far away in the parking lot of a playground and turns off the engine.

"What are we doing here?" I ask. The silence in the car is quickly becoming awkward.

"Lunch." He get out of the car without another word and opens the trunk.

When I get out, I see he has a box under his arm.

"What are we doing? Planting a bomb first?"

He looks at me like I'm nuts.

"Sorry," I say, embarrassed. "I guess all the talk of graves last night put me in a dark frame of mind."

He walks toward the swings, expecting me to follow. "Graves? Did you watch a horror movie with Teagan or something?"

"No. She showed me the grave she dug in the backyard."

He stops walking and stares at me. "A grave? Like a grave, grave?"

"Yes. It's for Charlie, apparently."

His expression goes softer. "You told her?"

"No. Well, yes, but not intentionally."

"Tell me over lunch," he says, walking again.

I follow behind, being careful not to trip over tree roots. We're under the biggest oak I think I've ever seen, and its legs stretch out in all directions.

Colin puts the box down and opens it up, pulling out a blanket that he spreads on the ground. It's wool, a red plaid that looks new. The lightbulb goes on in my head. "A picnic lunch?"

"Yep." He grins, obviously very happy with himself. "Awesome idea, right?"

I can't help but smile back. "Yes. Except for the part where I have to try and get up from the ground later." I can just picture it in my head. Instead of being a penguin, I'll be a turtle on its back.

"Don't worry. I'll help ya." He takes fast food bags out of the box next and puts them in the middle of the blanket. The upside down box serves as our table.

I laugh.

"Hey, no laughing. I'm not a cook."

I join him on the blanket, sitting opposite the food. Watching him fold his powerful legs into the same position second-graders around the world use every day makes me smile. He's way too adorable for his own good.

I can picture him as a small boy, and it slowly draws me into a melancholy mood. A fantasy of seeing him holding his own baby some day slides into my head. Some lucky girl is going to have that privilege, and I know it's not going to be me. I wonder if I'll still be around in his life to see it.

"You bummed about the food?" he asks, looking at me with a worried expression.

I yank myself out of my dreamworld. "No, don't be silly. I don't care. I'm starving. What'd you bring?"

"Chicken, coleslaw, hush puppies, and mashed potatoes with gravy."

My mouth starts watering. "I don't even know what a hush puppy is, but I'm pretty sure I want one."

He reaches into the bag and hands me what he pulls from inside: a brown, deep-fried ball of something.

"Try it. You'll love it."

I bite into what turns out to be crunchy on the outside and soft on the inside corn bread. "Mmmmm," I say, hoping I won't regret this later. I never know what my body is going to accept or reject anymore.

"So how did Teagan find out about Charlie?" he asks.

"They're spies. All of them." A piece of corn bread flies out of my mouth and lands on the white paper bag in front of Colin. My face flames up red.

He pretends he doesn't see it. "Seriously?"

"Kind of. Apparently the vent in the kitchen is somehow connected to the one in the attic and anything we say up there, they can hear downstairs."

"Oh. Bummer."

"Yeah. That's what I said."

"So what did she say about it?"

I shrug. "That she was so mad she dug a grave to put Charlie in." I smile at the memory. "And she says I need to get a lawyer and that everyone at Rebel Wheels has put money in to help me." I look up at him, hoping to read his mind. "Is that true?"

He looks down at his legs and tosses a napkin around a little. "Could be."

"Colin, seriously." I sigh in annoyance. "I'm so tired of you guys just doing things without talking to me first. Could you please just tell me what's going on?"

He looks up, abandoning his napkin. "I'd be happy to if I knew you'd be rational about listening and responding."

"Are you calling me irrational?"

"Do you hear your voice right now? We're veering into irrational territory already and I haven't even said anything yet."

I take a deep breath and close my eyes for a second. "Okay. I'm calm."

He leans forward and then shifts his body so he's closer to me. "Give me your hand." He holds his own out, waiting for me to comply.

"No."

"Why not?"

"Because. I can't think straight when you're doing that."

A slow smile moves into place. "Doing what?"

I slap at his hand. "You know exactly what. Just tell me."

"You think I'm just playing around with you, don't you?" His smile slowly disappears.

"No. Well, yes, actually, if you really want to know the truth."

"Why would I do that?"

I throw my hands up. "As if I know how your mind works, Colin!"

"No, I mean, generally speaking, why would anyone do that?"

I stare at him, trying to gauge where he's going with his questions. He just looks curious, nothing else.

"Colin, be honest, would you? You have no interest in me as anything but an employee, a friend, and someone to goof around with. Why keep trying to pretend it's something else? To be honest, it's kind of cruel." I shake my head. "I get that you're the kind of guy who always gets the girl. You always have people fawning all over you. I'm sure your whoooole life, that's what it's been like. So I'm the one girl not doing that. Obviously it's some sort of challenge or contest with you. I get that. But I just have to ask you right now, from the bottom of my heart, if you could quit playing this game with *me*, because I'm not in a good place to deal with it."

"You really think that."

"I really think that, yes."

"Talk about irrational."

I throw a hush puppy at him and it bounces off his chest. We both follow its path back toward my plate.

"You just assaulted me."

"Shut up. It was just a hush puppy."

"What are people going to say when I tell them I was just sitting there minding my own business and you threw a puppy at me?"

I laugh. "You'd better specify what breed of puppy that was. A *hush* puppy, not a . . . not a . . . wiener dog puppy or anything like that."

"You like wiener dogs?"

My heart goes soft. "I love wiener dogs. I've wanted one my whole life, but my dad always said no."

"No offense, but your dad sounds like a real . . . uh . . . not nice guy."

"I hate even thinking about him right now. He's not bad all the time, but he's very strict."

"Have you talked to him recently?"

"No. Not since I left. I can't. It's too painful right now. He said some very unkind things the last time we spoke. And my mother too. They are a very strong team, let's put it that way."

"I'm sorry about that."

"Don't be. It's my life. No use wishing it was different."

"So we got off track," Colin says. "You were abusing me with puppies."

"No, I wasn't. I was saying that you're a player and I'm not. So if you want to talk to me and be my friend, that's cool, but don't play with me."

He lies back in the grass and folds his hands behind his head. Staring up into the sky, he talks. "I'm not playing you."

It's easier to talk to him when he's not looking at me and I'm not looking at him either. I stare at the box of chicken. "Okay, good." I'm a little sad. Why a part of me wanted him to be playing me is a mystery. Must be my lack of self-confidence or something. Before Charlie, I used to think I had a lot of that. I used to think I knew myself really well. Boy, was I ever wrong.

"I really like you." He swivels his head to look at me.

I try to keep my eyes from bulging out of my head, but I'm pretty sure I fail at it. "Yeah, right."

"I'm serious."

"Like a sister, maybe."

"Nah. Guys don't try to picture their sisters naked."

I laugh and then snort. It's not pretty. "Ha. You're so full of it." I stare off into the distance, trying to keep calm.

"I'm serious as a heart attack. I tried to paint you naked the other day, but I couldn't. I can't see it. You need to come upstairs and take your clothes off for me."

I pick up a hush puppy and aim it at him threateningly. "Colin. I am dead serious. Stop playing games with me."

He holds up his hands in surrender. "I give up. I'm not going to say another word."

I'm more than a little disappointed as I lower my weapon. For a split second there, I was loving the idea of him wanting all that.

He rolls over and gets up onto his hands and knees.

"What are you doing?" I ask, watching him warily.

He starts coming my direction, still on hands and knees. He has a devious expression that has me gripping another hush puppy.

"Seriously, Colin. What are you doing?" I hold up my ammo. "Don't come any closer!" I'm frozen in place. I stay seated and don't move, even when his face is right next to mine.

"I'm coming over here to test a theory. Don't hurt me."

"Hurt you?" I try to laugh, but it comes out more like a high pitched giggle. "That's not even possible."

"Oh, don't bet on it," he says, putting his mouth near my neck.

"What are you doing?" I say, my voice moving to a whisper.

"I told you. I'm testing a theory." He kisses my neck with no warning. His lips are warm and his breath hot. The two opposing sensations make me shiver.

He kisses me again, closer to my jaw.

"You're kissing me." Queen of the obvious. Yeah, that's me.

His softened voice washes over me. Darkness mixed with heat. "Yes, I am. And if you'll turn your head over here, I'll do a much better job of it."

A raging battle takes place between my brain and my heart. My brain jumps in first. *Don't you dare turn your face! Think about your survival! He will destroy whatever it is inside you that you have left!* My heart makes her argument next. *He just wants to kiss you! What's it going to hurt? What's he ever done but be good to you? Maybe he really does like you. How will you know if you never take a chance?*

"Colin, this is not a game," I say. It's my last ditch attempt at remaining outside this whole thing, whatever it is.

"I know it's not. Come on. Just one kiss."

I huff out a breath of pent-up anxiety. *This is no big deal. It's just a kiss. Get it over with. Show him it's nothing to be all excited about so he can move on.*

I turn my face, and his lips are less than an inch from mine.

CHAPTER
FORTY

HE LEANS TOWARD ME SO our lips can touch. At first, it's
just a feathery lightness, barely there. It should mean absolutely nothing. He's a boy, I'm a girl, it's just a kiss.

Oh, God, who am I trying to fool? It's anything but just a kiss.
And as it deepens and our lips press more tightly together, I realize it's a mistake. A very big, very important mistake.

But I'm not strong enough to un-make it or stop it from getting
any worse. True to my self-destructive path, I lean into the place
where we're connected and let myself fall deeper into the feelings
that are rising up to drown me.

His tongue comes out and tickles my bottom lip as his hot
breath washes down past my chin. My mouth opens slowly, automatically, eager yet afraid to feel more of him. My breasts tingle
almost sharply and my nipples harden in seconds. I wait until his
tongue is passing my lips before I dare to let mine out too.

At the first touch of our tongues together, my breath hitches in
my throat. I've kissed Charlie hundreds of times, but not once did
it ever feel like this.

Colin's hand is on my shoulder and then my back. I feel myself drifting sideways and it's only when grass is tickling my ear that I realize I'm lying down. Colin is in front of me, lying down too.

He's kissing me first tenderly and then with more insistence and passion as his hand roams down from my shoulder to my hip. He tries to pull me closer but my belly bumps into his.

The sensation of the baby flipping around stills our kissing. Against my mouth, he whispers, "I felt her moving."

I break away, leaning back and looking down at my stomach. "Sorry."

He lifts my face back up and stares into my eyes. "Don't ever apologize to me for that. I love it. You are so beautiful."

Tears fill my eyes. "I'm a penguin with a beak."

He pinches my chin, not painfully. "No. You are a woman. A real, beautiful, intelligent, loving woman. You are not a penguin."

"You said . . ."

"Huh-uh. I said you walk like a penguin. And it's true, you do waddle a little. But you know what? I love it. It's cute. I've never said that about a girl before, I want you to know that. I love the way you waddle. It's adorable. And if you ever tell anyone I said that, I'll deny it."

I can't help but smile through my tears. "You are such a liar."

"No, I told you. I don't lie. Except for that one time you made me lie but it was for a good cause. Now stop talking and kiss me again." He starts leaning in, but I stop him.

"Hey. You were supposed to be testing a theory. One kiss you said." My heart is going wild. It's possible I'm about to have a heart attack, but I hope it doesn't happen before I hear what he has to say.

"My theory was proven. You can kiss me anytime you want now."

"What was the theory?"

"Well . . . I was wondering whether I was after your body because you're pregnant and I find the pregnant form so alluring - as an artist, I mean. Or whether I was after your body because I just like you so much."

"And the kiss was some sort of test?"

"Yeah."

"Doesn't sound very scientific to me."

"Well, if we had kissed and it sucked but I still wanted to see your body, then it would just be an art thing."

He pauses, but I have nothing to say to that. I'm too panicked that the kiss sucked.

"But if the kiss was amazing, like I thought it would be, then it's not just an artist thing."

I'm about to pee I'm so freaked out. But I ask anyway. "So . . .?"

"So . . . what?" He smiles all evil-like at me.

"Don't make me bean you with a hush puppy again."

He scootches in closer and puts his hand around on my butt, pulling my belly up to his. "I'm not sure. I think I need another kiss to make up my mind."

"Colin, I'm not sure this is such a good idea." This is his out. This is his chance to walk away, no harm no foul. I hold my breath as I wait for his answer.

"Anything that feels this good can't be wrong." He leans in and kisses me once gently and then pulls back again. "Every day when I wake up, I try to come up with ways to see you. I think about you and the baby every second of the day. I dream about you guys at night." His tone turns frustrated. "I know it's nuts and I'm not the right kind of guy for you. I know you probably don't want anything to do with me. But I can't stop myself. That's why I painted that picture. I was trying to exorcise you out of my head."

"Like a demon?"

"Like a muse. Like a habit. Like . . . someone I want around in my life but can't hope to have."

"I'm a burden."

"You are *not* a burden. You are a gift." He drops over onto his back, his mood darkening. "But listen . . . I'm not the right guy for you, I know that. I have a record. I drink too much sometimes. I fuck up a lot. I have a temper. I spend way too much time dreaming up revenge against that dick Charlie." He looks over at me. "You're way better off without me. Just tell me to fuck off, and I will. I swear to God, I'll leave you alone. I just can't do it all on my own. I need you to tell me to go and mean it."

My face is trembling all over. My chin, my lips, my cheeks even. Tears are streaming down my face and I quickly move to wipe them away. He thinks worse things about himself than I do of myself. We are quite a pair. "Do you really mean all that?"

"Yes. I really mean all that." He stares at the sky again. "Just don't ask me to explain it, because I can't. You're in my veins right now. I'm addicted. I want to be with you and only you. I haven't had sex in a month."

I laugh through my sadness. "I take it that's a bad thing?"

He shifts onto his side again and stares at me. "I would wait for you forever if you wanted me to. I don't give a shit about that. I told you before . . . I don't force myself on women. I would wait for you until you were ready. That is . . . if you wanted me at all." He grins with a sad tinge to it. "I'm not feeling all that confident right now to tell you the truth."

I shake my head. "You're crazy. You are the most adorable guy I've ever known."

"Yeah, but do you want to get naked with me or just pat me on the head like that wiener dog you've been dreaming of all your life? That's the question."

I can't stop giggling. "You know I'm waiting until I'm married for sex."

"It's just an expression." He rolls his eyes a second and mumbles to himself. "Low maintenance, my ass." Then he's looking at me again and getting on his knees. "You want to do this your way, fine. We'll do it your way."

"What's my way?" Panic sets up camp in my heart.

Colin settles back onto his heels and puts his hand on his chest like he's about to pledge allegiance to the flag. "Alissa, I like you. I want to be your boyfriend. I won't pressure you to have sex with me, but I wouldn't mind some fooling around if you can handle it. If not, I'll just wait." He huffs out a breath and drops his pledging hand to his side. "Okay? There. I said it. Please don't ever tell anyone I did this." He looks around to check and see if anyone's nearby.

My huge grin is giving me face cramps. "I can't believe you want to be my boyfriend."

"I know. So gay, right?"

Gay? No. How about romantic . . . adorable . . . risky . . . perfect. I hold out my arms, throwing all caution to the wind and ignoring my inner demons decrying this as a mistake of the worst kind. "Okay, you've convinced me. Come here and be my boyfriend."

He sticks the tip of his tongue out and bites it as he's coming closer, his eyebrows wiggling up and down. "That's what I'm talkin' about."

And then we're kissing again. I lose track of time and just let myself drown in the sensations. Later we can face reality and all the barriers that are in the way of our relationship actually working out; for now, I'm just going to keep on dreaming of happiness and being buried in the bosom of my new family.

CHAPTER
FORTY-ONE

I'M ON CLOUD NINE AS we go through the motions of con-firming everything at the gallery with Geraldine. Colin held my hand for almost the entire trip over here, there are no more sur-prise paintings of me in the mix, and Geraldine has agreed not to display the one that ended up on the postcard. Life is about as good as it can get for me right now.

Geraldine shakes her head, not happy that the painting of me isn't for sale. "We'll just tell anyone who asks about it that it's already been sold. But they'll want to see it anyway. I really think you should let me hang it. It shows a depth to your work that re-ally speaks to people, even those uninitiated in the arts."

"Nope." Colin shakes his head. "Not negotiable."

I put my hand on his arm, loving the fact that I'm allowed to be possessive of him since I'm now his girlfriend. I suppress the urge to giggle over it. "We'll see, okay? Maybe we can talk about it some more." I'm feeling very magnanimous for some reason.

He looks at me, confused. "You said . . ." He shakes his head and shifts his gaze to the gallery owner. "Never mind. We'll let you know, Geraldine."

"Good. You two talk about it and let me know."

Colin's phone rings and he takes the call, leaving me to chat with Geraldine on my own.

"So, what's the story with you two, hmmm?" She looks down at my belly and over at Colin.

My happy fog lifts and the fear comes back. I don't want my situation affecting his work reputation. I suddenly feel dirty. "No story. I work for him. That's it."

"Mmmm-hmmmm . . ."

She obviously doesn't believe me, but I'm not about to tell her that Colin just recently asked me to be his girlfriend. It's none of her business. I try not to feel guilty over it.

"Well, good for you, sweetie. He needs some help. He's going to have a great career if he can stay out of trouble long enough to do the work."

"He's not always in trouble." In fact, since I've known him, he's only been in one fight as far as I know, and that was because he was protecting me. The one with Mick doesn't count, since they're brothers. I'd hardly call that *trouble*. I guess he used to be in fights all the time, but that was before I came along. A thought niggles at the back of my mind. *Did I have anything to do with his life's change of pace?* I dismiss it as school-girl fantasy.

"Don't get me wrong, him getting into trouble is a good thing for his reputation. Bad boys sell more paintings, believe me. But if he's in jail, he can't do the work, you know what I mean? So he just needs to keep it to just a few events a year, nothing too serious, and that would be perfect."

"Events?" I'm almost afraid of what her explanation will be.

"Fights. Losses of temper in public places. He could trash a hotel room and that would be good, too. People love hearing about that kind of thing. Makes him seem very mysterious, don't you think?" She looks over at him and her eyes go all cougary. She's thinking about getting him naked, I'm sure of it.

I follow her gaze and all I can see is the man who put his hand on his heart and pledged himself on his knees to me less than an hour ago. He's not trouble. He's my guardian angel. When I turn back to Geraldine, I'm pissed.

"Colin is not a trained monkey, okay? He doesn't do anything just for publicity."

"Sure, darling. Whatever you say." She moves away, and I'm torn between following her to give her a piece of my mind and just leaving in a huff.

Colin makes the decision for me when he walks up, sliding his phone into his front pocket. "Feel like taking a drive?"

I lose sight of Geraldine. "A drive? Where?"

"Tegan asked that we come to her lawyer's appointment. I guess there's been some developments and she wants her family with her."

I try to not be too happy about being included in that description. It's not like she requested that I be there personally. "Okay. Let's go." Going to an appointment where I just sit and listen is probably way better than getting into a war of words with Cougar McShruger anyway.

Thirty minutes later, we're in the lawyer's conference room. The entire Rebel Wheels family is sitting there, and two lawyers are facing us, standing at the front of the room since there are no chairs remaining. We get there just in time to sit down and nod at everyone before the lawyers begin.

The older lawyer speaks first. "Thank you for coming on such short notice. Looks like you have your entire support network here."

"That's how I roll these days," Teagan says.

"Musketeers. All for one, one for all," Quin adds, holding Teagan's hand over the corner of the table. Mick is between them.

"Why don't we get started?" the lawyer says. "Basically, we have an offer on the table. We think it's pretty attractive, and counsel you to take it with some caveats, but of course, it's your decision."

"Okay." Teagan nods. "What is it? Lay it on me."

"First some background," the second lawyer says. He opens up a file folder and scans its contents. "The private investigator we hired, working on the information that you gathered for him, discovered some significant evidence. This went way beyond what we originally considered when we took the case. We're now looking at criminal charges. We have not yet, however, turned over our discovery to the district attorney's office."

I look at Teagan. She's really stressed, I can tell by the way her forehead is all wrinkled up. I wish there was something I could do or say to make her feel better. When she looks over at me, I get my chance; I blow her a quick kiss and she smiles. I'm proud of myself when I see some of her wrinkles smooth over.

"The conversation that . . . Mick . . . had with your father's assistant was very revealing. Apparently your father worked out at a gym with his wife's brother on a frequent basis. He had a locker there that still had his lock on it. Our investigator, following chain-of-evidence rules, gained access to the locker and its contents. Inside was your father's gym bag with some clothing and a half-empty bottle of sports drink."

I'm looking around at the faces at the table, surmising that they're all thinking the same thing I am: *What's the big deal about a gym bag?*

"We had the interior of that bottle tested at a lab and came up with some disturbing information."

"Disturbing how?" Teagan asks.

"There were traces of ethylene glycol inside it."

"What's that?" Quin asks.

"Antifreeze," Mick says.

When everyone turns to look at him, he shrugs. "What? We come across it in the garage all the time. We have to dispose of it a special way and report that stuff to the EPA. It's a pain in the ass."

"What does that mean?" Teagan asks. "Why was it in his drink?"

"It's unfortunately used as a poison, almost impossible to detect and sweet enough to be easily masked in a sports drink. Also the same bright yellow that several brands use to dye the liquid."

My ears are burning as I consider the ramifications. *Poor Teagan.*

"So you're saying someone poisoned her dad?" Quin says. "Holy shit."

"Would you like to hear the rest?" the older lawyer asks. "Or would you prefer to take a break first?"

Teagan shakes her head, holding Rebel's hand. "No. I want to hear it all now."

He continues. "We took this information along with some other facts that we learned of to the coroner who did the intake of your father's remains when he died. There, we found that they had actually taken some samples from his organs and kept them before the cremation was carried out. There's a period of time within which they keep and then destroy samples. Luckily, we showed up before that destruction period came due. They've agreed to hold onto the tissue indefinitely, so long as we pay for the storage, which we of course agreed to do. This means they can test for the poison being present in his system at the time of death, even though your father's remains have been otherwise destroyed."

"Thank you for doing that," Teagan says, a lot of her normal energy missing from her voice.

"Of course. Following this development, we approached your father's wife with the evidence we've gathered, along with some timeline information and some data we recovered from a hard drive that your father's former assistant provided us. Needless to say, we made a very convincing argument to her that she cooperate and do the right thing."

Teagan snorts. "Yeah, right. Like she's ever done the right thing in her entire life."

"We believe she realizes now the difficult situation she's put herself in. Her only hope is to do whatever she can with damage control so that when the DA comes knocking, she'll be in the best position she can be in to defend herself."

"If she poisoned my father, she has zero hope. She's not that stupid."

"We believe it wasn't her, that is was her brother, actually, who carried out the poisoning."

My jaw drops open. This just keeps getting weirder. *Poor, poor, poor Teagan!*

"How well do you know your stepmother?" the younger lawyer asks.

"Call her that to my face one more time and see what happens," Teagan says, glaring at him.

He puts his hand to his chest. "My apologies, Miss Cross. I meant to say how well do you know your father's wife?"

"Well enough to know I don't want anything to do with her."

"What I mean is, are you aware of her relationship with her brother?"

"No."

I squirm in my seat. I don't like the way he just said that last statement.

"Have you ever met him?"

"Maybe. Once or twice. I don't remember."

"We've interviewed several people who are privy to his private life. Suffice to say, he has a very . . . strong personality. He's the one pulling the strings, we're quite sure."

Teagan collapses back into her chair, slouching down. "I don't believe it. She's evil."

"Oh, make no mistake . . . we're not giving her a free pass. She had her hand in this for certain. But she's not the mastermind, if you will. She's a puppet, albeit a willing puppet."

"So what's that mean?" I ask, not realizing I was going to speak until the words are out. "Sorry," I say, looking around at everyone.

Teagan nods at me, as does Quin. Quin also gives me a thumbs up, making me feel not quite so embarrassed.

"It means that she's at least smart enough to see when the game is over and she's lost. And she's willing to sell her brother out to save her own . . . self." The young lawyer is smiling, and I get the distinct impression he'd be hell in the courtroom. I like him a lot more after I see this side of him.

"What's the offer?" Rebel asks.

The entire room goes quiet as we absorb the fact that The Quiet One has spoken.

The older lawyer puts on his reading glasses and looks inside another file. "The offer is as follows . . ." He glances up at Teagan before continuing. "Teagan retains all the shares in the company allotted to her father's wife, giving her control of the corporation. The former Mrs. Cross —not Teagan but her father's wife— agrees to testify truthfully to her brother's plans and turn over evidence to the district attorney as required by law. She has already given it to her attorneys as a show of good faith and I have verified they have possession of it."

"And what does *she* get?" Quin asks. "Besides a punch in the teeth and a bright orange jumpsuit."

"She wants to keep the life insurance money." The lawyer looks up.

"So let me get this straight," Teagan says, sitting forward. "She helps kill my father, tries to steal his company from me, and yet she still wants to keep five million dollars for her trouble?"

The lawyer clears his voice. "Yes. She does."

"Well, she can suck it. That's my answer. Tell her that." Teagan stands.

The older lawyer holds out a calming hand. "Please, wait. Just . . . have a seat and let's discuss this."

I stand up too, along with Quin, Mick, and Colin.

"I've heard enough," Colin says. His face is twitching and I can tell he wants to punch something. I reach out and take his hand. Caught off guard, he looks at me and his expression softens.

"There's nothing you can say that will change my mind," Teagan says.

"May I try?" the lawyer says.

Maybe it's the challenge there or something else, but Teagan hesitates.

"Hear him out," Rebel says from his seated position. "Can't hurt to listen."

Teagan folds her arms across her chest. "Okay, so I'm listening."

"She's going to go to prison. Nothing we say to her is going to change that. A person who is responsible for the death of another person cannot collect on his life insurance policy. The benefits will go to the secondary beneficiary."

"Which is . . .?" Teagan asks.

"You. It's you."

"So . . . what's the big deal then? Why is she asking for something she can't have?"

The lawyer shrugs. "Our best guess is that she thinks she's going to somehow convince the jury that she's not responsible. That she was an innocent pawn. However, we don't believe that's the case. If you want our recommendation . . . ?"

"I'm willing to hear it," Teagan says.

"We recommend that you come back with an offer to let her keep one million, but we word the settlement in such a way that if the court were to decide she's not entitled to it, that this one million would revert to you."

"But she'll spend it," says Quin, slowly taking her seat again. Mick follows suit.

"Perhaps. But it's unlikely that she'll liquidate her entire estate. In the end, you'll get your money either in cash or in liquidated assets. Or, perhaps you won't . . ." He shrugs. "Regardless, you'll be paying twenty percent of your cash holdings to gain four million dollars cash and a company worth vastly more than that."

"It's a measured risk," I say, bringing up vocabulary from one of my business classes. Everyone is back to sitting down around the table now.

"What if Teagan says no to everything?" Mick asks. "What happens then?"

"Worst case scenario?" the younger lawyer says. "This woman and her brother run the company into the ground. They steal from it, squeeze every penny they can from it, destroy it from the inside. It's about to go through an IPO. The shares could be worth many millions of dollars now, but after it's all over, they could dump them all on the exchange and then the whole thing would collapse when it was discovered what they'd done to the infrastructure. Teagan would be left with a shell and a company with a very bad reputation. Employees would leave in a mass exodus and then it would just be a fire-sale situation. That's worst case, of course, but it could happen."

I swallow the lump in my throat. I never liked gambling and I'm terrible at taking risks. This is a decision that I'm glad isn't mine to make. And I thought my life was tough.

"So you think I should negotiate with this bitch and tell her she can take a million bucks of my dad's death money, so that she'll just go down easy?"

"Yes. And so that we can turn over the evidence that we found and have her charged criminally for what she's done sooner rather than later."

"You'll do that anyway, right?"

"Of course. We're obligated to do it. It's a timing thing."

"Did she try to bribe you into not doing it at all?" Quin asks, sneering.

The lawyers look at each other, tight smiles on both their faces, before the older one responds. "There were . . . several rounds of negotiation that went back and forth to get us to this point."

"I knew it," Quin whispers.

I nod across the table at her. She and I are definitely thinking the same thing about this sorry excuse for a woman. She needs to be in that grave that Teagan dug. I wonder if there's room for two.

"I need a minute to discuss this with my family. Would you mind?" Teagan asks, looking at the lawyers and then the door.

"Not at all. Just press zero on that phone and get the receptionist on the line when you're ready."

As soon as they've left the room, Teagan turns in her chair to face all of us. "So, what do you guys think? Should I take what I can get and walk away or tell her to go fuck herself?"

Quin answers first. "Tell her to go fuck herself *and* take the money."

Teagan smiles. "Oh, she'll definitely get a few parting words from me, that's a given."

"I think you should take what you can get now and wait for the rest later," Mick says. "A million bucks is a lot of money, but it's a drop in the bucket compared to what you could have with no fight."

"I agree." Colin nods as he continues. "I mean, I'm all for fighting when it's worth it, but not in this case. Better to take the bird in the hand."

Mick turns to his brother. "Since when are you an advocate for peace?"

ELLE CASEY

"Shut up, dick."

Mick sees his brother's hand under the table by my knee and then looks at me. "Ohhhh, I get it. Never mind."

Colin scowls at him but doesn't rise to the bait. I squeeze his fingers and he looks at me, his growl turning into a slight smile. Our happy bubble is back, floating around us and keeping the ugliness out. For the first time in a long time I don't feel like I'm alone in battling the bad news that keeps coming at me.

"What do you think, Alissa?" Teagan asks. Suddenly all eyes are on me.

"Me? What do I think?"

"Yeah, you. I mean, would you take a small now, do the hard thing, and hope it all works out in the end, or would you just stick to your guns and take nothing, no matter what terrible things could happen and hope it all works out?"

I frown at her, wondering if I'm imagining the double meaning I sense in her words.

The words drag out of me as I wait for the trap to open beneath me. "I . . . would . . . take . . . a . . . risk . . .?"

"And . . .?" she pushes me.

I give up on waiting for the trap to be sprung. Nothing's going to stop Teagan from doing what she wants to do anyway. I roll my eyes. "Take the four million and the shares of stock and then give everything to the DA immediately. Get her arrested and her accounts blocked before she has a chance to spend any of it."

Teagan nods, and turns her attention to her boyfriend, making me think my paranoia was unfounded. "What about you, babe? What do you think?" She rests her hands on Rebel's knees.

"Take the money. Take the company. Take her down. In that order."

She leans in and kisses him. "That's my man."

She turns around and faces us again. "The family has spoken. Bring on the suits."

Quin leans over and presses zero, waiting for the receptionist to answer.

"And while we're here in the land of legal ass-kicking," Teagan says, her eyes sparkling, "we can get Alissa to talk to their family law division and maybe the criminal law guys and get the ball rolling for her stuff. Just a little risk. That's all it'll take."

Apparently my paranoia was not unfounded. My jaw drops open as I look at the faces around me. None of them look surprised. Not even Colin.

"What the . . ." I huff out my annoyance. "Ambushed. I've been ambushed!" I shove Colin. "And you're in on it, you jerk."

"Nah, babe, it's not like that."

I roll my chair away from him and the table. "Go to hell, Colin. Don't talk to me."

Before I can work myself up into a serious lather, the lawyers are back and then we're witnesses to Teagan being caught up in a whirlwind of phone calls, planning and paper-signing. Partway through the process, a woman in a black suit and pink blouse sticks her head into the room and signals to me. "Can I see you for a moment?"

I glare at Teagan, Quin, and Colin, but get up from my chair anyway. "You are so going to pay for this later," I whisper as I leave the room and follow the woman out into the hallway.

CHAPTER
FORTY-TWO

HI, I'M NATALIE," SHE SAYS over her shoulder as she swishes down the hallway, her pantyhose and skirt announcing her arrival long before she's at her destination. "I specialize in family law. I hear you need some legal advice." She stops outside an office and gestures for me to go in ahead of her. There's a desk with two chairs on one side and a single, high-backed, leather one on the other. Tasteful art decorates the walls and files are stacked neatly on a table behind the desk, just under a large window.

I'm tempted to throw a tantrum out here in the hallway, but decide it's best if I do it in private. This Natalie person has a lot to learn about ambushing pregnant ladies, and I'm not afraid to educate her on that.

She shuts the door behind us and sits down across from me. Before I can even open up my mouth, she starts talking way too fast for me to get a word in edgewise.

"So, your name's Alissa, you're twenty-one, you're a year away from a college degree, you were raped, you're pregnant, you're afraid your child's father is going to come after you and take your baby away, and you're without any money to care for your child who'll be born in the next few weeks. How am I doing so far?"

My ears are ringing so badly, I'm worried for my health. Does an aneurism give advance notice before it blows up in a person's brain? Can just hearing something dreadfully awful kill a person?

"Ahhh . . . you . . . ahhh . . . that's . . . that's none of your business," I finally manage to say. Sweat pops out on my forehead and upper lip. I grip the arms of the chair to keep myself from swinging out at everything on top of her desk. I could so totally sweep it all onto the floor right now, just like in the movies.

"I hear ya." She puts up her hands like stop signs. "I've been through it myself." She presses her fingertips onto the top of her desk. "I know how angry you are. How helpless you feel. How pissed you probably are that your friends shared your personal tragedy with me, some stranger in an office you don't want to be sitting in right now." She leans back in her chair and rests her hands on the arms of it.

Her confession takes some of the wind out of my sails. "You were raped? *You* personally?" I can't believe it. She's tough. She's pretty. She's completely no-nonsense. That kind of thing doesn't happen to women like her.

She smiles without any happiness to it. "Yes. By five men. All people I thought were my friends, one of whom was my stepbrother. Pretty awful, huh?"

"God." I swallow with difficulty. "Yes. That's . . . terrible." Now I feel like a jerk for planning to give her a hard time. She's already had a hard time; she doesn't need that from me or anyone else.

She leans closer, her hands gesticulating in rhythm with her words. "Terrible doesn't begin to cover it. It takes over your whole world. It diminishes you. It makes you feel worthless and dirty and unworthy of ever feeling anything good again. You question everyone, their motives, their words, their thoughts, even. You begin to hate yourself for being so stupid, for not seeing this coming, for being responsible."

I nod, the tears welling up as she's speaking directly to my soul.

She shakes her head at me slowly. "It's all a game. It's a mind-game you're playing with yourself and it has to stop."

"I'm not . . ."

"You *are*. You're doing it right now, just like I did it, just like women all over the world are doing it too. We are *women*. We believe in love and goodness and the kindness of others above all things. We are hard-wired to blame ourselves for things that other people do, even the bad, evil ones. That's why we're so good at compassion. It's also why we're our own worst enemies sometimes."

"Why are you telling me all this?" My anger is gone. Now I'm just lost and confused.

"Tough love. I'm good at that part of the equation. I'm also good at getting child support, spousal support, and fair visitation schedules. Your friends want you to hire me to take care of your legal needs . . . yours and your baby's. But you're the only one who can make the decision to hire an attorney."

My mouth flops open and snaps closed a few times before I can put together an actual sentence. "I can't pay you anything. I'm completely broke."

"Your friends have already taken care of that."

"I can't owe them like that. It's not right."

"Noooo . . . what's not right is denying people who care about you the chance to help you out when you need it most. Maybe you think I'm biased, but let me assure you . . . I have enough business to keep me in Jimmy Choos for the rest of my life. I've turned more cases down this week than I'll accept by a three to one margin. I'm busy because I'm good. I'm good because I'm passionate. I'm passionate because I believe very strongly in what I do. I'm the champion of the underdog, which is why after twenty years I'm still a Redskins fan, which is why I agreed to see you today. *You* are an underdog. I'd like to be your champion. You let me know if that's something you think you can handle." She stands suddenly and gestures toward the door. "I think your friends are waiting for you outside, and I have a client meeting starting five minutes ago."

I stand up, pretty much numb, her words still flowing around me like a veil of power. I'm pretty sure I was just hypnotized without my permission or awareness.

She holds her hand out as she comes around the desk. "Nice meeting you."

"Nice meeting you too," I say vaguely as my hand is clamped into her firm, confident grip.

Colin shows up in the doorway. "Ready to hit the road?"

I don't know whether to be angry at him or thank him. I school my expression to remain as neutral as possible with my mouth shut and follow him out of the office and down to the car. My ears are still ringing with what she said. *Rape. Underdog. Compassion. Champion. Redskins?*

"Are you mad at me?" he asks as he opens my door.

I sit in my seat and stare up at him, trying to read his expression. He looks worried, and it melts my angry heart just a little. That lady Natalie was right. People are trying to help me when I need it most. And I *have* been playing mind games with myself for way too long. "I'm not sure yet."

He leans down and gives me a thoroughly hot kiss. "How about now?"

"That's not going to work," I say, my belly full of happy butterflies.

He kisses me again, longer and deeper. "You sure?" he asks, pulling away only a little.

I smile. "No." Leaning forward, I grab the inside door handle and pull it closed, causing Colin to have to jump out of the way so he doesn't get caught in it.

"Bad girl," he says, pointing at me.

"Trouble," I say, shaking my head at him. I can't stop smiling as he walks around the back of the car to join me.

CHAPTER
FORTY-THREE

COLIN DROPS ME OFF AT the house with promises to return later. I'm still not ready to just forgive him for that surprise attack, but I'm also not angry anymore. He did what he thought was right for me, and I know that everything he and the others have done is coming right from the heart.

I just can't believe I fell for the ruse that the art show Colin is doing was to raise money for Teagan's legal bills. They really had me fooled. The money isn't in there yet, but Geraldine says he's already sold three paintings before the show and that's enough money to pay for five times the retainer Natalie requires. How can I possibly be mad at my friends for that?

I stop off at the mailbox and grab the few bills that are there. As I walk up to the porch, a slip of paper falls out of the stack and floats to the ground. Squatting down to pick it up is a challenge, but I manage. I grunt as I stand back up, reading the scrawled handwriting on one side of the paper as I waddle up the stairs.

'Call me. I lost your number. We need to talk about your problem.'

My heart picks up its pace. Flipping the paper over does me no good. This is the entire message and it's not signed. It's not even addressed. *Is it for me?* I look around, up and down the street. There's no one there, no cars parked on the side of the road.

As I open the door I take out my phone, wondering if I should call Charlie again. He's the only one who would leave me a note like this. But maybe this is a note for Teagan. She has problems. Maybe someone wants to help her or something.

But she has lawyers. And Rebel. She already has all the help she needs. For some reason, I think about Natalie. What would she do in this situation? I don't know about the Natalie that got attacked, but I'm pretty sure I know what that bulldog lawyer person who I met today would do.

I sigh. Might as well get the humiliation over with.

Dialing the phone, I take several long breaths in and out. As the number rings through, I walk into the kitchen and sit down at the table. I can hear my heart beating in between the phone rings in my ear.

Charlie answers after a few seconds. "Who's this?" he asks abruptly.

"The person who got a letter in her mailbox." If he's going to be rude, then so am I. I try not be hurt by his ugliness. He used to be so nice to me . . . *No! Do not go there. He's a criminal and an asshole and he doesn't deserve your kindness right now. Shut it down. Toughen up. Be strong.*

"We need to talk," he says, his voice going lower.

"Yeah, I got that." I'm somehow channeling the power of that lawyer lady. I'm feeling bold. I'm not going to let him intimidate me.

"What do you want from me?" he asks.

My mind draws a blank. It's too wide-open of a question. I want the moon, but I know I can't have that. And from him? Really, I want nothing. I just want to be left alone.

"Are you going to say something?" he prompts.

"I'm thinking."

He snorts. "Sure you're qualified to do that?"

The stark offensiveness of his statement is like a bucket of cold water on my face. Holy wake-up call. "Charlie, I don't know who you think you're talking to, but you'd better just back up and take a closer look before you get yourself into deeper trouble than you're already in." Where did that come from? I have no idea, but I'm going with it.

"Trouble? I'm not in trouble. You wish I was in trouble."

"No, what I wish is that you hadn't turned out to be a criminal. But wishes aren't fishes, so no matter how many times I cast that net, I'm not going to change reality."

"What?"

"Just shut up, Charlie, and listen for once in your life. You raped me. There's no getting around that. I'm pregnant, and there's no getting around that either. It's your baby, the DNA will prove it. The thing is, I don't want anything from you but nothing at all."

"What's that supposed to mean?"

"It means, I want nothing. I want you to stay away. I want you to write us both off and never have anything to do with either of us. Sign away your rights." I bite my lip as I wait for his reaction. Maybe I won't need to fight him after all. Maybe he'll just go quietly into the night never to be seen or heard from again.

"Fine with me. Except for one problem."

"What's that?"

"You keep calling me a rapist."

I'm instantly fuming. He's trying to pretend he didn't do what he did, and it's like calling me both a slut and a liar all in one shot. I struggle to keep my tone under control. "F . . . Y . . . I . . ., Charlie . . . when you *drug* a girl and have *sex* with her without her *permission*, while she's *unconscious*, that's *rape*. Okay? That's rape. Look it up, *jerk*."

"You're dreaming. You came on to me for months. I just gave you what you were begging for. And for the record, you weren't unconscious. You were moaning and groaning like a total whore the entire time. I have it on video, so don't even think about denying it."

I stand up so suddenly the chair tips over behind me and makes a loud banging sound on the floor, like a gunshot. "Don't you dare say that." My voice is raw. My stomach is churning and burning. My skin goes cold and sweat pops out of every pore on my body.

"What? You're going to try and deny it? Typical. Fucking chicks, man. Always playing games."

I abandon the phone on the table so I can make it to the sink on time. I vomit the entire contents of my stomach in a series of what feels like never-ending retches. I'm still clinging to the edge of the counter when Quin walks in.

"Hey, are you okay?" she asks.

I'm sliding to the floor when she appears behind me. She grabs me under the armpits and eases me down, making sure I'm leaning against the cabinets before letting me go.

"Holy shit on a stick, what is *wrong* with you? You look like a ghost." She puts her hand on my forehead and then pushes my sweaty bangs to the side.

I'm trembling all over, so much so that it almost feels like I'm having a seizure.

She turns around and runs over to the phone, grabbing it. She's about to press the buttons but then stops and stares at the screen quizzically.

I reach my hand out to stop her, but she's too fast.

She presses the phone to her ear. "Is someone there?"

"No!" I yell.

She's listening for a few seconds as I try to organize my limbs for action. Problem is, they won't cooperate. They're made of gelatin right now, apparently. My legs keep folding back under me and my arms aren't strong enough to lift me.

"Who is this? Is this Charlie?"

Her expression turns mean. "Ah-haaa, so you just tried to have a little intimidation conversation with my friend Alissa, is that right?"

She pauses.

"Okay, okay, Charlie, just shut your pie hole for a second so I can clear the air, okay? Here's what's happening. You . . . are a penis. You are a sick, diseased, full of rotten pus penis that needs to get chopped off. And guess what? We're going to do it, dude. We are going to come over there, to your house, and chop your shit off. And guess what else? If you ever, and I mean *ever*, call Alissa again . . . or try to make contact with her under any circumstances? We will hunt you down and take you out completely. Not just the penis, but the whoooole shebang. We have friends in dark places, and all of us put together have maybe one or two morals max. You are vermin. We are exterminators. Do not fuck with us."

She pauses and then laughs.

"Bring it, dude. Bring. It. Your shit does not scare her or us. We talked to a lawyer today. She is going to eat you and your family alive. Your shit is going down, like *all the way* down. No chick will touch your shit for the rest of your life, which is probably no big deal since you're going to be in jail anyway getting it up the ass on a daily basis from some dude named Bluto. But don't worry. Teagan will bake you some cookies."

She smirks as she hangs up the phone. Then she walks over to me, grinning. "He thinks that cookie thing was like an apology, but that's because he's never ever eaten one of those mofos."

She hooks her arms under my armpits and heaves me to my feet, grunting the whole time. "Holy . . . shit . . . woman . . . how much . . . do you . . . weigh?"

I start laughing and crying at the same time. This is madness. My life is a complete and utter mess. Whatever ideas I might have had about this whole thing fading into the past or blowing over are now blasted to pieces. I have a major fight on my hands, and there's no hiding from the fact that I'm going to have to face up to it and deal with it starting right now. Charlie is not just going to disappear and sign off on a paper giving me my life back. He's dangerous and he's mad, and that's a terrible combination.

Part of me wants to be angry at Quin for getting involved, but the bigger part of me wants to hug her and thank her from the bottom of my heart. So that's what I do. She was my guts when I didn't have any to use of my own. I squeeze her with everything I have.

"He says he has a video," I say, bawling into her neck. "He raped me on video."

"Shhhhh . . . shhhhh . . . don't worry about that right now. We're going to get that video. We're going to get him, I promise."

She's still patting me on the back and talking nonsense to get me to stop crying when Teagan, Mick, Rebel, and Colin all walk in the door together.

CHAPTER FORTY-FOUR

I'M IN BED WITH COLIN next to me. The entire family wanted to come sit on the bed too, but he kicked them out. It's amazing how well he already knows me. I'm proud to be a part of this group, but sometimes they're just too overwhelming for me.

"He took a video," I whisper. My face is pressed into Colin's chest. We're cuddling at an angle, our legs nowhere near each other to make room for my giant belly.

"Shhhh . . . I know it's awful, but it's really a good thing."

"How can you say that?" I cry, looking up at his chin.

"It's evidence, babe. He can't deny what he did."

Fear slithers through me. "He says I liked it. That I . . . that I . . . moaned." Just the idea of that makes me want to vomit again. Problem is, I have nothing left in my stomach but acid. It burns the back of my throat.

"I know it's pretty much impossible, but you have to forget what he said, okay? Just stop torturing yourself by thinking about it."

"I can't! I can't! It's all that I can think about."

"Come on, you can focus your mind on other things." He kisses my head. "Remember our picnic today?"

An image of him kneeling in the grass flashes across my mind. "Yes."

"Remember talking to me in the attic? Our first real talk?"

"Yes."

"What do you see?"

"You. Sitting on that stool. Wearing those jeans."

"Those jeans? What's wrong with those jeans?"

I wiggle a little. "Nothing. I like those jeans."

He looks down at me. "I look much better with them off. Want to see?"

I can't help but giggle. "Stop. I'm traumatized right now."

"Seeing my naked body is anti-trauma medication. You should take some."

Maybe I should be worse-off picturing Colin naked, but it's having the opposite effect. "Stop. I'm pregnant."

He kisses my forehead. "So? That's not going to stop me. The only thing that stops me is the word *no*."

"Okay then . . ." I should say no now, but I don't. I'm suddenly on fire and desperate to exorcise the ghost of Charlie out of my brain. I keep conjuring images of me on a video that I've never seen. It's ugly and awful and terrifying all at once.

"You're not saying no," Colin says. "Say no."

"Why? You want me to?"

"Hell no, I don't want you to. I just don't need you encouraging me by accident."

I wait three breaths before answering. "I'm not."

He backs away a little and stares into my eyes. "Babe, I don't want you to do anything you aren't ready for."

I hold onto his upper arms with surprising strength. Staring right back into his eyes I answer. "I'm afraid I'll never get that image that Charlie created out of my head. I have no real memory of anything pleasant, and he's turned my one experience into my worst nightmare."

"So you want to . . .?"

"Make a new memory. A good one."

He frowns, almost with an expression of pain. "I'm not sure about the psychology behind that."

"Me neither. But it feels right."

"I'll tell you what . . ." He pauses to kiss me on the forehead and then the cheek. "How about we take it real slow, and you just say stop whenever it gets to be too much?"

"But . . . that's not really fair to you," I say, suddenly very shy.

"Screw that. It's perfectly fair. Every second I get to touch you is a gift. Don't worry about me."

I put my hand on his cheek. "Are you for real?"

He shrugs. "I feel real when I'm with you. Only when I'm with you."

Then he leans down and kisses me and I'm lost in the warmth that begins to build.

CHAPTER
FORTY-FIVE

COLIN TAKES HIS SHIRT OFF and then immediately starts at my neck. I'm lying half on my side and half on my back. Shivers run all through my body as he places the gentlest of kisses at my throat. In the hollow of my neck, his breath tickles the sensitive skin, but then his scratchy shadow of a beard grinds into me as he sucks it, reminding me that this man is a dangerous man.

"Stop," I say, a little breathless.

He looks up. "Okay. I'm stopped."

I stare at his gorgeous face. He's not mad. He's not frustrated. He's just . . . Colin.

I let out the breath I was holding. "Okay. You can go again."

"You sure?"

I nod. "Yes."

He smiles and moves down to my breast, lifting the edge of my shirt and bra so he can lick my nipple, flicking it with his tongue.

I gasp. How is it that such a small thing can bring so much feeling to a person's entire body? Thank goodness the baby is sleeping and not moving. I don't think I could handle both sensations at the same time.

I moan when he takes my breast in his hand and sucks it while squeezing. As soon as I hear the sound come out of my throat, I freeze up. This is what Charlie said I did . . .

"Babe."

The darkness that was descending disappears at the sound of his voice. His expression is pure sadness.

"What?" I ask.

"You have to let go of that. Let go and relax."

"I was just thinking . . ."

"I know what you were thinking." He taps the side of my chin gently with his finger. "Listen . . . if you'll let me, I'll spend the next hour or so helping you forget the past and making you feel like a million bucks. I hope like hell that when I do that, you'll moan and shout and growl and scream and anything else that feels right. That's what happens when people make love, okay? They make noise. And it's not the same as what happened to you before. It's pleasure, not pain."

"Growl?" I giggle, too overwhelmed by his kindness to focus on what was freaking me out before. "I'm not sure I'm going to do that."

He cocks up an eyebrow. "We'll see."

We're both lying there, smiling at each other. Slowly but surely, the fear disappears and the idea of moaning and growling for an hour sounds like a really interesting plan.

"What are you going to do to me?" I whisper.

"Do you want a play-by-play? Because I don't usually plan it out. I'm more a go with the flow kind of guy."

I bite my lip as I imagine that for a moment. "Okay. Just go with the flow. That would probably be better."

He pushes himself up to kiss me on the mouth. "You're too cute." Then he slides back down to where he was. "Now can I get back to my business here?"

I nod. "Yes. Get back to whatever it was you were doing."

"You like it?" he asks, leaning down, his tongue coming out.

I have to look away. He's too sexy to watch. "Yes, I do."

Maybe I should be embarrassed talking to him like this, but I'm not. It's just the two of us. There are no cameras, no terrible people outside the door laughing behind my back. It's Colin and me and the great big unknown. I'm not a virgin, yet I have no idea what this is all about. But with him next to me, his leg draped over mine, I want to know. I want to learn. I want to replace the terrible nightmares with beautiful dreams.

Pretty soon, my lack of experience ceases to matter. As he kisses me and runs his hands all over me, squeezing, stroking, tickling . . . I become warmer and less inhibited. I reach out to touch him, amazed to find out how large he's become and how hard. *He must really want me.* His muscles are bulging and straining in his arms and back with the effort of being gentle. This knowledge makes me bolder and more excited. There's fear there too, but I won't let it take over because I know I can say *no* and Colin will listen.

"Wait!" I whisper loudly as his face drops lower, past my belly to my thighs. "Where are you going?"

"I want to kiss you down here. Is that okay?"

I can barely see him over my belly. It's so embarrassing to have this awkward body in the middle of us. "I'm not sure." I know that's a stupid answer, but it's an honest one.

"How about I give it a shot and you tell me to stop if you don't like it?"

"Okay." There's only a speck of hesitation on my part. I tell myself we can try anything tonight. This is my safe place. It thrills me to know this, and I relax as soon as he begins to touch me down there.

He pulls my pants and panties off, all the while being very soft with his touch. And then he's back between my legs with his mouth.

"Oh. Wow," I say as his tongue slides in. Then his fingers are doing something, and I feel cold air followed by hot breath on my most sensitive parts. "Oh. My." The words are barely there. I don't even know what I'm going to say next, and I don't care either.

His finger goes inside me while his tongue is touching me somewhere that's making me hot. I'm literally temperature hot and turned on too. I push the covers away from me. I need air.

A moan escapes my lips as a strange tension builds inside me, down between my legs and up in my chest too.

"What's happening?" I ask, my tone edging into the desperately worried zone.

"Want me to stop?" he asks.

"Yes."

He lifts his head, immediately causing me to feel bereft and abandoned.

"No! Don't stop."

His mouth is back on me in a second.

Relief washes through me. Losing that sensation was way worse than the nervousness that keeps niggling the back of my mind. I admonish myself, *Forget Charlie. Forget the past. Just relax and enjooyyyyy . . .*

"Oh, God, Colin. Something's happening." I grab the sheets with one hand and his arm with the other. "Something's happening!"

I'm desperate to feel more of it and less of it at the same time. This is what people talk about. This is what people are after when they have sex. This is the real thing. It's so much more than I ever imagined it could be.

He moans against me causing a deep vibration to join the process, and his mouth moves faster, his tongue flicking and licking and circling.

"Oh, no," I whisper over and over. *Oh no oh no oh no . . .*

"OH, YES! Colin! YES!" Wave after wave of pleasure surges through me, radiating out from the place where Colin's mouth is. I moan, I scream, I might even possibly growl. I have no idea. I'm lost somewhere in a bright cloud of exploding colors.

This can't really be happening, but it is. The bed was solid beneath me before, but I can't feel it anymore. I'm falling, falling, and falling . . .

CHAPTER FORTY-SIX

WHEN I CAN BREATHE AGAIN and Colin is back by my side, I finally get up the guts to open my eyes and look at him.

"I think I might have growled." My lips are trembling, either with nerves or adrenaline, I'm not sure which. But one thing I am sure of is that it's not embarrassment. I feel like I can totally be myself with Colin. This is a gift of the very best kind, one I've never been given before.

"You liked it, I know that," he says, smiling like a cocky fool. I adore him for that. He totally deserves to feel cocky all the time. He's hot, he's sweet, and he can do that thing he just did to me like some kind of expert.

I'm happy but then I feel bad. I had all this fun and he had nothing. It's not fair that he would have to pay for another guy's sins.

"I want to do something for you," I say shyly. My past experiences were mostly just kissing and some basic touching. I have no idea what I'm doing in the bedroom, and I was never one to read books about it or watch movies with those kinds of details. I'm a little worried that he'll laugh at my feeble attempts at seduction.

"Maybe we should just leave it at this for our first night together," he says, kissing my neck.

I try not to be paranoid and think he doesn't want me to do anything. "That's not very fair."

"All is fair in love and war."

My heart burns with the word *love*. I really do love him, but I don't want to say it now. I don't want him to think my love comes from between my legs. But the fact that he said love, even though it was in such a casual way, is enough to fuel my desire all over again.

"What can I do?" I reach down and rub the front of his jeans. He's still very hard, making me feel bolder. He must want me, right? That's what that means. I think. I'm pretty sure.

"Well . . .," he falls onto his back and stares at the ceiling, "you can do whatever you want or nothing at all." His head swivels to look at me. "Seriously, babe, we can do nothing. I just need a minute to collect myself."

"Collect yourself? I don't understand. I'm the one that had the . . . fun." I can't say the O-word. I sure can feel it, but I can't say it. "I haven't even really touched you yet."

"You don't need to touch me to turn me on. Doing that for you and watching and listening to you was fun for me. You just . . . get me going. All I have to do is look at you and I'm a mess."

"Really?" I can't stop the huge grin from taking over my face. "A mess? I turn you on?" I look down at my belly. "I think you need to see a therapist."

He rolls over onto his side and rubs my stomach all over. "You're gorgeous. I don't want to hear another word about it."

I keep my thoughts to myself. If he wants to like this body of mine, I'm not going to try and point out the errors in his judgment. Even if he's lying, I appreciate the thought behind it.

"Okay, so what can I do?" I say.

"You could . . . touch me. Lick me. Let me make love to you. It's your choice."

My heart beats double-time at his offerings. "We can't make love."

"Why? Are you too nervous? Is it the waiting until you're married thing?"

"No. None of that." My former plans for my future life seem very out of place right now. I can't even remember why I felt the way I did. "It's just . . . ." I look down at my belly. "There's something in the way."

"Tell you what. Turn over. On your other side."

I hesitate for a moment, but when I see the expression on his face, I do as he suggests. He's being patient and kind, but he's still hot and bothered. I can see the smoldering heat in his eyes. I want to do something about that. I feel powerful and sexy, which is some kind of miracle considering the fact that I'm a potbelly penguin.

I hear a zipper and look over my shoulder. He's off the bed and pulling his pants down. His erection springs loose from the fabric, and I quickly look away. *It's too big. This will never work. He better not think he's putting that somewhere weird.*

He's next to me a second later, his warm body pressing up against my back. The hair on his legs tickles my skin.

"I'm going to come into you from behind, okay?" His hot erection settles against my bare butt.

"Come into me where, exactly?"

He kisses the back of my neck. "Do you want the medical word or something a little dirtier?"

I giggle and then squirm a little bit. "Ummm . . . the dirty word. I want the dirty one." I'm on pins and needles waiting for him to speak. His tongue is on my neck swirling around and then his lips are kissing the wet spot he made. I have goosebumps everywhere.

"I'm going to put my dick into your pussy." He nips my shoulder. "How's that? Dirty enough for you?"

I try to answer, but I can't. My voice is stuck in my throat. I reach behind me and take his hard length in my hand, stroking it as best I can from my awkward position.

"I'll take that as a yes." He pushes closer to me and then takes himself in hand. I brace myself with a hand on the mattress up near my chest.

"I've always used a condom with other girls before. I know you're already pregnant, but I could still wear one if you want."

"No," I say, shaking my head. "If you always wore one before, there's no point now."

I don't know exactly how he's going to manage to do what he said he's going to do, but I wait with my heart hammering in my chest. I'm already getting wet down there again and he hasn't even really touched me yet.

"Lift up your leg a little."

I do as he asks, and then gasp as he comes sliding in toward me from behind. His body is hot and silky smooth. His hardness slips easily between us, and the tip of it pushes against the place where his fingers were earlier.

"Ready?" he asks.

"Yes," I whisper, not sure that I'm telling the truth. *I can say no whenever I want and he'll stop. Whenever I want. He'll stop . . .*

At first he goes in just the littlest bit. I'm breathing faster, waiting for pain. Waiting for shame. Waiting for something unpleasant to happen.

But it doesn't.

He's in deeper now, setting up a slow, easy rhythm.

I angle myself backward, enjoying the sensation but needing more. I can't believe how amazing it feels to have him sliding into me like this.

"Yeah, babe. That's it," he says, in a low, deep voice right next to my ear.

I push against him, tentatively at first but then more eagerly, meeting his rhythm stroke for stroke. I didn't know my hips could move like this. I feel sensual. Sexy. Like I know what I'm doing.

His body comes in closer and he presses his chest to my back. And then his hand is reaching around me, his fingers touching me in my tender place again.

"What are you doing?" I whisper, closing my eyes and falling into the sensations.

"I want you to come with me," he says against my neck. His finger is swirling around and pressing against me as he slides in and out of me. He feels impossibly big and long, and I cry out with the pleasure that's overwhelming me.

I don't know how long we're doing this before I reach the breaking point. I've lost all concept of time. "It's happening again," I say in a whimper. "It's happening again!"

"Shhhh . . . just let it happen." He goes faster, picking up the pace of his strokes.

My leg is trembling with the effort of keeping it up, but I don't want this to stop. I'm close to falling over that cliff again.

"Oh, babe," he grunts out, slamming into me from behind now. "Fuck!"

Everything is shaking. Me, the bed, our bodies. The pressure is building. Colin is growling and moaning. Just hearing him lose it like that is enough to make me lose it too.

Suddenly the fireworks are there. I'm filled to the core and I'm drowning. A strong pulsing starts between my legs, squeezing him over and over from inside my body.

He's falling with me as we both shout way louder than we probably should. And then he's jerking and slamming into me, his rhythm going hectic as he loses control. He's caught in some kind of seizure and I feel him pulsing into me now too.

I lower my leg, unable to hold it up anymore. Reaching behind me, I find his butt. I press him up against me, wishing this could keep going forever. I don't want to leave this place. Uninhibited. Sated. Intimate. I never had any idea that this could happen, let alone to someone like me.

He finally stills and kisses me loudly on the shoulder before slowly withdrawing and lying on his back.

I turn over with great effort, my belly feeling twice as heavy as normal. The baby shifts inside and makes her presence known. I'm so glad she waited until we were done.

"You okay?" he asks, looking worried.

I smile as I rub my belly. "Okay? Yeah. More than okay." I scootch over and put my head on his chest, snuggling in when his arm wraps around my back. I wish I could get closer but this giant balloon between us makes it impossible.

"More than okay, huh?"

"Yes." I can't stop smiling.

"Me too. Can I sleep here with you? I'm too tired to move."

I'm secretly thrilled. He wants to stay! "Yes. Sleep," I say, trying to sound all casual and cool, like I do this all the time. No big deal.

As I listen to his breathing even out, I'm sure he's fallen asleep. But then he startles me by speaking.

"Thanks."

"Thanks for what?" I try to look up at him but the angle isn't good.

"For trusting me with your body."

My lips tremble. The baby kicks. I'm suddenly back in that doctor's office with him sharing my intimate ultrasound moment. And now we have this thing we've shared too, him helping me move past my traumatic past sexual experience. He's been so good to me. Why do I have to be such a butthead sometimes?

I push off him and get out of bed.

"Where are you going?"

I walk over to the dresser and pull out the ultrasound pictures from the top drawer. Using the dim light from the window, I tear off the one that shows the baby in profile.

"Here," I say, coming back to the bed. I hand it to him before lying down by his side. I'm not as close to him now as I was before I got up.

He takes it from me. "What's this?"

"You wanted a picture. You said you did, anyway. I don't know why I didn't give it to you before. Sometimes I can be . . . a jerk."

He stares at the picture as he answers. "You're never a jerk. You're just dealing with a lot of stuff most people don't have to deal with." He looks at me. "Thank you. For this." He holds out his arm. "Get back in here, would ya?"

I smile and snuggle in as he reaches over and puts the picture down on the far corner of the bed. "I'll put that in my wallet tomorrow. I'm too tired to move right now."

"Okay." He's going to put my baby's picture in his wallet. I'm afraid to think of all the wonderful things that could mean.

I lie there as the night seeps in, wondering what tomorrow will be like. Will it be awkward? Will he regret what he did with me? Do I assume too much about what he's done and said?"

"What are you doing?" he asks.

"Doing? Nothing. Just thinking."

He spanks me lightly on the butt. "Just don't think yourself into a corner, 'kay?"

I smile, realizing that he knows me way better than probably anyone at this point. "Okay. G'night."

"Night."

He's snoring softly less than a minute later. It's the last thing I remember hearing before I'm asleep too.

CHAPTER
FORTY-SEVEN

I WAKE UP BRIGHT AND early and join my roommates down-stairs. Colin beat me to the shower and is sitting next to Rebel at the kitchen table, his hair still wet and slicked back. I grin at him shyly as Teagan walks up and hands me a mug of hot tea and a post-it note. "Made you an appointment at the lawyer's office." She pats my shoulder and takes the nearest seat.

I take a sip of the herbal tea and then smile at my friend. "Thank you for doing that for me, Tea-Tea." Easing my belly behind the table, I pick up a doughnut from out of the box in the center of the table.

I'm putting it up to my mouth and taking a bite before I realize the room is totally silent and everyone is staring at me.

I look around at their confused expressions. "Wha . . .?" I say, directly into the sweet, sweet goodness that is my breakfast. It comes out really muffled, so I laugh a little, causing a big poof of powdered sugar to fly out over the table. I lower the doughnut from my mouth and smile again. "Oopsy."

Teagan looks at Colin. "Did you drug her last night or what?"

He looks down at the newspaper and a hint of a smile appears on his face. "Nope. Not drugs."

My face is instantly on fire. Memories of his fingers sliding up my back and then down again, his hand grabbing my butt and squeezing . . . *God, I'm going to need a cold shower now.* I try not to look at him, but it's impossible. When he winks at me, I nearly have a heart attack.

"Oh my effing G, you did not . . ." Teagan looks at me and then him and then at me again. She points at my face, her own lighting up with happiness. "Ha! You totally did it! Pregnant lady sex! I thought I heard some shouting last night."

I slap at her finger. "Stop pointing. That's rude."

Rebel looks up over his paper first at me and then at Colin. It's possible he rolls his eyes before going back to his reading.

Teagan's chuckling as she picks up her doughnut. "Holy shit. You guys are nuts."

I kick her under the table. "Hey. Be nice."

She drops her breakfast on the plate and holds up her hands in surrender. "Hey, I'm good with it. No judgment here, no judgment." She pauses, cocks her head to the side and then goes serious, looking at me. "Is it hard to do it with your belly that big?"

"Teagan, come on," Rebel says, standing up, his chair making a loud dragging sound on the floor. "Time to go to work."

She pouts and stands with him. "Slave driver."

He comes around the table and grabs her, slamming her body into his and gripping her buttcheek with one hand. "Don't sass me," he says, before giving her the hottest kiss I've seen outside a rated-R movie. I have to turn away to ease my embarrassment.

Out of the corner of my eye I see her pushing herself away. "Holy alpha male alert. Save it for the bedroom, babe. I have filing to do." She leaves the kitchen after grabbing her purse off the counter. "Go to that appointment!" she yells from the foyer. "I'm not playing!"

"I'm going!" I yell back, staring at the note. I look up at Colin. "Can I get a ride from you? It's in a half hour."

"You bet. Just let me grab my wallet."

He leaves the kitchen but not before kissing the top of my head and rubbing my belly. I think he's gone but then he's there again, leaning down to kiss my stomach.

"What's that for?" I ask, my face warming.

"Gotta kiss the baby too."

I sit there at the table crying happy tears for a change, waiting for my boyfriend to take me to my appointment. I don't know how long it's going to last, but the ghosts that Charlie conjured have officially been removed from my brain. All I can think about now is how bright my future is.

CHAPTER
FORTY-EIGHT

WELL, THAT EUPHORIA DIDN'T LAST very long. *Thanks, Natalie.*

"I'm sorry to be the bearer of bad news, but it is what it is. You need me and you need my colleague William or someone like him. He's the civil torts guy. You need to file one suit for the child support issues and then a separate one for the assault and battery and whatever else he can come up with out of the statutes."

"But why can't you handle it all?" I ask, sick over the idea of this many lawyers in my life. One is more than enough, thank you very much.

"Because, I don't know that area of the law. You want an expert. That's not me. I can do the serious tango over child support, custody, and so on. But I'd lose and lose badly in a civil assault case. I'd be in over my head."

"I can't believe you're saying that." I just stare at her like she has two heads.

"Why?"

"Because you seem so . . . capable." My whole vision of her as a superhero is fizzling out.

"And I am. In family law." She comes around her desk and sits down next to me. Her penetrating stare is almost too much. "I'm good because I focus on what I know and what I like. Bringing justice to girls like you is my calling." She clasps her hands together and then points at me with her two first fingers pressed together. "You are running out of time. Now that you've exchanged heated words with your attacker and the father of your child, things are going to roll out fairly quickly. People like him do rash and stupid things without thinking. I want you to have all your ducks in a row before he gets his feet under him."

"What does that mean exactly? I mean, what will I have to do?"

"Give me the right to act as your lawyer. I'll get the ball rolling by filing papers in family court. When you give birth, you put Charlie's name on the birth certificate, not 'unknown'. If he wants to fight that, we'll do a paternity test. *You will win your case.* I don't know if he'll go to jail for what he did, but over my dead body will he get anything more than part custody."

"Part custody!" I yell. "Are you kidding me?!" I lean as far away from her as I can. The idea is positively abhorrent to me.

"Fact is, he's the father." She holds up a finger to keep me from exploding my anger all over her. "But, he's also a criminal. I'm going to leverage that as best I can to show that it's in the best interests of the child to be one hundred percent with you. If he wants visitation, I'm going to argue it needs to be supervised by an outside party." She puts her hand on my arm. "Hey . . . he might not want anything at all. My guess is he won't. But his parents . . . they might have other ideas."

"His parents?"

"They have no rights as grandparents, so don't get worried about that. But they have considerable influence over their child, so what he wants might not matter. We'll deal with that as it comes."

I shake my head, everything feeling like it's hopeless again. "I wish I'd never come."

"Why? So you can live with your head in the sand? Don't go there. He wins with that attitude."

"I don't want him to win, but this . . . this is . . . it's a nightmare."

"Yes. It's a nightmare. I'm not going to blow smoke up your dress and tell you differently. But we can control the outcome to some degree if we're smart, if we do everything right. That's where my team and I come in."

"Your team?"

"Yes. I have three paralegals and one associate who work with me. I call them the gators."

"Gators?"

"Yes. They lie in the water waiting, looking like harmless logs, but then when their prey least expects it, they leap out, grab 'em in their jaws and give 'em the old death roll. It's not pretty."

"Wow."

"They're very effective." She stands, holding out her hand to help me up.

"So what's next?" I ask.

"Sign my contract and I'll call Charlie today. I'm going to introduce myself and get the name and number of his lawyer so we can start a dialogue. I'll have papers ready to file in court in three days. Maybe even today if we're lucky."

"Three days is . . . Monday."

"Yep. We work weekends when it's necessary."

I'm in a mild state of shock. All this information. All the threats Charlie laid out, and my legal status as Natalie has explained it to me. It's too much to digest in one meeting. "Thank you. I mean. I guess. Yes. No. I do mean thank you. I appreciate your help."

"Get some rest. Relax. I'll contact you Monday and keep you posted as I learn anything new."

"Okay." I turn to leave and then stop. "About the money . . ."

"It's already taken care of. Talk to Colin."

I nod as I leave her office. Colin is waiting out in the lobby and the sense of relief that fills me as I see him stand to join me is palpable.

"All good?" he asks as we go outside.

"As good as it can be, I guess."

He holds my hand as he drives. "We're here for ya. You're not alone."

"I know that," I say, staring out the windshield. "I really do. Thanks."

My phone rings and startles me out of my mood. At first I'm terrified, thinking Charlie somehow knows what I just did, what I just started. But then I see it's Charity calling and relax.

"Hello?"

"Hey, Alissa! How are you, girl?"

I can't help but smile at her cheery tone. "Good. You sound happy."

"That's because I just signed all the papers with Barbara and Michael. It's done! It's a done deal! It all has to be finalized and stuff after the baby is born, but we have everything in writing now."

"Awww, congratulations! That's so cool! Wow, that was fast, too." My heart feels like it's floating it's so light. This totally beats hanging out in Natalie's office of doom and gloom.

"Yes, they just fast tracked everything as soon as the doofus officially agreed to sign off on his rights. And it's all because of you! I probably shouldn't tell you this, but I can't keep it to myself anymore . . . Barbara and Michael want us both to be the godparents. Squee!"

I almost can't swallow. "Really?" My voice is strained.

Colin reaches over and takes my hand. I smile at him so he knows I'm okay.

"Yes, really! Isn't that so cool? I have to google that godparent thing. I don't know exactly what it is I'm supposed to do. But I can learn!" She giggles. "Anywho, I'm about to go into class, so I just thought I'd let you know."

"Class? Isn't it too early for class?"

She snorts. "It's Lamaze class."

"Oh. You're doing that?"

"Yeah. You should do it too. They teach you breathing stuff. It's all kind of funny. My poor grandpa is in there doing it with me. Poor guy can't keep a counting rhythm to save his soul. But I appreciate the support so mum's the word."

"Maybe I'll sign up too."

"They have a new class starting next week. Better hurry! They fill up fast. Oh, crap. I gotta go. Hugs!"

"Hugs!" I say as the phone disconnects.

"What's up?" Colin asks.

"Charity did the adoption papers. Now all she needs to do is have the baby and her life is all good." I'm so jealous. I try not to feel that way, but it's impossible.

"Just like your life. All good," he says, glancing over.

"Yeah, right." I stare out the window, wondering what other surprises God has in store for me.

CHAPTER
FORTY-NINE

I SPEND ALL DAY SATURDAY staring at my phone. My dresser has been emptied, cleaned, filled, and emptied again while I moved it, all in an effort to keep my mind off my troubles. Sometimes free time feels like punishment of the worst sort.

A gift from Colin was delivered from Amazon this morning that included sheets and a quilt for the baby's crib, stuffed toys and a thing-a-ma-jig to attach to the side of it that has animals hanging down and music that plays. That only took me two hours to put up. I'm grateful not only for the gifts but for the distraction. I only wish Colin could be with me, but he has to work this weekend. Bringing me all over the place the past couple weeks has cut into his work schedule; it's just another thing for me to feel guilty about.

Are the lawyers working on my case? Did they call Charlie yet? Does he know? I peek out from behind the curtains for the hundredth time, almost expecting to see his car pulling up to the front and him striding across the front lawn. Will he have a gun? A baseball bat? An apology? Doubtful. He'll probably come armed with insults and hateful comments about my personality and morals.

I smile a little thinking about how the idea of that doesn't send me into quite as much of a panic as it used to. I have Colin now. I have friends who stick with me through thick and thin. Actually, I only know so far that they'll stick with me through thin times, but I have to assume they'll be there when my life is turned around too. It already feels like it's headed in that direction.

Leaning my forehead against the glass, I let my mind wander back to last night. Colin is the gentlest of men. He might beat the pulp out of people who make him angry, but those same hands that are sometimes fists touch me with a feather-lightness. They make me shiver and groan. They warm me and then still themselves to cool me down.

I don't know if this thing I have for him is bad, but if it is, I guess I'm just going to be a bad person. My parents would be shocked, but why should I care what they think? They abandoned me when I needed them most. Trying to please them is no longer one of my life goals.

I push thoughts of them out of my head. Rubbing my belly, I focus on happier thoughts. A bright new crib, an interview for a job in a few days, a court case that will settle my life once and for all. I made some hard decisions and I'm proud of myself. After almost nine months of hating myself and berating myself for being stupid, naive, worthless, and any number of other terrible things, I can finally look in the mirror and see someone beautiful there. Someone smart. And it's not a man who did that for me; it was *me* who did it.

I have Colin's support, but I know now that I can do this *life* thing. I can handle whatever it brings me. The time for pity-parties is over for good and it feels amazing to know that, to make that decision for myself.

I'm about to move away from the window when a car pulls into view. *Colin!* I'm about to take off running, but my eye goes back to the window. "Holy crud. What's wrong with his car?" I whisper out loud into the room. Maybe I'm talking to the crib, I don't know.

I don't wait to try and analyze his car problem from far away. Instead, I waddle as fast as my penguin legs will take me down the stairs and outside. He's getting out of the car as I walk up.

"Hey," he says. He's not happy.

"Hey." I look at the dents in his hood and the scratched paint. "What happened? It looks like you drove under a construction site and a ton of bricks dropped on you."

He doesn't answer me at first.

I walk up closer to him, cautious because I can see he's really mad. "Are you okay? Were you hurt?"

He jumps a little when I touch his arm, and he moves away. "Yeah, I'm fine."

"Colin, talk to me. What happened?"

He runs his fingers through his hair, frustrated. "I think your ex-boyfriend happened to me." He gestures to the hood. "Or I should say he happened to my car."

My heart sinks as I take in the damage along with this new information about its origins. "Oh, my god. I'm so sorry, Colin."

He lets out a long breath and tries to perk himself up. "Don't worry about it. It's not your fault."

"It feels like it is." I look at him, searching for signs that he no longer wants to be with me.

"Well, it's not." He walks closer, puts his arm around me, and guides me toward the house.

"What are we doing now?"

"Thought we'd give that lawyer of yours a call and see if she's talked to him."

I hold out my phone. "I've been waiting for her to call all day, but I figured she wouldn't contact me until Monday at the earliest."

He pauses on the front porch. "If you want to wait, you can wait."

I shake my head and press the contact for the lawyer, waiting as my phone automatically connects. "I'll just leave her a message." I'm standing in the foyer as the ringing starts.

But the message system doesn't come on. She does.

"Natalie Brustovski."

"Hi, Natalie. This is Alissa."

"Alissa, hello. What can I do for you?"

"Sorry to bother you on a Saturday. I thought I was going to leave a message on your voicemail." I cringe at the idea of having interrupted her weekend.

"I'm working all weekend. What's up?"

"Well," I sigh, trying to figure out how to word it, "I think Charlie vandalized my boyfriend's car."

"Tell me what happened."

"I'm going to hand the phone over to Colin. He can tell you more than I can." I give him the phone and listen in as best I can as we walk into the house.

"Hey, yeah, thanks . . . Okay . . . well, last night apparently while I was asleep someone decided to take out my windshield and back window, and left a few righteous dents in the hood. Slashed the tires, too."

He listens for a few seconds as I look over my shoulder. The glass looks fine to me, as do the tires.

"Nah, I had the car towed this morning and already replaced most of it. I just don't have time to do the bodywork right away. I'm slammed at work."

I can't believe I slept through all of that. I feel terrible that nobody woke me up and asked me to help. I don't know what I could have done, but I would have tried to do something.

We walk together down the hallway as Colin nods a few times, listening to Natalie's response.

"Yeah, okay. Got it," he says. "Thanks. Talk to you later."

When we reach the kitchen, he hands the phone back to me, so I put it to my ear and sit at the table.

"Hi. It's me again."

She jumps right in, going a hundred miles an hour. "Okay, so here's the deal. I need you to make sure Colin takes pictures of all that damage. I doubt there are any prints on the car, but I'm going to have someone come out and dust for them all the same. Can't hurt. Also, I don't want you going anywhere alone. Don't even stay home alone unless you have a dog and an alarm system that's hooked into the police department. Do you have a gun?"

My blood runs cold at her last sentence. "What? No, I don't have a gun. Do you really think I need one?"

"Probably not, but it doesn't hurt to be prepared. Charlie got served on Friday at his parents' house. The server stuck around long enough to hear some choice words flying around. His parents are aware of the claims we've made. Apparently his father read them aloud in their living room with the windows wide open."

"Oh no . . . I forgot Charlie was staying at home for the summer." My heart fills with dread. I know how much Charlie's parents rule his entire world. Life, as he knows it, is over. I don't feel one bit sorry for him, though. This was his doing, not mine.

"His parents know everything."

"They know everything? That means . . . what, exactly?" I'm too nervous to sit but too tired to stand. My toes are tapping like I'm practicing for Broadway or something.

"That you were drugged, raped, and impregnated. We said it with more flowery words but you get the idea. Cat's out of the bag. The district attorney is looking at the evidence we have and wants to speak with you as well. They're probably going to file criminal charges."

"Oh, God help me."

Colin hears my tone and comes over, stands behind me, and puts his hands on my shoulders. He kneads them softly as I listen to the rest of my nightmare unfolding.

"I suspect we're going to hear from his lawyers early this week. Just keep your phone nearby, go about your business, but be smart. If he did this to your boyfriend's car, I won't put anything past him."

I nod, then realize she can't see that. "Okay. Thanks." I'm not sure I'm really all that grateful at this point, but it's the polite thing to say.

She hangs up with a curt goodbye.

I look up at Colin. "She said I shouldn't be alone without a dog, an alarm and maybe a gun."

"Well, she's not an alarmist or anything, is she?" Colin sits down across from me. "What do you want to do?"

I try to smile. "Get a dog, an alarm, and a gun?" Just saying it seems silly. Charlie isn't dangerous. *Is he?* I guess that's a stupid question considering he is technically a rapist. Is being a murderer really that far removed?

Colin laughs gently. "How about you just come to work with me? I'll be your dog, your gun, *and* your alarm."

"And my guardian angel." I reach over and hug him as relief fills me to my toes.

He pats me on the back. "Pack up some stuff to keep you busy. I have about eight hours of work still ahead of me."

I leave him to go upstairs so I can grab my purse. After coming back down and stuffing it with snacks and my e-reader, I walk out the door with him ahead of me. "Sorry about all this," I say, getting into the car. "I'm trying really hard not to feel like a burden, but it's pretty much impossible at this point."

"Hey, don't talk like that. I get to work all day with my girl at my side. If I had known this was the way to do it, I might have smashed my own car up."

"Don't be ridiculous," I say, staring out the side window so I won't go all soppy on him. He's just too good to me sometimes. "All you ever have to do is ask and ye shall receive. From me, at least."

His answer and the low, dangerous tone to his voice makes me shiver with happiness. "I'll keep that in mind."

CHAPTER
FIFTY

I'M SITTING IN TEAGAN'S OFFICE, reading a book while she taps away at her computer keyboard when the outside door opens. This has already happened five times in the last two hours with customers coming and going, so I don't even look up.

"What in the holy hell do you want?" Teagan says, her voice almost vicious in tone.

I look up, completely confused. What kind of customer gets that kind of welcome? My face blanches when I realize it's not a customer standing just a few short feet away from me.

Charlie.

"Alissa. Thought I'd find you here. Can I talk to you for a minute? Outside?"

My mouth opens to answer, but Teagan beats me to it, yelling at the top of her lungs. "Colin! Rebel! Mick! Better get out here!" Before I can blink, she's on her feet, pulling a baseball bat out from under her desk.

She puts the Louisville Slugger up on her shoulder and stands with her feet slightly spread. "Dude, you have about two seconds to get the fuck outta here before I morph into Babe Ruth and send your ass into far left field."

"Shut up, cunt, I'm not talking to you." He looks at me, making attempts to smooth his features out and look friendly, which is impossible of course, now that he's dropped the c-bomb in my presence. "Alissa, I just want to talk."

Colin is the first to appear from the car bay area. "What's up . . ." His voice trails off when he sees who our visitor is. As soon as he makes eye contact with Charlie, his shoulders go back, his muscles bulge out, and his nostrils flare. He shakes his head slowly and his voice drops in volume and tenor. "Man, big mistake. Big fucking mistake, coming here." He moves into the room as smooth as a jungle cat, pushing his fists together and cracking his knuckles.

Mick is behind Colin and then Rebel appears, wiping his hands off casually on a blue rag.

"Aw, man, talk about stupid," Mick says, smiling and shaking his head. He points at my ex. "That's that Charlie guy, right?"

Teagan nods. "Yep, that's him, all right. Fucking loser is what I call him, though."

Charlie's not nearly as smart as I gave him credit for all those months I was with him. He talks when he should just shut up and leave. "I came here to talk to Alissa, not any of you. And I'd appreciate it if you would allow us to discuss our private business *alone*."

I stand up, tired of everyone else talking for me. "Charlie, if you have anything to say to me, you can say it through my lawyer. I have nothing left for you."

"Back off, Colin," Rebel says in a tired voice. "Give the guy a chance to leave on his own."

"Nah." Colin is hyped up. He's bouncing a little on his toes and his smile has a manic quality to it. "Dude's gotta pay. He came here looking for trouble and he's found it."

Charlie looks at him and sneers. "This isn't about you, grease monkey."

My jaw drops open at his rudeness and sheer stupidity. Anyone can see that Colin is about to blow and that he's built like a brick doo-doo house.

"Please, Alissa?" Charlie's back to talking to me. "We don't need lawyers. We can work this out." He holds out a hand toward me. "I've missed talking to you. Come on outside for just a minute and hear me out."

I can't help the expression on my face. It's like a terrible smell has moved through the office and I can barely breathe because of it. "God, Charlie, do you honestly think I'm that stupid? That I can't see right through you?"

"Don't be like that, Alissa . . .," he almost whines, " . . . I care about you."

I laugh bitterly, all his empty promises coming back to remind me how lucky I am to be rid of him. "Well, at least you didn't say you love me."

He takes a step toward me, and that's apparently all the excuse Colin needs to totally lose it. He grabs Charlie by the arm and drags him backward through the office and out toward the parking lot. A table falls over in the ruckus that ensues, papers go flying, and the door nearly gets torn from its hinges as they stumble outside.

Teagan drops her baseball bat and we both scream, a split second before all of us move in a mad rush to follow them. I try to get out the door, but Teagan turns around at the last moment to go the opposite direction and blocks my exit.

"Watch out!" I say, trying to push her away from me.

"No, *you* watch out! I forgot my bat!"

We finally separate and I make it out into the parking lot in time to see Colin land a horrifically powerful punch to Charlie's jaw.

Charlie goes flying backward and stumbles, but he doesn't fall. He recovers and lowers his head, coming at Colin's midsection while roaring like a bull.

Colin grabs him in a headlock when he's close enough and punches him in the ribs four times in quick succession.

Charlie grunts as his body pops up with the repeated impacts. He falls away and recovers enough to punch Colin in the thigh muscle, causing Colin to loosen his hold on Charlie's neck.

Charlie escapes and stands up, catching Colin who's bent over holding his leg with an uppercut.

I can see the change come over Colin as he backs up, rebalances himself, stands up straight, and then tilts his head down ever so slightly. His shoulders look almost twice their normal size as his muscles have gotten pumped up from the adrenaline or whatever other crazy chemicals his body is producing. He's gone from rational human being to killing machine in that instant, I know he has; I've seen enough fight scenes in the movies to recognize it.

Even without my cinema education, though, I'd know something was off about Colin right now. I don't know this man in front of me. I've slept with Colin, exchanged secrets, and let him feel my baby move inside me. This person standing here in front of Charlie ready to pound him into the pavement is someone else entirely.

"Colin. Easy," warns Rebel. I guess he sees it too.

"He ain't worth it," says Mick, holding up his hands, trying to calm Colin down.

Teagan has her bat up on her shoulder. "Just one hit. That's all I need."

I feel like I should say something to stop this madness. "Colin, wait!" I yell.

He doesn't even look at me.

"Just let him go," I beg. "He's not worth it."

Charlie sneers, oblivious to the danger in front of him, staring Colin down. "What's he defending your honor for? You figure out a way to blackmail him too? Too late, man. There's nothing to defend. She's all used up. I've got a sweet video I can show you if you want."

I open my mouth to tell him where to stick it, but it's too late. Nothing I say is going to stop the freight train that is Colin.

He flies across the space separating him from Charlie and tackles him.

Charlie is on his back with nothing but a grunt, before Colin starts punching him in the face, over and over.

Something in Charlies' face crunches and then blood is spraying everywhere.

Rebel and Mick run over to pull Colin off him. Charlie's barely conscious when they finally succeed.

Colin is breathing so hard he sounds like a bull. He's covered in Charlie's blood.

"Oh, God. Oh, God." My hand is stuck over my mouth as I stare at the carnage. Charlie's face looks like it was smashed into a truck going fifty miles an hour. I'm hoping I can keep myself from throwing up through sheer willpower. "Colin . . . what did you do?"

"He taught that asswipe a lesson, that's what he did. Don't fuck with us, that's the lesson." Teagan walks over and kicks Charlie in the leg a couple times before Mick is able to pull her away.

"Easy, tiger," he says, resting his arm over her shoulder. She tries to move away to go after Charlie again, but his grip is strong enough to keep her there.

"Let me go, Mickey Mouse!"

"Nope. Guy's been punished enough. Can't have two people going to jail today."

My heart freezes in my chest. "Jail?" I whisper.

"Better disappear," Rebel says to Colin. "Don't need you here when the cops show up."

"Cops? Fuck that." Teagan throws her bat toward the door. "Put this douche bucket in my car. I'll drive him home and dump him on his front lawn." She struggles out of Mick's grasp and walks over to Charlie who's lying on the ground, gingerly feeling the area around his broken nose and puffed up eye sockets. "And if he says anything to anyone about what happened here, we'll just inform them of the rape charge that's about to be laid on his stupid ass and the fact that he was here harassing the girl he raped." She kicks his ribs. "Get up, you piece of shit. We're going for a ride."

"I'm not sure that's the best idea," I say. But I look around at all the faces nearby and no one seems to agree with me.

"He has his car here," I say, pointing to the Porsche out on the street.

"You drive it," Teagan says, bending down and patting Charlie's pockets. She fishes out his keys. "Here." She tosses them in my direction and by some miracle, I catch them.

I look down at my hand. There's a keychain there with a locket on it. I can't help but open it. Inside is a picture of a girl with her big, naked boobs showing. Her eyes are closed. *God, what a pig.* I wonder if she has the same regrets that I do.

"Fine," I say. "I'll drive the Porsche." The poor, stupid girl in the locket. Maybe she was drugged when he took this picture. I feel like walking over and kicking him in the ribs too.

"Don't you fugging tudge my Borsch," Charlie yells, pointing at me. Blood is coagulated around his nose but it's still coming out and dripping down his chin to his shirt. I have to look away, his face is so nauseating.

Rebel and Mick bend down, hoisting Charlie to his feet as Colin backs away, wiping his jaw with the back of his hand. His eyes never leave Charlie. I get the feeling that Charlie is prey and Colin would like nothing better than to turn him into a pile of juicy pulp.

Mick laughs. "Yo, Alissa . . . dude doesn't want you touching his borchst."

I can't help but smile along with him. This whole situation is too ridiculous for words. "Ew. Like I'd touch his borchst. Not if it was the last one on earth." I can't believe it, but I'm actually finding humor in this horrible scene. Even Colin has a ghost of a smile on his face for me. The only one not finding the whole thing amusing is the guy with the speech impediment.

"You guys are gudda be really zorry when my lawyers are done wid you."

"So says the rapist," quips Teagan. "Why don't you do yourself a favor and shut your piehole until we get back to your place, huh? That way none of us will be tempted to kick it in again." She bends over and picks something up, throwing it at his back. "Oh, here's your tooth by the way. Better not forget that."

Rebel comes out of the office with a rag in his hand as Mick is pushing Charlie into the back of Teagan's car. He gives it to Mick who throws it at Charlie. "Don't get any blood on her car or you're going to pay for it," he warns.

Charlie sneers at him but takes the rag and wipes the blood from his face. Some of it stays because it's already dried. He looks like an actor in a horror movie. I can't even recognize his face anymore.

I walk over to Colin and stop in front of him, staring up into his eyes. "You probably shouldn't have done that." I reach up and wipe away some blood coming from a cut on his lip with my finger. He's still as handsome as ever.

"Are you mad at me?" he asks.

I think about it for a few seconds. "I probably should be, but I'm not. He deserved that. Maybe not for what he said today, but for . . . the past."

Colin tries to smile, but winces when his cut opens more. "Good. I was hoping you'd see it that way."

"But I really don't want you fighting anymore, okay?" I tap his chest with my fingertip, wanting to touch him in some way but also not wanting to embarrass him in front of all these people by being too affectionate. "It's not good for the baby."

He frowns. "I would never hurt your baby. Ever."

"I don't mean it like that. I mean that if you're in jail, who's going to bring me to my doctor appointments?" I smile to show him I'm kidding about using him for a taxi.

He puts his hands on my waist, and it warms me to my toes to know that he doesn't care about anyone seeing him do it. "What about the birth?" he asks.

"What?" I'm confused.

"Can I be there for that too? Or am I just the doctor appointment guy?"

My ears are on fire all of a sudden. "Uh . . ."

"Come on!" Teagan yells. "Gotta deliver this package! Get in his car and lead the way!"

I look over at her, realizing the big hole in our plan. "I don't know where he lives!" I look at Colin, feeling pitiful as I explain. "He never wanted me to meet his family."

"Don't worry," Mick says, jumping into Teagan's passenger seat. "He'll tell us or I'll pound it out of him."

"I should go with you," Colin says as I start walking to Charlie's car.

"No. Stay here. I don't want you getting in any more trouble than you're probably already in. His parents . . . aren't nice from what I gather."

"You'll be okay?" he asks, stopping me with a hand on my shoulder.

I smile. "Yeah. I'm going to be just fine."

He kisses me long enough to leave me dizzy before going back to work.

"Colin!" I say as he's walking through the door.

"Yeah?" He turns around to look at me.

"Yes."

"Yes what?"

"Yes, you can go. To the . . ." I look around. Everyone is staring at me. " . . .Birth," I finish lamely.

"Sweet." He grins big and it immediately starts his lips bleeding again. Grimacing, he waves and he's gone into the office.

Charlie's glaring at me through the back seat window as I walk to his car, but I don't care. I'm going to drive his stupid Porsche and deliver his idiotic backside to his front door and let his parents see what a piece of junk he is. And then I'm going to live my life without fear, because I have friends who have baseball bats and they aren't afraid to use them.

CHAPTER
FIFTY-ONE

I PULL INTO CHARLIE'S DRIVEWAY in the throes of what feels like a heart-attack. I'm pretty sure this event will rank up there as one of the most terrible ideas ever conceived. I cannot believe I am showing up at Charlie's house with his face pulverized not forty-eight hours after he was served with court papers. I must be insane. Why did I let Teagan talk me into this? I tap my fingers on the steering as I reflect on the last thirty minutes or so. Did she talk me into it, or did I jump at the chance of humiliating Charlie? I don't even remember at this point. I just want it to be over.

Shutting off the powerful engine, I hurry to undo my seatbelt. Before I'm even out of the low-slung driver's seat, the front door to Charlie's house is opening and a younger kid is coming out. He looks way too much like Charlie to be anything but a brother.

Oh, crud. And just when I thought things couldn't get any worse.

"Mom!" the boy yells as he sees his bother's face through Teagan's windshield. "Charlie's home! And he looks beat up!" The kid stares at all of us and then runs back into the house, his basketball forgotten in the front yard.

I feel terrible. The kid looked scared. I didn't want this to turn into a family drama. Leaving him lying on the front lawn would have been perfectly fine with me.

Mick is standing by the door of the car, waiting as Charlie gets out. He's not helping him, but he's not hindering either. Charlie looks stiff.

I walk up behind Teagan's Beetle and hold the Porsche keys out. "Here," I say.

Mick holds up his hand and I toss them to him gratefully. I don't want to get any closer to Charlie than I have to.

"Charlie?" a woman's voice comes out of the house, followed shortly thereafter by its owner, Charlie's mother. She's of medium height and thin, dressed in cream-colored linen. "Oh, my word, Charlie, what happened to your face?!" She goes down the two front steps with her feet at an angle and rushes over, hands held out.

"Back off," Charlie says, angrily. "Nothing happened to my face."

She stops short, her arms slowly lowering to her sides. She turns her head to the side. "Hal! Hal, would you come out here please?!"

"Mom, Jesus Christ!" Charlie yells. "Do you mind not doing this out here?!"

Charlie's younger brother appears in the doorway again, his eyes huge. He turns around and shouts, "Dad! Mom wants you."

"Shut the hell up, you little faggot!" Charlie growls.

"Charles Bentley Curtis don't you *dare* speak to your brother like that," his mother says, sounding shocked. "What's come over you? I don't understand where you're getting this stuff from lately."

"Save it, Linda." Charlie walks right past her like she's not even there.

A tall, broad-shouldered man appears in the doorway, and this is the first time I see Charlie's swagger adjust itself. Suddenly Charlie's not coming off as mister tough-guy anymore; his shoulders sag and his head drops just a little. It's like watching a dog lower on the food chain approaching the alpha male. It makes me feel just a tiny bit happy to see him cowed like this.

The man looks at his son, the cars, and then last, at me. He steps down from the house out onto this front sidewalk. "What's going on out here?" he asks no one in particular.

His wife walks back to stand next to her husband. Charlie stops in front of them both, turning sideways so he's looking out into some bushes on the edge of the property.

I can see that Teagan is about to answer, so I quickly walk over and step in front of her. "We were just bringing Charlie and his car back," I say. "He got into a fight and he hurt his nose, I think."

"Charlie, you got in a fight?" his mother asks. She seems genuinely surprised.

"I was attacked, Mom, okay? It wasn't a fight. It was an attack." He swings around to glare at Mick and then me.

"He's a fucking liar, is what he is," says Teagan.

I turn around and shush her. "Stop!" I say in a low voice. "Don't make it worse."

She lifts her eyebrows at me but says nothing more. Instead, she walks around her car and gets in the driver's seat.

I look back at his parents. "He was not attacked. He came to find me and maybe speak to me, but he was acting threatening so my friends stepped in to defend me. That's all it was. We're not going to press charges or anything, and we just wanted to be sure he got home okay." I'm not going to tell them the truth, that we wanted to be sure he wasn't going to go over and burn our house down.

His mother's expression turns to sheer disappointment. "Oh, Charlie . . . why?"

"Shut up, Mom, you don't understand."

His father takes three steps toward his son and grabs him by the back of the neck, shoving his son's shoulders down even farther than they already were. "Get in the house. But before you do that, apologize to your mother." He shakes him hard once. "And don't you *ever* let me hear you tell her to shut up again, you understand?" He jerks his son over to stand in front of his mother. "Say it," he demands.

"Sorry," Charlie mumbles.

She looks at him, tears in her eyes and her fingers playing with a necklace near the opening of her shirt collar. She doesn't say anything in response.

His father pushes him toward the house as he releases him. "Get inside. I'll deal with you later."

The atmosphere is darker than dark. I've never seen a parent treat a grown child like that before, and even though Charlie deserves that and worse, it's still disturbing. I'm wondering who's next to get a broken nose, and pray it's not going to be me or one of my friends. This guy is ten time scarier than Charlie ever was.

"Are you Alissa?" Charlie's dad is looking right at me, a storm in his eyes.

It's on the tip of my tongue to deny it, but at the last minute I don't. *Time to stop hiding. You've done nothing wrong. Stand up for yourself.* "Yes. I'm Alissa." I lift my chin just a little. I'm not going to let him intimidate me.

"And you're the one who filed a lawsuit against my son, is that right?"

Charlie's mom moves closer to her husband, taking him by the arm. "Honey, I'm not sure this is the best time or place for this . . ."

He pats her hand, disregarding her at the same time. All his focus is on me.

I feel Mick move in closer and it gives me a boost of confidence.

Hal speaks again. "Alissa, you have nothing to fear from me . . ." His eyes narrow. " . . . So long as you're telling the truth about your . . . liaisons with my son." He nods once.

I don't know why, but his choice of words sets me off, as does his supercilious tone. As if he can candy-coat what happened to me. *Nice try, butthead, but I'm not playing.* "I always tell the truth, first of all, and they weren't liaisons, for your information. What he did is called *rape*."

His voice softens. "Forgive me. I didn't mean it the way it sounded."

He gets only a polite smile from me. I wait to see if he has anything else to say, even though I should probably just leave.

"Would you like to come inside. Talk for a minute or two?" He gestures toward their house.

I'm struck with fear. A vision of them throwing a bag over my body and conking me over the head with a shovel flashes across my mind. Maybe they have a grave in their backyard too. "Um . . . no. Thank you. But . . . I don't think that's a good idea."

"Don't pressure her, Hal," says Charlie's mother. "Let her be on her way."

"I'm merely asking if she'd like an opportunity to speak with us, face-to-face, without the lawyers getting in the way." He smiles at me, and it's almost believable. Almost. "Sometimes it's better when people come to their own agreements outside of the courts. It's friendlier. Less stressful. Everyone can walk away happy."

I shake my head at him, while Mick pulls on my arm. I'm not ready to go yet, so I stand firm.

"Listen, Mr. Curtis, I know you're a lawyer. I know you know how this works. I'm not supposed to be talking to you, I'm pretty sure, and I don't think you're supposed to be talking to me either. I didn't come here to discuss this with any of you. I just came here to bring Charlie and his car back, even though he showed up at my work to harass me, even though he destroyed my boyfriend's car to the tune of several thousands of dollars of damage, even though he thinks it's okay to drug a girl, rape her, video tape it, and then call her a whore." I look down at my belly meaningfully and then back up at Charlie's parents. Tears sting my eyes, but I keep going. "Before your son did all this to me, I had plans. *Big* plans. College, a career, a family when I was married. I was a virgin." I cock my head, lost in the sarcasm and the pain. "Was that in the court papers? It should have been. He took that from me. He took my pride too. And my sense of self-worth. Is *that* in the papers? Probably not. But I'm not going to keep it to myself if I'm ever in front of a jury, I can tell you that much. And don't think for one second that you're going to buy me off or threaten me or do anything else that will get me to forget what he did and not go after him to make him pay for it. Because you know what? I have a responsibility. I have a responsibility to my child *and* I have to make sure he's never in a position to do this to another girl. Another *stupid* girl who believes his lies and his . . . his . . . *bullshit*." I walk over to the car and gesture to the back seat. "Get in, Mick. I can't fit back there."

I'm waiting for him to move my seat back into position from his spot in the back seat when I feel something touch my arm. I look up to see Charlie's mom there. She's crying.

"I'm so sorry," she says in a soft voice. "I want you to know, we didn't raise him to be this way."

I'm angry at her for apologizing, for not taking responsibility. Her apology actually hurts me, as if simple words can erase what happened. "Well, you didn't raise him *not* to, did you?" I jerk my arm away from her and get into the car. "Drive," I say to Teagan.

She's already gotten the car started and has the gear shift in reverse. "Yes, ma'am," she says, glee in her voice. As she backs down the driveway looking over her shoulder, she mumbles, "Do not fuck with the pregnant lady, people. She is fit to be tied and she's on a roll."

CHAPTER
FIFTY-TWO

JUST WHEN I THOUGHT MY weekend couldn't get any crappier, Mick comes home with a newspaper. Apparently, when you sue the son of a wealthy power-couple in our town, it makes headlines. He leaves me to my misery, disappearing into the backyard to finish some yard work Teagan conned him into doing.

I groan as Teagan reads the story aloud to me and Quin.

"Please, enough, already," I say, halting her after the opening paragraph. "I've heard enough."

"Hey, this stuff is great," she says, grinning from ear to ear, scanning the rest of the article. "He's coming off as a real douche canoe."

"That's because he is the captain of the douche canoe fleet," says Quin.

"Douche canoe, douche canoe, I'm going in a douche canoe. Down a river, down a river, down a lake, down a ocean . . ." Jersey, Quin's little brother, is playing with action figures on the living room floor near her feet while he sings his made-up song.

Quin rolls her eyes. "Stop saying that word." She gestures to something on the floor. "Go pull Han Solo's head off, would ya? He's looking at me funny. I don't like it."

Jersey grabs the action figure and complies, ripping the poor guy's head off like he's done it a thousand times. Then he launches the tiny bit of plastic across the room. It bounces off the wall and into a pile of magazines on the floor.

"He's doing pretty well," I say, trying to get my mind off that stupid article by commenting on Jersey's bandages. "His arm seems to be moving okay and the bandages are staying clean for a change." Apparently burn injuries are very . . . gooey. I'm happy to see he's out of that phase for my stomach's sake.

"Yeah, Jersey manages to play pretty much any game he wants, regardless of the fact that he still has to wear these bandages and the sling on his arm." Quin nudges him with her foot. "Punk is up my parents' assholes all day, so I thought I'd give them a break."

He turns around and glares at her. "I'm not up in anybody's asshole. There's poop up in there, not people. Not kids, just poop. And sometimes Legos. Some people have legos in their butts."

Quin frowns at him. "Legos?"

"Or racecars," Teagan mumbles.

I can't help but laugh. I try to hide my amusement behind the paper I yank out of Teagan's hands, but I'm too quickly distracted by the headlines to bother.

Scanning the article, I pick out words and phrases that make my blood start to boil. I have to rub my belly when it goes hard and crampy. *Stupid reporters.* The journalist doesn't get very far into her 'reporting' before she starts accusing me of being a gold digger looking for a payoff of some sort. I throw the paper down on the coffee table and pick up my phone.

"Who are you calling?" Quin asks. "Colin? Gonna tell him to go beat up the editor of the paper?"

"Shut up," I say. "I didn't tell him to beat up anybody." I wait for Natalie's voicemail to come on.

"Why not? You should sic his ass on Randy, too. Him and Charlie both need a good whoopin'." Quin sighs. "I just wish I could have been there to see Colin school that boy. That must have been epic."

"It was," says Teagan. She holds out a plate of several dark brown somethings. "Cookie?"

I wave it away, pretending I'm too busy or too pregnant or too *anything* to indulge.

Quin's eyes go wide with fear as the plate comes in her direction.

"Cookie?" Teagan asks.

"No, not me. I just ate a buffalo, so I'm full. Totally full." Quin waves her hands in front of her as if warding off something evil.

"You're a dick," Teagan says.

"I want a cookie!" Jersey says.

Quin grins evilly. "Go ahead, dude. Eat 'em up."

Teagan gives her the stink-eye as she holds the plate closer to Quin's little brother.

Jersey takes two, a big smile from ear to ear lighting up his face. "Thanks, Tea-Tea!"

"You're welcome, J-man." She frowns at me and Quin. "At least someone around here appreciates my cooking."

Natalie's voicemail comes on and I start talking. Jersey lifts the cookie to his mouth and takes a bite.

"Natalie, this is Alissa. Um, have you seen the newspaper? There's a big article about the lawsuit on the front page. You should read it. And also, Charlie came to see me today and he ended up getting hurt over it and we brought him to his house and . . . well, call me."

I hang up the phone and put it on the table, rubbing my stomach. The baby is stretching herself something awful, making me wish she'd just go to sleep. It's terribly uncomfortable to have her turning my belly into this weird, oblong shape.

Jersey catches my attention doing some exaggerated grimacing. His face twists around in several directions before the cookie starts reversing out of his mouth. "Cack . . . bleck . . .," he says as his tongue works to move the crumbs past his lips. They dribble with saliva down his chin and onto his shirt. "Caca doodie. Poo

poo caca pee pee." He looks at Quin, angry. "Why did you say that was a cookie, sister?" He slaps her knee, angry.

She's laughing too hard to answer. She just holds out her hands to protect herself in case Jersey decides to go after her more seriously.

"It *is* a cookie, you little twerp," Teagan says. She leans over and yanks the rest of the cookie out of his hand. "It's made with molasses for your information. It takes a very refined palate to appreciate this kind of food."

She gets up and goes into the kitchen, but I'm pretty sure she hears Jersey's response anyway. "How come she puts asses in her cookies? Asses don't taste that good to me." He uses one of his action figures to wipe his mouth out. Then he wipes the action figure on the rug. The second cookie he took from her plate goes flying across the room to rest on the floor with Han Solo's head.

I'm laughing so hard I feel a pop in my crotch and then I pee myself. I totally pee myself right there on the couch.

I struggle to stand as Quin points and laughs at me, probably way too entertained by my penguin-like struggles. She doesn't even know the worst of it yet. She's probably going to pee her pants too when she finds out what I've done.

"Shut up!" I say, snorting and laughing. I've lost it. "I just peed on myself. I totally just wet my pants."

She's gripping her stomach, gasping for air as Jersey points to my crotch and starts singing.

"You peed your paaaants, you peed your paaaants, you peed your paaaaants . . ."

I rest my hand on my belly as it goes hard as a rock. My laughter quickly peters out when a rush of warm liquid streams down my inner thighs.

"Oh, shit," I whisper, looking down.

Quin's still laughing. "What? You pee again? Or did you shit yourself this time?"

I look up at her, stark fear taking over. "No. I think my water just broke."

CHAPTER
FIFTY-THREE

QUIN JUMPS TO HER FEET. "Teeegaaaaan! Call nine one one! Call nine one one!"

I wave at her, annoyed at her spaziness. "No, you dope, don't tell her to do that."

More warm stuff runs down my legs. "Tell her to get a towel." I can't believe how calm I am. I wasn't ready for having a baby. I've just come to accept the fact that I'm pregnant, for poop's sake. I haven't even been to Lamaze yet. I don't have a birth partner, even.

Even so, I feel like I can do this. Everything is going to be okay, as long as I can get to the hospital on time. The nurses do everything, right? All I have to do is lie there and breathe. People have babies all the time. Some women squat out in a field and then go back to work, right? It's no big deal. *I can do this. I can do this. I can do this.*

"Towels! Hot towels and boiling water!" Quin yells, running out of the room.

Jersey stares at me from the floor. "You peed your paaants." He says it more softly this time with a hint of nervousness added to his voice.

"Actually, sweetie, I didn't pee my pants. I'm going to have a baby. Would you go to the bathroom and get me a towel please?"

"Uh-huh." He walks out of the room at a fast clip, an action figure in each hand. His corduroys sound like they're kicking up enough friction to start a fire.

Teagan shows up in the entrance to the room. "Is she serious? Is the baby coming?"

I look down at my legs and then at her. "My water broke on your couch. I'm so sorry."

"Gross. Does it smell? Okay, yeah, never mind, don't answer that question. Don't worry about it. What should I do?"

"Bring me some *dry* towels and then get the car. We need to get to the hospital."

"What about an ambulance?"

I shake my head. "No. It won't be a big deal, and ambulances are too expensive anyway. Labor takes hours and hours. They might even send me home once we get there, but I'd rather be safe than sorry."

A contraction starts, my belly tightening and gripping around the baby. It turns my stomach into a weird shape and more liquid comes out. I have to bend over a little to ease the tension.

I'm pretty sure I'm supposed to be timing these things, but I have no idea how. Am I supposed to time how long they last? How much time between the end of one and beginning of another? From the beginning of one to the beginning of another? It's all so confusing. I thought I'd have more time to do research. The baby isn't due for another few weeks. *Will she be okay?*

"You sure about that no ambulance thing?" Teagan asks, for the first time sounding scared.

I wave her away. "Just go." Reaching down to the table, I grab my phone. I flip it open and press the button for Colin's number.

"Hey, babe," he says after two rings.

"Hey," I say, almost grunting. *Whoa, these contractions are no joke. Holy . . . crud buckets.*

"Something wrong?" he asks.

"My water broke," I grunt out.

"What?!" he yells into the phone.

I hold it away from my head for a few seconds to protect my eardrums from any more outbursts.

When I'm sure he's done, I put it back to my head. "Easy, Colin. You just made me deaf in one ear."

"Stay there, I'm coming over."

"No, meet me at the hospital. Teagan is taking me."

"But . . ."

"Don't argue!" I yell, the pain from the contraction that doesn't want to end slicing into me. "Just go there!"

"Yes, ma'am," he says, sounding bewildered. "See you soon."

He hangs up and I waddle to the door, using the towel that Jersey brings me as a giant maxi-pad.

CHAPTER
FIFTY-FOUR

QUIN AND JERSEY ARE IN the back seat of the Beetle. Teagan's driving like a maniac and I'm her front seat passenger. My belly is squeezing itself over and over, almost without stopping. I did some reading about birth stories a couple weeks ago, but I don't remember any that sounded like this. It feels like it's going too fast.

"Shouldn't we be timing something?" Quin asks, her face appearing between the seats.

"Yeah. We should," Teagan says.

I have one hand on the dashboard and one on the windowsill next to me. I can't answer right now. I'm just trying not to explode with pain. I thought there would be breaks between the contractions, but either there aren't any breaks or this is just one big long one.

"Is this normal?" Quin asks. "Why isn't she talking?"

Jersey starts making a sound like a truck driving. Out of the corner of my eye I see a toy car coming at me from the back seat. Then I feel something rolling over the top of my head.

"Jersey, cut the crap," Quin says, smacking it off my head. Some of my hair goes with it.

"She likes it!" he yells. "It's rubbing her head. Daddy says it's nice to rub people's heads when they're sick."

The toy car goes back to my head as another contraction rips through me. I whimper when the pain reaches new heights.

The car leaves my head. "Oopsy. Sorry," Jersey says.

"Time it!" yells Teagan. "Time the contraction!"

Quin starts yelling right next to my ear. "One one thousand, two one thousand, three Mississippi, four Pennsylvanias!"

"Who the fuck taught you to count like that?" Teagan asks, twisting around to look at her.

"I'm under a lot of pressure! Shut up!"

I scream as the car swerves over to the side of the road. The side mirror hits a mailbox and goes flying off with a crash to the sidewalk below.

"Holy fuck-a-nutter," Teagan says, jerking the wheel back and getting the car straight again. "Phew! I almost just gave myself a heart-attack, I think."

"You drive! I'll count!" Quin puts her hand on my shoulder. "Tell me when to stop. One Mississippi, two Pennsylvania . . ."

I hold my hand up. "Stop. For the love of God, stop." I'm panting like a dog. Real breathing hurts too much. The baby is taking up all my lung room.

My phone rings. I grab it and throw it over my shoulder. "Answer it," I say weakly as another wave of pain starts to build.

"Hello! Alissa's phone!" Quin has gone deaf. That's the only explanation for her constant yelling.

"Brrrmmmm brrmmmmm," says Jersey. His toy car is on my shoulder now.

"Yeah, we're in Teagan's car! We're about ten minutes away." She twists around. "Hey! That's you back there? How'd you catch up so fast?" She leans closer to my ear. "Colin's right behind us. He wants to know if you want to get in his car."

I shake my head. "Pull over," I whisper. This is not going well. The gushing has lessened but the pressure is increasing. I'm pretty sure my entire uterus is about to fall out.

"Yeah, she wants to get in your car!"

"No!" I yell.

Teagan looks at me. "Am I pulling over or not?"

"Yes!"

Quin leans in-between the front seats, looking first at me and then at Teagan. "So is she getting in his car or what?"

"PULL THE FUCKING CAR OVER RIGHT NOW!" I scream, as I feel a bulging pressure coming from between my legs. Something inside me is ripping open. This makes round ligament pain feel like a friggin massage.

Teagan swerves to the right and pulls up onto a sidewalk. Cars honk and move out of our way. The one behind us screeches to a stop and then a guy starts yelling a stream of cusswords at us.

"What the fuck?!" Teagan yells. "All you had to do was ask! Don't yell like that or you'll make me crash!"

I'm struggling to find the door handle. "Out. Out. Out." It's all I can think. I'm about to have this baby and nobody is understanding me.

"You want out because you're getting in Colin's car?" Quin sounds confused and maybe a little nervous.

I hear some more screeching and honks and then as I'm getting the door to finally open, Colin's face appears next to me. The door opens and he's squatting down at my side.

"What's up, babe?"

"Baby . . ." I say in between panting breaths. "Baby coming . . ."

His face goes white. "Baby coming? Like now? Baby coming now?"

"You talk like a baby!" says Jersey, laughing. "Let's play baby, sister! Let's play baby. I'll be the baby, you be the momma."

"Shut up, Jersey! Not right now!" Her voice is in my ear again. "Are you having the baby right now?"

"Get my pants off," I say, practically crying. "Get them off right now." All I can picture is my baby getting turned into an accordion because my jeans are in the way of her coming. *Why didn't I wear a dress today? Ugh, they're wet! They won't come off!*

Colin turns me sideways and yanks my shoes off. He gets one leg of my pants off by pulling it from the bottom. As he reaches for the other side, I hold my hand up. There's no way my leg is moving over there.

"Leave it," I say, swiping at his hand. "Underwear." I can't say anything more. I'm out of breath and another monster contraction is about to tear me in two.

My underwear disappears about three seconds after Colin produces a knife from his pants pocket. The pieces fall to the seat, trapped under me. I now have a free path for the baby to use. *Thank God. No baby accordions today.*

Colin holds my hand and looks into my eyes. I can barely see him through the haze of pain.

"You ready for this?" he asks.

"No choice," I say, right before I scream like a wild woman. The pressure is too much. I feel like I'm being torn in two.

"Holy mother fucking miracle of life . . . you're having a baby in my Beetle," Teagan says. She takes off her seatbelt and gets on her knees on the seat, leaning over to be in front of me. "You can do this! Just breathe, okay! Just breathe!" She puts her hand on my shoulder and looks down at my crotch. "Oh, God. That is just . . . that is just . . ." Her face goes pale too.

"What? What is it?!" Quin yells. "I can't see! Tell me!"

"Is that . . ." Teagan points to my crotch. "Is that . . . the baby?"

I close my eyes and lean my head back against the seat. The pain is gone for two seconds and then it comes back, full force. And things start to move inside me.

"Oh, man. That's the head, I think," Colin says. "Quin, call nine-one-one."

Quin gets busy following his orders, but I don't have the presence of mind to hear everything she's saying. I have the strongest urge to push, but I know it won't matter whether I do or not. This baby is coming, and it's happening *now.*

I grab Colin's bicep and Teagan's forearm. "She's coming," I say. "Somebody catch her."

"I got you, babe," Colin says. He looks terrified. "I got you. Just do what you need to do."

I can feel warm fluids slipping out of me as the pressure builds.

The smell of iron and I don't even want to know what else fills the car. *Please, God, don't let me poop in Colin's hands!*

"Ooooohhh Goooood!" I cry. And then my air is cut off as I bear down, pushing with everything I have. "Aaahh!" I scream as I feel something stretch too far, to the point of tearing apart, and then . . .

Kachow!

The baby is zooming out of me and into Colin's hands.

I can breathe again.

I'm burning something fierce down there, but the pressure is gone.

I'm crying and laughing and trying to gasp for air all at the same time.

"It stinks in here," Jersey says. "Pewey. Somebody farted."

"Oh my god," Teagan says in a really high, silly voice. "You just had a fucking baby in my Beetle! Holy fuck of all fucks. What the . . ."

"Hold her up! Hold her up so I can see!" Quin yells next to my head.

Colin looks up at me and smiles, his eyes filled with tears. "You just had a baby and I caught it."

I smile at him, suddenly very tired. "Thanks for being there for me." I loosen my grip on their arms and hold out my hands. "Can I have her?"

She's covered in all kinds of goop. Blood and creamy white stuff are smeared everywhere. And this giant purple and white, lumpy-looking cord is still connecting her to me. She is so very beautiful. I can't stop crying.

Colin settles her into my arms and I stare down into her puffy face. She looks like she's trying to open her eyes, but it's too bright or something. I carefully brush the goo away from her lids. The tears are hot on my face. I'm so deliriously happy. And I'm in pain. More contractions are coming, bringing goop and God knows what else with it.

"What are we supposed to do next?" Teagan asks, sliding back down into her seat. "Do we cut the cord or something? I have a shoelace." She rolls down her window and cracks her door open.

"I'll call nine-one-one and ask them. I think I hung up on them too soon," Quin says.

The rest of the event passes in a blur. The ambulance shows up and loads me and the baby inside where they cut the cord off and wrap the baby up. I think Colin and the girls are behind us on the way to the hospital. I'm wheeled on a gurney up to a room, and nurses clean me and the baby off. My clothes are bagged up and I'm put into a hospital gown open in the back. I have no underwear. Someone comes in and gives me some stitches in my nether regions. But none of it matters to me much. I can't take my eyes off my daughter. She's drinking from my breast. A real live itty bitty person, perfectly formed, is lying in my arms, staring up at me with dark blue eyes like she's lost.

"I'm here, baby girl." I say, stroking her fuzzy down-covered cheek. "I'm here. You don't need to worry. You're not alone." She closes her eyes and falls asleep, and I join her a few minutes later.

CHAPTER
FIFTY-FIVE

I WAKE UP TO FIND Colin next to me. As soon as he sees I'm awake, he smiles. "Hey." His voice is rough, so he clears it. "How're you feeling?"

I smile. "Tired. I don't know why. It all happened so fast."

His eyebrows go up. "You did the concentrated version, I think. If I had to do what you did, I'd sleep for a week."

"How long have I been here?" I ask, looking around. The table near the foot of the bed has three bouquets of flowers on it and two silver balloons.

"Few hours. You have lots of fans," he says, following my gaze. "The newspaper wants to interview you."

I sigh and just stare at the flowers for a while. Then I look at Colin. I feel like I'm in another world. My baby is nestled in my arms, wrapped in hospital blankets with her eyes closed.

He moves his chair closer. "She's real pretty," he says, looking down at her.

"You think so?" I move the blanket away from her face. "She's got dark skin. Like a tan."

"The nurse said all babies look like that. She said they'll put her under some lights to make it go away."

"Is it bad?" I ask, suddenly fearing for my baby's health.

"No, I don't think so." He strokes her forehead with a finger. His hand is huge in comparison to her tiny features. "She's so soft," he whispers.

"Yeah," I whisper back. "Like velvet."

He seems mesmerized by her. My heart squeezes painfully in my chest. "Thank you, Colin. Thank you for catching her."

He smiles. "We have a hell of a story to tell her some day, don't we?"

I can only nod. His choice of words suggests that he'll be there, when she's grown up. How did I get so lucky?

The door opens and a nurse sticks her head inside. "Hi. Grandparents are here to say hello. Can they come in?"

My body goes ice cold and I grip the baby tighter. She squeaks and squirms but quickly settles back down as I relax my hold a little.

I look at Colin as he stands.

"Who is it?" he asks.

The nurse frowns. "Father's parents. Yours maybe?"

Colin looks down at me. "I'll go see what's going on. Just wait here."

I have to laugh. "It's not like I'm going anywhere."

"Oh. Yeah. Right." He pats me on the shoulder and is halfway across the room before he stops, turns around and comes back. "Be right back," he says, kissing me on the forehead and then the baby on the cheek.

My lips tremble in a smile as I watch her face twist up in annoyance.

He's gone and back again before I have time to decide how I feel about these strangers coming into my hospital room. How did they find out? If Charlie's with them I'm going to have Colin beat his butt all over again. He's not coming anywhere near my baby. Over my dead body.

Colin stops at the foot of my bed. "It's Charlie's parents. He's not with them."

REBEL WHEELS - TROUBLE

I breathe out a sigh of relief.

"How did they find out?" I ask.

"Apparently someone who works in this hospital is a friend of theirs and has decided that privacy laws mean absolutely nothing where you're concerned. And when I find out who that person is, I'll re-educate them on that law, but in the meantime, they say they want to see you to see if you and the baby are okay."

I grimace. "They're going to ruin my afterglow."

Half of Colin's mouth goes up in a smile. "No one can ruin your afterglow, babe. No one. And I talked to them. I don't think they mean you any harm. I think they want to make things right. As right as they can."

My lips set into a firm line. "I'm not going to stop the lawsuit. I don't care what they say."

"Agreed." Colin nods. "And I'll be right here with you the whole time. They'll be out on their asses if they say anything out of line."

I take a deep breath and let it out, gazing down at my daughter. "Fine. But if they don't tell me how beautiful she is within the first ten seconds, they're outta here."

Colin opens the door and gestures to someone outside.

I school my features to look unconcerned as Charlie's parents walk into the room.

CHAPTER
FIFTY-SIX

ITHINK CHARLIE'S PARENTS ARE as nervous as I am. They walk into the room cautiously, nodding to Colin first and then stopping at the foot of my bed. Hal looks around at the flowers, but Charlie's mother only has eyes for the baby.

I hold my daughter closer, my protective instincts going into overdrive. If she comes too close and tries to make a grab for the baby, I will rip this woman's eyes out and feed them to her with my fist through her stomach. I resist the strong urge to growl like a mother bear.

"Congratulations," Charlie's mom says. "She is *just* beautiful."

I flick my gaze over to Colin. He nods at me and smiles.

"Did Colin tell you to say that?" I ask.

She looks confused for a moment. "Say what, dear?"

I shake my head. "Never mind."

"Pretty flowers," Hal says, reaching out to touch the petals of one of the pink roses.

"Thanks." The atmosphere in the room could not be more awkward.

Charlie's mom moves carefully around the side of the bed. "May I see her? Is she sleeping?"

She's moving slow enough that I don't feel threatened. Besides, Colin is standing right behind her. I know he'll protect us.

I move the blanket away from the baby's face a little. "She's sleeping. She just ate." I feel so proud of myself, that I was the one to feed her. I've never done that before, sustained another human life like that.

"Oh, my goodness. She looks just like you. So pretty." She smiles at me. "I won't ask you if I can hold her this time, because I know you're a new mom and it's hard to share right away, but I can't promise I won't ask next time."

I don't know how I feel about that . . . seeing them more than once or ever again. It makes me nervous to think these people are going to be in my life or even that they want to be in it.

Hal leaves his study of the flowers and looks somewhere up near my headboard. "So, you're feeling okay?"

"Yes, I'm fine."

"We heard you had the baby in a car on the way over," Charlie's mom exclaims. "That's so exciting. Probably at the time it seemed scary, but boy oh boy what a story you will have to tell later."

"That's what Colin said." I smile over at him. He's standing in front of his chair, his arms crossed over his chest.

"Were you there?" Hal asks Colin.

Colin nods at the baby. "I showed up just before she arrived."

Hal nods and presses his lips together, turning his mouth down at the corners. "Good."

Colin drops his folded arms and lets them swing at his sides.

Hal clears his throat a few times. He's plainly uncomfortable. We all wait for him to work up the nerve to say whatever's on his mind.

"So, we received your court papers," he says. "As you can imagine, we were quite shocked."

I can't look at him or respond and be polite, so I keep my mouth shut. My fingers go automatically to cover the baby more with her blanket. Charlie's mom turns to face her husband.

He continues. "We were in denial at first, but then we had a talk with Charlie and we did a search of his bedroom and vehicle ..." Hal sighs and his voice gets rough. "Suffice to say, we have reason to believe everything you've claimed in the court documents to be true."

I want to cry with relief. These people are not here to hurt me. At least, I hope they're not.

Charlie's mom speaks next. She's very sad, that much is obvious. All of her joy over the baby has disappeared. She rests her hand lightly on the blankets covering my legs. "There is nothing I could possibly say to you to adequately express my sorrow over learning about what my son has done to you. This is a mother's worst nightmare, and now that you have a child of your own, perhaps you can get a small feeling for what that means. My heart is broken in two, and I'm quite sure it will never be the same again."

Hal puts his arm around her and draws her close. "You never think your kid will be the one that you read about in the papers," he says. "The one who hurts another human being. You raise him up, you try to teach him right from wrong, you try to give him the things he needs to be a better person than you are ..."

"But sometimes, you give too much," Charlie's mother says, looking down at the bed. "Sometimes you spoil them and then they lose that sense of themselves and where they fit in with the rest of the world."

"Charlie was spoiled rotten," Hal says. He sounds angry. "He was given everything and worked for nothing. We are guilty of allowing him to believe he was somehow better than his fellow man. And it's too late to apologize, because the damage is done, but we'd like to do that anyway." Hal finally looks right at me. "Please accept our sincerest apologies for what our son has done to you. We know it doesn't change things and we know it won't make it better, but we felt like it needed to be said anyway."

"Yes," his wife adds. "Please. And if you could just think about perhaps letting us be a part of your life and our grandchild's life ... I know it's a lot to ask and we really have no right ... but we would be so ... happy ..." She can't continue. She's crying too much and her husband takes her in his arms so she can bury her face in his shoulder.

I can't help but cry right along with her. Silent tears leave salty tracks down my face. I sure wish I had met her under different circumstances. I wonder if she would have liked me. I think she might have.

"Thanks for coming over," Colin says, walking over and holding his hand out. "It can't have been easy."

Hal leans over and takes his hand, shaking it for longer than normal. "Happy to."

Hal finishes the handshake and looks at me. "I'm going to leave you our cell numbers." He puts two business cards on the table with the flowers. "You call us anytime, for anything. I mean it. Anything you need, you call. Money, food, a babysitter . . ." He smiles, looking almost shy. "If you don't trust us for anything like that, we'll take our lumps. But maybe we can all do a trip to the zoo or something some day."

I nod. I can't speak. There are too many conflicting thoughts and emotions bombarding my brain and heart right now.

"I need to go now," Charlie's mom says.

Hal turns to the side, leading her out, but she pauses at the door. Turning back to me, her eyes red rimmed and her make-up leaking down her face, she attempts a smile. "I know this seems like a terrible thing . . . what Charlie's done . . . and it surely is . . . but I hope you'll eventually see that in some ways, even bad things work out for the best. Your daughter . . . she's a miracle. Congratulations."

And then they're gone, leaving me, my daughter, and the guy I adore alone in the room together.

Colin climbs into bed with us and we all fall asleep exhausted, and for the first time in a long time, I don't have a nightmare about Charlie.

CHAPTER
FIFTY-SEVEN

BEING WITHOUT INSURANCE, I'M ON the fast track to get out of the hospital. As soon as the staff is happy with my baby's feeding schedule, which takes less than twenty-four hours, we are out the door and headed back home. I'm glad to be leaving. That place is way too sterile for my taste. I miss my pink bedroom.

Colin is driving and I'm in the backseat with the baby. We're using the surprise baby gift car seat that Quin and Mick gave us, and the baby is swaddled in the clothes and blankets that Charlie's parents gave us. The gifts from them started arriving not long after they left and pretty much didn't stop until I checked out. There was a delivery guy out in the parking lot as we drove away who I'm almost positive was there for the baby too.

"You excited to bring her home?" Colin asks.

"Yes. I need to name her soon, though, or someone from the state is going to hunt me down, and I'm not in the mood for anyone else to be bossing me around."

"Don't worry. I'll guard the door." He smiles at me in the rear-view mirror.

I wink at him. "I know you will." I stare at my sleeping angel the rest of the way home. For some reason I haven't quite found the right name for her. It has to be something special. Something that means something to me, not just any old name. She's my little miracle baby. I'm so happy to be bringing her home.

Home. I love the sound of that word, especially knowing who will be in it with me.

I thought my heart was as full as it could get, but when we pull up to the front of the house and I see the big banner over the front porch, I know there's still room for more.

WELCOME HOME MOMMA AND BABY [INSERT NAME HERE] !

I laugh. "They are not going to stop harassing me until I name her."

Colin opens the back door. "Do *not* name her Teagan or Quin, whatever you do."

"Why not?" I ask, sliding out after the car seat that Colin has in his strong grip. I take it from him when I'm out. I can't stand to be too far away from her for more than two seconds. I even take her into the bathroom with me.

"Because, if you only use one of their names, the other will have a tantrum for the next fifty years. And if you use them both, the one who's first will constantly harass the other one and rub her nose in it. You can't win with that one. Just avoid it completely."

As soon as we're in the door, the party starts. The baby wakes up, startled by all the noise, and then whimpers for the thirty seconds it takes me to get her out of the carseat and onto my breast. I sit on the couch and just soak up the love as my friends blow noisemakers, drink beer, and eat pizza around me.

Colin drops down onto the couch next to me. "You good?" he asks, putting a plate full of pizza down in front of me next to a cup of water. He's always making sure I have food to eat and water to stay hydrated. It's kind of cute how he's become the mother hen.

"Yeah. I'm good."

"There are more gifts from Hal and Linda here," he says. "Rebel put them in your room."

"More? I think they have baby fever or something."

"I think they do too. Are you going to let them visit?"

I sigh. "I guess so. I don't know when, though."

He leans in closer and stares down at the baby's face. "Just give it time. Do it when it feels right." He moves her blankets up higher, closer to her neck.

I kiss Colin on the side of the face.

He turns a little to look at me. "What was that for?"

"For being you."

He slides an arm behind my back and slides me closer to him. "I don't know if there's ever been anyone outside of my mom and sister who liked me just for being me."

"Not like . . . *Love*." My face goes pink with the admission, but I hold my head up anyway.

"Yeah. Love." He leans in and kisses me gently. "I love you and that cute baby you made." He tickles the baby under her ear and she stops drinking for a few seconds before going back to it with a frown.

"You do? Both of us? Even though . . ." I can't say it, but it doesn't matter. Colin seems to be able to read my mind these days.

"Yeah. Even though her daddy is a fool, I still love you both. How could I not?"

"Awwww, look at the love birds," Teagan says. "Aren't they just adorbs?"

"Totes ma gotes," says Quin in an obnoxious Valley accent.

I roll my eyes and shift myself forward, scootching closer to the edge of the couch. "Want to go upstairs?" I ask Colin. Just the idea of my bedroom makes me tired enough to take a nap. This mothering stuff is exhausting.

Colin widens his eyes just a little and smiles. "Thought you'd never ask."

"Not like that," I say, suddenly shy.

"Of course not," he says, but he still has a devilish glint in his eye.

I'm not worried. Colin is no Charlie, that's for sure. Not even close. I've never felt safer than when I've been in Colin's arms. *Thank you, God, for that.*

CHAPTER
FIFTY-EIGHT

IT'S MORNING AND TODAY MY baby is officially a month old. How time flies when you only get three hours of sleep a day. I don't need an alarm clock to tell me it's time to get up because I have a baby who sleeps in my arms and wakes up every morning at six thirty wanting to eat.

"Time to get up?" Colin asks in his sleepy voice.

I smile at him as the baby latches on. "Yep. The princess says it's time to get up."

"Big day today," Colin says, opening his eyes.

I love looking at him in the morning when he's still half-asleep. He's the most handsome guy I've ever seen in my life, but in the morning, he's just plain adorable. His dragon tattoo is showing above the covers and I reach over to trace it with my finger.

"Yep. Big day." My mind starts whirling with all the plans that still need to be followed up on.

"Uh-oh," he says, grabbing my finger.

"What?"

"You have that look in your eye."

I pull my hand away. "Stop."

"Seriously. Just let the dynamic duo handle it, would you?"

"If I let them handle everything something will go wrong. We'll end up with an internet priest from the Church of the Anti-Christ or something."

"Really?" Colin sits up halfway.

I laugh. "No. Not really. But I can't let them do all the work."

"Sure you can." Colin lays down. "That's what godmothers are for."

The baby takes that moment to let out a diaperful of gas and Colin leaps out of bed. "Well! That's my cue, I guess!"

"Hey, where do you think you're going?" I ask, watching him snag clothes out of the dresser and closet for himself.

"Shower, shave, and barbecue grill setup."

"You guys already did that!" I yell as he disappears out the door.

"A man's work is never done!" he says, just before banging the bathroom door shut.

I give up on corralling him back in here for a diaper change. He'll do it if I ask, but he's not a big fan. I can't blame him. This girl is a real ripper.

I take my time getting ready. The baby lies like a lump of cuteness in the middle of the bed. She's still not moving a whole lot and she's just now tracking things around her face, acknowledging that there's more than her in the universe. I'm enjoying every moment. The fact that I didn't get that job at the accounting firm is not making me all that upset. Besides, with the child support money I'm getting from Charlie, I have everything I need to take care of the baby. And Colin takes care of me. For now, I can live with that.

"You ready?" Teagan says, sticking her head in the door.

"Almost," I say, reaching behind me.

"Let me help," she says, coming into the room.

"Wow." I say, freezing in place.

"What?" she says, looking down at herself.

"You look . . . hot."

She smiles. "You think so? I just got these heels. Rebel says red is sexy."

"Rebel is right."

Teagan twirls once for me and then moves her finger in a circle. "Turn around. Let me button you."

"It's a zipper."

She's behind me fixing my dress when she starts in on me again. "So I know today is the big naming and christening day and all, and I know you've planned for this big reveal, but I thought maybe you could break the news to Quin beforehand so she doesn't make a big scene during the ceremony. You know. Like break it to her easy."

I can't keep the smile off my face as I plan my revenge. "So . . . you think if someone's going to be let down, I should tell them ahead of time?"

"Yeah, I mean, it's only fair, right?"

I turn around slowly and make my expression go serious. "Yes. It is the only fair thing. I'm really glad you see it that way, Teagan. That's very mature of you."

Her hands fall to her sides. "I am mature."

I nod. "Good thing. I know I can count on you."

She narrows her eyes. "So what are you saying?"

I press my lips together and nod. "Teagan . . . there's something I have to tell you."

Her face falls. "There is?"

I put my hand on her arm. "Yes. There is. I'm sorry . . . but . . ."

"But what?"

"But . . .," I rub her arm a little and try to look as sad as possible, " . . . I can't tell you anything ahead of time because that would be cheating!" I grin big.

She slaps me lightly on the arm. "You are a twat monster. You almost had me fooled." She walks out of the room backward, shaking a finger at me. "Payback's a bitch, yo. Better watch your back." She pauses just before going out the door. "I mean that in the nicest way possible. Just in case you're thinking of using my name for the baby, and all." And then she's gone.

ELLE CASEY

Quin is not far behind. The door hasn't even shut all the way and she's there. "Hey, baby momma! You ready?"

"Yep." I slip my shoes onto my feet. "Now I am."

"Wow, I can't believe how you've lost all that baby weight. Already? Must be all that hot sex you're having."

"Please." I roll my eyes. Like I'd share the intimate secrets of my love life with her. No way, no how. Colin is my confidante.

"So, the big reveal, eh?"

"Teagan already tried and failed, Quin. Just let it go. You only have to wait another hour or so."

"An hour? You're going to make us wait an hour? That's ridiculous. That's . . . torture." She closes the door and talks in a near-whisper. "If it's not Teagan, you should tell me now so I can, you know, control my initial reaction so it doesn't upset her."

"Give it up, Quin. Not gonna happen." I put on the earrings that Colin gave me - a gift for becoming a new mom. He doesn't need much to find an excuse to give me something. Everything I'm wearing today came from him, for being a mother, a girlfriend, a roommate, an employee, the cutest brunette on the block. He's very creative.

"Fine. Want me to take the baby down?"

"Nope. I've got her." I look over at my bundle of joy. She's wearing a white frilly dress her grandparents bought her.

"Okee dokee. Don't keep her fans waiting too much longer. The house is getting packed and they're already drinking."

"Seriously?"

She smiles. "No. That was a lie."

I shake my head. "Take the diaper bag down there. I'll be right with you guys."

She takes the bag without another word and disappears.

I take one more look in the mirror and smile. Perfection. Hair smoothed and gently over my ears. Makeup simple but tasteful. Lipstick a perfect shade for my skin. Dark blue eyes, a perfect match to my daughter's. And to top it off, I have a huge smile because for the first time in a really long time, I'm truly happy with my life. Now I'm living it for myself and my baby, not parents, not people who don't care about me or even think about me. I'm in love with a man who stands guard at my door and doesn't fall asleep until he's sure I'm set for the night.

I gather the baby up from the bed with her soft blanket around her and go downstairs, resting my nose on her head for a few seconds when I get to the bottom. She smells like heaven to me.

The first person to see me is Linda, Charlie's mother.

"There she is! The beautiful girl!" She puts her hands on either side of my face and kisses me on the cheek. "Gorgeous, gorgeous!" She shifts her attention to the baby. "Aaaand, here's the baaabyyyy!"

I happily hand her over. Hal joins his wife and they both look down at their granddaughter with shining, adoring expressions. I cannot believe how lucky I am that they turned out to be so normal. I'm really not sure how Charlie came out of their nest. I've decided he must have fallen out of it and landed on his stupid head.

I'm both happy and sad that he's in jail. He deserves to be there, but now that I'm a mother, I can appreciate how devastating that must be for his parents. It makes me a lot more tolerant of their desire to spend time with their granddaughter.

Charity is in the corner of the room with Rat. With Rat now working at Rebel Wheels on weekends, I'm seeing more and more of them. High school romance is so adorable. I'm so happy for them and for Barbara and Michael. Charity's baby has been nothing but a blessing to them. Now I understand why they were so desperate to be parents. It's the best, most amazing thing I've ever done.

"Hello, Alissa," says a female voice off to my right. She hands me a glass of orange juice.

"Natalie! Hi! Thanks for coming." I give my lawyer and friend a hug. "You look pretty fabulous."

She does a quick modeling move for me. "Bought it yesterday. Paid full price."

I laugh. "Clothes like that never go on sale."

She winks. "So . . . we happy?" She surveys the room with me. "Yes. Very."

"I think all things considered, the case went very well."

I nod. "Well, him admitting what he did, and the D.A. having all the videotape evidence didn't hurt, did it?"

"What I didn't see coming was the friend," says Natalie, frowning.

"Who, Randy?"

"Yes. Usually, those guys stick together. All the crim law guys in the firm were surprised too. Lucky break, I guess."

"Teagan says Randy was a jealous b-word and finally had enough of Charlie's nonsense. Hell hath no fury like a scorned best friend or something like that."

"Nonsense meaning he was tired of Charlie messing with girls or something else?"

I shrug.

"What are you guys talking about?" Quin asks, coming up behind us.

"Randy, the jealous twerp who came up with all those videos of Charlie for the D.A."

"Know what I heard?" Quin drops her voice. "Lindey said that *apparently* one night when there was way too much alcohol involved, there was something that happened between Charlie and Randy . . . so I guess Randy felt his emotions were justified . . . he was punishing Charlie for blowing him off for all those girls."

I look at her, shocked to be hearing this. Charlie was a homophobe from the word go. Imagining him with Randy makes my head hurt with confusion. "Are you serious?"

Quin waves her hand around carelessly. "Well, it was Lindey saying it, so you never know. She had those posters on her wall. Shawn Cassidy? Please."

I frown, confused about what posters have to do with anything. *Is that code for something?*

Quin smiles and walks away never filling me in. But I don't care. Randy is part of my past. Charlie . . . he's part of my past too. Yes, to some degree he'll always be a part of my life, but from now on, it will be on my terms, not his. I can live with that.

"Every day I work in this field I have one universal truth that keeps coming up and reminding me of its existence," Natalie says.

"Oh, yeah? What's that?"

"Truth is stranger than fiction." She winks at me. "I'm going to go mingle with the Curtises. They're good referral sources for me. Talk to you soon."

Teagan comes over and puts her arm around me as Natalie drifts off. "All's well that ends well, right?" she says.

"Yes. Are you good?"

"Hell to the fuck yes, I'm happy. My lawyers took that bitch downtown. She thinks she's going to keep my one million bucks? *Pffft*. Riiight." Teagan grins at me. "Did I tell you they froze all her assets? Every last penny. Boom! Now I just need to wait for the D.A. to nail her ass to the wall and I can get the last of her ill-gotten gains. Otherwise, I got everything, right? Stocks, my dad's house, the cars, the artwork, most of the insurance money, blah, blah, blah . . ."

"What are you going to do with all of it, though? Are you going to run the company? Move away?" The idea of her no longer harassing me or dropping F-bombs all over my life is positively depressing.

She bumps me with her hip. "Why? You gonna miss me?"

"Heck yes, I'll miss you." I bump her back. "So will your goddaughter."

"Good. Because I'm not leaving. I already got an offer to buy the company from some egghead in Seattle."

"But what about the IPO?"

"Nah. I don't have the chops for that. I'll take my fifty million cash and skeedaddle. Let them handle all that jizz."

I choke on my orange juice. "Fifty . . . fuck . . . what?"

She points at me and bends over, laughing her butt off. "You just said fuck!" She stumbles away to share my faux pas with Quin. Soon they're both laughing.

I can't believe I'm looking at a mulit-millionaire right now. Her favorite present ever is a karaoke machine that Rebel bought her last week and she just downloaded a fart app onto her phone which she's been using judiciously at the most inopportune times. She's been torturing us with both items for hours every day. *What's she going to do with all that money?* I laugh imagining the answer to my question.

"It's time, everyone!" Mick yells from the back door. "Everyone in the backyard, pronto. Father Tim ain't got all day."

Linda comes over with the baby. "Here you are, dear. We'll see you out there." She winks and leaves for the backyard with Hal right behind her. Quin's parents and siblings are next. I'm the last one leaving the living room when the doorbell rings.

"I'll get it!" I say, watching as Colin waves from the back door. He's watching me, making sure I'm okay.

I'm still smiling over his protectiveness when I open the door to greet the late arrivals. I can't imagine who it will be. Everyone I care about is already here.

The door swings open and I see who it is.

My face falls.

My heart stops beating.

I can feel the blood draining from my face.

"Hello, Alissa."

CHAPTER
FIFTY-NINE

MY MOUTH WANTS TO RESPOND but it can't. It's not working anymore.

It's only when I hear Colin's quick footsteps behind me that I can breathe again.

"Hello," Colin says, putting his arm around my shoulders. "I assume you're Alissa's parents?"

My father nods. "Yes. We are. I'm Jim and this is Mary."

My mother just stares at me. She looks worse than I do, I'm pretty sure. She's lost a lot of weight and has dark circles under her eyes.

"What are you doing here?" I ask, my voice barely above a whisper. I'm a little girl again, looking at the people who brought me into this world. I feel vulnerable and scared. This was a sneak attack of the worst kind.

"Your friends invited us," my father says.

I grit my teeth together. "What are you doing here, Mom?" I'm mad at her. Furious. She looks sad, like she's sorry, but she's just standing there saying nothing, letting my father speak for her as usual.

"I came to see you. To see the baby," she finally says.

I'm trying so hard not to cry. I'm not really succeeding, though. But I'll be darned if I'm going to let those traitor tears fall. I blink over and over, willing them to go away.

"Colin told us over the phone that you were having a baptism and a naming ceremony and we wanted to take part," my father explains. "To bear witness."

"As long as it was okay with you," my mom adds. "We'd really like to be a part of it."

I lift my chin. "You haven't been a part of anything I've done for the last eight months. Why the sudden interest now?"

My father drops his gaze to his feet. This is the first sign he's given me that he feels any remorse. "We made a mistake."

"A very grave, very serious mistake," my mom says, her eyes pleading with me. She's wringing her hands, a sure sign she's worried. "We shut you out when we should have drawn you in. We ignored you when you needed us. We pushed you away when you needed arms wrapped around you in love and under-standing." She's crying pretty badly, barely able to get the words out. "Can you ever forgive us? Do you still have room in your heart for your parents, as flawed as they might be?"

I can't answer. I'm happy now without them. And they caused me so much pain. It's not something a girl just gets over.

Colin clears his throat. "I lost my mom a while back."

We all look at him.

"Every day I wish I could have her for just another hour or even a minute, so I can tell her how much she meant to me. I hope you guys can fix this so that you don't have to live with regret like I do."

He walks away, to the back of the house.

I turn fully around, shocked that I'm alone in front of these people who abandoned me. "You're leaving me?" I sound so pitiful, but I can't help it. He's my guardian angel. Why is he going away?

He shakes his head. "Hell no, I'm not leaving you. I'm just giving you the space you need to stand on your own, babe. I'll be waiting outside. Shout if you need me."

And just like that, he makes it all okay. I turn back to face my parents, pride in my boyfriend and pride in myself giving me the strength I need to say what needs to be said.

I stare at them both, one by one, refusing to let them look away. "I lived on my own for *eight months*. It was only through the grace of God and generosity of my friends that I survived to have this baby. You kicked me out . . . an unmarried pregnant girl who suffered a brutal rape . . . because I didn't fit your mold of what a perfect woman should be. I am *never* going to forget that. I know you want me to, but I'm sorry, I can't."

I huff out a sigh, looking down at my daughter, feeling as if with that one big breath I somehow let the demons escape my system that had been haunting me and controlling my head and my heart for more than half a year.

My baby girl is looking up at me with her innocent face, her blue eyes like the deepest of oceans, her skin like the richest of creams, and in her, I see my ancestors. My parents. All the people who are responsible for me standing here on this porch today, preparing to celebrate the entry of my baby into the world.

I continue, still staring at her beautiful face. "But I'm not going to keep punishing you for what you did. For the mistakes you made. Life's too short to live with that kind of darkness." I look at my mom. "Mom, you and Dad are welcome here anytime, but it's going to be on my terms. No more judging me, criticizing me, or using your love as a weapon against me."

She nods. "That's fair."

I look up. "And Dad, no more bullying. No more judging me or Mom. Loosen up that choke hold, or you will lose me. And next time, it will be forever. I'm a mother now. I don't have the time or the patience to play games with anyone."

"Life is not a game," my father says.

"No, it's not."

"I wasn't playing games with you before. I was doing what I thought was right. But I was angry. I was focused on the wrong things, what I imagined people would think of our family, instead of what was best for you. And for that, I will always be regretful."

I nod. This is as good as an apology as I will ever get from this man. And as many faults as he has, he's still my dad. He's the guy who taught me how to ride a bike, to throw a ball, and to plant a tree. Someday, I hope Colin will do that for my children. And today is the first step toward getting us there. Life is not about holding grudges. It's about forgiving and letting go.

"Come on out to the backyard," I say, moving out of the doorway so they can pass. "Everyone's waiting."

CHAPTER
SIXTY

MY PARENTS FIND A SPOT to stand behind Charlie's parents. *That's going to be an interesting introduction*, I say to myself as I walk by. I'll save it for later, though, because I have fun things ahead of me that I can't wait any longer for.

The priest is waiting at the front of the small crowd, a pedestal and a silver bowl in front of him. There's a flowered arbor over his head and those of Colin, Teagan, and Quin too. All of them are there waiting for me and the baby, dressed in their finest. Mick and Rebel are off to the side, both of them wearing suits with their hair freshly spiked. I can hear Jersey in the crowd somewhere running his toy car, probably over someone's head.

The priest smiles at me. "Good morning," he says, his face glowing with happiness. I'm not sure if it's that smile or his flaming red hair that has me grinning back.

"Good morning," I say, stopping next to Colin.

"I was told you wanted something short and sweet," the priest says.

I'm glad to see he's not offended by my request. "Yes. I'm not big on long ceremonies and she gets hungry a *lot*."

Everyone laughs and my face feels hot as I realize I just kind of talked about my boobs in front of a crowd.

"Okay, then. How about we all hold hands to start . . ."

I can't help but giggle at Rebel holding Mick's hand. He does it without complaint but it looks so out of character for him. I think Teagan's about to melt with goofiness over it the way her face is all sappy looking.

"Friends . . . brothers and sisters, mothers and fathers, grand-mothers and grandfathers . . . we are gathered here today to celebrate the birth of this beautiful baby with her mother Alissa. A child so loved and so cherished, that all of her friends have come together to witness both her naming and her baptism. Let us take a moment to gaze upon her beautiful face, a shining ex-ample of God's love."

I take her blankets off and angle her up so everyone can see her. I'm teary-eyed with pride. She really is the prettiest baby that was ever born. When everyone oohs and aaahs, I'm absolutely sure it's completely genuine. I'm glad none of them have babies right now so they won't become horribly jealous of me having one so much cuter.

"Have you selected a name for this lovely angel?" the priest asks me.

"Yes, I have," I say, facing my friends one at a time.

The priest continues. "Please announce to her and to all her friends what you have chosen."

I lean down and whisper in my baby girl's ear the name I picked out especially for her. When she doesn't cry, I take that as a signal that she's okay with it. I lift my head to face my friends.

"From this day forward, my baby girl shall be known as Col-leen Teaquin Benson."

Both Teagan and Quin start squealing and jumping up and down. The small bouquets of flowers they were holding are quickly shredded in the process and the petals rain down to cov-er their feet.

The priest's voice takes on a booming quality, making me almost think he has a microphone hidden somewhere. "Welcome! Colleen Teaquin Benson, into our world. May you always find blessed happiness, enduring friendships, and supportive love from those here today." He puts his hands together. "Who are the godparents?"

I sweep my arm to the right. "They're right there. Mick, Rebel, Colin, Teagan, and Quin."

Colin's face looks all warped. It's only when he's closer that I realize it's because he's fighting emotion but losing the battle.

"You okay, babe?" I whisper in his ear.

He looks off into the distance. "Yeah." The word barely makes it out.

I put my hand on his arm as the priest is giving Colleen's other godparents some instructions. "Are you sure? Are you mad? You look mad." I feel sick over it. Did I make a mistake? Did I make the wrong choice? Did I misunderstand something?

He finally looks at me and his face starts spasming even worse. "You named her . . . Colleen."

I smile, feeling both happy and sad at the same time. "Are you mad?"

"Is it . . . is it . . . for me?"

I nod. "It was the closest I could get to Colin without it sounding like a boy name."

His face crumbles and he takes me into a bear hug, squishing the baby between us.

I pat him on the back, more than a little surprised at his strong reaction. "It's okay, babe. Really. It's okay."

He pulls away. "Yeah. I'm fine. I'm fine." He wipes his face, takes a few deep breaths, growls a little, and then looks off into the distance again.

I reach up and touch his cheek. "I owe you so much."

He shakes his head but says nothing. His jaw muscles are clenching and unclenching over and over. He looks like he's ready to punch something.

"You make me feel . . . strong again. Strong maybe for the first time. You helped me find *me* again. Every time I look at my daughter, no matter what happens between us, I want to remember that. I want to know that because of you, I had her and I loved her the minute she was born. I wasn't scared, I wasn't hating the world, I wasn't feeling sorry for myself anymore."

He looks down at me again. "You did that." He clears the frog out of his throat. "It wasn't me." He smiles gently. "But I'm gonna go ahead and let you give me credit because maybe then you'll stick around."

I laugh. "Stick around? What makes you think I'm going anywhere?"

He shrugs and looks down at the ground. "When I love people this much, they go. Forever. They go away forever."

I grab him to me and hug him so hard I almost strangle him. "I'm not going anywhere." I kiss his neck loudly. "Come on. Let's go baptize this monster."

Before I know what's happening, he sweeps me up into his arms and carries Colleen and me over to the priest and the silver bowl.

"Well, special delivery, I guess," the priest says, chuckling. He holds his arms out for the baby and I pass her over. Taking out a silver seashell from the bowl, he gently dips it down into the water, collecting some in the bottom of it.

The priest raises the shell of water up over the baby's head. "I baptize you, Colleen . . ." Quin and Teagan join him in a chorus of voices, " . . . *Teaquin Benson!*" The priest continues on his own, letting the water run out of the shell and down Colleen's head. "In the name of the Father, and of the Son, and of the Holy Ghost."

The entire group finishes the ceremony all together. "Amen!"

CHAPTER
SIXTY-ONE

THE DAY WAS LONG AND although everything went off without a hitch, with no one punching anyone's lights out, I'm happy to be in bed for the night, snuggled under the covers with my two most favorite people in the world. Colin and Colleen.

"You happy?" Colin asks.

"Yeah, I'm happy." I could stare at his face forever and never get tired of it. I reach out and touch his eyebrows, smoothing them down a couple times before pulling my arm back inside the warm covers.

"Think you'll ever want to marry me?" he asks.

I'm stunned into silence. For about three seconds. Then I reach out of the covers and smack him.

"Hey! What was that for?" He's laughing.

"That is *not* how you ask a girl to marry you, you big dope." I'm angry and thrilled. He is too much. I never know what he's going to do or say next.

"I was just checking for indications of interest." He ducks under the covers before I can get him again.

"Indications of interest?" I grumble. "I'll give you an indication of interest . . .

He crawls under the covers and grabs me around my waist.

"Hey!" I whisper-shout, trying to wriggle away. "Stop! You'll wake the baby."

His head pops out of the covers by my stomach. "I'm putting her in her crib."

A hot jolt of excitement runs through me. Baby in the crib is totally code. "No, you're not."

"Oh, yes I am. Just for thirty minutes."

I can't help but smile, feeling really naughty. "Why? You got plans?"

"Yeah, you know it, baby." He buries his face between my legs, and I squeal with surprise. "Fine! Put her in her crib," I whisper. "And hurry up. She's going to wake up soon."

Colin hurries to put her down, tucking her in with blankets, before doing a flying leap back into the bed.

I squeal again, this time with anticipation.

"You love me," he says, grabbing me into his arms and flipping me over on top of him.

"Yes. I do." I'm lying on his chest staring down at his face.

"You just said I do." He grins.

"Oooh, no you don't. It's not going to be that easy, trust me," I say, using my most evil grin.

"Oh, yeah?" He flips me over and then starts going down below the covers. "We'll just see about that."

What to read next …

For more of the humor, romance, and writing style you enjoyed in the REBEL WHEELS series, try BY DEGREES, available at all major on-line book retailers or through your local bookstore.!

Being an independent author, I depend entirely on *you*, the reader, to get the word out about my books. If you liked this book, won't you please leave a review online and recommend it to a friend? The more you spread the word, the more books I can write, and nothing would please me more than to put a new book in your hands every single month.

I read all my reviews!

Find more Elle Casey books at the following retailers:

Amazon
iBooks
Barnes & Noble
Google Play
Kobo
Walmart
Your Local Library via the OverDrive ebook platform

ABOUT THE AUTHOR

Elle Casey, a former attorney and teacher, is a NEW YORK TIMES, USA TODAY, *and Amazon bestselling American author who lives in France with her husband, three kids, and a number of horses, dogs, and cats. She has written more than 40 novels in less than 5 years and likes to say she offers fiction in several flavors. These flavors include romance, science fiction, urban fantasy, action adventure, suspense, and paranormal.*

A PERSONAL NOTE FROM ELLE ...

If you enjoyed this book, please take a moment to leave a review on the site where you bought this book, Goodreads, or any book blogs you participate in, and tell your friends! I love interacting with my readers, so if you feel like shooting the breeze or talking about books or your family or pets, please visit me. You can find me at ...

www.ingramcontent.com/pod-product-compliance
Lightning Source LLC
Chambersburg PA
CBHW021524250626
47154CB00006BA/1969